For more information please visit:

www.fishkorn.com

www.facebook.com/fishkorn

NOCTURNE
IN
BLACK AND WHITE

ERIK BELCARZ

FISHKORN PUBLISHING

Novi

To Mom- thanks for taking me to the James Whistler exhibit at the DIA

To Rinka- thanks for prodding me to finally do this

To M and A- may we leave you a better world than the one we inherited

Fishkorn Publishing
P.O. Box 278
Novi, MI 48376

Though portions of this book are inspired by real events, it is a work of fiction. Names, characters, places, and incidents either are the products of the author's imagination or are used fictitiously. Any resemblance to actual persons, living or dead, businesses, companies, events, or locales is entirely coincidental.

First Edition, 2018
Printed in the U.S.A.
ISBN: 978-1-7323-166-0-7
ISBN: 978-1-7323-166-1-4 (ebook)

FISHKORN
PUBLISHING

PART I

CHAPTER I
MAY 9, 2008

"It's too late."

They were all around the room, hanging in frames between Victorian inspired, serpentine wall sconces and hand crafted mahogany bookshelves.

"There is no fixing this," they added, mocking Martin Kerner with their static, lifeless eyes.

Earlier that morning, he'd felt confident about his chances of arguing his way into the University of Ann Arbor's law program, the most prestigious in the state of Michigan. But that was before he'd been left alone in the dean's cavernous office with a collection of mounted dignitaries.

Unable to find a comfortable position in the unforgiving high back chair, he shifted and fidgeted and started playing his right knee like a drum.

Tap, t-t-tap, t-t-tap.

The room's air was stifling and when Martin ran his hand through his short, well kempt hair it came back coated with a fine glaze. And though a peek at the thermostat behind the dean's monstrosity of a desk informed him that that it was only seventy-one degrees, Martin swore it was at least twenty degrees hotter.

Tap, t-t-tap, t-t-tap.

Just then, perched above the fireplace, a long dead Secretary of State seemed to question Martin's mere presence in their rarefied air, let alone his worthiness of becoming one of their peers.

Or maybe it was all in his mind.

Tap, t-t-tap, t-t-ta-.

At last, Dean Cavanaugh walked in with a reputation as a bit of curmudgeon preceding him. He was well over six feet and thin, with a

1

frame of white hair running the perimeter of his face. He resembled Santa Claus, albeit a wiry and joyless version.

He sat behind his desk in a brown leather executive chair with a brass nail head trim, but said nothing. Rocking ever so slightly, he breathed deep, prolonged breaths, each accompanied with an audible wheeze. There was something hypnotic about the sound. The air passing in and out, synced up with a slight creak from the chair's rocking.

Foreboding, as well.

Martin found himself becoming mesmerized by it until, all of a sudden, it ceased.

When he looked up into the dean's eyes he saw something there that he wished he hadn't. Not quite anger, but close. More like profound annoyance.

"Sir, I-," Martin started, but Cavanaugh cut him off with a simple raise of his hand.

"Forgive me, Mr. Kerner, for not immediately speaking when I entered the room," the dean said in a deep, rumbling baritone.

"Oh, it's no prob-,"

"I needed time to think," he said, his glare just as severe as those in the portraits. "And now that I have, I still cannot figure out why you are here."

Martin, briefly taken aback by the dean's forthright tone, forged on. "Sir, the reason I'm here is-,"

"You were not admitted to the law program due to insufficient GPA, and now you're here to plead your case as to how it's all so unfair, and how you should have received a higher grade in such and such class and so on and so forth. Does that about sum it up?"

Martin absently squeezed the folder in his lap.

"Well, yes it involves my GPA, but it's not exactly how you say. There were...extenuating circumstances. I-,"

"Ahh, yes," Cavanaugh said. "It's always the same. Mr. Kerner, I'm sure your circumstances are somehow unique compared to all the other failed applicants we had this year. Do you know how many applicants that is?"

Martin shook his head. The situation looked grim and he was not in the mood for guessing games.

"About five thousand, of which we admit roughly one fourth. How many failures does that leave, Mr. Kerner?"

"Thirty-seven fifty, sir."

"Very good. Apparently it wasn't math that dragged down your GPA. So, that's three thousand, seven hundred and fifty sets of extenuating circumstances then, is it not?"

"I suppose so," Martin said with an air of indignation.

"I'm sorry. Did I offend you?" the dean said. The look on his face did not suggest he was all that sorry.

Martin let out an exasperated sigh. "No, sir. You didn't offend me. It's just…"

"Just what, Mr. Kerner?"

He had given everything the last two years to rectify the mistakes he had made. Had it not been for that woeful sophomore year, he would have had a perfect 4.0 grade point average.

He pulled his transcript from the folder and set it down on the dean's desk. Cavanaugh did not so much as glance at it.

"If you take a look at my junior and senior years, you'll notice straight 'A's. I have worked my tail off just to get to the point where I felt I wouldn't be wasting my time getting an audience with you."

"That's the crux of it right there, Mr. Kerner. I don't feel there is *any* point that an applicant deserves an audience with me. What I think does not and *should* not matter. It's all quite simple. If your GPA and LSAT scores are among the very best, then you are in. If not, then…"

"Well, my LSAT was-,"

"171."

Martin was confused. The dean still had not addressed the transcript. "How did you know?"

"You don't think I've reached this position by being ill-prepared, do you?"

"No, sir."

"If that is all, Mr. Kerner," Cavanaugh said, offering the transcript back to Martin. "I must ask you to excuse me as I have a number of pressing matters to attend to."

"But sir-,"

The dean cut him off with a groan. "Why is it always like this with you grade grubbers? How about an analogy, Mr. Kerner? Two runners.

One maintains a steady pace and finishes a marathon first, arms up through the ribbon. The other runs faster over the last mile, but finishes much later. Who is the winner?"

Martin bit his lower lip but said nothing.

"Who deserves the accolades?"

Sensing the imminent demise of his lifelong dream, the prevailing emotion Martin felt was anger, not depression as he would have predicted. It was an anger so raw and visceral that it took everything in his power to fight off the vitriol that gurgled at the back of his throat.

He was halfway to the door when Cavanaugh let forth with a loud "Ahem..."

Martin turned and saw the dean still holding the transcript out and seeming very irritated for doing so.

"Keep it," Martin managed.

"All right," the dean said, crumpling it up and tossing it aside.

That final act of disrespect was too much.

"Bullshit," he said, slightly over a whisper.

"Excuse me?" the dean said.

Martin continued his exit in silence. He had the door slightly ajar when Cavanaugh exploded.

"EXCUSE ME?"

"I SAID IT'S BULLSHIT!" Martin shouted, spinning around to face him.

The dean's eyes nearly escaped their sockets. He was not a man accustomed to being yelled at.

"Close the door," he said.

Martin did not immediately comply. He was trembling, not in fear, but from shock at how quickly and fabulously the situation had decomposed.

"CLOSE IT!"

Martin pulled it shut.

"WHAT..." Cavanaugh shouted, before exhaling and trying to redeem some of his earlier decorum. "What do you find to be bullshit?"

"This whole charade."

"I don't follow."

"You. This school. All of it."

"The school you so desperately want to attend."

"I did."

"And now you don't? That is the quickest I've ever seen grapes go sour."

"I came in here to argue my case. I had done my due diligence and prepared myself for almost any possible line of inquiry you might have thrown my way. I did it exactly the way a lawyer might."

"I know of no lawyers that include obscenity in their arguments."

"What difference did it make? You'd made your mind up before I even walked in the door. You took one look at my GPA and that was that. Well, you know, things aren't always so black and white."

"In this case, Mr. Kerner, they are."

"All right then, tell me something. Him, right there," Martin said, pointing at one of the portraits.

"Clarence Darrow?"

"Yeah, him."

"What of him?"

"What was his GPA?"

The dean said nothing. His face trumpeted impatience, though Martin thought he saw a sprinkle of curiosity in there, as well.

"And him, over there. Branch Rickey. What do you think? 3.7? 3.8 maybe?"

Cavanaugh shifted uncomfortably in his seat. "Ok. You've made your-"

"And the guy in the black robes? Supreme Court Justice Sutherland? He must have been at least a 3.9."

The dean sprang to his feet, appearing a full foot taller than just minutes ago. He slammed his palms on the desk. "I THINK THAT'S ENOU-"

"AND YOU," Martin countered, unfettered. Aiming an accusatory finger, he said "You, the most revered and respected dean of The University of Ann Arbor Law School, what was your GPA?"

Cavanaugh could only stare at the thin young man in awe while he racked his brain for the two digits in question that, for the life of him, he could not recall.

He reached back to find the armrest of his chair. Slowly, he descended into it, the stoicism returning to his face. He took a moment to gain control of his breathing, all the while never taking his eyes from the young man across him.

He slid open the top drawer of his desk and pulled out a pair of reading glasses before gathering the crumpled ball of a transcript. Slowly he unfolded it, taking care to smooth out the creases.

"In your sophomore year, you earned a D in Contemporary Social Issues," he said, again rocking the chair. "If you were to replace that D with an A, your GPA would rise to the sixtieth percentile of all applicants. With your LSAT…that would be enough, I believe."

Martin thought his ears had deceived him. "It would?"

"Yes. You could enter this fall."

Martin was staggered. "Seriously?"

The look on the dean's face was all Martin needed to confirm that he was, indeed, serious.

"Do you know if there are classes still available this spring?"

"That is hardly my concern," he said, again holding out the transcript. "And like I said before, Mr. Kerner, I am very busy today."

"Oh, yes. Of course," Martin said. He crept back across the room in a dream-like state. When he reached out to take the transcript, he almost expected it to pass right through his hand.

He gripped it, but Cavanaugh did not release the paper. "Don't make me regret this," he said.

"I won't."

He extended his right hand to the dean who accepted it.

"Thank you, sir."

Cavanaugh nodded and Martin left the office. He was fairly certain he saw a hint of a smile briefly pass over the dean's face.

Jack Kerner was in the same place he was every day at 4:30pm; sitting behind the wheel of his 1967 Pontiac GTO. He had no destination; in fact the GTO had not left the garage in years. Jack's companion was a six-pack of beer on the passenger side of the parchment colored bench seat. He reached over and liberated a can from its plastic ringlet. The cold cylinder immediately began to numb his dry and calloused hands. He stared ahead, down the driveway, over the narrow pentagonal scoop emerging from the center of the GTO's hood. Slowly, he lifted the tab on the can.

He did this without thought, like an automaton, just as he had done for most nights since she died. He took a large gulp, hoping to wash her from his thoughts, to no avail.

He shifted uncomfortably in the seat, trying to focus on nothing but the burn as the beer slid down his throat.

Something moved out of the corner of his eye. It was that old bastard Robinson, his neighbor. He was stooping over his lilacs that hugged the chain link fence along the property line their homes shared. He held pruning shears in his hand but they were merely a prop. His attention was focused squarely on Jack. His squinty eyes implied disapproval at Jack's solo happy hour. Jack glared right back at the old man indignantly and slowly raised his right middle finger above dashboard level so the old man could see. Robinson's mouth dropped agape as if his jaw had somehow spontaneously unhinged. Jack's finger continued its ascension until it met the garage remote attached to the visor. He pushed the button to lower the door, but held his finger up until Robinson's stupefied face was obscured from view.

He finished off the beer and tossed its carcass out the driver's side window. With the garage closed, a flickering, dust covered fluorescent bulb that hung above the GTO's white convertible top provided only the vaguest hint of light. Jack caught a glimpse of his own face in the rear view mirror for a fleeting moment during the flicker. The creased skin and perpetually graying hair did not bother him in the slightest.

It was his eyes.

They were vacant. A split second looking into them was more disconcerting than any glare that Robinson, or anyone else for that matter, could have thrown his way. Jack shifted the mirror so all he could see was the empty, depthless dark behind the GTO. He stared into it, allowing the black to swallow him up.

Martin found a seat near the window at the Starbucks on University Ave and popped open his laptop. He felt revived after his meeting with the dean. All that was left to do was enjoy a tall caramel Frappuccino and then find a social awareness course to replace his D. His optimism faded soon after he searched the summer course registry and realized each and every potential class was already full.

"You gotta be kidding me!" Martin muttered a little louder than he realized.

A few heads turned and looked, and then quickly dismissed the skinny kid bent over his computer. He pressed his palms into his temples, exasperated. Just then, two girls walked in carrying with them a conversation from outside. Unintentionally eavesdropping, Martin determined their words to be tedious drivel regarding their end of semester travel plans. One said to the other, "I got the 3:15 Amtrak to Chicago, and then transferring to…"

There was more to it than that, but Martin got stuck on the word 'transfer'. He immediately began searching for transferrable courses at nearby Universities. Eastern Michigan was a dead end. So was Oakland.

With most spring/summer courses beginning in a mere three days, pickings were beyond slim. He grimaced when he typed Detroit State University into the search bar. It was smack dab in the middle of the city, a place he'd avoided like the plague ever since the incident. He'd almost hoped he wouldn't find anything available there either but, sure enough, there it was: *Race relations in America. Professor Marid Abdul-Tawaab. Focusing on the historical and contemporary patterns of race and ethnic relations, using Detroit as a model city.*

Despite his trepidation about returning to the city that had played a significant role in his current predicament, he was at that moment a beggar, and therefore did not have the luxury of also being a chooser.

As he began clicking his way through the prompts on the university's online registration page, a thought occurred to him. He had neither a vehicle to transport himself the forty or so miles each way from Ann Arbor to Detroit for class, nor the additional funds to find a temporary residence near campus, not that he'd ever entertain the idea of living in Detroit anyways. He was operating on a very tight budget as it was; in fact the money he had intended on using to pay for his summer rent in Ann Arbor barely covered the cost of the course. He was going to have to get creative.

He put his laptop away and tipped his head back, emptying the remains of his beverage down his gullet. He dropped his cup into the trash bin on his way out the door and an icy shiver ran up his spine. The sensation was strange, but he wrote it off as some full bodied 'brain freeze'.

NOCTURNE IN BLACK AND WHITE

By the time he returned to his apartment it was 4:30, or just about the time Jack Kerner cracked open his first beer. After tossing his keys on the kitchen counter, he made a bee-line for his futon. Finding no answer to his problem within the chipped and water stained stucco ceiling, he flipped over on his side and noticed the photo of him and his mother on his bedside table. It was from his graduation day. Her smile was brighter than he could ever remember it. He took the frame in his hands and stared deeply into the eyes of his younger self knowing full well what had to be done. His eyelids became intolerably heavy and the frame fell to his side as he slept.

CHAPTER II
JUNE 5, 2004

"Good afternoon fellow classmates, distinguished faculty, family and friends. Today is a day that we will not soon forget. It is the day we let go of mommy's hand and go forth into the world on our own. I, for one, am not frightened by this. I…"

There was a gentle tapping at the bedroom door.

"Martin?"

"Yes?"

"I have your gown," Diane Kerner said.

"Ok. Come on in."

She wore a radiant grin as she walked into the room.

"Oh, look at you all cleaned up and raring to go. How's the speech coming?"

"Fine. I just want to go over it some more. We only have an hour or so before we have to go."

"I know, I know. I'll let you get back to it, but first…" She held the gown, still warm from the iron, against Martin's chest and examined him.

"Mom, what are you doing?"

"Nope. It's not working for me. Try it on."

Martin grimaced and his shoulders sagged.

"Seriously? It's a gown. It'll look the same as everybody else's on stage."

"Not at all. Yours'll have this."

She held up a sash with the word 'valedictorian' emblazoned on it. Her smile somehow got larger as she played keep-away, dangling it in front of Martin's face. He snagged it on the third attempt, and she chuckled and then wrapped Martin up in her arms.

"I'm so proud of you."

"I know. You already told me."

She broke their embrace with a wince, and put her hands to her temples. She reached back for Martin's bed and sat at the edge.

"What's wrong?" Martin said.

"Another headache. It's nothing to worry about. I'll take an Advil and I'll be fine."

"I thought you went to the doctor."

"He said it was nothing. Stress, maybe."

"From what? Dad?"

"No...Don't worry about it," she said.

"Where is he, anyway?"

"Out in the garage, I believe."

Martin shook his head. "Of course he is. Why did I ask?"

Diane rose from the bed with a forced smile and put her hand on Martin's shoulder. "Never mind that now. If I'm stressed, it's probably from my little baby growing up and leaving me."

"I haven't left yet, but *you* need to. I have to practice."

At this point the front door swung open, and Jack Kerner entered the house with a grace not unlike a Pamplonan bull. "DIANE!" he bellowed.

"Oh, God!" she said, rushing out of the room.

She came upon him as he stumbled over the stoop, crashing into the wall. He somehow managed to stay off the floor, his body at a near forty-five degree angle.

"Jack! What the hell? Are you drunk?"

"Hell no!" he said, though his slurred speech suggested otherwise.

He pushed his body up the wall and regained his footing. In the process, his shoulder dislodged the family photo from the wall. It fell to the floor, the cover glass shattering.

"Goddamnit! Why'sa picture right there? Huh, Diane? Huh? N'wonder I knocked the sonofabitch off. Get the broom."

"No leave it, Jack. I'll get it"

"THE GODDAMN BROOM"

She didn't move.

Jack bobbed and weaved like a stunned prize fighter, his expression shifting back and forth from anger to bewilderment.

"Ah, hell. I don't need it."

He failed in his attempt to squat, and ended up on his ass. Undeterred, he scooped the broken glass up with his bare hands.

"Goodness, Jack! Stop that!"

Diane grabbed him by the wrists and he dropped the shards to the hardwood floor.

Martin watched all of this from the hallway, arms crossed. He had seen it all before and was not at all surprised that his father had chosen one of the most important days of his life to get shitfaced. That was his M.O. When a strong, supportive father would be at his most valuable, Jack Kerner became a burden.

He went to his mother, and put a hand on her shoulder.

"Let's get him to the bedroom," he said.

They got him upright and, after the three of them ricocheted off the hallway walls, they dropped him on the bed he had shared with Diane for almost twenty years. Martin untied his father's shoes and swung his legs up on the bed.

"On his side, Martin," Diane said.

"I know the drill."

Once settled, Jack started to mumble into his pillow. Most of it was incoherent but, just before he passed out, the words became more intelligible.

"Reggie Howard. I'll fix his black ass…,"

"Ok, Jack. Shhh," Diane said, quickly rushing to his side and pulling a blanket over him.

"Wow! He's even racist with his brain functioning at two percent capacity," Martin said.

"He doesn't know what he's saying."

"He knows. Who's Reggie Howard, anyway?"

"I don't know. Probably no one."

"Why do you put up with his bullshit? He contributes nothing. He just sits out in that car, getting drunk-,"

"You shouldn't talk about him that way. He's your father. He's only going through a rough patch."

"How many rough patches is this for him now?"

"What do you mean?"

"C'mon, mom. This is no anomaly. This is the norm. I mean, don't you remember when I was a kid? When Grandpa Kerner died?"

Diane solemnly nodded.

"He came in from the garage, plastered, and started tossing plates against the wall. You, still in your black funeral dress, cleaning it all up."

"Losing his father was very hard on him."

"He hadn't spoken to him in years! He found out about his death in the obituaries. How hard could it have been?"

"I'm surprised you remember that. You were only four."

"Yeah, well, I do. And then the fire. When we had to live at that shitty motel in Warren for a month. All I remember, other than the stuffy room and stiff comforter, is him being drunk and useless the whole time."

"Yes, well…"

"And then-,"

"That's enough."

"Look, even if he *was* going through something. It doesn't give him a free pass to be as abusive as he wants."

"He's never laid a hand on either of us."

"There are other kinds of abuse."

"I said that's enough. It's a rough patch. That's all."

"Whatever. I'll be gone in three months and I won't have to deal with him anymore."

"Martin."

"What?" Martin said.

She wanted to say that she could see so much of Jack in him and that in many ways they were very much alike, but she dared not.

"Nothing. Go practice your speech," she said, shooing him out of the room.

He went, closing his door behind him. Diane lingered, laying a hand on Jack's cool and clammy forehead. She watched his chest, waiting for it to rise. Somehow, after everything, she was relieved when it did. She wanted to be furious with him. She wanted to hate him for doing this on Martin's big day, but felt only sympathy. After all, she knew who he was when she married him.

She gently closed the door, not wanting to wake him, even though she knew a marching band couldn't shake him from his alcohol induced slumber.

She went to the closet and retrieved the broom and dustpan. Squatting over the mess he had created, she couldn't take her eyes off of the picture lying amongst the glass. Their smiling faces looked fraudulent, foreign.

A single tear coursed down the side of her nose and dropped onto the floor only to be swept up, as well.

"Here. Take this," Martin said from over her shoulder. She hadn't heard him come down the hall, but there he was with a glass of water and two Advil.

"Thank you, honey."

Diane waited until he had returned to his room before she slipped the pills in her pocket. She took the loaded dustpan to the bathroom and dumped the glass in the wastebasket. She then opened the medicine cabinet and took out two bottles; the Advil, which she opened and replaced the pills that Martin had given her, and another smaller one. Its label read; *oxycodone 10mg: take 1 tablet every twelve hours as needed for pain.* She shook two tablets out into her palm and, after a deep breath, downed them with a swig of water. Looking into the mirror, she saw that her eyeliner had run down her right cheek. She dipped her finger in the water, and rubbed it out.

Martin stood in shadow to the left of the stage behind the thick, velour curtains as the superintendent addressed the crowd. He could see the man's mouth moving but heard nothing.

Up until a few minutes prior, he had been holding it together, despite the auditorium's sweatbox-like atmosphere that had made his tank top cling uncomfortably to his back underneath the polyester gown.

He had made the mistake of peeking through a slit in the curtain to find his mother. After being momentarily blinded by the sunlight piercing the windows that circled the base of the domed ceiling, his eyes adjusted and he could see all the faces. In front were his three hundred seventy-four classmates and, behind them, their families. All the little brothers and sisters looked restless while the parents and grandparents at least feigned interest in the superintendent's droning.

He didn't find his mother until he reached the back row. She bore a pained expression and was slumped to the side, fanning herself with her program. Next to her was the source of his distress.

A single, empty chair.

While there were other empty chairs in the auditorium, as the lengthy ceremony tested even the most resilient of bladders, to Martin, that one was somehow emptier. Looking at it incensed him. Deep down, he knew it could have been the heat, or her headache that made his mother appear so miserable, but he blamed it on that empty seat, or more specifically the man who should have been sitting in it.

At that moment, the superintendent said something that caused the crowd to rise and applaud.

"Hey, that's your cue," said Tanisha Johnson, the salutatorian, from just over Martin's shoulder. She had just previously delivered a near flawless, if cliché-riddled, speech of her own. "Huh?" Martin said. He had been so lost in thought that he had no idea she'd been standing there.

"You're up!"

"Oh."

He pulled his notecards from his pocket and began mindlessly shuffling through them.

"Are you ok?" she asked, finding his behavior unsettling.

"Yeah…"

"Well, go knock 'em dead."

He held the cards out to her, and, though perplexed, she took them.

"What do you want me to do with these? Now's a little late for me to proofread your spee-,"

Before she could finish her sentence, Martin had already walked onstage. He strode quickly and purposefully right by the superintendent and his outstretched hand. It dangled there unfulfilled, before the man, stunned at the affront to his position, dropped it to his side. He had no recourse but to skulk away to his seat behind the podium with the other faculty.

Martin gave the microphone a gentle tap and the corresponding thud came through the p.a. system. He took a deep breath and began.

"I suppose this is where I am supposed to champion the significance of this charade. I am supposed to stand up here, and look into all of your faces and reflect on how magnificent an achievement graduating from high school is. That *is* why we're all here, right? It certainly isn't for the ambience."

Nary a response came from the sea of dumbfounded faces.

"All right, then. Well, how's this sound?"

He straightened up and cleared his throat.

"Fellow students, faculty, friends and family. We gather here on the precipice of a new day…"

He stopped and shook his head, "No, no. That's not right."

The crowd began to murmur. Martin struck a fist-to-chin pose à la Rodin's Thinker and looked up to the ceiling.

"Ahh, yes!" he exclaimed, with a raised finger symbolizing his epiphany.

"We are embarking on a journey to new horizons. A journey that will lead us to the promise of a new blah, blah, blah…"

The murmurs grew louder. The superintendent, recognizing something amiss, rose from his chair.

"Martin, I, uh…," he said, with a false smile. "I'm not sure what you're-,"

"Sit down. You already had your turn," Martin said.

"Excuse me?" the smile wiped away.

"SIT…DOWN."

The crowd let out a collective gasp. The superintendent, in shock, meekly sat back down.

"You!" Martin barked at someone behind the velour curtains. "Yeah, you. Bring me one of those."

A very skittish underclassman slowly walked towards Martin and handed him one of the diploma scrolls that all the graduates received.

"Thanks," Martin said. The young man nearly leapt back behind the curtain.

"This is it," Martin said, holding the scroll up high. "This is the proof that we are now fit for society. Except, I don't see it that way. What I see is a piece of paper and some dollar store ribbon."

He lowered the scroll and absently fiddled with the bow.

"What it *does* represent is our competency in memorizing and spitting out a bunch of information that some politicians in Lansing think is important."

His words produced nothing but more puzzled looks. Steadfast in his righteousness, he continued.

"A.P. English, for example. We read Homer's Iliad and then analyzed it and then analyzed our analyses for weeks and for what? What relevance does some ancient poem have to my life here, now in the twenty-first century?"

There were a few scattered claps dispersed through the crowd, but he was preaching to a mostly unenthusiastic congregation.

"And Mrs. Szymanski's social studies class…no offense to her, but who gives a shit about the hunting patterns of the Bushmen of the Kalahari?"

"What's your point?" an angry voice rang out from the crowd. "The point…" Martin said, pausing to collect his thoughts. "The point is that this piece of paper holds no real value. This *ceremony* holds no real value. What does it matter if you know how to calculate the area of an equilateral triangle or what the Oedipus complex is? I mean really? In society?"

"Get off the stage!" someone cried out.

As he unsuccessfully searched for the heckler, several others voiced their displeasure from the audience.

Dauntless, he centered his gaze on that one empty chair, way in the back, and when he began again, his voice was louder, manic.

"What matters…what *truly* matters is who you are, deep down, as a person. Show me a paper that says you are good and kind and capable of basic fucking human decency!"

The crowd was frenzied. Mothers, fathers and grandparents alike joined in the uproar, shaking their fists and screaming from the top of their lungs. Balled up programs flew like cannonballs, littering the stage. The superintendent, having had enough, sprang from his seat.

"And not just to some people," Martin continued, "to all people. Rich, poor. Tall, short. Blue eyed, brown eyed. Black or white!"

The superintendent closed in on Martin.

"And not some of the time. All the time!"

He gripped Martin by the arm and tugged, but he would not release the microphone.

"And lastly…that you're a loving husband and father…NOT AN ALCOHOLIC ASSHOLE!"

The microphone broke free from its support and Martin and the superintendent tumbled to the floor.

The room fell silent.

The superintendent rose first.

"Let's go, pal. You're done here," he said, pulling Martin to his feet.

"DON'T TOUCH ME, MAN!" Martin said, shaking him off.

The superintendent let go, but his stern gaze was enough for Martin to know that he was indeed finished. After a few steps toward the shadows he became aware of the scroll in his right hand. He opened it.

It was blank.

He held it up for the crowd to see, and smiled before disappearing behind the curtain. He threw open the door of the backstage restroom and leaned against the tiled wall. He could barely hear it over the soft hum of the exhaust fan, but mixed in with all of the angry shouting was a smattering of cheers. At first, he thought it was only his ears deceiving him, but the more he focused on it, it became all he heard.

The superintendent pulled a handkerchief from his pocket and blotted the beads of sweat from his brow. Ever the professional, his expression quickly changed from one of exasperation to one of a competent calm. He stood behind the podium saying nothing and within a few moments, everyone was seated again as if nothing had happened.

The ceremony had reached the point where he would normally wish the newly graduated the best of luck in their future endeavors and wrap it all up with a quote from a great thinker or an amusing anecdote. But after the hullabaloo, he just wanted it to be over. He thanked those who had attended and directed everybody outside where photo ops would be aplenty.

One by one, they gathered their belongings and quietly made their way outside, seemingly still in a bit of shock. The graduates lingered, trying to squeeze every last bit of the moment.

The superintendent watched them embrace and laugh and cry with an almost paternal pride. He stepped away from the podium and into shadow behind the curtains where he spotted Martin exiting the bathroom.

"Stop right there!" he shouted. Martin obliged. The superintendent advanced on him to the point where they were nearly nose to nose.

"You must be very proud of yourself," he said, seething.

"I don't follow, sir," Martin said, backing up a step.

"I've been doing these things since before you were born, and every year it's the same thing. Diplomas, handshakes, a couple of coming of age speeches from the valedictorian and salutatorian, and bingo, we're done. Tanisha did her part, but you-,"

"I was just speaking from the heart, sir."

"Bullshit!" he shouted, spittle flying. "You were airing your family's dirty laundry. Even if your father is as big of a prick as you say, this was not the forum to discuss it."

"The applause seems to contradict that."

"You smug, little bastard. You think you know everything. Ninety-nine percent of the people out there were appalled. The only idiots clapping for that garbage were the burnouts."

"That's fine. Maybe it wasn't for everyone. That doesn't make it wrong."

"And the children. That language."

"I'm sure they've heard worse, and if not, they will."

Martin turned away but the superintendent grabbed his shoulder and spun him back around.

"I told you not to touch me," he said, defiantly.

"One other thing, you insolent little shit. When a man extends his hand to you, you look that man in the eye and you accept it."

Martin stepped back from the superintendent, straightened his posture, and extended his hand.

The superintendent breathed a disgusted sigh.

"Get out of my sight."

Once outside, Martin scanned the terrace for his mother. She was nowhere to be found amongst the smiling graduates and their families.

He sought higher ground near an elevated row of pines beyond the terrace to get a better perspective. After only a few steps he was cut off by Dan Schoenfeld.

"Hey, man. That was epic, yo!" Dan said, running his right hand, with a smoldering Camel perched between his index and middle fingers, through his matted, greasy hair.

Martin had not spoken to Dan since elementary school. They ran in different circles. Dan was not in the national honors society and Martin never smoked pot behind the auto shop.

"Oh, thanks man," Martin said, trying to seem as disinterested in the conversation as possible so he could resume his search.

"Yeah, me and my boys went off during that shit. We were all screaming and cheering and shit. It was crazy, dog!"

"That was you?"

"Hell yeah! My dad's a drunk, too. I wish he was here and heard your speech, 'cuz I woulda turned around and flipped that asshole off. I'da been all, FUCK YOU DAD!" Dan said, providing a visual by extending his middle finger out in space. He laughed and took a drag off his cigarette.

Dan walked away leaving Martin alone again. All of a sudden he felt ill. Without thought, he drifted into the sea of people. Conversations ceased as he passed by. Heads turned as if humiliation was transmissible via direct eye contact. Behind him, the more popular kids snickered and he didn't blame them. They weren't his friends. They were barely acquaintances. They didn't owe him any benefit of the doubt.

He pushed on through the crowd and saw, just a few paces away, were some of his Science Olympiad teammates. Surely, he felt, they would offer him sanctuary. When he reached them, though, he realized that they too were lost to him. Their solemn faces did not mock so much as pity him. Somehow it was worse than the laughter.

He needed to find his mother and even more so, to get out of the crowd. He nudged and pushed through the mass of people, unable to evade the sideways glances and hushed derision. He squinted into the low hanging sun, which washed out the detail on all but the most near of faces. Each second, he could feel panic rise up in him a little bit more.

He was suffocating.

He unbuttoned his collar and loosened his tie, but it was of no help. There was no end to the bodies. It was as if the crowd moved along with him, conspiring to keep him from getting free. Just as he thought he may pass out, he saw her seated on a bench near the pines. A wave of relief came and suddenly, a plethora of exit routes opened up to him. He took one and approached the bench.

Arms open prepared for an embrace, he stood before her. Diane looked away, failing to recognize his presence.

"Mom?"

She continued to pay him no mind.

"What's wrong with you?" he asked.

Diane finally addressed him. "With me? What the hell is wrong with you?"

"You too, huh," Martin said, falling in a heap onto the bench beside her.

"I will *always* love you and I will *always* support you, but…"

She paused before continuing. "I just don't understand why you chose your valedictorian speech as an outlet for anger towards your father."

Martin leaned his head back and noticed storm clouds were slowly infiltrating.

"I don't know. I looked out into the crowd and I saw you there and that empty chair and you looked so miserable."

"Oh, Martin," Diane said, shaking her head.

They sat in silence for several minutes until the first raindrops fell. Martin watched everyone scurrying about, snapping one last photo before retreating to their vehicles. Despite the rain, they seemed happy and he hated them for it.

"Can we go? I have no desire to be here anymore," he said.

"Fine," Diane said. She stood up and slung her purse over her shoulder.

"Not until we get a family photo," Jack Kerner said from behind them.

"Jack!" Diane said, startled.

"What the…?" Martin said.

Diane went to her husband and hugged him. She stepped back, and with a condescending eye, she said, "How did you?"

"Don't worry. I took a cab."

"How long have you been here?" she asked.

"Umm…not long."

"Well, you missed everything," Martin interjected, not wholly pleased to see him.

"Yes, well…," he hesitated and said, "I'm here now. Let's take a picture and get some dinner to celebrate."

"Yes, that sounds nice, doesn't it Marty?" Diane pleaded.

"Whatever," he said.

Martin called out to the first person he saw within earshot.

"Tanisha!"

She came to them, although her slow pace suggested she was unsure if she should.

"Yes?"

"Can you snap a quick pic of my family before it really starts to get nasty out here?"

"Sure."

"Thank you, dear," Diane followed. "I must say you did a wonderful job with your speech. Very poised."

"Oh, thanks. Martin, yours was very…um. Very, passionate."

Diane reached in her purse and retrieved her camera. As she passed it to Tanisha, Jack swiped it from her outstretched hand. "It's fine sweetheart, but I think we have it under control," he said.

She stood by, confused.

"Go run along now," Jack said, treating her like a fly at a picnic.

Tanisha walked away muttering under her breath.

"What the hell, dad?" Martin said.

"All I want is a goddamn family picture. She was liable to run off with the camera and sell it for drugs or some shit. You know how their kind are."

"Their kind?"

"Don't be coy with me, boy."

"That's it. I'm outta here," Martin said, storming away. Diane shot her husband a disapproving look.

"Really, Jack?" she said, before chasing Martin down. She caught up to him on the terrace which had mostly emptied save for a small group of Martin's peers smoking by the auditorium's exit. They stood there indifferent to the falling rain taking drag after drag.

"Martin…" she said.

"Did you see what he just did?"

"He's being unreasonable, but, despite himself, he's here and so are we, and goddamnit, we are still a family."

She was on the edge of breaking down. Her lip quivered, but she managed to fight off any more tears. "Now, let's go back and take the picture, and we can all go home."

"I'll take one with you, but not him."

"Martin…what if, one day, it's just you and him."

"Don't say stupid things."

"But what if? It can't be like this. You need to accept his deficiencies. He's your father. Like it or not, there will probably be a time when you'll need him."

"I will never need him for anything."

She put her hand on his shoulder. "For me then."

Martin looked at his mother, her makeup running down her face, and knew that he couldn't deny her this simple request.

"For you. But first, you gotta fix your mascara, or eyeliner or whatever it's called."

Diane pulled a pocket mirror and tissue from her handbag.

"Oh, my! I look awful!"

They walked together back towards Jack, who'd sought refuge under the auditorium's overhang. By the time they had reached him, Diane had remedied the makeup situation and they were ready to take the photo. Martin called out to the one smoker he recognized, Dan Schoenfeld. He ambled over to them and quickly lined the Kerners up with Diane and Jack flanking Martin on each side.

"Cheese," Dan said, almost out of obligation, and he snapped the photo.

It came out as good as it could have, considering the circumstances. Martin's smile was not really a smile, at all. It was more of a subtle upturn at the corners of his mouth. Jack, standing a safe distance away from his son, paired a toothy, remorseless grin with his bloodshot eyes. Diane, on the other hand, was beaming. She, in her pearls and favorite dress, had her arm wrapped tightly around Martin with the biggest smile she could muster. In that moment, she was truly happy. It was the first time in a while she was able to ignore the fact that she was dying.

CHAPTER III
MAY 9, 2008

It was 8:32 and Martin sat at the edge of his bed, breathing deeply, slowly emerging from his post-nap daze. The sleep was unfulfilling and longer than he intended.

Once he felt composed, he focused his attention back on the picture. He held the frame in his hands, tapping his fingers on its brushed steel edges. He then flipped it over and loosened the metallic tabs holding the backing board and took out the photo. Unfolding it along a hidden crease revealed his father. It was the first time Martin had seen Jack Kerner's face since his mother's funeral in May of 2005. It was surprising to him that he was unaffected by it. There was no false nostalgia.

Nothing tingled inside.

He grabbed his cell phone and scrolled through the contacts until he found 'Home'. His thumb hovered over the 'send' button momentarily before pressing it. Within seconds, he could hear ringing. Relief washed over him when he heard the click of the answering machine picking up. That is, until he heard his mother's voice.

"Hi. You have reached the Kerners. Leave a message after the beep and we'll call ya' back. Unless you're one of them telemarketers, then don't bother. Bye, now."

Martin hurriedly pressed 'end'.

"Why hadn't he changed the message on the machine?" he said, but there was no one there to answer. Again he scrolled through his contacts until he found 'Jack-cell'. He pressed 'send'.

Jack Kerner was eighteen again and it was a pristine summer day. He was in the GTO cruising down West Grand Boulevard. The convertible top was down and he could feel the heat radiating against his face and arms. He slowed to a stop at Woodward, he and the car engulfed by the pall cast down by the Fisher building on the left. Using only his index finger along the metallic spoke emerging from the center horn button, he guided the Pontiac into a right turn. Gravel crunched underneath the redline tires. The polished chrome on the rally wheels glimmered. Southbound on Woodward, he turned to his passenger and said, "You better hold onto somethin', babe."

She offered him a coquettish smile.

He squeezed the wheel with both hands before driving his right foot down on the accelerator. The rumble of the Ram Air equipped, four hundred cubic inch engine turned heads as he passed. Next to him, she squealed with a mix of excitement and apprehension as the rapid acceleration drove her back in her seat.

"Jack! Slow down!" she implored him, not really wanting him to.

"Not yet!" he said, watching the needle creep past sixty, then seventy.

"Baby!" she screamed again.

"Ok, ok. Don't have a cow!" he said, recognizing some actual distress in her tone.

The light ahead at Baltimore changed from yellow to red and he brought the GTO to a stop. Her chest heaved in and out and she playfully slapped him on the arm.

"Don't do that! You scared me half to death!"

"Sorry, sorry," Jack said, still grinning. "Hey, grab something from the glove compartment, will ya?"

"What?" she asked, sensing a ruse afoot.

"Go on."

She pushed the button and the GTO's glove compartment popped open, revealing two items. The owner's manual, and a small, felt covered cube. On its side were the words 'Simmons and Clark Jewelers.'

Her eyes nearly popped from their sockets.

"OH MY GOD!" she squealed over and over in a pitch that would make dogs howl.

"Well, are you gonna look inside?" Jack said, full on smiling.

Her hands shook as she slowly lifted the lid of the box along its hinge. Inside was a gold band equipped with a modest, but brilliant diamond. She looked at him as if asking permission to try it on.

"Go ahead. It's yours."

She slid it onto the appropriate finger and held it up, turning her wrist left and right, watching it capture and release the midday sun.

"So…whaddya say?"

There were tears in her eyes. "I say yes, Jack."

"Yes?"

"YES! YES! OF COURSE, YES!" She bounded from her seat, narrowly missing the GTO's Hurst shifter, and wrapped her arms around his neck. She kissed him all about the face and lips.

"Be careful. You almost knocked it out of gear."

"Oh, sorry." She sat back, and bounced ever so slightly in her chair, unable to sit still from the excitement. She stuck her arm out again, right in front of Jack's face this time. "Just look at it Jack! Isn't it so beautiful?"

He laughed and said, "I know it is. I picked it out, but you can't put your hand there. I can't see the road."

"Can I put it here?" she said, placing her hand on his right leg, just above the knee.

"Umm…yeah. I suppose that would be ok." His heart beating faster, he looked away from her dark brown eyes only for a second to check the light's status. It was still red. He begged it to stay that way as her hand began to inch up his thigh. The closer she got the more his glutes and thighs tightened. He tilted his head back, and peered into the clear blue expanse. He was holding his breath, his teeth clenched, bracing for contact. Her fingers crawled across his shorts, inches away, and then, strangely, her hand vibrated on his thigh; not at all the sensation he had expected.

"What the…?" Jack yelped, and the sky went black. He looked to his right and she was gone. He was still in the GTO, but he was alone, in the garage. He was no longer eighteen, but fifty-nine. Disoriented, it took him a moment to realize everything other than the vibration had been a fabrication of his mind.

His cell phone continued to shake.

He leaned over to pull it out and a sharp pain shot down his leg. His hip had stiffened from sitting in a forty-one year old chair for over four hours.

Wincing, he held the phone up to see who had so rudely interrupted his dream. It was all a blur and his readers were on his nightstand. He answered anyway.

"Hello?"

26

"Hello. Jack?"

"Yeah. Who's this?"

"It's Martin."

Still slightly buzzed from the six-pack, the name didn't immediately resonate.

"Who?"

A sigh came over the line. "Martin...your son."

Jack opened his mouth but nothing came out. He shifted in the chair and again felt an excruciating pain in his hip.

"DAMNIT!" he shouted. Reflexively he had reached for his hip and in the process dropped the phone.

"SHIT...HOLD ON A SEC!" he yelled out, hoping Martin heard him. "Where are you, you sonofabitch?" he said, blindly reaching down to the floor mat, finding nothing. He sat back and saw a glimmer of light emanating from underneath the clutch pedal. Jack nudged it with his shoe towards his outstretched hand and grabbed it.

"Martin?"

"What the hell is going on?" Martin said, annoyed.

"I just dropped the damn phone on the floor mat when my leg cramped up and-,"

"Floor mat? Wow. You're still doing that?"

"Did you call now, after three years, just to antagonize me, boy?"

"You know, if I blew my hip out falling down some stairs, I'd find a more comfortable place to pass out."

"That's enough. What do you want?"

"A favor."

"Well, if its money, you're shit outta-,"

"I need to take a class at Detroit State-,"

"So do it. What does that have to do with me?"

"If you'd let me finish, you'd know."

"All right. Go on with it."

"It's a car. I'll need to borrow one to get down there."

"Why Detroit State?"

"Because the class I need is not available here."

"That'll be a change from Ann Arbor. Detroit's a lot...darker if you know what I mean."

"Do you have one I can use, or not?" Martin said, irritated.

"I suppose you can use your mom's Chrysler. I never did get around to sellin' it."

"Great. I'll be there tomorrow with my things. Will you be home?"

"Things?"

"Yeah…I had to give up my apartment lease to pay for the class. Why? Is that a problem?"

"No, no. It's just…"

"You haven't burned the place down in some alcoholic stupor, have you?"

"Now wait a second, here. I'm confused. Didn't you get a nice chunk of change when your mother died?"

"Ann Arbor's expensive, Jack. What's left I'll need for four years of law school. I'm living on coffee and ramen noodles as it is."

"Student loans?"

"Maxed out."

"Huh…Seems like there should still be some money unless you've been livin' high on the hog."

"Well, there's not. I don't know why we're discussing this. Are you gonna help me or not?"

"Tomorrow, huh? Kinda short notice."

"It's not like I planned this. Classes start Monday."

"Well…I guess I'll see you tomorrow."

"Ok. Good," Martin said, matter of factly, and he hung up.

Jack held the phone to his ear for a moment as his brain toiled away trying to process what had just happened. After a few seconds he put it down and closed his eyes, attempting to go back to that day on sun drenched Woodward Ave. No matter how hard he clenched his lids, though, he remained alone in the garage.

Discouraged, he pressed the button on the visor, and, on command, the garage door rose. Robinson was gone. The lilacs pruned. Night had come, and with it a light mist. Jack collected the empties strewn across the garage floor, and dumped them in a trash bin in the corner that was filled with dozens of others just like them.

CHAPTER IV
MAY 10, 2008

In the two years that Martin had lived in his apartment on South Forest, the only person in the building he had spoken to was Abigail Joplin. He had initially written her off as another pretentious Ann Arbor hipster, with her pale skin, white girl dreads and an affinity for consignment shop attire. He soon came to find that, despite this she was also impossibly friendly. Their first "hello", and every little tête-à-tête in the halls since, was initiated by her. It amazed him how she never failed to ask him how things were, and how she seemed to be genuinely interested in the answer. She was the closest thing to a friend Martin had in Ann Arbor and that was why he was knocking on her door.

She opened it wearing a stretched out sweater emblazoned with an obese Calico cat paired with black and white striped leggings.

"Marty!" she squealed, springing forth and wrapping her arms high up around his neck.

"Abby!" Martin said, trying to match her enthusiasm, but failing miserably.

She released him and stepped back.

"I haven't seen you in forever."

"Finals," he said with a shrug.

"Ahh. Well, c'mon in," she said, waving him inside.

"No, no. I'd like to, but I really just came over to ask you for a favor, but don't worry if you can't do it. It's no big deal."

"What is it?"

"It's kind of a long story, but…I'm leaving today."

"Where?" she said, concerned.

"Back ho…to, uh, my dad's place. Hazel Park."

"Aww, you didn't get in? I thought you were doing well?"

"I was, and I got in-,"

"Yay!"

"Sort of. I have to take a class. It's a formality, really."

"Why back home then?"

"The class is at Detroit State."

"Confused."

"There wasn't anything left here that fulfilled the requirements."

"Bummer," she said, pushing out a pouty lower lip.

"Yeah, it is, 'cuz the class wasn't in my budget so I had to give up my summer lease to pay for it."

"So…do you have, like, a truck coming to get your stuff?"

"That's the thing…"

"You need somewhere to *put* your stuff."

"Yeah. Just the big stuff, really. Futon, table, desk. And only until the fall."

"I got plenty of room. Bring it over."

"Really?"

"Yeah."

"You're awesome. I really appreciate it."

"Shut up. So when're you leavin'…actually, *how* are you leaving?"

"Bus."

"To Hazel Park?"

"Detroit. Another one to Hazel Park after."

"That sounds awful."

"Not looking forward to it."

"I'm heading back to Port Huron today around 4:00. If you want, you can hitch with me."

"That…yeah. That would be way better."

"Throw me a couple bucks towards gas and it's a deal."

"Will do, and I'll be by later with the stuff."

"I'll be here."

It was just after 4:00 when Martin and Abigail finished relocating Martin's things to her living room. She offered him a diet pop, which he graciously declined, and then suggested they hit the road.

"My chariot awaits," she said as she led him out of the building towards the resident parking lot. Her chariot, in this case, was a 2005 silver Toyota Prius. She popped the hatchback, and he deposited his only Earthly belongings, other than the furniture, in the trunk; a sack of clothes, a backpack filled with briefing cases he was supposed to study prior to the upcoming law semester, and his laptop. After doing this, he settled into the surprisingly roomy shotgun seat.

"Off we go!" she said, and they quietly zoomed down Forest Street. Martin watched as the only home he had known for the last three years grew smaller in the side view mirror, getting anxious about returning to the home he had spent those last three years trying to forget.

"So where's your house?"

"It's my dad's house, actually."

"Okay—so where's your dad's house, then?" she replied, wondering why he felt the need to specify.

"Off Nine Mile. You can grab 94 ag-,"

"Nope. I'm horrible with directions and road names and all that. Just plug it in the GPS please and thank you."

He did as she asked and pulled his phone from his pocket. He sent the words 'on the way' to his father via text message and resumed gazing out the window at the passing landscape. It wasn't long before the conversation stalled, despite Abigail's valiant effort to the contrary, due to Martin's distant, one-word responses.

By the time they passed I-275, the vertical stretch of highway bisecting Detroit's western suburbs the atmosphere in the car had grown uncomfortable. Trying to circumvent this, Abigail said, "Music?" with an upward inflection of her voice at the end, intimating a question.

"What about it?"

"Did you want me to turn some on, duh?"

"Sure," Martin said, knowing the alternative would be to sit in awkward silence with a girl, while friendly, who was still hardly more than an acquaintance, with nothing to occupy his thoughts other than the sting of bile rising up in his throat from the thought of seeing his drunkard, callous, racist father again, but also from the fact that he was about to attend a strange school in a city he'd been indoctrinated to fear, and the passing of the class held in the balance his future as a lawyer, something he had spent the majority of his life striving towards.

"Music would be great."

"Cool," she said, and plugged her mp3 player into an auxiliary cable. "I just downloaded an album from this indie band from New York. It's a guy and a girl. She does the keyboards, and he's on drums, or is it the other way around? I can't remember, but they are *so* good. You will love it!"

Martin did not love it. In fact, he thought it may have been the worst hipster garbage he had ever heard. It resembled the sound of nails on a chalkboard, if only those nails belonged to a dying cat. He made it through about five songs before he reached over and shut it off. "I'm sorry. I can't…" he said.

"What?"

"No music right now. Is that ok?"

"Sure. What, though? Did you not like it?"

"No, no. It was great. It's me. My mind is kinda spinning is all."

"It *is* great, isn't it? I'll burn you a copy."

"Thanks," he said, feigning a smile.

"Why's your mind spinning?"

He waved her off. "No. It's no big deal. I'll be fine."

"Uh uh. You can't shut off my music and then expect me to drive in silence. You gotta talk to me or else I'll go narco and just pass out."

"It's only like twenty more minutes to Hazel Park."

"Music or talking. Pick one."

Weighing the pros and cons, Martin decided talking was better than any more of that dreck she called music. Plus, if he was being completely honest with himself, he needed to get some of what was bothering him off his chest, and he would have been hard pressed to find a more receptive set of ears than Abigail's.

"Fine. Let's talk."

"All right. How long has it been since you've been home?" she asked, getting right to the crux of it like it was written on his face.

"A lifetime."

Martin could feel Abigail's eyes on him, knowing that she was looking for a more specific answer.

"As in…"

"When I called my dad yesterday, it was the first time I'd spoken to him in years."

"Oh," she said. There was something in her voice that suggested she was aware of the Pandora's Box she'd opened. For a good thirty seconds, nobody said anything. Abigail, afraid to dig any deeper, resigned herself to the fact that the trip would be done in silence.

Then, quite suddenly, Martin spun his body towards her and erupted with words.

"It's just that he...he..." Martin said, his palms turned up as if waiting for the end of the sentence to drop from the sky.

"He what?"

"He just let her waste away. He was never there for her or me for that matter. I had to go to school. What was I supposed to do? Drop out? She wouldn't have wanted that."

"I...I don't know. Who are you talking about?" Abigail said, thoroughly confused, and just a wee bit startled. Martin exhaled deeply and settled back into his chair. After a moment, seeming more in control of himself, he continued.

"It was March 6, 2005. A Sunday."

Jack Kerner spent an inordinate amount of his Saturday deciding what to wear. After trimming the scraggly, gray hairs that protruded from his face, and combing the mess of follicles on top of his head, he did two loads of laundry, and sifted through it all for the right outfit. He normally paid little mind to his attire, but on that day, he had wanted to make sure his clothes did not send the wrong message. A black shirt was tossed aside for being too dark, too imposing. Then a crisp white button down was bypassed for suggesting surrender. Finally, after he scolded himself over being concerned with such trivialities, he put on a brown and yellow striped flannel shirt with blue jeans. He could think of no emotion implied by brown and yellow stripes.

When Martin's text arrived, he made his way to the single car garage that sat unattached at the culmination of a fifty foot driveway just to the right of the humble eleven-hundred square foot bungalow. It, like most of the property, existed under the canopy of the surrounding ash. He stopped briefly to pry a few weeds from between the cracks in the cement before arriving at the GTO. He eased himself into the driver's seat, and set a six-pack of beer down next to him. He was in good cover, as the descending sun had already made its way to the westward sky, casting a thick shadow in front of the garage. From his perch, he had an excellent view of the street.

It was quiet in the car. Jack took a deep breath, and looked at his watch. It was 4:35. Martin was expected to arrive within the hour. He unsheathed one of the beers and lifted the tab but did not crack the seal. He put it back down on the seat, and wiped the condensation off on his pant leg.

As he watched the street in silence, a calm came over him and he recalled the countless stakeouts he had undertaken as a detective for the Detroit Police Department.

"That was another life," he told the empty car.

He reached over and opened up the glove compartment. On top of the dog eared owner's manual was an old, faded Polaroid. It was from July 21, 1967, just days before the Detroit race riot. Three people were standing in front of his Pontiac GTO convertible. He had just brought it home that day from the dealer. Jack was in the middle of the threesome, with the twins, Frank and Pamela King on each side. They were smiling. Not like the 'say cheese' forced smiles found in many photographs, but real, caught in the precise moment of true happiness smiles.

Jack's eyes lingered over Frank's face. They were best friends back then, but it had been over two years since they'd spoken, and that conversation had not gone well.

The sound of an approaching car snapped Jack back into the here and now. He put the photograph back in the glove compartment and watched a 2002 Crown Victoria come to a stop in front of the house. The driver was looking in his direction. It was his neighbor, Robinson.

"Keep moving. I don't have time for your bullshit today," he said.

"You remember the exact date?" Abigail asked.

"It was the last day of spring break. My ride was about to pick me up to go back to Ann Arbor for the rest of the winter semester. She was in the back bedroom in the hospital bed they set up for her. The whole time I'd been home, she'd been in and out of consciousness."

"Are you talking about your mom?"

Martin nodded. "It was hard for me to look at her. The chemo ravaged her. By that point, she couldn't have weighed more than ninety pounds. The bed…it seemed to engulf her. Her lips were chapped. Her skin, pale and blotchy. She wore a blue headscarf with lilies on it. They were her favorite. Out of all of it, though, the worst part was her eyes. They looked like they were sinking into her skull."

"That's horrible," Abigail said.

NOCTURNE IN BLACK AND WHITE

"It was. Chemo is shit. It's almost worse than the cancer, in my opinion. Anyways, I decided to sit by her side until my ride arrived. I brought a bowl of ice cream for her because it was the only thing she seemed to be able to keep down. When I walked in, though, she was asleep so I started to talk to her instead."

"What did you say?"

"Small talk. The weather. I remember it was nice that day. Like fifty degrees, and sunny. She didn't respond, so I just sat by for as long as I could take it, watching her sleep, then I got up and told her I was leaving for school and kissed her goodbye on the forehead."

"And..."

"I didn't make it to the door. Either the kiss woke her up, or she was up the whole time. She said, 'You know it's cruel to bring me a bowl of Ray's mint chocolate chip, only to set it out of my reach.'"

"What did you do?"

"I sat back down and fed it to her, one spoonful at a time. 'Ooh, it's cold,' she'd say."

"Isn't it supposed to be?"

"That's what I said."

"And what did she say?"

"She called me a smart ass."

Abigail chuckled, and so, in turn, did Martin.

"It went on for a while. I told her about school. She mostly listened, smiling as best as she could, but then, all of a sudden, her expression soured. I thought she was in pain, but that wasn't it."

"What was it?"

"She had to tell me something that she really didn't want to tell me. The story of how she met my father."

"She had never talked about it before?"

"Bits and pieces, but not the real meat of it. She felt she needed to get it off her chest right then because she knew she was dying."

"She said that?"

"Yeah, and I got mad at her for it. I was naïve enough to think that she still might pull out of it, you know? But she was very matter of fact about death. 'Everybody dies,' she said. 'I can't fathom why anyone would want it any other way.'"

"Well..."

"I know. She was right. She always was."

"So what was the story," Abigail said.

"She said she met him at the hospital after his accident."

"What kind of accident?"

"That's the thing. My whole life I'd heard about my father's 'accident.' Any time his hip bothered him, he'd mention it. In '86, a few months or so after I was born, he fell down a set of stairs and shattered his pelvis at an axle plant he had been working at as a night watchman."

"Ouch!"

"Yeah. Apparently the lighting in the stairwell wasn't up to code and he bit it hard. Ripped up his shoulder good, too. He never worked again. Got a nice settlement, though."

"That sucks."

"Apparently this other 'accident' occurred in July of '82."

"What happened?"

"My mom was a nurse at Detroit General. My dad initially was in the ICU and then got shifted into her ward after his condition stabilized. The psych ward."

"Psych? Why?"

"He tried to kill himself."

Abigail's eyes widened and her mouth fell agape. For the first time since Martin knew her, she seemed to be at a loss for words.

"It's ok. He obviously survived," Martin said.

"I know, but…I just…I don't know how I'd feel if I knew that my father had tried to do that. You seem so cavalier."

"The shock has worn off for me, I guess."

"Oh. Well…how did he, you know…"

"With his gun. He used to be a cop, so he always had one. Probably still does."

"Oh. So he got transferred to the psych ward and…"

"Well, she told me he didn't feel like he belonged there, that's for sure. He was very upset that they wouldn't let him go, but he couldn't be released until it was determined that he wasn't going to be a danger to himself or anybody else. When the doctors would ask him to talk about the suicide attempt he said that he couldn't remember trying to do it, and it must have been a drunken accident."

"Well, how do you know it wasn't?"

"Apparently, they had him on some strong painkillers and sedatives while he was there, and they loosened his tongue. She called the few minutes before he passed out his 'magic interval'."

"What did he say?"

"My mom said it was nonsense, mostly, but she was so intrigued by him that she'd sit by while he slept and listen for little nuggets. Apparently women like mysterious types."

"Well, yeah," she said, her tone suggesting that it was a universal truth.

"Anyways, one day he mumbled some actual sentences. He said, 'Fuck Reggie Howard' and 'let me go, I need her.'"

"Who is Reggie Howard?"

"No clue. All I know is that he mentioned him again when he was shitfaced the day I graduated high school."

"What about the other part? Who's the 'her' he needed?" Abigail asked.

Martin shrugged. "My mom initially thought it was *his* mom, my grandma, who he was talking about, but she died during childbirth. It couldn't have been her. He never knew her."

"Did your mom ever ask him?"

"The next day, when he was coherent, and so did the doctors. He denied saying it."

"Hmm. Very mysterious."

"Uh huh. So, after a few weeks, they determined that he was not a danger to himself and released him. I guess my mom had grown quite fond of him and was upset to see him go. She said, and I'm paraphrasing, 'It was my face he woke up to most mornings, and when he opened those dark eyes and looked at me, I melted.'"

"Wow. Romantic."

"Yeah, and stupid."

"What, what?"

"Her words, not mine. She told me that she was young and impressionable and may have only been in love with the mystery. It was like the fact that he'd been admitted for attempted suicide failed to register with her twenty-three year old brain."

"She said that?"

"Yeah. So, she slipped her phone number into the pocket of his jeans on the day he was to be released, not really thinking he'd call. They dated for two months or so before he proposed Christmas Eve that year."

"How'd he do it?"

"He didn't get down on one knee, or anything. He told her that he needed her to help him feel 'normal' again."

"Not very romantic."

"No, but the part about him needing her struck a chord. Being a nurse, she always had a soft spot for the weak and wounded, which is fine, but not something to build a marriage on."

"It's a good thing for you that they did."

"I suppose."

"Did she say anything else?"

"Yeah. She was always covering for him until the day she died, making excuses for his alcoholism, racism, and all his other 'isms.' She said something along the lines of, 'Beneath his exterior, there's a man whose demons take over and he drinks and hurts himself and those he loves.' She said that whatever took place before he shot himself must have been truly terrible and that she believed there was always a reason for his actions."

"So she never found out who Reggie Howard or this anonymous woman was?"

"No, but she told me that when I find out who they are, I'll find out who my father is."

"Are you gonna ask him?"

"No. I don't need to. I know enough."

"So that was it?"

"Basically. I guess she just wanted to get everything out there, so he and I could start building some kind of relationship. She wanted to die knowing that we'd be there for each other."

"And you haven't spoken to him in how many years?"

"Almost three. Since her funeral and even then I might have said two or three sentences."

"Oh," Abigail said. Again, Martin could feel her eyes upon him, and with them, judgment.

"What?"

"She wanted you to-,"

"To what? Be best friends? To go fishing and watch baseball and whatever it is that guys do with their dads? How could I? Were you listening to the story?" Martin said, defensively. He continued, more animated, "I'm talking about a man who loved alcohol more than his own wife and kid. A man who disappeared when needed the most. I mean, he got plastered on the most important day of my life and missed the whole thing! I'm supposed to forget that? I'm supposed to forget her dry lips on my cheek and her jagged shoulder blades, all the while he was boozing and shirking his responsibilities? I'm sorry. I can't. I can't just forgi-,"

"Martin," Abigail interrupted.

"What?"

"We're here."

"What?"

The sight of his childhood home shook him. He took it all in; on the left, the ash trees he used to pepper with rocks. On the right, Robinson's finely pruned azaleas that more than once he'd lost a baseball in. And straight ahead, up the driveway, the open garage, and inside it, the GTO shrouded in darkness.

His body tensed up.

He closed his eyes and took a few deep breaths, trying to take solace in the fact that he'd be back in Ann Arbor in a few months.

"This is it, right?" Abigail said, trying to pull Martin back into the moment. He didn't respond.

"Martin," she said, this time giving him a little shoulder shake.

He opened his eyes and said, "Yeah, yeah. This is it."

"Good. I thought I lost you there for a sec."

"I just needed a moment."

"Understandable," Abigail said, popping the hatchback.

"Thanks, um…for the ride, and storing my stuff. I appreciate it." He handed her a ten dollar bill, which she directed him to drop in the cup holder.

"No prob."

He retrieved his things and closed the hatch. Before approaching the house, he stopped and tapped on the window.

"What's up?" Abigail said.

"To get to 94 you have to-,"

"I'll put it in the ol' GPS. Thanks, though."

"Of course."

"I'll see you when you start lawyering in the fall then, right?"

"Barring some catastrophe…"

She pulled out onto the street, and quietly drove away leaving Martin alone in the driveway, frozen.

The AM oldies station was playing "Standing in the Shadows of Love" by the Four Tops, and Jack hummed along, tapping the steering wheel. A minivan drove by, then a Jeep, then nothing for a few minutes. The Four Tops finished their serenade, and an advertisement for an erectile dysfunction drug came on. Jack switched off the radio and pulled the key from the ignition.

The anticipation was driving him batty. The fact that he had no idea what car Martin would be arriving in made every car a possibility, and therefore, most of them heart-wrenching disappointments. He pulled his cell phone out of his pocket to check the time.

It was 4:55.

He set it down on the console, only too near to the edge, and it fell to the floor. "Goddamnit!" he said, cursing his clumsiness.

The phone wedged itself under the seat. Jack felt around blindly, finding nothing but the supports until his hand struck a cold, metallic object. He pulled it free.

"Hello, there. I forgot about you," Jack said to his police issue Smith and Wesson .38 revolver.

Typically an officer leaving active duty must relinquish his gun, but Jack's exit from the force was anything but typical.

His fingers wrapped around the walnut grip and he delicately caressed the hammer with his thumb. He ran his left hand up and down the blue steeled finish on the barrel. Just the act of holding the gun again rekindled so many feelings. He felt a sense of purpose and power, more so than at any time in years.

There were five rounds in the cylinder, though how old the ammo was, he could not say. He could not even remember when he placed the gun under that seat. He clicked the cylinder into position and raised the gun up. He closed his left eye, and peered down the sight, right at a silver Toyota Prius.

"Shit!" he said, sliding the gun back under the seat. He crouched further into the shadow and waited. Nothing happened for it seemed like an eternity, until finally Martin emerged. The Prius drove off, leaving him alone in the driveway, his steely gaze aimed at the garage briefly before he made his way inside.

Everything was the same, yet it felt somehow different. His mother's absence was palpable, though traces of her were everywhere. She was in the duck print wallpaper covering the kitchen walls. She was in the collection of ceramic figurines in the curio cabinet. She definitely was in the gray brain cancer magnet on the refrigerator.

Martin set his things down and stepped deeper into the kitchen, dragging his fingertips lightly across the Formica counter, the only sound a creaking from the seventy year old floorboards under his weight. He walked into the living room and looked towards the front door. The picture that Jack had knocked over during his drunken outburst was hanging again, the glass replaced. He could still see his mother stooped over those shards.

The tears in her eyes.

Down the hall he went, towards the room she died in. He put a hand on the knob, but couldn't will himself to turn it. His chest began to heave and panic started to build up in him. His old bedroom was on his left, offering him an escape, but he resisted. He knew there was no point delaying the inevitable.

Jack wanted nothing more than to greet his son as soon as he popped out of that hybrid, but he thought an ambush might only frighten the boy. He wanted to give Martin some space. Some time to get reacclimated. But, when Martin burst forth from the house, hard stepping towards the shadowy garage, Jack knew he'd made a mistake not meeting him in the house. With Martin approaching the passenger side of the GTO, Jack pressed the button to lower the window, to no avail. Repeated attempts produced the same result. Martin, having reached, looked in, agitated.

"This damn thing isn't working for some reason," Jack said.

"The key," Martin replied.

Jack realized his error, and inserted the key, turning it halfway and lowered the window. Father and son met eyes for the first time in three years.

"Hello, Martin."

"Jack."

Jack had a million things to say to his son, but couldn't find one of them. Instead he sat waiting for Martin to break the silence which he did after noticing the six-pack on the passenger seat.

"Un-fucking-believable!" Martin said, smacking the door in disgust.

"Hey, goddamnit! You could of…did you scratch the paint?"

Martin said nothing as he stormed down the driveway.

"HEY!" Jack shouted throwing the door open and rushing after him.

Martin stopped, but did not turn to face him. Jack put his hand on Martin's shoulder to turn him around, but was startled when Martin spun away.

"Don't touch me, man!"

"Hey…calm down."

"Calm down?"

"This isn't…let's just take a minute and…now, I haven't had a drop all day. I-,"

Martin interrupted him and said, "Let me stop you right there. This is no happy ending where the estranged son comes running home with arms wide open. This is necessity. You hear me? This is born of desperation."

"Ok, ok," Jack said, palms out.

"I didn't want this. To be here with you. I'm sure you didn't want it either."

"I never said-,"

"Let me finish. For three months, I will come and go as I please. I will rely on you for a bed, and the use of my mother's car. That is all. We will not speak. We will not eat together. Ideally, we won't even see each other. Ok?"

Jack's realized right then that Martin had grown. He was looking up, albeit slightly, into his son's eyes.

"Have you gotten taller?"

"What?"

"You gotta be at least six foot," Jack said.

Martin cocked his head to the side, confused. "I'm going to my room," he said. "Please leave me to my studies. I have a reading list ten miles long for law school, which is where I intend to be in September."

Jack nodded and Martin went inside. He slowly crept back to the garage, and the GTO. He examined the door for any scratches, and felt relieved to find nothing but a handprint. He pulled the corner of his shirt from his pants, and wiped it clean, blowing any remaining dust off that the shirt didn't catch. After collecting the six-pack, he closed the garage and walked towards the house.

He cracked open the can he'd freed earlier and, right there in the middle of the driveway, he closed his eyes, cocked his head back and emptied the contents down his throat. He inhaled deeply, holding it, embracing the burn and waiting for the medicine to take effect. When he opened his eyes, they were wet with tears. He stood there, trying to convince himself that they were caused by the beer's sting, dumbfounded, not so much as how Martin reacted to seeing him again, but as to why he thought he deserved anything different.

CHAPTER V
JULY 21, 1967

Jack Kerner eased the GTO onto Detroit's West Philadelphia Street and parked in front of the duplex he had always called home. He closed his eyes and felt the summer sun skittering on his face. He could have stayed that way for hours. When he opened his eyes, they dropped to the instrument panel. He touched the odometer, to ensure that the fourteen miles it read was not an illusion.

"How 'bout a ride?" said Pamela King, as she leapt down the steps of her family's half of the duplex. Her twin brother and Jack's best friend, Frank, followed behind.

"Hey, now. Ain't no way you can afford something this cherry," Frank said, smiling.

"I must. They let me drive it off the lot," Jack replied, wearing a grin of his own.

Frank walked around behind the car and put his hands on Jack's shoulders. "Well, that only leaves one explanation. You must be doing some streetwalking late nights on the Boulevard," he said.

"Ha ha. You slay me. You know I've been bussing tables at Carl's."

"If you got this picking up rich folk's chewed up fat, why am I going to college?"

Jack looked over at Pamela. "You say you want a ride, huh?"

"You got the time?" she said, her hands in the back pockets of her cut-off shorts.

"Always time for an angel like you."

Frank rolled his eyes, figuring he should at least feign disgust.

Pamela got in and Jack started the car. The engine roared to life, making Pamela flinch when Jack revved it up.

"She gets the first ride? I see where I stand," Frank said.

"You can drive it when we get back."

"Far out!" Frank said, with a fist pump. He hopped onto the curb and watched them off towards Third St and out of sight.

"Was that Kerner?" a deep, booming voice said behind him.

"Shit, Reggie. Don't be creepin' up on a brother like that!"

Reggie Howard had been watching the whole exchange from his porch a few houses down the block. The Kerner, King and Howard families had been mainstays on West Philadelphia for years, and the twins, Reggie and Jack all had grown up together.

"That's right. You are a *brother*. How you let a cracker mess 'round with your sister?"

Frank, still a little disquieted, took a step back, to get out of Reggie's shadow. Though no dwarf, at six feet and one hundred eighty pounds, Frank paled in size compared to Reggie's six feet four inches and two hundred twenty-five pounds.

"Cracker? You're calling Jack, your friend since forever, a cracker?"

"He ain't my friend. Yours neither."

"News to me."

"You should be tryin' to set her up with a brother."

"Yeah, like who? You?"

"Shit yeah, like me. Pammie and me's a better fit, anyhow."

"I couldn't do that to my best friend."

"What I tell you? He ain't your friend. He leave your ass at the first sign of trouble. Believe me."

"Well, even if I wanted to set you up with her, I couldn't. Who Pammie dates ain't up to me. What's gotten into you, anyway?"

"The truth. My brother been educatin' me."

"Your brother? Isaac?"

"Yeah. Ice been back a couple days now."

"I thought he was...you know," Frank said.

"In prison? Yeah, he was out in Cali. Folsom. But they let him out. Overcrowded, I guess."

"They let murderers out on overcrowding?"

Reggie reached out and grabbed Frank by the collar of his t-shirt.

"ATTEMPTED murder!"

"Sorry, sorry! I know. Attempted murder. Just don't hit me," Frank pleaded.

Reggie released Frank from his grip, and sat down on the curb. "Sorry. It's just…"

"No. It's fine. You just done stretched out my shirt," Frank said, taking a seat on the curb a safe distance from Reggie.

"So, anyway, 'bout six months ago, Ice was out in Oakland and met up with these guys, Huey and Bobby. They teaching brothers and sisters to stand up for they selves."

"Nice."

"Nice? It's a goddamn revolution, like Malcolm preached. Not this Dr. King 'let's all get along' bullshit."

"You got a problem with the Doctor?"

"You don't? Look around you, brother! This is a white man's world. He don't want to share with us, so if we want somethin', we gotta take it."

Frank shook his head, which drew a slant-eye look from Reggie.

"What you shakin' yo' head fo'?"

Frank chose his words wisely, looking to avoid any further stretching of his shirt.

"It's just funny to me you never said anything like this before. Even how you're talkin', like, your words…"

"What?"

"Sounds like, maybe, Ice is talkin' through you."

"What? You think I can't decide shit for myself? Think I listen to anything Ice be tellin' me? Forget you then," he said, popping up off the curb and back towards his house.

"Wait," Frank shouted, knowing he had hit a nerve. "Come back."

Reggie stopped but didn't turn around.

"Tell me 'bout Oakland."

It took a few seconds, but Reggie sat back down on the curb. With vigor, he continued. "They policin' the police, shotguns out, in uniform like a goddamn army. Ice says it's beautiful."

"Shotguns?"

"Yeah. They tired of the pigs pushin' them around, and tired of bein' forced to live in these ghettos, cops doin' what they want. They takin' the power back." Frank had never seen Reggie so excited about anything before in his life.

"So how come your brother came back?"

"Well, he says that one night while they were out on patrol, he took a pot shot at this pig as he drove by. This Huey and Bobby, they said with it already bein' a powder keg over there they didn't want him bein' all hot headed, startin' shit before they was ready."

"So...they kicked him out?"

"They ain't kick shit out! He left. Figured he was better served comin' home and startin' a movement here. Detroit's like ninety percent white cops, even though the city's thirty percent black. You believe that? And that whore, the sister that got killed a couple weeks back? Everybody knows it was them pigs did it, not no damn mafia, like they sayin'."

"You believe all that?"

"Why shouldn't I? I was asleep to the reality, or foolin' myself that things weren't bad as they are, but now I see."

"I don't know, man. This ain't Oakland. DPD ain't never bothered me none."

"You've never had one of them pigs stop you for no reason at all?"

"Naw, man. At least not to a point I'd start runnin' round with a shotgun. College is more my style. Accounting. Hey, maybe I can get back at the white man by screwin' him out of some deductions," Frank said, laughing.

"Joke now, but come the revolution, you either with us, or you ain't."

"Here comes the white man, now."

The GTO came rumbling down the street. Jack parked next to the curb, flexing the V8's muscles a few extra times before shutting it down. Reggie walked over to the passenger side and opened Pamela's door.

"Thanks, Reg. When did you get here?"

"I been around. So, where'd ya get this lead sled, Kerner?"

"Lead sled? This baby purrs, just ask Pam."

She nodded in approval and Reggie slammed the door a little harder than necessary, drawing a raised eyebrow from Jack.

"Don't know your own strength?" Frank asked.

"I know exactly how strong I am," he snapped with a menacing glare.

Jack got out and reached into the backseat. He pulled out a camera and tossed it to Reggie, who fumbled and caught it.

"Mind takin' a Polaroid of us, man? I want to get a shot of me with my two girls," Jack said, nuzzling up to Pamela.

"What?"

"Pammie and the GTO, of course," Jack said, chuckling.

"Man, I ain't no photographer."

"What photographer? Just point and click. A monkey could do it."

"The hell's that supposed to mean?" Reggie said, advancing on Jack, whose smile was replaced by a look of utter confusion and fear.

"Nothin' man. I'm just sayin' it's easy."

Frank wedged himself between them.

"It's an innocent comment. We're all friends here."

"Man, you such an Uncle Tom and a disgrace to that 'fro on top yo' head!" Reggie said, backing off.

Pamela walked over to Reggie, smiling all the while.

"Reg baby, don't get all riled up, now. Can't you just take the picture? For me?"

The little voice inside Reggie's head said to walk away and smash the camera to bits on the sidewalk in the process, but it was no match for Pamela. When it came to her, every bit of his hulking six feet four inches was powerless.

"For you, Pammie," he said, meekly.

"Good," Jack said. "Frank, why don't you get in on this, too?"

Frank met his sister and best friend at the GTO. He put his arm around Pamela, who stood between the boys. Reggie lifted the camera to his eye, and counted backward from three. At one, Frank yelled, "STOP!" He stepped aside and slid a pick out of his pocket, and began pulling out his afro.

"Franklin King, you fool! Get back in this photo. We don't got all day," Pamela managed through bursts of laughter. Frank got back in line, and leaned on her shoulder. Everybody smiled but Reggie. He clenched his teeth and centered the trio in the view.

"Snap it, baby!" Pam said.

He pressed the button. The picture slid out of the groove, and the image began to materialize. He walked over to Jack, and shoved the camera into his chest, and said, "Snapped."

They all watched as he walked away.

"What was that all about?" Jack said to the others, puzzled.

"Ice been fillin' his head with shit," Frank said.

"Ice?"

"Yeah. He's back preachin' revolution. You know how Reggie always looked up to him. He'd jump off the Ambassador if Ice said to. I wouldn't worry about it. In a few days, I'm sure Ice will split town or get pinched, and Reggie'll be back to normal."

"Hope so. Well, you ready?"

"For?"

"For the one and only time I'll let you behind the wheel," Jack said, dangling the keys in Frank's face. He snatched them and sprinted around the car, vaulting over the door and into the driver's seat.

"Hey, watch the upholstery!"

"Hush now. I got this."

Frank started the engine and revved it several times.

"Ooh, that's nice," he said.

"If there's a scratch on her, it's comin' out of your ass!"

Frank left twin rubber patches behind as he darted off. Jack and Pamela walked over to the porch and sat down. She reached for his hand, and intertwined their fingers.

"Can I put it back on now?" she asked, squirming.

"You crazy?" Jack said.

"Why not?"

"Someone could see."

"So, am I never supposed to tell my folks?"

"We'll tell everybody soon enough. Let's just get down to D.C. and get settled first."

"What are you gonna do when I'm takin' classes at Howard?"

"I'll find work. They have to have factories down there, too."

"Is your dad gonna be mad you won't be taking that job he got you at GM?"

"He'll be mad, but for a whole different reason."

Her eyes dropped to the tops of her shoes.

"Hey," Jack said, lifting her chin. "Nobody said this is gonna be easy."

"I know."

"I love you."

"I love you, too."

He smiled at her, and she barely returned it. At that moment a police cruiser zoomed by, traveling at a higher speed than usual for a residential area.

"If I let you put it on again, would that make you happy?"

The wattage of her smile increased tenfold.

Jack looked left and right. The street looked free of any nosey neighbor types.

"Ok. Ten seconds, and be discreet about it."

She dug into her pocket and pulled out the ring. Once it was on her finger, she couldn't seem to be able to sit still. She sprang forward and wrapped her arms around Jack. Out of the corner of his eye, Jack thought he saw the curtains shift in the front window of his half of the duplex. He pried her arms free from his neck and looked again, but there was no one there.

"Ok. Ten seconds up."

She pouted but ultimately returned the ring to her pocket.

"How I see it is, I'll tell my pops I can't start at GM until September because I want to help you guys move in to your new digs in D.C. Then, when you leave, I have an excuse to come with you. Once we're down there, we can find a justice of the peace."

"Justice of the peace?" Pamela said, with a troubled look on her face.

"What do you think? Your daddy will happily walk you down the aisle when he knows it'll be me waitin' there at the end?"

"I guess not. I just…I always pictured my wedding different, is all."

"If you wanna back out, let me know."

She leaned over and gave him a peck on the cheek. "Sorry, Kerner. You are mine now. Forever and ever."

Jack watched her get up and cross the porch to her side of the duplex, waiting for the screen door to slowly pull shut before going into his. He was startled when he saw his father sitting in the den.

August Kerner was a stern man. His hands rough and calloused from years on the line. His penchant for cheap whiskey could be read in his jaundice yellowed eyes and his proclivity for cheap cigars was audible in each harsh and phlegmy cough.

"Jack. A word?"

The throes of childbirth stole his wife from him and left him alone to raise a boy he never loved. Every time he looked at his son, he saw loss.

Pain. Regret.

Add to that a perpetual foul mood borne from working midnights on the assembly line and it became easy to see why the pair spent most days actively avoiding each other.

"I'm kinda busy, dad"

"Sit down."

Jack sat on the sofa, but refrained from making eye contact with his father.

"I see you got the GTO. Ol' Ace give you a deal?"

"Yes, sir."

"Good. Well, hopefully he will on the next one, too."

"Why would I need another one?"

"When your colored friend never comes back."

Jack noticed a half empty bottle of bourbon on the table beside his father.

"Frank would never…" he started, but was cut off.

"We should have moved to the suburbs years ago."

"Why?"

"Why? Because it's only right to be with your own kind. This city is getting far too black. If they want it, they can have it."

"Too black?"

"And that's not the worst of it. I could tolerate you experimenting with dark meat. A little suck and fuck."

He took a swig from the bottle, and slammed it back down on the table.

"But I look out that window, and…" he paused, grimacing, seemingly overcome with disgust.

"What?" Jack said. The little hairs on the back of his neck began to stand up.

"Did you propose to that nigger girl?"

"Don't call her that!" Jack yelled.

"YOU LISTEN HERE, BOY!" August bellowed, heaving the bottle against the wall.

It shattered, flinging shards and brown liquor everywhere. Jack bolted for his room. August followed behind as quickly as his battered knees would allow and cut his son off in the hall. He grabbed Jack and threw him against the wall, emphatically shoving a finger into his sternum.

"I will not have you sully the Kerner name by gallivanting around with one of them. I-"

Jack pushed August back, and then advanced on him, pressing his nose into his father's.

"No, you listen, old man! I will marry who I want, when I want, and there's nothing you can do about it."

August stared into his son's eyes saying nothing. Somehow what he did next, though, was worse than any words.

He started to laugh.

"What are you laughing about?" Jack said, thoroughly confused. He continued, albeit with diminished fervor. "Maybe in your day it-,"

August let out another burst of laughter.

"But this is a new time…"

The laughter grew louder, intermixed with wheezing.

"You're a dinosaur, man! A relic!" Jack shouted, fleeing to his room.

Reggie Howard was furious. He had tried to talk some sense into that Franklin King but instead he was made a fool. He stomped up the steps to his house without noticing his brother on the porch swing.

"You a goddamn disgrace," Isaac said. He was wearing a white tank top and jeans. His arms bulged from afternoons spent pumping iron in the yard.

Reggie, looking small in comparison, turned to him and shrugged. "What am I supposed to do, huh?"

"I tell you to recruit a young brother, and you over there takin' pictures."

"I tried but…he's an ignorant fool. He thinks Jack is his friend. And Pamela…"

"That bitch."

"She ain't no bitch."

"Oh, she a bitch. Foolin' round with the enemy…"

Reggie fell silent.

There was an object wrapped in a towel on the seat next to Isaac. He put it on his lap and directed Reggie to sit. The pair barely fit on the swing.

"Look over there. She hangin' all over that cracker and Frankie sittin' in the car lettin' it happen. He's all, 'Yes massa, you can have m'sister, if I c'n ride in yo fancy car.'"

Reggie hung his head. Ever since he was born, he was always the shadow Isaac never wanted. He'd have followed his brother anywhere, and in return all he wanted was the thing that seemed the most unattainable; his brother's respect.

"Look at this shit, here," Isaac said, unwrapping the object in his lap.

Franklin burned rubber down the street.

"Holy shit, Ice! You can't be wavin' no shotgun 'round in public!"

"In Oakland, this was how we did it, my brother. That's whitey's rule, anyways. Soon, we'll make the rules."

"When will that be?"

"Any time now. I can feel it. Felt it out in Oakland, and I can feel it here. Brothers be itchin' to fuck shit up, know what I'm sayin'"

He didn't.

"Yeah. I know."

Isaac looked at his brother, and shook his head. "Naw, you don't know shit, lil' brother. Never did. That's how come you blew it so bad just now. You don't truly believe. You happy bein' a second class citizen."

"You're wrong, man. I believe. I'm ready to fight."

"You tellin' me you ready to walk away from that honkey, and them honkey lovin' twins?"

"I'm ready to do whatever it takes, Ice. Teach me what you learned."

At that moment, a police cruiser pulled onto the street. Isaac tucked the gun under the swing and got up so quickly that the swing's recoil nearly dumped Reggie to the ground.

"Geez! Where you goin'?" he said, grabbing the rail to stabilize himself.

Isaac ignored him and continued down the approach waving his arms frantically until the cruiser stopped.

"Officer! Officer!"

"What, boy?" the cop said.

"This man, he just stopped by here tryin' to sell me and my lil' brother drugs. He's in a blue convertible. I told him no, of course. We's innocent and never mess 'round with no drugs, no sir."

"He did, eh?"

"Yes sir. Young brother pulls up and waves me to come over to the car and when I gets there he shows me these funny lookin' cigarettes. I says, 'What's that', and he tells me they's cannabis cigarettes."

The cop raised an eyebrow, seemingly having a hard time believing the giant decorated with a myriad of prison tattoos.

"You playin' with me, boy?"

Isaac conjured the most angelic look he could, raised his right hand and shook his head vehemently. "No, sir. I'd never lie to no officer of the law. I's only tryin' to keep my neighborhood clean. If you leave now you can probably catch him. He turned up there, at Third."

The cop gauged him one last time before turning his attention down the street and beginning pursuit.

Isaac watched him speed down the street beaming with pride like an artist before his latest masterwork. He twisted the disheveled hair on his chin, and leisurely sauntered back up the walk.

"Are you out yo' damn mind? What are you doin' foolin' with that cracker cop when you got a shotgun up here on this porch?" a nervous Reggie inquired.

Isaac disregarded his question, and plopped himself back down on the porch swing, again almost sending Reggie flying off.

"Ice man. What wh-."

"You asked me to teach you. Now watch and learn."

Frank turned left on Third and hit the gas. In a flash, he was doing fifty miles per hour.

"Hot damn!" he said, slamming through the gears. The light at Seward was red, so he begrudgingly stopped. Marvin and Tammi were on the radio, and Frank happily tapped his fingers on the wheel and sang along.

That's when he noticed a set of legs moving by on his right. His eyes worked their way up past the short shorts, and the tube top, and he saw the owner of that impeccable body was one Martha Ross. She only happened to be his high school crush, one that he never had the courage to talk to before. Something about being behind that wheel, though, made him feel invincible. He channeled that feeling, and directed it right at her.

"Ain't no mountain indeed…"

She stopped in her tracks, and turned to get a look at her catcaller.

"Is that you Franklin?" she said, shielding her eyes from the ruthless sun.

"The one and only."

She ambled over to the passenger side and leaned on the door. Her long black hair tumbled across her eyes. She tucked the wayward strands behind her ear. "Your wheels?"

"I wish. Kerner's. I'm helpin' break it in."

"Oh."

"I must say you are lookin' mighty good this fine summer day."

"Why, thank you. I never thought you one to notice."

"You kiddin'? Every day, that's all I do is be noticin'."

"You never said nothin'."

"I'm sayin' it now. Whatchu been doin' lately?"

"Not much. Aren't you leavin' for school in D.C. soon?"

"Supposed to go next month, but that was before I saw those legs. They give me all the education I need."

She laughed, and Frank thought he saw a hint of a blush sneak across her face. "You are bad, Franklin King."

"Bad as you want it, baby."

He had no idea from what depths this suave and confident voice had risen, but he decided to roll with it. She reached in her purse and pulled out a gum wrapper and a pen. She scribbled something and handed the wrapper to Frank.

"Here's my number. You call me if you wanna grab a hot fudge sundae at Sanders or…something."

He took the paper, and as he slid it in his pocket, a police cruiser screeched to a stop behind the car. Martha jumped back onto the curb.

"HANDS IN THE AIR!" the cop shouted, springing from the car, gun drawn.

Martha, frightened at what was transpiring, shuffled away down Seward.

"I SAID HANDS IN THE AIR, NOW!"

Frank reached for the sky.

"AND SHUT IT DOWN!"

He lowered his right hand and did as he was told.

"HANDS UP! I'M NOT GONNA SAY IT AGAIN!"

He again reached up and shouted back to the officer, "Yes sir. I don't know what this is-."

"SHUT UP! YOU WILL SPEAK WHEN SPOKEN TOO!"

Frank had never been more scared in his life. He closed his eyes and waited for the next instruction.

"License and registration," the officer shouted, from just over Frank's left shoulder.

"NOW!"

Franklin did not move. He just squeezed his eyes shut and reached for the clouds.

"You hard a hearing, boy?"

"Nn…No sir. I can't-,"

"LOUDER, BOY!"

"I CAN'T KEEP MY HANDS UP AND GET THE PAPERWORK AT THE SAME TIME!"

The officer grabbed Frank's hair and slammed his head backwards. He pressed the gun hard into his temple, leaving an imprint in the skin.

"You're all the same, ain't you? No respect for authority."

Frank opened his eyes and looked at the cop, but only could see his own petrified face in the officer's mirrored aviator sunglasses.

"I respect you, sir. It's not my car. I don't know where the paperwork is."

"You are useless, ain't you?"

The cop crowned him with the butt of his revolver, and dragged him out of the car. Frank crumpled in a heap on Third Street; blood trickled from behind his ear to the pavement.

"Get up, boy!"

Frank made it to his feet, only to be shoved into the fender. The cop holstered his weapon, and bent him over the hood, wrenching Frank's arm behind his back.

"Ahh!" he screamed. The pain was so intense that he feared the bones might snap.

"You holdin', punk?"

"What?"

"Grass! Where is it?"

The cop reached into Frank's back pocket and pulled out his wallet. Finding nothing but a driver's license and four dollars, he flung it to the ground. In the front pocket was only Martha's gum wrapper.

"This one of your rolling papers?"

"No, sir. That's-,"

The cop cut him off, and wrenched a little harder on his arm.

"SHUT UP!"

The cop tossed the paper to the breeze. Frank saw it sail away down Seward out of the corner of his tear-blurred eye.

"Hands on that hood! Don't move a muscle."

Frank did as he was told, feeling the warmth of his own blood as it slid down his neck and pooled in a crimson spot on his collar. The cop searched first the trunk then the glove box. The temporary registration was there, as was the owner's manual, but nothing else. After a cursory glance of the back seat he walked to where Frank stood frozen, legs spread, fingers splayed on the driver's side fender. The cop leaned over his shoulder and whispered in Frank's ear, "You toss it?"

"T-t-toss what, sir?"

"Don't play with me, boy. The marijuana."

"Sir, I...I didn't have no marijuana."

The cop lingered there. His warm breath left a thin layer of moisture on the skin. Frank cringed with each exhale. Finally, the cop backed off.

"Well, then. I suggest you keep it that way," he said, with a pat on Franklin's back. "You have a good day, now."

And that was all. He walked back to his car and drove off. Stunned, it took Frank a moment to realize he was free to go. He picked his wallet up and got back in the car and started it. After wiping the tears from his eyes, he looked up at the light. It was red.

Reggie and Isaac remained on the porch until Frank pulled back onto West Philadelphia.

"Let's go," Isaac said, jumping up at first sight of the GTO.

"Where?"

"Shut up and follow me."

They walked down the street until they had a good view of the Kerner/King duplex. Isaac leaned against the trunk of a giant birch, and

Reggie stood beside him. The GTO came to a screeching halt in front of the house, and Frank got out of the car.

"What are we doing?" Reggie asked.

"When you want to get the ball rollin', you gotta give it a little push."

"What are you-,"

"SHHH!"

The pair watched Frank run up the porch steps to the Kerner's door. He pounded on it and within seconds Jack opened up. From their position, Isaac and Reggie could hear the conversation. Jack said, "Whaddya think about the-. Hey, is that blood on your shirt?"

"Your goddamn keys," Frank said, tossing them at Jack's chest. He stormed away.

"Hey man! What happened?" Jack said.

He followed Frank to the other door, but it was slammed in his face. Jack knocked and waited for a minute, but when Frank did not come back out he returned to his house.

"That is how you do it, little brother."

"What did you do?"

"Taught that young Negro a lesson."

"What lesson was that?"

"I taught him what happens when you fuck with the Howard brothers," Isaac said with pure mania in his eyes. "And I'm a teach Jack and his lil' bitch next."

"What's that mean?"

Isaac offered only a nod and walked away. Reggie stayed behind, in the shadow of the birch, his stomach turning as that nod replayed over and over in his head.

CHAPTER VI
MAY 12, 2008

Martin woke to the pitter-patter of raindrops against his bedroom window. A meager light poked through the slats of the blinds. It had been a restless sleep with fits of tossing and turning. Martin, wanting nothing to do with the day, flipped onto his side, tucked his knees in to his chest and closed his eyes.

He tried, unsuccessfully, to return to his dreams. Shapes and shadows flirted with each other, only hinting at a concrete image. A strong sense of dread emerged, but it dissipated, leaving no context or detail. He opened his eyes, knowing any further attempts to conjure his dreams would be fruitless, or at least contaminated by his present consciousness.

The clock read 7:44.

The alarm was set to go off at 7:45. Martin contemplated shutting it off, but chose instead to wait. Anticipation built inside him as the seconds clicked off in his head. Finally, after what seemed like much longer than possible, the buzz filled the room. Martin's arm came forth from his blanket cocoon to shut it off.

After a shower, he dressed and made his way to the kitchen. It was empty as he had predicted, figuring his father to sleep off his latest hangover until past noon. With the Chrysler's keys in hand, he slung his laptop over his shoulder and walked out into the rainy morning.

Cursing himself for not grabbing an umbrella, he hopscotched down the driveway around the puddles. He made it to the 2002 Concorde being only moderately drenched. Sitting in the driver's seat, *her* seat, was surreal and summoned feelings that he had no interest in dealing with at that moment. Seeing her *Proud Parent of a University of Ann Arbor Student* sticker in the rearview mirror didn't help.

It was 8:12.

With the class starting at 9:00am, he needed to get going. A quick perusal of the directions he'd printed suggested he take I-75 south and

exit at Warren. After that, it was a short jaunt until he would reach
Higgins Hall, the building his class was in, on Cass Ave.

Merging onto the freeway from Nine Mile, he recalled his father
mentioning the 'Cass Corridor' years ago.

"There are only three things you can get in the 'corridor'," he said.
"Crack, AIDS, and shot."

Martin wondered how a university could exist in a neighborhood like
that. His imagination ran wild, picturing this Higgins Hall as some
dilapidated remnant from a time when Detroit was a living, breathing
city. He saw classrooms without ceilings, water dripping down on the
students as they sat cross-legged on the floor gathered around raging
trashcan fires. They would listen to some degenerate "professor" ramble
incoherently about nothing while drifters, rats and vermin wandered in
for the heat.

A horn blast.

Martin swerved back into his lane and made the obligatory apologetic
wave to the incensed driver beside him. Just ahead, the highway rose up
over the surround near the exit for the Davison freeway. Between swipes
of the windshield wipers, Martin could see the Detroit skyline in the
distance. On the left, the Renaissance Center's modernistic towers
guarded the riverfront with aplomb while the Fisher Building stood alone
on the right, a shining example of Art Deco opulence. He slowed the
speed of the wiper motor, allowing the rain to bead up on the windshield.
The water distorted the skyline, transforming it into a Renoir-esque
impressionistic landscape until the blade swiped it clear again.

He took the exit for Warren Ave. and waited at the light to turn right
towards campus. On the curb was a grizzled old man soaked through his
clothes holding a sign that read "WILL BUILD CARS FOR FOOD."
Martin avoided making eye contact with the man, instead darting his
eyes to and fro, searching for would be carjackers. His heart nearly leapt
out of his chest when a tapping came on his passenger window. The
vagrant had approached the car, water dripping down his disheveled
beard. He was clamoring, palms up, for a handout. Martin panicked and
slammed on the gas, nearly side-swiping a westbound Buick. Only the
vagrant's quick reflexes kept him from losing a toe. The Chrysler raced
down Warren rapidly approaching the intersection at St. Antoine.

The light was red.

Martin slammed on the brakes. The tires skidded against the wet pavement, bringing the car to a halt in the middle of the intersection. Martin tried to collect himself, breathing deeply. He knew that if he didn't assuage his fear of the city, he would wind up getting killed.

He backed out of the intersection and ended up right next to the Buick he had nearly side-swiped. The driver, a middle aged black woman, looked at Martin and shook her head. For the second time that morning he held up his hand to a fellow driver in apology.

When the light turned green, Martin waited for the Buick to move first before gently applying the gas. He managed to avoid further incident all the way to the campus and pulled into a spot on the second deck of the student garage on Cass. He shut the engine off, but couldn't will himself out of the car.

In his mind, Detroit equated with the darkest period of his life. The rational part of him knew it wasn't Detroit that caused his pain. It couldn't have been. Detroit is a city, and while cities hum and move with a rhythm of living, breathing organism, they are inherently no more than an idea, a concept with imaginary walls incapable of causing pain, joy or any other emotion.

He closed his eyes and took a deep breath, letting the silence and calm inside the car wallow over him. He breathed it in until, slowly, he regained his nerve.

The campus was busy with students. Martin had anticipated that he would be one of the few whites, but roughly half of the faces looked just like his. Though he couldn't justify any reasoning for it and hated admitting so, this provided a sense of comfort.

With his laptop overhead to shield him from the rain, he headed to Higgins Hall. It stood, regally, at the corner of Cass and Warren.

He was instantly impressed.

He had not figured Detroit State to have any historical buildings to rival his beloved University of Ann Arbor, especially after the reputation that the "corridor" had, but there Higgins Hall stood in all of its brick and limestone glory. He scampered across the wide thoroughfare to get a better look at the spires reaching up toward the low, cloud filled sky and the intricate lion's head carvings in the building's façade. Craning his neck up with drops beating his face, he took in the central tower, and its clock.

It read 8:58.

"Shit!" he said, before sprinting up the stairs and throwing open the doors.

His wet shoes squeaked all the way down the hall until he reached the room he was looking for. He was relieved when he found only students, and no professor, inside.

The auditorium was small compared to those he was accustomed to in Ann Arbor. It had four levels of alternating gray and blue chairs and tall windows in the back, all of which had the shades drawn. Martin found an open seat in the back corner of the room and sat, surveying the class of about forty people. It was an ethnically diverse group, which was unsurprising considering the subject matter.

All conversations halted when a tall, burly African American man walked in and set a briefcase down on the desk at the front of the room. Martin wondered who the man was, as the course registry clearly stated the professor to be a man of a Middle Eastern background named Marid Abdul-Tawaab. He figured perhaps there had been a last minute change, or potentially Abdul-Tawaab had fallen ill.

The man, who Martin gauged to be about sixty, stood behind the desk, and pulled a marker from his briefcase. On the whiteboard, he wrote in large block letters, MARID ABDUL-TAWAAB, PHD.

"My name," he turned and bellowed, "is Doctor Abdul-Tawaab. You will refer to me as such. 'Sir' is equally acceptable."

His face was round and framed by a receding hairline up top and graying Van Dyke beard below. His wide set eyes locked on a mousy, waifish redhead seated in front of Martin.

"Do you understand?" he said in a deep, imposing timbre.

The girl looked positively petrified.

"Yes," she squeaked.

"Yes, what?"

"Yes, sir," she corrected.

"Good," he said, pulling a sheet of paper from his briefcase. "I do not lecture on the first day of class. I have only one goal for today; to get acquainted."

This news seemed to please the crowd, as Martin saw many smiling faces. He, however, was annoyed. Why someone who is paying to be educated would celebrate a wasted day was beyond him.

Abdul-Tawaab, now seated behind the desk, clicked his pen and held it hovering over the paper.

"I have here your names. When I point to you, you will state your name. I will then ask you a question, and if you successfully answer it you will be given extra credit."

This news perked Martin back up. Surely some early extra credit would bolster his chances for that all-important 'A'.

"You. Who are you?" Abdul-Tawaab barked at a young black man in the front row. He wore a hooded sweatshirt with large headphones draped around his neck.

"Darius Rhodes, sir," the young man said.

Abdul-Tawaab found him on his sheet and placed a check next to his name.

"Mr. Rhodes, who gave the famous 'I have a dream' speech?"

"That's easy, sir. Martin Luther King."

"Doctor," Abdul-Tawaab said.

"Oh, yeah. That's what I meant," Darius said.

"I will give you the credit, but don't disrespect the man's memory by omitting his title."

"Yes, sir."

"You," Abdul-Tawaab said, moving on the next person in the row.

"Me?" said the African American girl seated next to Darius.

"Yes, you? People!" he said, addressing the whole class. "When I point at you, state your name, first then last. It isn't that difficult."

"Danielle Denson, sir."

"Better. All right, Ms. Denson. What degree did Dr. Martin Luther King hold?"

"Doctorate, sir?"

"Of what, Ms. Denson."

"He held a PhD in theology, sir."

"Very good."

The questions kept coming, and it didn't take long before Martin noticed a disturbing trend. They alternated between ridiculously simple or ridiculously challenging. The disturbing part was that it looked like he was in line for the latter.

"Who is Rosa Parks?" Abdul-Tawaab said.

"The woman who wouldn't get out of her seat on the bus, sir?" said the waifish redhead.

"Correct. Next!" the professor said, marking something on his sheet.

"Himal Patel, sir."

"Who is Claudette Colvin?"

"Who?"

"Yes, that is the question."

"I'm sorry. I do not know her."

"Then you get no credit. Next!"

"Amber McInerney, sir"

"What was Malcolm Little also known as?"

"Malcolm X?"

"Correct, although that sounded more like a question rather than an answer. Next!"

"Jake Whitfield, sir."

"Where did Dr. King first deliver his 'I have a dream' speech? The transcendent discourse of one of the twentieth century's most influential and important men. The fervent plea to the people of a broken nation to unite amongst their similarities and embrace their differences."

"The March on Washington, sir."

"Incorrect. Next!"

It went on like that until finally he reached Martin.

"And last but certainly not least..." Abdul-Tawaab said.

"Martin Kerner, sir."

The professor slowly lowered his sheet of paper and peered deeply into Martin's eyes.

"Martin what?" he said after a pause that bordered on the uncomfortable.

"Kerner, sir."

"Kerner," Abdul-Tawaab said barely above a whisper. He seemed dazed, and the class recognized it, exchanging puzzled looks of their own. It was brief though, as his expression quickly changed to one of subtle malevolence.

"Your question is this; What does the term 'long hot summer' allude to as it pertains to this course?"

"The long hot summer refers to the summer of '67 when race riots erupted all over the country."

"Very good."

Martin pumped his fist under his desk.

"Where?" Abdul-Tawaab said, freezing Martin's fist mid-pump.

"Sir?" he asked.

"Where were they, these riots?"

"Detroit, sir."

"And?"

"And..." Martin said, trying to locate the crevice in his brain that held Mrs. Szymanski's social studies class from six years prior.

"Newark, sir," he blurted out, feeling ninety-five percent confident.

"Good. And?"

"Another one, sir?" he asked, getting exasperated.

"Yes. Another one."

"Oh, man. Umm...Chicago?" he said, down to about twenty percent confidence.

"Impressive." Abdul-Tawaab said.

A wave of relief came over Martin, that is until he noticed Abdul-Tawaab was still looking at him.

"And?"

Martin sighed. He was done. Anything else would be purely a guess.

"Baltimore?"

"Incorrect."

Abdul-Tawaab placed the sheet with all the marks on it back into his briefcase and closed it.

"That is all. For Wednesday, I would have you read the first three chapters. Good day," he said and rose from his desk. Martin watched, slack-jawed as the class followed Abdul-Tawaab's lead and gathered their things. Martin quickly stuffed his laptop in its case and bounded down the stairs.

"Doctor Abdul-Tawaab," he said.

"Yes?" the professor said, looking at his watch.

"Will I be receiving the extra credit?"

"No."

"But I answered the question correctly."

"That is not accurate."

"Long hot summer. I got it right."

"But you could not name the cities. You failed. There is no need to discuss it any further."

"Nobody else had to answer two, three or four part questions."

"Your point?"

"My point is that it's a bit unfair."

"Unfair?" he chuckled. "Son, I'm sure I'm not the first to tell that life is not fair. That's simply not a credible argument."

"Sir, I need an A in this class and some extra credit could really help out. It's tyrannical to take it from me over some triviality."

Every single member of the class stood by watching the spectacle but nobody spoke up in his defense.

"Downright oppressive, I'm sure," Abdul-Tawaab said.

"Let me answer another one," Martin said, beginning to panic. "Or, better yet, I'll answer questions that people missed.

Abdul-Tawaab only shook his head.

"Dr. King first delivered much of the 'I have a dream' refrain right here in Detroit just months prior to the March on Washington. Cobo Hall after the Great Walk to Freedom in June of '63."

Abdul-Tawaab turned and resumed his walk to the door.

"Claudette Colvin. She refused to give up her bus seat nine months before Rosa Parks, but the NAACP didn't want her as the face of their movement because she was an unmarried, pregnant teen."

"I'm sorry, Mr. Kerner," Abdul-Tawaab said, almost to the door.

"This is garbage!" Martin shouted. He pointed, one by one, at the chairs, starting at the gray one that Darius had sat in and said, "Easy one, hard one, easy one, hard one. It's like you arbitrarily decided who was gonna get screwed just by the color of their seat!"

Abdul-Tawaab froze.

The light bulb went on in Martin's head.

"Oh my God. That's it, isn't it?" he said.

Abdul-Tawaab pivoted to face him and the rest of the fascinated onlookers. He said nothing.

"Was this all some sort of game?"

"No game. More like an exercise in prejudice." Abdul-Tawaab said, stepping back into the room.

"So…I'll bet there never was any extra credit. Am I right?"

Abdul-Tawaab looked around at all of the eyes upon him and stood tall, defiant.

"No. I don't believe in it."

Some of those who had answered their questions correctly began to complain. Several were quite vociferous, even going so far as to threaten reporting Abdul-Tawaab to the dean. Then those who had answered incorrectly joined in, obviously displeased with having been played.

"Then what was the point?" Martin said.

"The point!" Abdul-Tawaab shouted, slamming his fist down on the desk. The room fell alarmingly silent. The professor breathed deeply and exhaled.

"The point, Mr. Kerner, was to teach you how horrific it is when something independent of your intelligence, character, or ability—something that you had absolutely no control of and cannot change, is used to hold you back. I wanted you to see that in such a situation, the only recourse may be to fight, just for that small chance that your actions would affect real change. And you know what? It worked. Just look at you all. I can see it on your pampered little faces. I trampled on what you felt was your inalienable right to extra credit, just once, and you come at me with a barrage of insults and threats. ME! YOUR PROFESSOR WHO WIELDS COMPLETE CONTROL OVER YOUR ACADEMIC FUTURE!"

Sheepish looks and shoegazing took over everyone in the classroom, including Martin.

"I have begun every semester for the last nine years with this exercise, and for nine years I have seen the downtrodden faces of those who'd answered incorrectly march one by one out that door. I could sense that they felt an injustice had occurred, but not one of them said a word. Not one of them had the self-respect to stand up for what is right."

He made his way to the door, but once again stopped before exiting. Instead he turned and looked Martin square in the eye.

"I'm just surprised that you, of all people, were the first," and he was gone.

Martin lingered until each of his classmates had slowly filtered out of the room, contemplating that last sentence.

As he stepped out onto Cass Ave., he lifted the laptop case over his head again, to protect himself from the rain.

"Martin! Hey, wait up!" he heard a female voice call to him.

It was the girl who had answered Abdul-Tawaab's question about Martin Luther King's field of study. Now that she stood before him, he noticed how breathtaking she was. Five feet four inches, slender with curves in all the right areas and the most intoxicating brown eyes Martin had ever seen. He had to tell himself to blink occasionally lest he seemed creepy.

"It is Martin, right?" she said, approaching him.

"What? Oh…yeah. Martin. I'm Martin."

"Hi," she said, extending her hand. "Danielle."

"Hi. I'm Martin," he said, accepting her hand with his own clammy one.

"Yeah. Umm-we've established that."

"Sorry."

"I just wanted to say that was pretty impressive back there."

Martin wanted to say that he was impressed by her too, not only with her knowledge of Dr. King but with her stunning beauty that even the blind could appreciate.

"Uhh-thanks," was all he could manage.

"I knew somethin' was up with those questions, but I never woulda put two and two together like that."

"Yeah, well, now he hates me and there's no way in Hell I'm getting an 'A'."

"Nope. Probably not," she said, chuckling. Her nose wrinkled a little when she laughed, which Martin found only amplified her beauty.

"We're all just pawns in his game, I guess," he said, not really knowing where to take the conversation.

"Yeah, or rooks."

"For sure."

She laughed again and said, "Why did you agree? That didn't even make sense."

"What? Oh, yeah. I don't know"

Neither said anything for a few seconds, which made Martin even more nervous.

Finally, Danielle spoke up. "Hey, so a bunch of us from class are going to the Corridor Café. You interested?"

"Who?"

"Me, Darius and a few others. You should come."

"Darius. The guy who sat next to you?"

"Yeah."

"Is he your boyfriend?" he blurted out without thought. Something about her seemed to cause his verbal filter to malfunction. He winced, waiting for her to inevitably call him strange and walk away.

"No, we just met. Why? You interested?" she said.

"What? No. I don't know. I just, uh…"

"You are funny, Martin Kerner!"

"Yeah…," he said, feeling like he dodged a bullet.

"So, you coming?"

He wanted to go, but there was a stack of cases waiting to be briefed calling his name back in Hazel Park. "I would, but I have a ton of reading to do."

"Oh, ok. Some other time then?"

"Sure."

"Well, nice meeting you," she said, offering a gentle squeeze to his arm. "Bye."

"Bye," he said.

He watched her walk away, keeping his eyes on her backside for an ungentlemanly long period of time. He thought she caught him when she turned around and shouted back, "You know, you can probably take that computer off your head." She smiled again, and waved. He lowered the laptop to his side, and waved back. He hadn't noticed the rain had stopped.

CHAPTER VII
MAY 14, 2008

Martin drove from Hazel Park without incident and parked in the same garage off Cass that he had before. This time, though, he exited the car with a spring in his step. He told himself his exuberance was probably due to the alleviation of many of his concerns about the school, or because the sun was shining or any number of other falsehoods. Deep down, though, he knew the real reason he had been looking forward to this moment for the prior forty-six hours.

Danielle.

Her smile, her voice, her long black hair all commandeered his thoughts. It made it challenging for him to concentrate on his case briefings at the Starbucks in Royal Oak the day before. He even found himself subconsciously rubbing at the spot on his arm that she had touched.

Never before had he considered a black girl to be a romantic option. In his household, it would have been blasphemous. While he'd found black woman attractive before, they'd been actresses, singers and other unattainables. He even had a Destiny's Child poster in his dorm room freshman year. Dating a black girl, though, had never seriously crossed his mind, that is until Danielle.

Eager to see her, he moved spritely through the masses on Warren and into Higgins Hall. He took the steps to the second floor two at a time, and walked into class, immediately scanning the room for her. He became dejected when he found that all the seats in her vicinity were already occupied.

He sat down in an open seat in the corner of the room and glanced in her direction. She was talking to the waifish redhead. Martin was enamored with everything about her; how she absently twirled a strand of that long black hair around her finger during conversation, the way her sandal slapped at her heel while she bounced her knee, and especially her voice. Over the din in the bustling classroom, it was all he could hear. She turned her head towards him, and made eye contact.

And waved.

He waved back. Her eyes stayed on him for only a moment, but it didn't matter. He was smitten.

It was then that Abdul-Tawaab entered the room. As seemed to be his modus operandi, he said not a word and showed no expression. He set his briefcase down on the desk and removed a DVD. He inserted it into the player on the utility cart next to the desk. He turned on the TV, pushed play, and left, turning the lights out behind him.

The unsupervised class muttered and whispered amongst themselves until the program began. It was one in a series of PBS documentaries on psychology. It opened with the host, a Dr. Zimbardi, announcing the topic to be behavioral development before jumping to an old black and white video from the '20s of an infant surrounded by researchers. This infant, Baby Albert as Zimbardi referred to him, seemed to be unafraid of a number of objects that were offered to him, whether it was a white rat, cotton or even burning newspapers. Zimbardi went on to state that the researchers had already determined the infant, and by extension all humans, demonstrated an innate fear of loud noises. The next time they presented the objects to Baby Albert, they struck a steel bar with a hammer. Not surprisingly, Baby Albert cried whether he was holding the cotton or the rat. This scene drew some gasps from the students who, while not psych majors, recognized the ethical questions raised by such research.

Lastly, Zimbardi said the researchers presented the objects a third time, this time without the loud banging, yet the child burst into tears at the mere sight of them. This, he stated, was an example of classical conditioning, or pairing the innate fear of the noise, with the previously non-threatening objects. The show then moved on to discussing classical conditioning in "modern times", which seemed to be the late '80s according to the hairstyles. These drew almost as many gasps as the questionable experiment did.

Some forty minutes later, Abdul-Tawaab returned from wherever he had gone, and watched the end of the program from one of the empty seats. When the credits rolled, he removed the DVD and put it back in his briefcase. He walked around the desk and sat on it, picking lint off of his slacks and balling it up between his fingers. He raised his head and said in his monotone, "Why did I show you this?"

Nobody answered. He repeated the question. Again no response. He stood up and said, "Come on, people. Somebody give me something. This is not behavioral psych, right? So, why did I show you the video?"

Martin raised his hand. Abdul-Tawaab regarded him with a sneer.

"I think it is because the theory of classical conditioning will tie in somehow with your discussion on race relations, sir."

"Not specific enough. You said you need an 'A' in this course. Earn it."

"Ok. I thought you showed us the video to demonstrate that there are innate and learned emotional responses. In the case of Baby Albert, the emotion was fear. Seeing as this is a race relations course, my guess is that you are going to suggest that fear is the source of most racial divide, sir."

"Better. Do you concur?"

"Sure. If they had Baby Albert play with a black baby, then struck the hammer, I don't doubt that the black baby would have then evoked the same response that the rat or cotton did."

"So, what pray tell would be the hammer in our society, specifically 1960s Detroit?"

"I don't know, sir."

"No? Does anybody have a guess?"

Danielle raised her hand.

"Was there really only one event that we could refer to as the 'hammer'? Racial issues didn't all of a sudden come about in the '60s. They have been going on for centuries, I mean, that's what the civil war was all about."

Martin, impressed by her commentary, gave her a thumbs up which she responded to with a wink.

"Well, you're wrong about the civil war. Yes, racial issues, specifically slavery, were part of it, but it was predominantly about what most wars are about. Money. The wealthy southern plantation owners were trying to protect their investment. You were right about Detroit, though. Racial strife was an ongoing thing, but one singular event seemed to really drive the wedge between the people of this city. What was it?"

Several hands went up this time.

"Ahh, good. There are some people awake in here besides Martin and Danielle. Well, all of you with your hands raised…"

Simultaneously, they said, "the riot."

"Correct. Which brings me to next week's assignment. I'd like you to read chapters four and five, which cover the 1967 Detroit riot, for Friday. You are dismissed."

With that, the students packed up their things and filed out of the room. Martin sorted through his laptop bag for nothing in particular, all the while keeping his eye on Danielle. When she made a move for the door, he ended his pseudo-search and followed her.

"Hey, Danielle," he said just as they reached the exit.

"Oh, hey. How's it goin'?"

"Good. How 'bout-um, I mean, how's it goin' with you?"

"Good," she said, drawn out with an upward inflection at the end.

They were outside now, standing in front of Higgins Hall.

"Beautiful day out today," Martin said, rocking back on his heels. "Much better than Monday. Warm, too."

He cursed his nervousness and inability to come up with something more interesting.

"Did you stop me to talk about the weather?"

"What? No, no. I, uh, I just wanted to say that you are two for two. Another impressive answer in there today."

"Thanks. Walk with me?"

He nodded and she lead them north on Cass. "You were pretty good, too. It seems he likes to pick on you," she said.

"Yeah, well I take it as a compliment. He must think I can handle it."

They crossed Warren at the corner and passed the campus bookstore in silence.

"This is me, here," Martin said when they reached his garage.

"What are you doing now?"

"Now? Why? I was gonna go…uhh, oh, I don't know. What are you doing?" Martin couldn't believe how stupid he sounded.

She chuckled. "I was going to get a head start on the assigned reading."

"Oh. Yeah, me too. Where?"

"At the library."

"The library? Where is the library?"

She raised her eyebrow at him a second time. "You're joking, right?"

"No. Why?"

She pointed to the block-long, marble building behind her. It gleamed in the sunshine. The smooth, white walls popped against the neatly trimmed Kentucky bluegrass.

"That's the library?"

She nodded slowly.

"Seriously? Where did that come from?"

"It's been there for like a hundred years."

"That's marble, isn't it? I had no idea this was here." He wandered ahead towards the entrance on Cass. Danielle laughed and followed behind.

"The roof, the windows. It looks like Italian renaissance," he said, standing at the circular driveway of the Detroit Public Library.

"Sure," Danielle said, shrugging her shoulders. "Are you an architecture major?"

"No. I've always kind of been into it, though. As a kid, whenever we'd go up north on 75, I'd always stare at the skyscrapers there in Troy where the highway curves near Big Beaver."

"You'd obsess over those generic suburban towers but didn't know about the library?"

He shrugged. "I've never thought much about Detroit. Chicago, sure. New York. But I have to say, first Higgins and now this…."

He pointed to tile mosaic above the entryway featuring five figures with quotes beneath them. "What is all that?"

"It's a mosaic. If I remember correctly, they call it the River of Knowledge. I like the Whitman quote," she said.

He found it beneath a figure in full battle regalia encircled by, what looked like to Martin, a torso halo, or possibly a hula hoop. Below the figure it read, *Darest thou now o soul, walk out with me toward the unknown region, where neither ground is for the feet nor any path to follow?*

He pondered the quote for a full thirty seconds.

"Why that one?" he asked.

She was gone.

He went inside. He wandered through the central building east towards the Woodward entrance half searching for her and half gawking like a tourist. He was drawn to an important looking set of stone stairs up ahead on his left. The stairwell led to a corridor, dimly lit by two spherical chandeliers and two fifteen foot tall stained glass windows at the north and south ends. On his right was an equally large mural recessed into the marble wall. It depicted a confluence of artists and nobles on Earth and above, cherubs watched from the heavens. Martin gazed at the gold leaf embellishments on the intricately carved arched ceiling.

The west doorway led to a cavernous room. He slowly walked in, each step falling with an echo. It was essentially empty save for benches against the walls. A trifle of sunlight filtered in through even more stained glass. A mural in three pieces greeted him on the westward wall. In the center was a man looking skyward with rockets and shooting stars exploding behind him. The side murals were of his large open hands and little people atop them using antiquated modes of transportation; steam engines, horse carriages, and early automobiles.

Words circumnavigated the room at the top of the walls. The deep shadow, especially in the corners, made it difficult to read. Martin squinted and was able to decipher the East wall. It read, *through seas of knowledge, we our course advance discovering still new worlds of ignorance.*

He left the room and walked downstairs. In the central building he found Danielle seated at a desk, studying. She saw him and yelled out, "Hey, Kerner!" which drew a "shush" from a librarian behind the reference counter.

Martin sat at her table and took out his book.

"Why'd you ditch me?" he said quietly, so as not to draw further ire from the librarian.

"I didn't ditch you. I wanted to give you some time. I figured you'd come find me when you were ready."

"Oh," Martin said, feeling better. "This building is really impressive. I never knew Detroit had one this nice. The architecture rivals the best from anywhere in the U.S."

"Ok, Frank Lloyd Wright, less architecture and more riots," she said, tapping her textbook.

"Done," Martin said.

Danielle, still nose deep in her book, looked up at him through the top of her eyes. "I've been done for a while."

"Whatever," he scoffed.

"I didn't want you to feel bad, so I started over."

He shook his head. "Ok, speedo. I'm hungry. Where's a good place to eat nearby?"

"Speedo?"

"I'm sorry," Martin said. "It sounded better in my head."

They gathered their things and made their way to the exit.

"There's a little shawarma place on the corner by the bookstore. It's good, if you don't mind having garlic breath for a week," Danielle said.

"That's fine. I won't be kissing anybody any time soon," Martin said with immediate regret. She gave him an awkward, closed mouth grin.

"That's not what I meant," he said.

"No?"

"I mean I could kiss someone…or…not that I will be, but I…I'm gonna shut up now," he said, giving up.

"Oh…my…God, Kerner!"

As she walked ahead Martin watched, realizing that the more time he spent with her, the more she intrigued and confused him.

They reached the fast casual restaurant, ordered and within minutes they were seated in a booth with their sandwiches. Danielle unwrapped the end of hers, but before biting in, she said, "So, Kerner, what's your story?"

"My story?"

"Yeah, you know. Where you're from, what you wanna be when you grow up…"

"Oh, well, I'm from Hazel Park."

"A suburbanite. Figures."

"What is that supposed to mean?" Martin asked, unsure of whether to take offense to that remark.

"It's not because you're white. It's because you didn't know where the library is."

"Touché."

"So, what is your major?"

"I'm entering law school in the fall, at UAA."

"Ooh la la! You must be a smart cookie. I heard it's hard to get in, there."

"Yeah, well, I'm not technically in, per se."

Danielle washed down a mouthful of shawarma with a healthy gulp of pop.

"Per se?" she said, dabbing at her balm-coated lips with a napkin.

"Well, I need to get an 'A' in this race class in order to get in."

"Did you need to replace a grade from a class you failed or something?"

"I didn't fail. I just underperformed in a few courses, and an 'A' will raise my GPA to an acceptable level."

"Underperformed, huh? You don't seem like an underperforming kind of guy."

Martin's face took on an air of seriousness, and he stiffened up in his seat. "Yeah, well…"

Feeling she'd hit a nerve, Danielle did not press him any further, choosing instead to continue eating and do a bit of window gazing.

"Anyways," Martin said, sensing a brewing awkwardness, "I checked for a class there, but nothing was available. Ditto Oakland and Eastern. So I came here."

"I see," she said, her eyes fixed on the students mingling outside of the science building. "So, Detroit wasn't your first choice."

"No. So far, though, I'm glad I ended up here."

She smiled, but her gaze never left the window. "Can you imagine it?"

"Imagine what?"

"The riots. I mean, here in Detroit. People looting and fighting and killing each other. Houses and businesses, up in flames. National Guard. Paratroopers. Tanks! Like a third world country!"

"Up until a few days ago, I always thought of Detroit as a third world country. So, I guess, yeah. I could imagine it."

"Not me. Not my city. I know I just read it, but I can't imagine it. It's too horrible."

She took another sip of her pop. The sound of air burbling up her straw indicated that she was done. Martin looked down at her tray and noticed that her sandwich was gone, too. She set her empty cup down on the tray, and slung the strap of her purse over her shoulder.

"Well, Martin. It's been real, but I gotta-,"

"Wait a sec. That's not fair."

"What?"

"I tell you my story, and then you just up and leave?"

"Yep."

"I don't think so."

She tightened her lips and put her hand on her hip, feigning annoyance. "One question, cuz I gotta go. I have afternoon classes, ya know."

Martin pondered the options knowing he could ask her anything in the world.

"Hello! I haven't got all day," Danielle said.

"Ok, ok. Umm-do you have any siblings?" he stumbled.

"Really?" she said, with an expression of total disappointment.

"What?"

"That's what you want to ask me? You could have asked me anything. Like, what is my biggest fear, or my secret fantasy?"

"Like I would ask about your fantasies on a first date."

Another filter malfunction. He scanned the room for the quickest exit. He could feel himself blushing and wondered what shade of tomato his face looked like.

"Date?"

"Umm, no. I was joking. Obviously this isn't-,"

"This can be a date," she said.

"It can?"

"Yeah, only you didn't pay. Usually the guy pays."

Martin was thoroughly befuddled, which could be the only explanation for why he said what he did. "Uh, did you want me to give you the seven bucks?"

"Arrrggh! I have to go, for reals this time. See you next class?"

"Oh, yeah. I'll be there."

She dumped her trash out in the bin, and left. Martin's internal clock began clicking down the excruciatingly long two days until he would see her again.

A tap on the window.

It was her. She shouted something that Martin couldn't decipher. He cupped his ear. She leaned in closer to the window and shouted again. This time, though muffled, Martin heard, "One brother."

He nodded, and smiled. She waved and was gone again, down Cass Avenue. Martin watched her down the street, until she was lost in a swarm of bodies at the corner.

CHAPTER VIII
JULY 23, 1967

"Isn't it supposed to cool off when the goddamn sun goes down?" Isaac said. His light green t-shirt was stained dark with perspiration.

"Look at this shit," he said, peeling it from his chest.

"Me too, Ice," Reggie said with arms raised, showing he shared his brother's affliction.

They had been on the porch for the better part of two hours with Isaac alternating between extended periods of silence and long-winded, manic diatribes on the necessity and benefit of black revolution. Reggie, just happy to be noticed, did nothing more than sip his beer and nod when appropriate.

The Howard brothers had never been particularly close. In Reggie's case, this was not for lack of trying. From birth, he had looked up to Isaac with an intensity that bordered on hero worship. Isaac, though, had seven years with his parents all to himself and resented Reggie from day one. He even wrongfully attributed their father's unannounced and permanent exit from their home to Reggie's existence, when, in fact, the whole neighborhood knew it had been born of precipitous infidelity and general dead beatedness.

For the first few years, Reggie tottled along behind his older brother to only be recognized when on the receiving end of a shove. Things only got worse as he entered his teen years and it became apparent that he was clearly the brighter Howard. With each gleaming report card, Isaac treated Reggie with something much worse than resentment; apathy.

Isaac entered his twenties and with them, several jail cells and halfway homes. When nary a letter or phone call came, Reggie moved on, emptily collecting academic awards and spending time with Jack and the twins.

But on that steamy, July night things were different. They were on the porch, talking. Really talking, like brothers.

Isaac raised a Stroh's beer to his lips but received only a single drop. He looked inside the bottle and confirmed its emptiness.

"Reggie, get me another Stroh's."

The cooler was also empty.

"Sorry, Ice. All's left is my half bottle, here."

"Hmm...ok. Kill it. We going."

"Where?"

"To get more beer, dummy. Where else?"

Reggie took a glance at his watch. "Uhh, Ice, maybe you don't realize, but it's like 2:30 in the morning."

"Uhh, no shit," Ice said, mocking him. "I know a place."

"Where?"

"Up Clairmount. Party for some brothers just got back from 'Nam."

"What kind of bar is still serving? It's illegal after 2:00."

"My God. I been preachin' all night, and you ain't learned a damn thing. It's illegal. Shit. You think it's legal for you to be drinkin' that beer?"

"No, I guess not."

"Well then, like I says before. Kill it and let's go."

Reggie guzzled the last half of his beer, and off they went down the sidewalk. After a few paces, Reggie stopped and turned back to the house.

"What you doin?" Isaac said.

"Gonna change my shirt. I'm all sweaty and there might be ladies there."

"It's hot as shit. You think you won't sweat up the next shirt just walkin'?"

Reggie thought it over, and said, "You're probably right."

"Course I'm right. I'm always right, lil' brother. Sooner you realize, better off you'll be."

Off they went. At Third St, Isaac stopped and said, "On second thought, maybe you should go back and change."

Reggie was confused. "I should?"

"Yeah, cuz I don't know about them pants."

Reggie looked at his red bell bottom slacks without noting any perceivable flaw.

"Why, what's wrong with them?"

"Red? You look like some hippie queer, but maybe that's the look you goin' for." He started laughing.

"I like these pants."

"What you like about 'em? How they so tight, yo' bulge be poppin' out?" Isaac started laughing even louder, bent over, hands on knees.

"No it's not!" Reggie said, though he pulled the inseam down a little lower for good measure.

"Or is it…" Isaac continued through bursts of laughter, "The ass. Ooh wee, yo ass lookin' good in these pants!"

He pulled Reggie to him and smacked his backside with all of the force he could muster.

"Shit, man!" Reggie said, feeling his brother had left a permanent imprint of his hand.

Isaac then swept Reggie's legs and they fell onto the grass. In-between guffaws, he slapped about Reggie's face.

"Stop it!" Reggie shouted.

"What are you gonna do?" Isaac said, playfully.

"I'm gonna shut you up, that's what. I ain't some little kid no more."

He grabbed his brother's wrists and they grappled, rolling across the lawn. Reggie managed to get the top position, and delivered some unsuccessful body blows to his still laughing brother. Finally, a punch landed just below Isaac's ribs.

He stopped laughing.

Isaac grabbed Reggie's shoulders and flipped him to the ground instantly reminding him who the stronger brother was. Reggie's hands were pinned to the grass. He struggled but could not slip free from his grip.

"Well, go ahead. Shut me up," Isaac said, no longer smiling.

"Let me up, Ice. I was just foolin'."

"Naw, you was shutting me up. That's what you was doing." He dug his fingers deep into Reggie's wrists. The pain grew and grew until Reggie nearly burst into tears. Just when he thought Isaac might snap his wrists, it was over. Isaac released him and playfully ran his hands roughshod through Reggie's hair.

"Ha! Look at that shit! Good luck gettin' pussy with that hair." He stood up, chuckling.

Reggie, still in shock, pulled himself up and swept the grass from his clothes. Isaac put his arm around Reggie and said, "You know what? I actually like those pants."

"You asshole," Reggie said.

He gave Isaac a little shove and the two continued towards Clairmount.

Isaac stopped in front of the Budget Printing Co. It was a two story brick building, long vacant, on the northeast corner of Twelfth and Clairmount. Faint rock and roll could be heard coming from the top floor.

"We here," he said.

"We are? This place is empty."

"Empty, my ass."

Isaac walked over to the front door and knocked. A behemoth of a black man came to the door. He had a full beard and a supersized afro. He was wearing a leather vest, aviators and bell bottom jeans. He said nothing.

"Hey, brother. You gonna stand there or you gonna let me and my lil' man here in?"

The large man took a deep breath, and then slammed the door in Isaac's face. Isaac, undeterred, pounded on the door. Again, the man opened the door. Isaac puffed out his chest and said, "Don't make me go all Folsom on yo' ass."

Reggie feared for both their lives when the man grabbed Isaac by the collar and yanked him inside. The giant then pointed at Reggie and grunted. Taking it as an invitation, he sprang through the doorway. Once inside, the man grunted again and pointed up a dimly lit stairwell. Isaac looked back at him and said, "Much obliged."

The two walked up the stairs and opened the door at the top. Like Dorothy's first step into Oz, they passed from a grimy unoccupied print shop and into a bustling party. The single room, rectangular in shape, was dangerously overcrowded and stiflingly hot, though the patrons didn't seem to mind. Isaac promptly walked over to the makeshift bar in the corner and got two beers. He paid the busty, purple eye shadowed bartender and returned to Reggie, who had not left the doorway.

"Man, drink this quick. You crampin' my style."

"Sorry, Ice. I just, I never been to an after-hours place."

"Well, I been to plenty. This is how *we* get down. Though, I gotta say, most the time, it ain't this crowded. Must be like, eighty, ninety motherfuckers in here. Lot of fine tail, too. Play your cards right, you might even score yo' self some, even with that 'fro."

"Yeah. That would be far out."

"Speaking of cards, I'm 'bout to play me some right now. I see a table goin'. You mingle. See if you got any of that Howard charm."

"Ok, man."

Reggie took a sip of his beer and squinted through the thick clouds of smoke. There was a group of girls dancing near the Hi Fi. Amongst them was Florence Wilson. She lived in the neighborhood and had graduated a year earlier. Reggie had always had a bit of a thing for her, but he'd always been afraid to approach.

"No better time than the present," he mumbled to himself.

Halfway to her he became mesmerized by her braless bosom gyrating to and fro with the music. She must have noticed him gawking, because she crossed her arms over her chest and stopped dancing.

"Can I help you?" she said.

Embarrassed, Reggie said the first thing that came to his mind. "Umm. Good song, huh?"

"Good? It's Jimi. He's the best," she said, turning away from him.

He tapped her on the shoulder. She spun back around, looking mildly annoyed. "What?" she said.

"You ever wonder why he says, 'scuse me while I kiss this guy'? I mean, what's that about?"

She looked at him like he was diseased. "It's kiss the sky, you dope!"

"Oh…well, yeah. I know. I was just foolin'."

"Sure, kid. Ain't it past your bedtime?"

When she and her girlfriends began pointing and snickering, Reggie scanned the room for the spot that was geographically as far away as possible.

He settled on the ledge of a window looking out over Twelfth St.

Suddenly feeling the need for air, he yanked it open. It screeched and whined all the way up.

"Close that Goddamn window!" a very angry man shouted at him from the card table.

Reggie froze. Every eye was on him.

"I was just try-" he stammered.

"You tryin' to get us busted is what you doin'!"

Reggie closed the window, though he contemplated jumping out of it first.

"Willie, man. He's cool. Don't let it kill your buzz," Isaac said to the man.

Willie calmed down, but not before giving Reggie some very threatening looks. It didn't take long before all seemed to be forgotten and the party was rocking again, at least for everybody other than Reggie. He resigned himself to window-gazing until Isaac determined it was time for them to go.

There were many interesting people roaming the streets at 3:00 in the morning. Reggie killed time guessing the people's occupations from their attire. By his account he saw two pimps, five prostitutes, at least three dealers and one or two honest looking men.

One such man, wearing a bright red shirt, approached the print shop. Reggie watched him try, unsuccessfully, to negotiate entry with the behemoth before eventually giving up and walking off northbound on Twelfth.

At that moment, Willie stood up and told Florence and the girls dancing by the Hi-Fi to shut off the music. They did and the room got quiet.

"All right now. Y'all know why we here tonight. We got some real honored guests and I wanted to take a minute to recognize 'em. C'mon on over here, boys."

Three young men got up from their seats in different parts of the room, and made their way to Willie. He put his arms around two of them and said, "Right here we got two heroes. These boys just got back from Viet-fuckin-nam! Give 'em a hand, would ya?"

The gathering put their drinks and joints down long enough to muster some rather enthusiastic applause.

"And this one, over here," he said, pointing to the third guy. "He's goin' over there. Let's hear it that this young brother gets back safe."

Again, the applause filled the room. People stood up to shake the hands of the honored guests, who seemed to appreciate the recognition.

After the applause dwindled down, Willie said, "Ok, then. Bartender! Free drinks for our troops, here!"

Again, the party roared back to life. The Hi-Fi was rocking and the girls were dancing, all the while demanding that passers-by sock it to them, just like Aretha taught. Reggie looked down at his watch, and noted that it was 3:45.

He yawned.

He looked back out the window and again saw the man in the red shirt. He was two blocks up Twelfth leaning on a four door Plymouth sedan, talking to whoever was inside. Reggie couldn't get a look at them as the car was parked perfectly between two streetlights on the darkest part of the street. Just then, two girls Reggie had made for prostitutes were approaching the door to the bar. This caught red shirt's eye apparently, because he broke off his conversation and trotted down the street after them.

Within moments the door opened and in he walked with the two girls.

Upon closer examination, there was nothing particularly special about him but, for some reason, Reggie couldn't look away. He was in his late twenties. Good shape, about six feet tall. He was black, but so was everyone else there. At first, Reggie thought the man knew the girls he had come in with, but after they got in they all went their separate ways. Red shirt didn't seem to know anybody at the party. He wandered around aimlessly, not saying anything to anyone.

Reggie panicked when he realized the man had caught him staring. He looked angry and approached with zeal.

"Hey, you got a problem?" he said, with a jab to Reggie's chest.

"No, man. Why?"

"'Cuz you been eyeballin' me. Way I see it, you either got a problem or you want to fuck. Which is it?"

Reggie scooted down the ledge trying to escape. "Neither, man. I didn't realize I was starin'. We cool."

"I'm cool. Don't know about yo' ass," red shirt said, lingering in Reggie's face before backing off in the direction of the bar.

Reggie wanted to go. He waited until red shirt was a safe distance away and walked over to the card table where Isaac was in mid conversation with Willie.

"Hey, Ice. Let's get outta here," Reggie said.

"Not now," he said, waving Reggie off.

"Brutha man, all's I'm sayin' is, don't get me wrong, these boys are heroes, but they fightin' a war to free a bunch of goddamn gooks on the other side of the world when the war is right here on these streets. Every able bodied brother should be fightin' to free us here, man. They dyin' for the wrong cause."

Willie shook his head. "Have you ever been to another country? Do you even know what it's like? We got it pretty good here, ya know. Not great, I know, but it's a slow process. Dr. King's doin' his thing. It's happenin', brutha. You gots ta give it time, not run around with guns in your hands thinking people gonna respect you."

"Ice, man. Let's go. I-,"

"Shut up, Reggie!"

"Listen," Willie said, standing from the table. "Don't be spreadin' none of that black power bullshit tonight. We just tryin' to have a good time."

"Brutha, I'm tellin' you-,"

Willie waved Isaac off, and walked away. Reggie sat down in his chair.

"We ain't never gonna get nowhere with ignorant ass brothers like that," Isaac said. He downed a mostly full bottle of Stroh's, and slammed the empty down on the card table. Red shirt was over at the bar, ordering a drink. He turned and looked in Reggie and Isaac's direction. Reggie quickly diverted his eyes.

"Can we go?" he said.

"What's your problem?"

"It's late, I'm pissing people off, the girls want nothin' to do with me, and-,"

"And what?"

"I don't know. There's somethin' off about that guy over there in the red. Just looks like he don't belong, or somethin'"

Isaac examined the man from afar. "Look normal to me. You been smokin'? You paranoid as hell."

"No."

"Then I'm getting' you another drink," Isaac said and off to the bar he went.

Reggie sank in his chair and, against his better judgment, he let his eyes follow the man in the red shirt around the room. The man went straight to the ledge that had been Reggie's seat for most of the evening and casually looked out the window, or, at least to Reggie, he looked out the window in a manner as to seem casual. Then he did something strange. He held his beer up to the glass and waved it around. He then placed the untouched beer next to him on the ledge and leaned back, looking very satisfied.

Reggie met Isaac over by the bar. The busty bartender had just given Isaac two beers.

"Here," Isaac said.

"Naw, man. I just wanna get going."

Isaac put the beer in his brother's hand. "Take this goddamn beer. I told you, I ain't leavin' 'til I either set some of these brothers straight, or I get some tail. One of the two. And you ain't leavin' 'til I leave, ya dig?"

As Isaac sat down at the card table, to wait for the next deal, Reggie wandered to the back of the room and peered out a window that looked out over the alley. He pressed his beer to his lips, and froze when he heard the sound of shattering glass. It had happened right at that perfect moment when one song ended, and before the next began. He looked around to see if anyone else had heard it but nobody seemed to notice. The only person whose expression had changed was red shirt. He was looking right at Reggie with a self-important grin slathered over his face. At that moment the door flew open and a parade of cops entered the room.

"It's a raid!"

Pandemonium ensued. Drinks and bodies flew every which way. Isaac launched the card table in the direction on the infiltrating cops. Playing cards pirouetted through the smoky air. A five of spades landed on Reggie's shoulder but he didn't notice. His eyes were locked on red shirt, who was carousing with the cops. One of the uniformed police offered him a gun and a slap on the back.

A frozen Reggie was immediately roused when a panicked girl dashed by and singed his arm with her lit cigarette. He frantically scanned the room for Isaac. He found him to his right battling with the release on a window looking alleyside.

"Ice! Ice!"

"Reggie, get your ass over here and help me!"

"I'm comin'!"

Reggie took a step towards Isaac, but slipped on the remnants of an orange juice and gin. He went sprawling to the ground, taking a frantic Willie out in the process. He landed on top of Reggie with a thud.

"You sonofabitch! I'll kill you!" he said with murder in his eyes.

Reggie was able to block the blows to his face, but Willie landed several to his ribs. Isaac witnessed it all and quickly came to his little brother's aid. He pulled Willie up by the scruff of his collar and delivered a thunderous punch to the left side of his jaw.

"Hey you!" shouted an officer. He was closing in on them, baton out ready to do damage. Isaac shoved Willie in the cop's direction and bolted for the window. A still dazed Willie collapsed on the cop's legs, undercutting him. The officer grabbed at his knee and screamed in pain.

Reggie leapt up and met his brother at the stubborn window. With their combined strength, they pried it open. Isaac stepped through and prepared to drop.

"Ice, man! It's too far!" Reggie said, grabbing Isaac's arm.

"Reggie, what else we gonna do? I ain't goin' back in, man. I done my time. Now let me go!"

Reggie complied, and Isaac fell, limbs flailing, into a pile of garbage some fifteen feet down.

Reggie poked his head through the window and yelled out, "You ok?"

"I'm fine, fine," he said, working at his lower back. "Get your ass down here!"

Reggie looked down and his stomach somersaulted, but when he looked back, what he saw wasn't much better. The white cops were rounding all the blacks up while the captain, or at least the cop Reggie assumed to be the captain because he was the one barking out orders, stood near the door.

"Round every last one up, boys!" he yelled out over the commotion.

A uniformed officer had Willie, still stunned from Isaac's punch, down on the floor, his knee pressed in to the small of his back. The officer, while wrenching Willie's arms around to cuff him, shouted back, "All of 'em, Cap?"

"All of 'em. I recognize some of these scumbags. I love repeat offenders," the captain said.

Isaac yelled up to Reggie from the ground, "Quit daydreamin' and jump!"

Reggie, deciding the risk of a broken ankle was better than spending the rest of the night in jail, gingerly lifted one leg over the ledge and tucked his head underneath the raised pane. Straddling the ledge, he saw red shirt coming right for him. "Freeze!" he commanded, gun drawn.

Reggie panicked and nearly fell, but managed to grab the ledge with both hands. He hung there, legs dangling nine feet from the garbage pile.

"Let go!" Isaac shouted.

Reggie put his feet on the bricks and pushed off just as red shirt reached the window. Reggie watched the man's dejected expression as he plummeted. He braced for impact on the unforgiving cement ground, but instead felt himself being corralled by his brother. They tumbled to the ground, but were unharmed.

"Thanks, man," Reggie said.

"Thank me later," Isaac said. He got up and looked left down the alley towards Clairmount, before heading northbound towards the dead end of the alley.

"Where you goin'? Our house is the other way!" Reggie shouted, following behind.

"Pigs'll be crawlin' all over Clairmount. Let's loop around and come back up Twelfth," Isaac said.

"What? No! Let's get our asses home."

"Naw. I wanna see what they gonna do."

"They'll arrest everyone, including us! That's why we just jumped out the window!" Reggie said, stupefied.

"No way. There's too many. You do what the hell you want, brother. I'm watchin'," Isaac said. He then quickly overtook the six foot high chain link fence and took off north towards Atkinson.

Reggie lingered for a moment watching him disappear into the darkness. He begrudgingly followed, running through the backyards of homes whose owners soundly slept. It was absolutely not what he wanted to be doing at that moment. He wanted to go home, but feared he'd lose any chance at his brother's respect if he did. He ran as fast as he could to catch up, with only the occasional fleeting glimpse of his brother's form against the shadowless night to guide him.

When he reached the corner of Atkinson and Twelfth, he spotted his brother across from the blind pig. He was not alone. A small group of people had gathered, watching the goings-on at the vacant print shop.

After he had caught up to his brother, Reggie said, "Why are we stickin' around? What do you think is gonna happen?"

"I don't know, man, but they ain't enough cops to bring in that many people. I wanna see how they think they gonna do it."

At that moment, a paddy wagon pulled up and two uniformed police popped out of the cab. One went up the steps to the party, while the other went behind and opened the van's back doors.

"Right there, that's how they gonna do it," Reggie said.

"Naw, man. Even crowdin' 'em in like cattle, only like fourteen, fifteen people gonna fit. They gonna need like four more of them things."

A pot-bellied, middle aged black man in loafers and shorts and nothing else wandered up. He overheard their conversation and asked, "What's goin' on in there?"

"These goddamn pigs come bustin' in, smashin' heads. They won't be happy 'til every last Negro either dead or in jail," Isaac replied, without taking his eyes off the front door of the print shop.

"Well, you a damn fool, havin' a party there. Place been busted up couple times already this year. Good thing, too. Brings around the seedy types," he said, with a pejorative glance at Isaac.

"You got a problem with me old man?"

Isaac made a move to advance on the man, but stopped when Reggie grabbed him by the shoulder. The old man stumbled over the curb while retreating from Isaac, but caught his balance. He melded back in with the growing crowd, now near fifty people.

Isaac pushed Reggie's hand off of his shoulder.

"Can you believe that old fool? We got whitey pushin' us around, and he's callin' me out?"

"Never mind him."

"Naw, man. That's the problem. These old brothers been pushed around they whole life to the point they don't even realize when they getting' pushed no more. They just lie down and take it like a dog. Well, not me."

The first group of arrestees were paraded out of the print shop and led to the paddy wagon. One of them, a small-time drug pusher Reggie recognized from the neighborhood, fell to the ground just before entering the van. Unable to protect himself with his hands cuffed behind his back, he landed face first on the pavement. This drew gasps from the crowd. Isaac took this as an opportunity to rabble-rouse. He stood on top of a bus-stop bench and addressed the growing horde.

"Look at what they are doing to our people! Are we gonna stand here and watch as they beat us senseless?"

The shirtless old man shouted back at Isaac, "Oh, you quiet down now. That boy tripped. Probably drunk as a skunk, anyhow."

A smattering of laughter could be heard permeating the crowd. An incensed Isaac jumped back off of the bus bench, and began pacing and muttering to himself. Reggie recognized the fury rising up in his brother and knew from years of experience that it would be good for nobody to allow it to continue. He purposely stood right in the path of his brother's frantic pacing.

"Ice man, cool it for a second. Now's not the time to play Stokely Carmichael and start an uprising."

"It's not? Than tell me, when will it be?"

Reggie could tell that his attempts at taming the beast inside his brother would be for naught. He tried to at least distract him.

"How's your back?"

"Forget my back! It's fine, unlike that brother who just face-planted on the cement when that cop pushed his ass down."

"I don't know, man. It looked like he tripped on the curb."

Isaac pierced Reggie with an unflinching stare. A stare that meant that nothing, not even blood ties, would stop him tonight and that Reggie had better decide right then and there whose side he was on.

Another paddy wagon pulled up in front of the print shop just as the first one left. A uniformed policeman hopped out of the cab and approached the captain who was overseeing the operation from just outside the print shop's entrance. Isaac walked away from Reggie and the crowd, approaching the captain and his cohorts. Reggie watched him go, realizing that the night was slipping away.

Isaac stopped about ten feet away from the police. He heard the patrolman say, "The other wagons are tied up. It's gonna be at least an hour before they can get everyone to the precinct."

"So be it," said the captain.

"Are you sure this is the best way, Cap? I mean, what are we gonna do with 'em once we get 'em there?"

The captain, visibly frazzled from the night's events, unleashed on his underling. "What is this? Are you giving orders, now?"

"N-no, Cap."

"We will continue on as planned, officer!"

"Yes, cap," the patrolman said and up the stairs he ran.

The captain took off his hat, and wiped the beads of sweat from his brow with a handkerchief. He stuffed it into his back pocket, and that's when he noticed Isaac standing by.

"What are you doing, green sleeves? Get outta here, now. Ain't nothin' for you here."

Isaac smiled.

"I said, scram before I round you up with the rest of them, boy!"

Isaac turned and strolled back over to the growing crowd. He called Reggie to him.

"Lil brother, they have no idea what they doin'. This is the time. I can feel it. Can you feel it?"

"I guess so."

"Oh yes. It's it the air," he said taking a deep dual-nostriled pull. "That electricity. It's like right before a lightning strike. We gonna bring the lightning. We gonna bring a goddamn hurricane."

Another group of people were being led to the paddy wagon by the police. One of them was Willie. His eye was purple and closed up from Isaac's punch. He resisted the arresting officer when he attempted to get him to step up in the van.

"Hell, no pig. I ain't getting' in," he screamed.

"Oh, yes you are!" the cop demanded.

He shoved Willie hard and he crashed into the van's door and collapsed to the ground. The cop reached down and lifted him back up, where Willie struggled against him some more. He lurched forward, chin raised.

"Look at his face!" Isaac yelled, jumping back up on the bench.

"They beat him! Look at him! He can't even open his eye! Are we gonna allow this, in our neighborhood? Tell me, people! If we was in Grosse Pointe, shit wouldn't be like this!"

"Ice, his eye's black from-,"

"Shut up, Reggie!"

Reggie watched as the crowd started to liven up. His message had fallen on deaf ears before, but that puffed up eye made the crowd more receptive. With each surge of Willie's handcuffed body came a cheer from the now hundreds strong throng. Another cop came to the aid of the first, and together they were able to subdue Willie and put him in the van. This drew a chorus of boos that only grew with each additional person led to the wagon. Isaac, atop the bench, chanted "black power" repeatedly. The crowd slowly joined in. Reggie watched his brother, beaming with pride, lead them, a maestro sans baton.

The paddy wagon filled with prisoners left, and about five minutes later, another took its place. Most of those arrested cooperated with the police, and were handled fairly. Those that resisted met with the business end of a nightstick, or worse, the butt of a gun. Isaac welcomed these physical altercations. They fueled his congregation, and the louder they were, the more the windows in the cramped second story apartments up and down Clairmount and Twelfth Streets lit up. Sleepy eyed and weary, people emerged from their homes and joined in.

When that paddy wagon left, none came to replace it. The captain was looking much less self-assured than he had upon breaking into the party. A uniformed officer came to him and whispered in his ear. Incensed, the captain threw his cap against the brick wall of the print shop.

"How the hell do you work for the Detroit Police and not know where Twelfth and Clairmount is? How long 'til he's here?"

The uniformed cop shrugged his shoulders and backed away from the captain, hoping to avoid any further projectiles.

"What's wrong, pig? Lost your van?" Isaac shouted.

The captain watched nervously as the mob laughed in unison, their caterwauling heard for blocks. The captain pulled his sweat drenched collar from his neck, his claustrophobia choking him off as he could feel the mass of humanity closing in on him.

"Oh hell yeah! We gon' kill all you whitey motherfuckers!" Isaac shouted. The crowd responded orgasmically.

Reggie could not believe it. His brother had just endorsed murder, of the police nonetheless, and they cheered. All thoughts humane and decent were lost on them. His brother's enthusiasm was viral and it had robbed them of their sensibilities.

The last paddy wagon came speeding down Clairmount. At the turn onto Twelfth St, the back end of the van slid out behind it, leaving rubber on the pavement. The driver regained control and slammed on the brakes, skidding to a halt in front of the print shop. He jumped out of the van, and was met with immediate scorn from the captain, before running up the stairs to help in rounding up the remaining prisoners. One by one the cops came down the steps with them, filling the last van.

"Are we gonna let these peckerwood crackers push us around?" Isaac screamed to the mob.

"Hell no!"

"Are we gonna take what's rightfully ours?"

"Hell yes!"

A scream could be heard from the stairwell of the print shop. Seconds later, an overmatched cop tried to escort the busty bartender with the barely there tube top to the van.

"Let me go, you honkey pig," she yelled, twisting and kicking in his grip.

He had her in position to enter the van when she raised her right leg up high, and brought the pointed heel of her go-go boot down with such force on his foot that he cried out in pain. She tried to escape his clutches, but, though hurting, he managed to grab her from the back of her top. The thin material gave way in his hands, and tore away from her body, leaving her standing in the street bare-chested. She wobbled in her heels in shock, her arms cuffed behind her back, like an unfortunate Venus De Milo. Another officer corralled her before she could run, and shoved her into the van. The crowd, which was angry before, reached a level of ire so intense that it was palpable.

"Now they tryin' to rape our women! Let's rain hell down on these motherfuckers!" Isaac commanded.

The people picked up rocks and pebbles from the street and began pelting the van with them. They pinged off the sheet metal, a hail storm of street justice. An old wino stood by Isaac watching the uprising, guzzling from a bottle of cheap whiskey. Isaac grabbed it from the man, and took a swig. He handed the bottle to Reggie, and said, "Throw it, brother. Join your people."

"I'm not throwing any-,"

"You throw this goddamn bottle!"

Reggie took the bottle and watched the cops hurrying to escort the last man into the van. He looked at the bottle, and back at the van.

"DO IT!"

"I...I can't, man."

Isaac leaped onto the bench and started chanting, "DO IT! DO IT! DO IT!"

His followers joined in. Their chants rattled in Reggie's head. He couldn't concentrate. It's all he could hear. He closed his eyes so he wouldn't have to see them shout it, but this only amplified the sound. Then one voice rose up over the rest. The girl in the van, poked her head out of the window, and screamed, "BRUTALITY!"

He opened his eyes. Her tear streak face struck something inside that he didn't know was there.

"BAPTIZE THAT MOTHERFUCKER!" Isaac demanded.

Reggie unleashed the bottle at the captain. It sailed with a velocity that surprised even him. The captain, recognizing it at the last possible moment, was able to evade the bottle, feeling a slight breeze as it passed his cheek. It slammed into the brick wall inches behind him and rained shards and whiskey upon him. The crowd let loose a Vesuvian eruption. More bottles and rocks filled the sky. They crashed at the feet of the police, dashing to their vehicles. Isaac rared back and let loose a large rock that shattered the back window of the captain's squad car. They cheered and cheered as they watched the police leave the scene. Isaac hopped down from the bench, the eyes of the people on him, waiting for their next command. Reggie watched him, too. He had become one of them, intoxicated by Isaac's siren song. Isaac raised his fist in the air, quieting the crowd.

"Let's burn this motherfucker down."

A man picked up the garbage can at the corner, and catapulted it through the plate glass window of the black owned neighborhood drug store. Looters infiltrated the store. Isaac sat back with a self-satisfied grin on his face. The riot had begun.

CHAPTER IX
MAY 21, 2008

It was seven o'clock, and Martin had been studying cases for over five hours at the Starbucks in Royal Oak. His eyes were strained and his brain was fried and it seemed to him that every single person on Main Street was enjoying their Wednesday much more than he was. They were riding bikes, sipping drinks, licking ice cream cones. He was nose deep in law texts and had been consistently for weeks.

Before continuing on with Brown v. Board of Education, he tilted his coffee cup to his lips hoping for some caffeine fueled rejuvenation.

The cup was empty.

Undeterred, he forged on. Two sentences in, the words began to melt into a text soup no longer resembling the English language. He threw out the cup, got into the Chrysler and headed home.

On the way, his mind drifted. He thought mostly about the class. Danielle.

Other than his living arrangement, things were going well. The tension between him and his father, though, was profound and going out of his was to avoid him had grown tiresome. He was not sure how long he would be able to do it.

Martin parked the car and walked in the house. He was surprised to see his father in the living room watching baseball instead of the garage, though not everything was out of order; Jack's trusty beer was by his side.

Jack turned his head when Martin came in. He looked like he wanted to say something, but did not, choosing instead to sip his beer and resume watching the game.

Martin had loved baseball as a kid. In the early nineties it seemed like every kid did. His interest waned as he devoted more time to studying in high school. By college, he'd even stopped reading the box scores online.

"Who's winning?" he asked Jack. He was surprised at how easily the words had sailed out his mouth. His hibernating love of baseball had trumped the boycott of his father.

"What? Oh, uh. No score."

"Oh."

"I don't suppose you'd want to-," Jack said.

"Want to what?"

"I don't know. Watch the game?"

"No," Martin said, momentarily giving it some thought. "I don't think so."

"Oh…all right," Jack said, melancholic.

Martin passed through the kitchen on into his bedroom. He set his laptop case down on the desk and lied on his bed. He picked at his fingernails and twiddled his thumbs, hearing, over and over, that hint of sadness in his father's voice.

"Just watch the game with him. Would it kill you? " he could hear his mother say.

"A couple hours. That's all. "

He resisted at first, watching the leaves gentle sway through the window, but ultimately, he caved. He would do anything for her.

On his way to the living room, he paused at the fridge giving himself one final opportunity to reconsider and turn back.

"It's not hard. Only beer, salami and Faygo in there," Jack shouted.

"I'm thinking."

"Think with that door closed. Electricity isn't free."

Martin grabbed a can of Rock & Rye and took a seat on the plush brown couch he used to fall asleep on as a child. Only an oak side table separated him from his father.

"Changed your mind?" Jack said.

"It would appear so."

The broadcaster announced that the game was scoreless in the bottom of the second inning, and for a while his voice was the only one to be heard in the room. Jack raised his beer can to his mouth. Martin did the same with his pop.

Detroit got two men on base, and up to the plate stepped Detroit's third baseman.

"All right, little bingo here. Couple ducks on the pond," Jack blurted out.

Martin knew that this was directed at the television, or more specifically to the man playing baseball twelve miles away, but thought maybe it was also his father's not so subtle way of breaking the awkward tension in the room.

"Yes! We're on the board," Jack said, as the man, a white player, ripped a double down the leftfield line, scoring the two men on base.

Martin braved a glance in his father's direction. He had a big smile on his face, and he was leaning forward on the edge of his seat.

"Damnit. Left a guy in scoring position," Martin chimed in, when the next batter weakly lined out to second base to end the inning.

Jack nodded. "Yeah. Sure did."

He finished off his beer and got up out of the recliner. He walked into the kitchen and opened up the fridge.

"You want anything else? Some salami?"

"No thanks."

Within moments, Jack returned with two cans of beer and the salami.

"Here. I brought you something a little harder than that pop."

He offered the beer to Martin.

"I'm all set. Thanks."

"More for me," Jack said, shrugging. He set the can down on the side table.

"How many is that today, Jack?"

He didn't answer.

A commercial came on the television. Black words emerged against a white background. "We can replace fear...with hope," they read. Then came a voiceover about the economy, healthcare, and many other hot button topics. The commercial ended with "believe again" on the screen. It was an advertisement for Barack Obama, the black presidential candidate.

"That's all we need," Jack said.

"What are you talking about?"

"President Coon."

Martin scoffed. "Well, that didn't take long."

"What? You want a black president?"

"I don't think his performance in office will have much to do with his skin tone, if that's what you're asking, but, geopolitically, yes, I think it would be a good thing."

"Geo-what?"

"I'm saying it may be perceived globally as a progressive choice. Certainly it couldn't hurt our standing more than the previous administration."

"It could do more damage than you know. Look at this Kwame Kilpatrick."

"What about him?"

"You hear that 'n' bomb he dropped in the state of the city address?"

Martin sighed. "Yeah. I heard it." His argument for the merits of black leadership was not bolstered by discussing Detroit Mayor Kwame Kilpatrick.

"That's serious race baiting. You think that doesn't do harm? And what about all these allegations? Couple hundred grand for expenses, that crazy party at Manoogian...that stripper-,"

"Allegations. The party stuff...the stripper. That was never proven."

"Yeah, yeah. Either way, he got himself reelected, didn't he? Show's how bright the average Detroiter is."

"Yeah, well, that's just one example."

"Marion Barry?"

"That was almost twenty years ago."

"Still..."

"Ok. If were gonna sit here and list black politicians, how about Dennis Archer?"

"Mayor Archer? He's almost as white as you or me."

"That's just plain ignorance."

"Maybe I'm ignorant. I'm not in some fancy race class like you."

Martin shook his head. "Why don't we just watch the game?"

"Fine by me."

Other than some cursing from Jack when Seattle's leadoff man hit a home run, neither of them spoke again until the bottom of the third inning. Detroit had once again mounted a threat, loading the bases for their African American journeyman leftfielder. He quickly crushed a pitch deep over the left field wall for a grand slam.

"Yes! I love this kid!" Jack said, moving on to the beer he'd brought for Martin.

"You love him?"

"Yeah, he's a great ballplayer."

"But he's black."

Jack cleared his throat. "What does that have to do with anything?"

Martin let out an exasperated chuckle. "Wow. The color of their skin matters when they want to move in next door, take your picture, cook your food or run for president, but not if they play baseball?"

"I love him as a ballplayer. He could be purple or green or polka dotted for all I care, as long as he can hit that ball. Hell, Willie Horton was my favorite player when I was young."

"That's the problem. You can't decide when being racist is ok and when it isn't."

"I'm not racist."

"Oh, no? What are you then?"

Jack looked away from Martin and took a sip of his beer. "Must be nice to know everything at such a young age," he said.

"Sarcasm. Nice."

Jack's expression grew dour, pensive. "Did you ever think that possibly, just possibly, people think a certain way because of things that happened to them in their lives?"

Martin immediately thought of Baby Albert and the ping of hammer on steel.

"Ok, I'll bite. What happened?"

Jack didn't respond. He was no longer there. He had drifted through the television, past the drywall and framing. He was through the bricks and over the backyard, in an alley behind a motel miles away and forty-one years in the past.

"Whatever," Martin said, taking Jack's silence as obstinacy.

Detroit tacked on another run, ending the third inning up 9-1. Jack rose from his chair, and wobbled into the kitchen.

"Another one?" Martin said.

"No. I gotta piss. That ok with you?" Jack shouted.

It was obvious to Martin after three innings of baseball that he just wasn't meant to be in the same room as his father. That, and the fact that the game was a blowout, had him considering calling it an early night, but the stack of empties on the side table kept him on the couch.

The magic interval.

The haphazardly constructed tower of cans suggested that it wouldn't be long before Jack would achieve that special kind of drunkenness his mother had told him about and he himself had witnessed on his graduation day. The possibility of getting answers to questions that had long bothered him was too attractive to pass up.

Jack returned just as a promo for a local hardware store ended and the scene cut back to game.

"What'd I miss?" he said, while he poked his head into the fridge.

"Nothing. Commercials."

Jack closed the fridge and walked over to his recliner and sat down. He had two beer cans in his hands.

"Was it another boner pill commercial? I swear every man in America must have a limp noodle for how much they play those ads."

"No. It wasn't one of those," Martin said, fighting a smile.

Jack popped open one of the cans and took a hearty gulp. He had it finished by bottom of the fourth inning and finished the other one during a Seattle mini-rally in the top of the fifth. Martin sat quietly and watched his father's armchair managing become less and less shrewd.

By the top of the ninth, the sun had gone down, taking with it all of the light in the living room but that from the television, and Jack consumed five more beers. When he started calling the players by the wrong names, Martin knew the time had come.

"Hey Jack," he said.

"Huh?"

"What's with the GTO?"

"Love that car."

"I know, but how can you sit in it every day for hours?"

"She rode in it."

"Who? Mom?"

"She was so beautiful," Jack mumbled, his eyelids drooping. His breathing became more erratic. On the television, Seattle's shortstop flied out to center field.

"Who are you talking about? Mom?"

"You hungry? I'm hungry," Jack said, lunging forward suddenly. He clumsily grabbed the package of salami off the table and fumbled it open. He held a single slice in front of his face, turning it, examining both sides.

"Look at this salami. The marbling and the…"

"Huh?"

"You know what? It's gonna get ripped up and shredded to pieces."

He put the slice in his mouth, whole. His jaws swiveled side to side, tearing the meat apart.

He swallowed.

"Now it's in a pit of acid. Sloshing around, being broken down even more. Then…then it'll get squeezed through these tunnels, anything good stripped away. Pushed through further…and further…until any hope, any promise…gone."

Martin gazed on his father unsure of what to say.

"And the useless leftover junk'll be packed together into shit and then it'll…it'll…"

Martin sat stupefied.

"What are you talking about?" he asked.

Jack slumped into the recliner and closed his eyes.

"I used to be good at baseball. Damn good," he said, sighing.

"Well, it's a hard sport to play drunk."

"Day you were born, told Diane I'd teach you everything I knew. Quit the booze that day, cold."

"It obviously didn't take."

"She worked days. Me, nights at the plant. All day you'd cry. Colicky."

"I was? Mom never-,"

"Tried everything. You'd scream…pained screams for hours. Agonizing…Woulda gave anything…switch places," Jack, said. He was losing his grip on consciousness.

"And?" Martin said.

"Huh?"

"You tried everything?"

"Seven straight hours…Held you…rocked you. Couldn't take it anymore. Bottle on the way to work."

Jack's eyes closed and his body slumped over to the side.

"Is that why you fell? It wasn't the lighting at all, was it?"

"Kindofafather…," Jack mumbled. His face wrenched and contorted.

"Jack…" Martin pleaded as Seattle's third baseman meekly lined out. "…"

He grabbed his father by the shirt and yanked his slack body forward.

"Jack!" he shouted again, garnering nothing more than a flutter of his father's eyelids.

"Who is Reggie Howard?" Martin said.

Like he'd been pumped full of adrenaline, Jack lurched forward, his eyes wide open.

"Whaddayou doing?" he said.

"Tell me!"

"Let go!"

His hands wrapped around Martin's wrists, but he could not break Martin's grip on his shirt.

"TELL ME!" Martin implored.

"NO, YOU TELL ME!"

"Tell you what?"

Jack came within an inch of his son's face. With beer-tinged breath he uttered a name Martin hoped he'd never hear again.

"T-Mar."

Martin's arms became jelly.

"Wait…how do you…"

He stumbled backwards into the side table, knocking over the stack of beer cans and flopping onto the couch. He made no attempt to get back up. He couldn't.

Jack propped himself up from the recliner and shuffled into the kitchen, bumping into the wall and knocking over a dining chair. He turned the corner around the Formica counter to the kitchen sink where his body violently rejected the poison. With each retch, Martin struggled against his own urge to vomit. On the television, Seattle's second baseman grounded out. The game was over.

CHAPTER X
FEBRUARY 6, 2006

Martin was seated at the computer desk underneath his bunk in his West Quad dorm room. The space was small with four sterile white and unadorned cinder block walls and illuminated only by the monitor's glow. Laughter drifted over from his neighbor's room, down the hall and through his open door, along with the faint smell of marijuana.

His fingers twitched over the mouse button to pull up his grades from the fall semester online.

Click.

Within seconds, the grade for his Contemporary Social Issues course emerged. Martin was flabbergasted. No amount of blinking or eye rubbing could change the fact that before him, plain as day was a letter that had never been next to his name in his whole life.

'D'

He leaned back in his mesh, swivel desk chair with the adjustable lumbar support and took a swig from a pint of bourbon. The brown elixir should have been harsh to take straight, but as he'd already finished half the bottle, it went down smooth as glass.

He propelled himself across the linoleum floor to the window and pulled back the sheer curtain. Snow was falling heavily. The flag on top of the student union building whipped to and fro high above the white blanketed landscape. A single girl trudged along, her books held tightly to her chest and her head down in attempt to shield her face from the biting cold.

Martin took another swig.

After the girl was out of sight, he slid back to his desk. A sideways glance at the screen reaffirmed what he feared; it was still there, the D, just the same as before.

The sad fact was he could not remember even taking the final exam that earned him that meager grade. The only memory he could pull from that day was waking up on a couch after a rager at the Chi Phi house with a colossal migraine that he'd attempted to chase with Jameson. No final exam. Yet, right there on the screen it said he'd scored a fifty-two percent.

Unfortunately, these blackouts had become commonplace. The first time he'd woken up missing a portion of his yesterday, he was terrified. Paranoia filled the gaping hole in his memory with all sorts of heinous actions to the point that he vowed never to get drunk again. The next time it happened, he was remorseful, but less so.

The next time, even less.

Eventually, alcohol induced amnesia would become the rule rather than the exception.

Martin maneuvered the little arrow on the screen to the x in the corner. With a click of the mouse the proof of his lost semester vanished. He was left with his desktop image from his graduation day staring him in the face. His mother was still smiling, though she'd been dead for months, while his father was obscured by a myriad of icons. For a moment, a wave of shame overcame him. He turned the monitor off and the shame, as well as his mother's image, faded.

In the dark now, he became aware of the whiskey filling his head with helium. It was comfortable, calming to the point where it almost made him forget the gravity of that letter 'D'.

Almost.

In the hall, his neighbor's door opened and Martin heard two men exchange good byes. Not wanting any interruption to the solo wake he was holding for his grade point average, he quickly went to close the door. He reached it just as a thin, Caucasian man walked by. He had medium length, straw-like hair that looked as if it hadn't been washed in weeks. He appeared to be about Martin's age and looked vaguely familiar. He stopped when he saw Martin in the doorway.

"Oh, sorry dude. Were we gettin' a little loud?"

Martin, who had not spoken to another human being in several days, took a moment to respond. "What? No, I was just closing my d-,"

"Hey, do I know you?"

Martin thought that he might, as the twinge of familiarity grew stronger as they conversed. "I don't think so."

"You look like this guy I went to high school with. You go to Hazel Park? "

"I did," Martin said.

"Ha! I knew it! Martin, right?"

"Yeah. How are you…I'm sorry, I can't-."

"Shit, it's ok, man. It's Dan. Dan Schoenfeld."

It came flooding back to Martin. This was the Dan who took the picture on his computer desktop. The Dan that was one of the few supporters of his ill-fated commencement speech.

"Oh yeah. What have you been up to?" Martin said out of social convention rather than actual interest.

"Chillin' man. Just chillin'. You?"

"Classes. Do you go to school here?" Martin said, though he was fairly certain that he did not.

"No. My cousin does. Your neighbor. I just came by to smoke a little with him."

"Oh."

Martin searched for something more to say, but was at a loss. He and Dan had just as much in common then as they had two years prior, which is to say, very little.

"Well, it was nice seein' you," he said. He started to close the door, but Dan stuck his foot in the way.

"Hey, what do you got there?" Dan said.

Martin pulled the door open again. "What?"

"In your hand. You partyin'?"

Martin looked down at his hand and saw the bottle. He hadn't considered what he was doing as partying.

"No, I was just-,"

"Aww, don't hold out on me, bro. What else you got in there?"

Dan squeezed past Martin and flipped the switch to the overhead fluorescent bulbs. The room was filled with a blinding brilliance. Martin shielded his eyes from it.

His temples pulsated.

Dan walked around the room, soaking in his surroundings. There were the corpses of liquor bottles bearing the names of long dead men all over the room.

Johnny Walker, Jim Beam, Jack Daniel.

Dan stepped over one and his foot bumped into another. It rattled against the linoleum floor, before settling on its side. By Dan's estimate, there were forty to fifty of them. Some on the sill. A few on top of the armoire. Others indiscriminately placed on the floor.

"Holy shit, man! You *have* been partying. Aren't you afraid of the R.A."

"Dan, Look, it's nice to catch up and everything, but-,"

"You wanna smoke?" Dan said, patting his shirt pocket.

Martin stood with his hand on the doorknob. A voice inside his head told him to rid himself of this interloper, but the voice was not alone. Another told him to go ahead. That he had nothing to lose.

That voice was louder.

"Sure," he said, closing the door.

Dan sat at Martin's desk.

"Whoa, this chair's comfortable as shit!"

"Yeah," Martin said, taking a gulp from his bottle. It was three quarters gone.

"So, are you like rich, or something?"

"No. Why?"

"Duh, look around. You get this sick ass chair and about two grand in booze scattered around."

"I'm not rich."

"Sure seems like it."

Dan rocked back and forth nervously clicked his tongue against the roof of his mouth. He turned his attention to the black screen on the computer monitor, and powered it on. It flashed bright, and Diane's smiling face returned.

"Hey, that's graduation. Didn't I take that pic?"

Martin shot off the couch and pushed to the button to shut the monitor off again. "Don't fucking touch the computer!"

Dan cringed and pushed the chair as far back against the wall as it would go. "Whoa, man! Ok! I won't."

Martin closed his eyes and took a deep breath and sat back down on the couch.

"You really need to get a hit of this shit. It will mellow you out," Dan said, reaching into his shirt pocket.

"What else do you got?"

"What do you mean?"

"Do you have anything else?"

"Drugs?"

"What the hell else would I be talking about?"

Dan leaned forward in the chair. "What, you want something harder?"

"Maybe."

"Like what? What have you done?"

"Nothing, really."

"Well, why don't we start with the weed then?"

"What does it do?"

"It just, I don't know, gets you high, man. You feel, like chilled out."

"I don't want it then."

"Why not?"

"It's not what I'm looking for."

"What are you looking for then?"

Martin didn't say anything. He just looked out the window into the snowstorm.

Dan scratched at his greasy straw follicles. After a few moments, he said, "I think I know what you need, but I don't have anything like that on me."

"Oh, ok," Martin said, disappointed.

"But, I know a guy."

Martin's eyes opened wide.

"This guy, he's got everything, but he's not around here."

"Where is he?"

"In Detroit. If it weren't snowing so bad I'd say-"

"You got a car?"

"Umm…yeah, I got a car."

"Call him."

"I'm not driving all the way down there."

"I'll drive."

"I don't know, man," Dan said, wishing he hadn't mentioned it. In fact he was starting to regret even talking to Martin to begin with. He was just looking for a good time, and Martin seemed morose, even a little disturbed.

"Even if I can get ahold of the guy, the shit ain't cheap," he said.

Martin stood up from the couch and loomed over Dan. "Make the call."

Dan swallowed hard. He reached into his pocket and pulled out his cell phone. Martin backed off.

Dan dialed the number.

A man answered. The conversation was short and direct.

"T-Mar?" Dan said. "You around? ...Yeah. A little somethin'. Whatever you got, I guess... Yeah, we got money...Me and another guy...No, he's not a cop...All right, we'll see y-,"

Dan flipped the phone closed.

"He hung up."

"T-Mar?" Martin said. "What's he like?"

Dan shrugged. "I don't know, man. A drug dealer. A little unhinged. Seems more put together than the big guy, though."

"The big guy?"

"Flip, T-Mar's cousin. He's nuts."

"Why do you say that?"

"I only saw him once, but I heard some stuff. He's got that crazy eye, y'know? Plus, he had like three of those teardrop tattoos on his face."

"What?"

"You know, it's like a notch in the bedpost for killers."

"T-Mar doesn't have one?"

"No...at least he didn't the last time I saw him."

Martin nodded. "Good to know."

He grabbed his jacket and walked into the bathroom.

"You might want to wash your face while you're in there. I mean, no offense, but you look like shit," Dan shouted.

Martin took off the t-shirt he'd been wearing and stood in front of the mirror. Dan was right. The man in the mirror looked like hell. He was a pale, bearded recluse with dark circles under his eyes. His arms frail; his ribs exposed.

Martin decided that he didn't want to see the man anymore, so he pulled on a sweater and turned out the light. He left the bathroom, and walked over to the armoire. Out of a drawer he pulled a wad of cash.

"Let's go."

The third time Martin veered the Dodge Dakota onto the rumble strip, Dan reached over and grabbed the wheel.

"What the hell? Don't touch the wheel when I'm driving," Martin said.

"Well stay in the lane, then. You're freakin' me out like we're gonna fly into a damn ditch."

"We're fine. I'm fine."

"I shoulda drove, I think. You're drunk as shit."

"Yeah, well, you're high."

"Pull off at the Southfield exit and we'll switch."

Martin didn't say anything. He kept his eyes on the road, trying his hardest to keep the car perfectly between the lines. It was a constant battle to look beyond the flying snow to the jet black highway. He gripped the wheel hard, his back two inches from the seat cushion. His eyes cycled from the speedometer to the rearview mirror to the road. Dan watched Martin from the passenger seat. He tugged at his seatbelt, ensuring that it was securely fastened. He reached for the controls for the radio, but Martin slapped his hand away.

"No radio," Martin said.

"What? Why?"

"Concentrating."

"Well, you ain't talkin' to me, and I can't listen to the radio, so what the hell am I supposed to do?"

"Not my problem."

"Can I at least burn one?"

"Go ahead."

Dan pulled one of the joints out of his pocket and lit it up. He took a long, slow drag.

"Ahh, that's better," he said, slowly releasing the smoke from his lungs. The cab of the small truck quickly took on an aroma of oily, burnt herbs.

"So where am I going, anyways?"

"What?"

"Where is the guy?"

"Just get off at Chene and I'll direct you from there."

Martin nodded. He had no idea where the Chene exit was. He had spent very little time in the city as a boy. His knowledge of Detroit locations were limited to what he could see out of his window as he passed through on I-75.

"Are we close?" he asked.

Dan was in the middle of another toke. He released it and said, "Not far. It's abou-, HOLY SHIT!" he yelled.

His outburst caused Martin to veer across the middle lane and into the far left before regaining control.

"WHAT?" he said, his heart thumping against the wall of his chest.

"That was a big fuckin' tire!" Dan said.

"What? That's why you screamed? Because you saw the giant Uniroyal tire?"

"That thing was real?"

"Yes, you dipshit. Don't scream again. I almost killed us. In fact, don't talk at all. Just point to where I should go."

Dan mimed a zipping of his lips. He then bumped the joint repeatedly into his symbolically closed mouth before bursting into laughter.

"I said shut up!" Martin said.

For the remaining fifteen minutes on I-94, Dan did not say a word. He smoked his joint, and relaxed, enjoying the snowflake ballet on the other side of the windshield.

A green sign emerged in the distance. It was the exit for Chene St. Dan pointed at it as he'd been instructed.

"I see it," Martin said, directing the truck to the off-ramp.

"Turn right just before that gas station."

Martin approached the intersection with far too much velocity considering the road conditions. The pickup began to lose traction on the slick pavement.

"Slow down, man! Black ice!" Dan shouted. He reached for the support grip on the ceiling.

Martin attempted to steer into the slide, but he was too late. The rear end swung around and they entered the intersection backwards. Dan screamed, though the joint stayed tucked safely in the corner of his mouth. A pizza place flew by on the right, then the freeway off ramp. The truck showed no sign of coming out of the spin. The gas station rapidly approached, but then it also passed by the right. The second time Martin saw the pizza place, he had to shut his eyes. The centripetal force glued his body against the door.

They continued to spin until the curb put an end to it. Martin's head slammed against the window and then they were leaning. He opened his eyes and saw the sign for the gas station through the windshield. It was slowly tilting. Dan fell across the seat almost into Martin's lap, screaming. The sign reached a forty-five degree crescendo. The axle of the truck whined beneath them. The truck teetered, and then began its rapid descent to the Earth. The airborne tires slammed into the icy pavement, rocking the shocks, and the truck's inhabitants.

They were still.

The truck had settled in front of the gas station on the east side of Chene. They were facing south, into what would have been oncoming traffic had there actually been anyone else on the deserted road.

Dan sat up and readjusted his seatbelt. He had the look of a man who'd just escaped death. He tried to say something, but only the breath he'd been holding in came out. He tried again.

"That…," he said, pausing to take a hit from the joint. "…was fucking awesome!"

Martin was stunned. There were many words in the English language that he'd of used to describe that experience. Harrowing, maybe. Terrifying, possibly. Awesome, no.

"That was like that old ride at Boblo Island. The Rotor."

Martin could do nothing but stare at his dimwitted riding mate.

"Did you ever ride that one? You know it spun around and then the floor dropped out, and you're like hangin' there and shit."

"What is wrong with you?"

"What?" Dan said.

"Who gives a shit about some ride? We almost died."

"No, we didn't. We're fine. I could do that shit again."

Martin shook his head. "We should get back on the freeway and head back to Ann Arbor."

Dan's jubilant expression changed to one of dread. "Oh, no, no. We can't do that. T-Mar'll kill me."

"I thought you said he didn't have one of those teardrops."

"Don't mean he ain't dangerous."

With a look of complete seriousness, he continued. "Anyways, he could always call Flip. That dude…I swear if we'd died just now, he'd a found our corpses and killed us again."

CHAPTER XI
FEBRUARY 7, 2006

"You want anything else?" said the Chaldean man behind the bullet-proof glass. Franklin King did not answer as his attention was on a dusty, old clock hanging above the top shelf liquor. His eyes clicked along with the second hand as it crept closer and closer to its brethren patiently waiting at the twelve. They eventually met, signaling the passing of another day without fanfare.

"Hey, you! Is that all?"

"Sorry, yeah. Just the coffee," Franklin said, reaching for his wallet.

"You fine. No charge."

"No charge? Why?"

"You police, right?"

"Yeah."

"I give you coffee, you drive by every now and then. Check on the place."

Franklin King had been a cop for thirty-nine years. Over that time he'd been offered many things in exchange for special treatment: coffee, donuts, baseball tickets and once, a trip to the V.I.P. room at a gentleman's club in Greektown, which he of course declined. He'd have felt Martha's wrath if he'd have come home with even the hint of another woman's perfume on his clothes.

"Sure, I'll keep an eye out."

He grabbed the coffee from the counter and made his way to the door. Lifting the steaming cup to his mouth, he saw a small pickup speeding down Harper. It hit a patch of black ice and entered a tailspin. It did two complete 360°s before slamming into the curb and nearly toppling over.

"You see! Crazy drunks and hopped up fools almost crashing into my station all the time. That's what you look out for. Arrest them!" the man behind the counter said.

Franklin took a sip of his coffee. It was too hot, taking the top layer of his tongue down his throat with it. He kept his eyes on the two kids in the cab of the truck. They were talking. Nobody looked hurt.

"Why you stand there? Arrest them!"

"You worry about your business, and I'll worry about mine."

"No free coffee for you then."

Franklin pushed the door open and was met with a wall of frigid air. The wind nipped at his crow's feet and chafed at his bald head. He shuffled his feet across the salted ground wishing he still had that afro of his youth.

He closed the door on the unmarked cruiser and relaxed. Ever since Martha's passing, that seat felt more like home than his house in Woodbridge did.

He took another sip. The coffee burned less going down the second time. He punched the Dakota's license plate number into the police computer. It was registered to a Daniel Schoenfeld of Hazel Park. Not reported stolen.

A quick check revealed Mr. Schoenfeld had a prior for Minor in Possession back in '03 and an arrest for possession of narcotics in '05. He served six months of probation, but no jail time. A suburbanite, especially one with priors, cruising the East side at 11:30pm on a Monday night in a snowstorm set Franklin's police sense all atwitter. Throw in the spinout and he made up his mind to follow that truck for a little while.

Martin gingerly hit the gas, moving the Dakota southbound down Chene. He never seriously threatened the speed limit, partially due to his trepidation at another spinout, but also because he was mesmerized by the devastation around him.

"Oh my God," he said.

"What?"

"It looks like Hiroshima around here."

Dan laughed. "Yeah. This city is a shithole. Only reason I ever come down here is drugs. Oh, and coneys. They got good coneys."

"I mean, seriously look at that place. And that one!"

They passed by one dilapidated monstrosity after another. At Hendrie St. they saw what looked like an old saloon. The door was boarded up and the upstairs windows were gone. On the left was another similar two story building. The only difference was that this one was missing the southwest wall. It its place lied a pile of rubble. And just before the East Palmer intersection was what appeared to have once been a thriving strip of businesses. An old marquee hung over a vacant lounge. Next to it was a store with the name 'Zanefski' on the façade, their wares long since gone. All that remained was plywood and wreckage and a spray painted warning to 'keep out.'

Having been sheltered first in suburbia and then economically isolated Ann Arbor, Martin had never seen anything like it.

"It's like a ghost town. Sad, really," he said.

"Sad? Why? Who gives a shit? We don't live down here."

There was not a soul in sight, only snow covered lots and the remnants of a once vibrant neighborhood.

"Why don't they knock these buildings down?" Martin asked.

"You need money for that."

At Farnsworth was another pile of rubble. Martin began to think that the snow was actually a blessing as it at least partially covered some of the blight.

"Look, that one got knocked down, but they must have run out of money to remove the debris," Dan said.

"How is that safe? Don't people complain that there's a big pile of wood and nails there that kids could get hurt in? It's dangerous."

"There are worse things for kids in this city than wood and nails," Dan said, trying to relight his joint.

"Where are we going anyway? It doesn't look like anyone lives around here," Martin asked.

"Turn left here."

Martin turned down Farnsworth. It was more of the same: snow, potholes and empty husks of street lights. Dan gestured ahead and Martin pulled into an alley next to a small garage with peeling white paint. Long, finger like extensions of the overgrowth scraped against the side of the truck.

"He told me to text and he'd come out."

"Which house is his?" Martin asked.

"Hell if I know. He always makes me meet him in the alley."

Dan sent the text and then put the phone in his pocket.

"Now we wait," he said.

"How long?"

"As long as he wants. Sometimes it's like five minutes. I've waited three hours once. I was too scared to leave."

"Hopefully he's punctual tonight," Martin said.

"Yeah. It's balls cold out here."

Franklin King idled down the near-abandoned thoroughfare, sipping his coffee. He found it adorable that the suburban kids kept stopping at the stop signs. Even if he hadn't pulled up their info on the computer, that alone would have suggested their origins were north of Eight Mile.

He paid no mind to the blight around him. He'd driven every square inch of the city and it no longer surprised him; in fact it failed to register at all. Like most Detroiters, he'd become desensitized. Since they'd all been sold the bill of goods of urban renewal, only to see nothing ever change, he figured it best to not waste another bit of mental energy on it.

That isn't to say he didn't still cling to some hope for change. The feeling would usually rekindle in the winter when the snow would fall and bury at least the low lying ruins. He'd cross his fingers that the snow would act like some kind of magical solvent, seeping into the city's core and melting away in the spring leaving the Detroit he remembered from his youth, free of dilapidated buildings, vacant lots and dormant streetlamps.

When the thaw did come, though, nothing ever transformed. In fact, everything usually looked worse for having endured another brutal Michigan winter.

It was what it was.

His job wasn't to raze vacant properties or to find businesses to occupy them. He didn't mow lawns, clean debris, or replace bulbs, either. His job was to fight crime, in hopes that the few who did those things would have a shot at success.

The Dakota turned left at Farnsworth and he followed. When they turned into the alley before McDougall, he drove past and turned right at the intersection and then another right at Theodore. With the headlights off, he eased the cruiser into the opposite end of the alley that they had parked and killed the engine.

It was completely dark. He could barely make out the silhouette of the truck a block away.

"This is King. I'm in the alley west of McDougall between Theodore and Farnsworth. Following a pickup, make Dodge, license CQB 241. Over," he said over the police radio.

A voice crackled through the speaker. "Do you need back up? Over."

"No, but inform any nearby cruisers of my location. Over."

"Affirmative, King. Over."

He tucked the walkie in his coat pocket, making sure to turn off the volume. After finishing his coffee, he got out, gently closing the door behind him. His hand instinctively went to his hip, just to be certain that his gun was there. He unclipped the holster and started walking, taking extreme caution with each step to subdue the crunch of the fresh snow beneath his boots. After about fifteen paces, he was able to make out some detail. He tucked behind a utility pole and waited.

"Where is this guy? It's been twenty minutes," Martin asked.

"I thought I saw him comin' up the alley awhile back, but my eyes musta been playin' tricks on me. Probably the weed. Anyways, I told you, this nigger operates on his own schedule. He'll get here when he gets here."

"Why do you keep saying that?"

"Saying what?"

"The 'n' word."

Dan scoffed. "Uhh…'cuz he's a nigger."

"That's racist."

"No it's not. If I said 'I hate niggers' that would be racist, but I didn't say that. I love them. In fact, I used to have a lot of nigger friends but my dad sold them." He started laughing.

"You're an idiot," Martin said, unamused.

Dan took another hit from his joint and blew the smoke in Martin's direction. "Fuck you! Who are you anyways? Jesse Jackass? Louis Farracoon?"

"My God, don't you shut up?" Martin closed his eyes and hoped that when he opened them he'd be back in his dorm room instead of a poorly lit alley on Detroit's east side in a pick-up truck with an ignorant acquaintance trying to purchase drugs he no longer wanted from a potentially homicidal dealer.

"Text him again," he said.

"No way."

"I'm leaving then," Martin said, opening the door.

"How? You gonna walk?"

Martin hadn't thought that far ahead. "I'll get a cab."

"Here? Good luck!"

"I'll figure it out."

Dan grabbed his arm.

"You can't throw me under the bus with this guy. He's expecting to move drugs tonight and I got no money."

"Sorry," Martin said, peeling Dan's fingers from his sleeve. He got out of the car and started walking towards Farnsworth.

Dan put his joint out in the ashtray and jumped out of the truck.

"Get back here!" he shouted. "He'll call Flip, man! And he'll kill me, I swear! He's fuckin' crazy!"

"Who crazy?" a voice said from the alley.

Martin and Dan froze.

"Who mu'fuckin' crazy? Huh?" the voice said, again. Martin turned to see a man slowly emerge from the darkness.

T-Mar was in his early-twenties and thin. He stood about five feet nine inches and looked like a drug dealer cliché; jeans that hung low on the backside exposing designer boxers beneath, an oversized plain white t-shirt, and fresh white sneakers. He had a heavy leather jacket on as well, embroidered with the logos of all the NBA teams.

He grabbed Dan by the shoulders and shoved him down near the Dakota's passenger front tire. Looming over him, he lifted his shirt up to expose the black matte finish on the grip of a 9mm Glock above his waistband.

"You see this shit? You think I won't blast you? Talkin' shit about my family!"

He let fly a fearsome kick into Dan's ribs.

"AHHH!" he squealed, curling into a ball.

Martin glanced down Farnsworth, towards Chene and a potential escape, but his conscience got the best of him.

"Hey!" he shouted.

T-Mar delivered another crushing kick before taking a moment to soak in the frail, bearded white boy standing in the street.

"Who the hell is you?"

Afraid of saying the wrong thing, but having no idea what the right thing might possibly be, Martin chose honesty.

"Martin."

"He's the guy that wants to-," he said.

"Weren't talkin at you!" T-Mar said, bringing the heel of his glistening white shoe down on Dan's kneecap. He howled in pain.

"I…I'm the guy that Dan told you about. I wanted to get some, you know, stuff from you."

"You got paper?"

"Excuse me?"

"Money, dipshit!"

"Oh, yeah. I got money."

"Well, why didn't you say so? Let's do some bidness," T-Mar said, his demeanor instantly sunnier.

Martin cautiously approached, stopping at the truck's tailgate. That was as close as he wanted to get.

"C'mon, now. Don't be scared. I ain't gon' bite," T-Mar said.

"I…I think I'll just stand here if that's ok with you."

"Suit yo'self."

T-Mar took out his cell phone and took a photo of Martin.

"What…why did you do that?" Martin asked.

T-Mar said nothing, returning the phone to his pocket.

"He took my picture my first ti-," Dan said until the throb in his knee reminded him it was in his best interest to shut up.

"So whatchu want?" T-Mar said to Martin.

"Yeah…about that. See, the thing is, I was drinking and Dan offered me some weed, and, at the time, I thought I wanted to try something harder, but…"

"But what?" T-Mar sniped back, his newfound pleasantness vanishing as quickly as it had come.

"I…I think I'm good."

"You good?"

"Yeah. I mean, don't get me wrong. I appreciate your time and everything, as a businessman, and I'll compensate you accordingly."

"You gon' compensate me?"

"Yeah, of course."

T-Mar chuckled. He shook his head and then took in a long deep breath. Martin smiled, foolishly thinking that he'd appealed to the dealer's more rational sensibilities.

T-Mar charged at him.

Martin slipped trying to run, allowing T-Mar to quickly close the gap. He clenched his hand on Martin's shoulder and yanked him down to the cold, hard pavement.

"You two motherfuckers," T-Mar said as he dragged Martin over to where Dan lay, useless. "You get my ass out here in the cold…"

He started pacing back and forth, visibly agitated, with his fingers tracing the butt of his pistol.

"Fuck I'mma do witchu?" he asked, rhetorically.

Martin had never been more frightened in his life.

Franklin King wished he hadn't downed that coffee. He had stood next to the utility pole out of sight for what seemed like an eternity for nothing. Having had enough, he pulled out his walkie.

"This is King. Still in the alley. No action. About to abort. Over," he whispered.

Within seconds, a voice came quietly over the speaker. "Should we send a patrol through? Over"

"No. It was a false al-,"

At that moment the driver's door opened and, after a brief struggle, he exited the truck. Immediately, the passenger followed, and the two men argued briefly before a man seemingly emerged from thin air behind them. Franklin could not hear what anyone was saying, but from the looks of it, the truck's passengers were not happy to see the third man.

When the first kick fell, Franklin got on the radio. "This is King. Anybody nearby? Over."

Another blow was delivered to the man on the ground. The voice crackled in Franklin's ear, "We have a cruiser southbound McDougall and Palmer. Over."

"Tell them to hang on McDougall, north of Farnsworth. I may need backup. Over."

At that moment, the driver made a break for it, falling in the process. The third man dragged him around the truck by his collar. Franklin didn't like the way things were unfolding, but he had to wait. An arrest for battery was small potatoes. He felt if he was patient, he'd have something else. Something substantial. He just hoped he didn't wait too long.

"I know what I'mma do," T-Mar said to himself.

"Wha-," Dan started, but stopped when Martin smacked him in the arm.

T-Mar leaned down into Martin's face. They were so close that it was hard to tell whose breath was whose. "You wanted sump'm, right?"

"Excuse me?" Martin said.

"Dope, crack, whatever. You wanted the shit, I got it."

"Yeah, that's why we came, I guess."

"And you got the green?"

Martin glanced over at Dan, who nodded.

"Yes, and, like I said, I'll pay you for your time. How much do you think is fa-,"

T-Mar reached under Martin's backside, probing for his wallet.

"What're you do-,"

"Where is it?" T-Mar said, becoming agitated with each empty pocket.

"Hey, come on. I think we can be civil about this," Martin said, sliding his jacket zipper up to its apex.

T-Mar smiled.

"It's all I have," Martin pleaded.

T-Mar grabbed the zipper and slowly slid it down. He reached inside and pulled out what he was looking for.

"Holy shit! I'm getting' paid!" he shouted, counting the bills.

"There's over two 'g's here! What the hell was you thinkin'?"

Then, in his best white person impression, he said, "Uhh…Mr. drug dealer? My name's Whitey. I need a hit of something good. How's two 'g's sound? Is that enough? Oh, splendid."

He cackled and stood up to leave.

Martin looked over at Dan, shocked. Dan shook his head vehemently, impressing on Martin to let it go, but he couldn't. That money was his. It had come to him from his mother's foresight and concern that her son wouldn't have to work while in school. He had spent some of it, a lot, foolishly over the previous six months, but he was not about to lose the rest of what she had toiled so hard for to some pusher.

"That's a fucked up way to do business!" Martin said, standing up.

T-Mar turned around, surprised.

"What's that?"

"You heard me."

T-Mar nodded slowly. He took a few steps back towards the two of them. "No, you right. You right."

"I know I am," Martin said, surprised nonetheless.

"No, you guys came down to get some shit, and I jack your cash. That ain't cool."

Martin and Dan watched as T-Mar got closer and closer.

"And I ain't even give you nothin' back. I just up 'n jacked it, he said, steps away. Martin raised his chin to meet T-Mar's manic gaze.

"Well, let me give you sump'm then."

He raised his shirt.

Franklin King got his wish. He waited patiently and now could add larceny to the third man's charges.

"Sgt. King to backup, on my call, make a move to the alley."

The third man, having appeared to be leaving the scene, turned around.

"This is car 67. Stationed at Farnsworth and McDougall. Say the word. Over."

The third man made a move to his waistline.

"Now, now, now!" King barked into the radio.

T-Mar's hand reached past the Glock and into his jean pocket. He pulled out a plastic baggie filled with little blue pills.

"Ain't no bidnessman 'fy don't deliver," he said with a wry smile.

Suddenly, he leapt forth, body checking Martin into the truck. Martin's head slammed back against the passenger window, spiderwebbing it. Dazed, he fell back to the ground.

T-Mar, seizing the opportunity, pounced, his weight on Martin's chest and his knees pinning Martin's arms to the snowy alley floor.

Martin, weakened from months of self-abuse, could offer no resistance and Dan was equally useless, fear and cowardice filling his boots with cement.

"Open wide," T-Mar said, grabbing Martin by the mouth. Martin struggled against his fingers as they penetrated his lips and pried apart his jaws.

Then came the pills.

A seemingly endless avalanche of them, ecstasy to be more specific, quickly filled his oral cavity. His tongue writhed back and forth, trying woefully to expel them, but they were incessant.

"Chew, motherfucker," T-Mar said, working Martin's lower jaw up and down. Martin did all he could to avoid swallowing, but the forced chewing was grinding the pills up. He could taste the venom slipping down his throat.

A siren blared and flashing lights enveloped the street. A police cruiser came roaring down Farnsworth and slid behind the Dakota, blocking the north exit of the alley. A uniformed officer popped out, gun drawn.

"Freeze!"

T-Mar sprang up, eyes darting in every direction. To his left and right were eight foot high chain link fences that he knew he'd never ascend before the cop could fire. With the north exit blocked, he had only one choice. He spun around and ran south down the alley, pulling the Glock from his pants. After about thirty feet, he snuck a peak over his shoulder. The cop chose not to follow, instead tending to the two by the truck.

Just then, a figure came from out of nowhere and struck T-Mar across the chest. He tumbled to the ground, the gun flying from his grip and landing harmlessly several yards away. He laid face first in the snow stunned, wheezing for air when he felt his arms being wrenched behind his back.

"Where you think you goin'?" Franklin King asked, cuffing him.

"Wha-," T-Mar mumbled.

"On your feet."

Sgt. King dragged his prisoner up off the ground and examined him.

"I know you. T-Mar, right? I think we got you a few years back on a possession."

"I didn't do nothin'," he croaked.

124

"Of course you didn't," King said.

He nudged his reluctant prisoner along to the scene of his crime where the backseat of a cruiser awaited. After a bit of a struggle, T-Mar was secured, though his repeated cries of innocence were easily heard through the glass.

King then turned his attention to Martin. He was on all fours, his face inches above a mound of partially digested pills. He spat repeatedly, lest one contaminated drop remain. Tears streamed down his face and froze to his cheeks. He cupped snow from the ground and put it in his mouth, swishing it around and spitting it out as well.

"You. Get off the ground and come sit up here," King said, lowering the Dakota's tailgate.

Martin managed to get to his feet and do as he was told.

"You Schoenfeld?"

Martin shook his head. His whole body was trembling.

"You speak when spoken too, boy. Understand?"

"Y-yes, s-sir."

"What's your name then?"

"Martin."

"Well, Martin, what the hell are you boys doing out here at this hour."

"Don't say a word," Dan shouted, finally deciding to join the festivities.

"You shut your mouth! I ain't talkin' to you," King said, pointing an authoritative finger at Dan.

"Let's try again. Martin, why are you here?"

Martin's head was throbbing, his jaw ached, and there was an unpleasant, medicine-like taste in his mouth. He couldn't foresee a scenario where lying to a cop would better his situation.

"We came to buy drugs."

"What's with you suburban kids comin' here for drugs? Ain't you got drugs north of Eight Mile?"

"Actually, we drove in from Ann Arbor. I go to school there."

"You in school in Ann Arbor? You a smart kid, then. Why go an' do somethin' foolish like this?"

Martin shook his head.

"Your parents know where you are?"

"My mother died nine months ago, and my dad…" Martin said, with a shrug.

Franklin leaned back and looked up into the falling snow. He called the uniformed officer over to him. "The perp dropped his piece in a bank when I tackled him. It's up the alley on the right. Grab it and tag it."

The officer left and King turned back to Martin.

"You got I.D.?"

Martin handed him his driver's license. King looked it over and was about to hand it back, but froze.

"Kerner? Martin Kerner?"

"Yes, sir."

"What's your dad's name?"

"Why?"

"What is his goddamn name?"

"Jack."

Franklin hadn't heard that name for years, but he hadn't forgotten it. It's hard to forget the name of your best friend, no matter how much time has passed.

"You think you need a doctor?" he asked, giving the license back.

"No. I'll be ok."

"If I ever see you in Detroit again, you won't be. Follow?"

He pointed at Dan and said, "That goes for you, too."

Behind him T-Mar was still writhing and yelling in the back of the cruiser. The officer, who had returned with the gun, smacked the window with the nightstick to shut him up.

"Schoenfeld, you drive. Get your asses in that truck, and back down 94," King said.

Dan went around to the driver's side and Martin took shotgun. Dan started the truck, but before slipping it in gear he said, "Hey, man. What about your money?"

Martin turned his head. Through the splintered glass his eyes met T-Mar's, and in them he saw nothing but unbridled rage.

"Forget it," he said.

"What? That was like two grand! Just go ask that c-,"

"I said forget it. It's over. I just want to leave this city and never come back."

It was far from over.

King watched the truck squeeze past his cruiser at the far end of the alley, and then out of sight down Theodore.

"Why'd you let them go?" the uniformed officer asked him.

"We got T-Mar on the 'E', and if not that, I'm bettin' that gun ain't registered. Even without their testimony, he'll be goin' away for a while."

"I meant…weren't they tryin' to buy? Shouldn't we have bust-,"

"Take your prisoner down to the precinct and get him processed, officer."

The officer lingered for a moment, but ultimately got in his cruiser and pulled away. King slowly made his way back down the alley, pulling his coat tight across his body. He opened his car door and collapsed into his chair. The blinking cursor on his computer monitor was practically begging him to type it in, so he did. In the search bar he entered a name.

Jack Kerner.

Within moments an address and home phone number popped up. He pulled his phone from his coat pocket and typed in the number. After a short delay, he pressed send.

It rang several times without an answer. Franklin was about to disconnect when he heard a tired, gruff voice on the line.

"Hello."

"Uh…Is this Jack Kerner?"

"Who is it at this hour?"

"Sgt. King. Detroit Police. Is this Jack Kerner?"

"Yeah. What do you want?"

"Sgt. Franklin King."

Nothing but breath came over the line.

"Jack?"

"Yeah?"

"Did you hear me?"

"What do you want, Frank? It's late."

"It's been a long time, Jack."

"It has. What can I do for you?"

Franklin didn't know what he'd expected when he made the call, but he couldn't help but feel let down by Jack's apparent disinterest.

"I'm on a drug bust. Chene and Farnsworth. Nothing big. Perp's a small time banger. Name's T-Mar. One of these little street gangs. No leadership. No organization. Ain't nothing like the Flynns from years back, or even the Young Boys or Chambers, but of course that was more after you'd already left the force…"

He was rambling and he knew it, but he couldn't do anything to stop himself.

"Just a buncha punks, runnin' around. But they mean. Goddamn, they are mean. No respect for life."

"Mmhmm."

"Reason I call you is…the buyer. He's your son."

No response. Only more breathing, though heavier.

"You hear me, Jack?"

"Yes."

"I let him go. He seems like a good kid, just confused. He's shook up somethin' fierce. He mentioned his mom passing."

"Is there anything else, Frank?"

"No, Jack. I guess not." He paused. "How are y-,"

There was a click and Jack was gone. Franklin sighed and dropped the phone on the seat beside him. He thought about how they say time heals all wounds.

Bullshit.

Thirty-four years hadn't done a damn thing for Jack Kerner.

CHAPTER XII
JULY 7, 2008

'Lunch plans?' was all it said, but it had Martin positively titillated. The handwriting, while clean and mildly effervescent, was nothing spectacular nor was the message itself novel in any way. But it was Danielle who had written it in the top corner of his paper and that alone was noteworthy. To Martin, the words implied she was ready, after two months of flirtation and countless hours studying together in the library, to take things to the next level.

Feeling mildly embarrassed it was she that made the next move, he leaned over and scrawled 'Second date?' on her notebook in response. She chuckled a little too loudly and covered her mouth a little too late.

"Something funny?" Abdul-Tawaab barked, stopping mid-sentence. He glared at her with an expression relaying his complete lack of amusement.

"No, sir," Danielle said.

"And what about you, Mr. Kerner? Do you find the Algiers Motel events humorous?"

"No, sir."

"Tell me, Martin. What happened at the Algiers Motel? You must be an expert on the topic since you don't need to pay attention."

Martin looked around at a room filled with sympathetic eyes.

He cleared his throat. "Well, sir, the Algiers was a seedy motel off Woodward where three blacks were murdered during the riot."

"When?"

"The early morning of July 26, 1967, sir."

Abdul-Tawaab looked down his nose at Martin.

"Yes. That is correct," he said, with an air of disappointment about him. He turned and sat at the edge of his desk.

"Two were shot by either the police or guardsmen, while there are questions about the third."

"What happened?" Darius asked.

"The Algiers was a haven for pimps, prostitutes, and the like. The lowest common denominator. That night, the police got a report of sniper fire coming from the hotel's annex, which was an old manor house converted into separate dwellings. Whether a shot was ever fired from the building was never determined, but the cops, white cops, showed up to find out and they were not in the best states of mind."

"Why?" waifish redhead asked.

"They were tired from working fourteen, sixteen sometimes twenty hour shifts and they were angry over losing one of their own just hours before. Oh, and many of them were unapologetically racist."

"What did they do?" Himal Patel questioned from the back row.

"They raided the annex looking for the sniper. They found nine people, according to reports; seven black males and two white women. White whores, more specifically. During this initial assault is presumably when the first man was killed, although other accounts refute this. Another man was shot and killed by law enforcement who claimed he went for their weapons. But the most disturbing thing about the Algiers is what took place after the first two slayings."

The class was silent and perched at the edges of their chairs, fully engaged. As an orator, Abdul-Tawaab had few peers.

"The police and guardsmen brought everybody out of their rooms and lined them up, facing the wall of the lobby. They were interrogated about where any weapons were and who shot out the window, the questions accompanied by blows to the backs of their heads with rifle butts. One man claimed that a cop put the barrel up into his crotch and threatened to, and I quote, 'blow his testicles off'."

"Goddamn!" Darius said, as he and the rest of the males in the class squirmed in their chairs.

"And the women…they hated them even more. They could not fathom why white women, or 'nigger lovers' as they called them, would ever choose to be with black men."

"That's horrible," Danielle said.

"Oh, it gets worse. Then the cops threw a knife on the ground, baiting the suspects to pick it up in hopes somebody would. It'd give them a reason to shoot. When no one bit, they started taking them back, one by one, into the rooms for questioning. The first man taken back came forth from the room minutes later looking like he'd gone ten rounds with Ali."

The class whispered amongst themselves and shook their heads in disbelief.

Abdul-Tawaab continued, becoming more animated as he went on. "After taking another prisoner on a search for weapons that were never found, the cops started to play a death game."

"What's a death game, sir?" Darius asked.

"One cop would take a prisoner back, beat him a little, ask him about the guns, and then fire a few shots off into the ceiling or wall. He'd then leave the room and tell the prisoner to be completely quiet."

"What's the point of that?" Danielle asked.

"The point, Ms. Denson, was they wanted to scare the other prisoners into thinking they were killing people in those rooms. So, the cop came out, and when asked by another cop if he'd killed the guy, he'd confirm it, though the prisoner was really alive."

"That's sick," Danielle said.

"What's sick is that the last cop to play didn't realize it was a game at all. He was told to take his prisoner into a different room than the one that was previously used. That room had two supposedly dead prisoners in it, lying down on the floor quietly. Had he gone in there, he'd have realized it was a game. Now, it depends on whose story you believe, he may or may not have been provoked, but a third black man died in that room, a shotgun blast to the chest."

He paused.

"A little bit of the soul of this great city died that night."

The class collectively dropped their heads for a man and a city they never knew. Abdul-Tawaab looked at his watch, and got up from the desk.

"That's all then. Read up on it in your book, and I suggest you do, because it will be on Wednesday's test."

This spurred the group to rise. Martin gathered his things and then gave Danielle a playful nudge.

"Hey, watch it, bud," she said, in mock annoyance.

"So, are we on?"

She smiled and nodded. Martin couldn't help but smile, as well. He could feel the muscles pulling his lips apart and exposing his teeth. It was strange. Good but, strange. He hadn't smiled much since his mother had died.

"Where too?" she said, slinging her purse over her shoulder.

"Hell if I know. The only restaurant I've eaten at around here is that Middle Eastern place."

"No, no, no. That won't work. I'm not feelin' the garlic right now. I need somethin' a little less, you know, garlicy."

"How about the Garlic Hut, around the corner?" Martin said.

"There's no such place, you smart ass."

They walked down the steps to the front of the room where Abdul-Tawaab was organizing his papers. They were unaware he was watching them.

"But seriously, what should we eat?"

"I told you. I don't know. I've never been anywhere around here."

"You know, if I had a nickel for every time you said 'I've never' about something in Detroit, the city you've lived five minutes away from for most of your life, I'd have-,"

"About a dollar twenty."

"You keepin' track?"

"I guess. Maybe one day you can take me around and show me all of the things I've been missing in this glorious metropolis."

"Maybe I will. Let's start with the Corridor Café. The food's good and they have all this local art to look at. You'll like it."

"Lead the way."

Just as he was to enter the hall, he was entrapped by Abdul-Tawaab's stare. Like a tractor beam, it had him, slowing his pace through the door. And the professor did not relent, instead dropping his chin ever slightly to further amplify the gaze's ferocity and purposefulness. It was shiver-inducing. Martin was relieved when he passed through the doorway and was released from its grasp.

"That was weird," he said, jogging forward to catch up with Danielle. "What?"

"Abdul-Tawaab was really eyeballing me back there."

"When?"

"Just now. He looked like he wanted to kick my ass or something."

"Why would he want to do that?"

"I don't know."

They passed through the main doors onto Cass Ave. It was cool and the sky was low with dark clouds.

"You know," Danielle said. "He did look upset when you knew about the Algiers Motel. Like he really wanted to make an example of you."

"Great."

"I wouldn't worry. You're getting 'A's on everything so far. I'm sure you'll be fine."

"I guess. So where's this café?" he asked.

"Up there a bit, but we better hurry. Looks like rain."

They walked briskly in silence for the first block. Martin felt anxiety creeping up in him. Each time there was even the slightest break in conversation it would. The insecure part of him thought that she'd deem him uninteresting and she'd bolt away, down Forest Ave. and out of his life. Then again, the anxiety may have derived from the possibility that she wouldn't.

"So you have a brother?" he blurted out.

She looked at him, somewhat surprised. "Yeah, what brought that up?"

"Well…um, I figured if this is to be our second date, we should pick up where the first one left off."

She smiled. "Ahh, ok. Yes. One brother. Seventeen."

"Cool."

"You?"

"Only child."

"Cool."

The conversation stalled again. Martin painstakingly searched for words but nothing came. All he could think about was his own social ineptitude and how it seemed to be only a recent phenomenon spontaneously arising while in the presence of Danielle. He'd actually had a modest amount of success with girls in Ann Arbor, though mostly during the dark period when he was perpetually drunk. In retrospect, it occurred to him that most of his conquests had also been inebriated. Loosened inhibitions and proximity probably had more to do with their willingness than his charm or looks.

His palms began to sweat.

"Hey," Danielle said, waving her hand in front of his face.

"What?"

"Where are you?"

"What do you mean?"

"I'm standing in front of the café. I have no idea where you went."

"I'm sorry. I was thinking and-,"

"Stop."

"Stop what?"

"Trying so hard."

Martin looked at her, confused. "I wasn't."

"You were."

She turned to face him and grabbed each of hands. She showed no revulsion over their dampness.

"And you don't have to."

And just like that, it all drifted away. He got lost in her sparkling brown eyes. He floated on a cloud of her delicate vanilla aroma. She closed her eyes and leaned forward, offering her lips to him. They were plump and glistening. Martin could almost taste the strawberry lip gloss. He leaned in.

"Dani!"

Martin turned to see a black 2002 Pontiac Grand Prix idling in the southbound lane. The trunk, fastened to the bumper by bungee cords, rattled from the bass exploding from the sound system. A thin, black male with an ill-defined goatee and dark, wide-set eyes was behind the wheel. He wore a navy blue baseball cap, tilted off-kilter to the left.

"Tyreke?" she said.

Tyreke turned down the radio. "What you doin'?" he said. His eyes were on Martin.

Danielle let go of Martin's hands and wiped hers on the front of her shorts.

"Uhh…nothin'. I was just going to get lunch."

Tyreke's eyes poked holes in Martin. "Who dis?"

"Oh, this is Martin."

"You was goin' to lunch with him?"

"Yeah," she said.

Martin, having had enough of being stared down for one afternoon, stepped away from Danielle and pretended to be interested in a flyer posted on the outside of the café advertising an upcoming poetry reading.

"Not today. I need you for somethin'," Tyreke said.

"What?"

"Somethin'. Just get in the car. Don't wanna play no twenty questions."

Danielle turned back to Martin, who was still facing the posters.

"Hey, I'm sorry. My brother needs me for something," she said, putting a soft hand on his shoulder.

"That's your brother?"

"Yeah. Funny we just talked about him."

"Funny," Martin said. He waved at Tyreke, who did not reciprocate.

"So…we'll have to postpone our date. Are you super mad?" Danielle asked.

He didn't think he could ever be mad at her. "Mad? No, it's cool. I understand."

"For reals?"

"Go on. I'll see you Wednesday."

She hugged him, which normally he would have been ecstatic for, but over her silky, black hair he could see Tyreke watching them.

Martin broke the embrace.

Before getting in her brother's car, she shouted, "You should still eat there. Get the lentil burger. You'll love it!"

Martin watched them speed down Cass and, for a moment, considered doing just as she said, even going so far as to open the door a crack, before realizing he no longer was hungry.

The sky rumbled.

A horizontal bolt of lightning shot across the darkened sky. Martin felt first one, than many drops of rain against his face. He lifted his laptop case above his head, and ran north towards the parking garage where his mother's Chrysler was. When he reached Hancock, he could see the students outside of Higgins Hall scatter from the rain like cockroaches from light. They were foolish, running this way and that. They were going to get wet and that was just the way it was and the way it always had been. Their insignificant desires were no match for the natural order of things. Another lightning bolt ripped across the city's sky. He dropped the laptop to his side and walked on, indifferent to it all.

The Grand Prix sped down Cass, darting across the lines to avoid potholes. The stereo was booming. The song was from native Detroiter

Obie Trice. Tyreke rapped along with Obie, threatening violence and boasting about his manliness.

"Tyreke!" Danielle yelled over the music. Her insides rattled with the beat.

"…gun in my hand…" he continued, unwavering.

Danielle reached over and shut off the radio. Tyreke looked at her with disdain.

"What the fuck? Why you shut my shit off?"

"Don't speak to me like that," she said, firmly.

"Sorry. What's up witchu? I was jammin'."

"I was talking to you, but you couldn't hear me."

"A'ight. Whatchu want?"

"You wanted *me*, remember?"

He chuckled and leaned back in his seat, which was reclined all the way. His right arm was fully extended to reach the wheel.

"What's so funny?" she asked. "And what's with this gangsta lean? You look like a fool."

"Whatever," he said. He sat up a little.

"Tell me. What did you want?"

"Nothin'. I was just cruisin' and I saw you with that…" He cleared his throat. "That guy."

"So?"

He raised his eyebrow at her. "Don't play."

"How am I playin'?"

"Dani."

"What? 'Cuz he's white?"

"Hells yeah, 'cuz he's white. Whatchu thinkin'?"

"He's smart and cute and he likes me is what I'm thinkin'."

The rain started to beat against the window. He leaned forward and flipped first the wiper motor on, then the radio. Obie Trice came roaring through the speakers. Danielle immediately reached over and shut the radio off again.

"Hey!" he shouted.

"You turn this car around and take me back there."

"What? You serious?"

"Yes. Now."

"I can't. It's raining."

"Boy, don't play with me! Since mom died, I am the boss, and you will do as I say."

"I ain't got to listen to shit," he muttered under his breath.

"What was that?"

He didn't repeat it. He scowled but did not heed her.

"Now, Tyreke," Danielle said, glaring at him.

He pouted like a petulant child and pulled into the driveway of an empty lot near Martin Luther King Blvd, slammed into reverse, and squealed the tires backing out onto Cass. He floored the accelerator, and sped north back towards the café.

"What's your problem?" Danielle asked.

"What?"

"You don't have to drive like a maniac."

He turned from her slightly before slowing the vehicle down to the speed limit.

"Thank you," she said.

He didn't say anything. Within minutes, they were in front of the café again. He stopped the car. The wipers raced back and forth across the cracked windshield.

"See you at home?" she said.

He nodded. The rain was falling in sheets.

"I love you," she said.

"Mmmhmm," he mumbled.

"Hey!"

"Love you, too."

He pressed the stereo's power button, and again the bass rattled the vehicle. Danielle stepped out into the rain and ran into the café. She had a big smile on her face upon entering, but it slowly faded as she scanned the room and didn't find Martin. She ran upstairs and again found nothing. Dejected, she sat alone at a table in the corner and opened her book to the chapter about the Algiers Motel.

CHAPTER XIII
JULY 25, 1967

It was 8:45 and Jack Kerner needed out. Out of his room. Out of the house. Out of Detroit.

That morning, he saw tanks rolling down West Grand Boulevard on the small black and white screen he and his father shared. He knew then that waiting until the fall to leave with Pamela was no longer an option. They would go in a few days once they got their affairs in order.

Then came the fires.

The first came at about 2:00pm. The Platchkes, who lived two doors down West Philadelphia towards Woodward, had a small fire that was contained in the garage and slowly petered out, but Mrs. Falkler wasn't so lucky.

Gladys Falkler had lived sixty-three of her eighty-one years on West Philadelphia, the last six of which were spent alone after Mr. Falkler's heart attack. A very suspicious fire started in her back bedroom at around 4:30. The fire inspector later confirmed the source to be a cigarette, but Gladys herself had never taken a single puff in her life. Regardless, the fire quickly took over the house. Her impassioned screams were heart wrenching as her son pulled her from the inferno. She fell to her knees in the front yard, clinging to a couple photo albums and a small jewelry box, and watched everything else succumb to the flames. Everybody on the street watched. There was nothing to be done. By the time the firetruck showed up an hour later, there was nothing left but a pile of smoldering ash and debris.

It was then that Jack bumped their departure to midnight.

At first, Pamela was hesitant but with some gentle needling, she came on board. They planned it all out. His father would be off to work by ten as the big three automakers had announced that day that they would resume normal working hours. As for Pamela's parents, they'd be asleep by eleven. They always were, even during the previous few days' hullabaloo. He and Pamela would hit the open road in the GTO and not look back.

So he'd spent the rest of the evening in his hotbox of a bedroom, fans awhirl, staring at the clock in an attempt to make the hands spin around more quickly.

A scraping sound from outside.

Jack went to the window. He felt a modest amount of relief when he saw that nothing was ablaze. He did notice something odd, though. Initially it looked like a large cardboard box was walking down the sidewalk. Things had gotten topsy-turvy during the riot, but Jack was not ready to believe that boxes had developed the ability move on their own.

When the box finally made it in front the house to the left of his, Jack saw a balding middle aged man pop up from behind it.

"Goddamn, this heavy," the man said, pressing his hands into the small of his back.

He pulled a handkerchief from his back pocket and wiped his brow. It was Mr. Jaczynski, Jack's neighbor to the right.

Mr. Jaczynski was a teenager when he moved to Detroit from Poland with his parents just before the Nazi invasion. He had lived next door to Jack for the past twelve years and was seemingly quite normal, which is why it perplexed Jack to see him in his current state.

"What is that thing?" Jack heard coming from his right. It was Mr. Jaczynski's wife, Petronela. She was a big woman and looked quite menacing, standing there on the sidewalk, brawny arms crossed over her kitchen apron. She was dusted with a white powder. Jack assumed she must have been in the middle of another batch of her famous dumplings.

"What you mean?" Mr. Jaczynski said. Despite thirty years in America, he still had a thick Polish accent.

"It says dryer on box."

"And?"

"I said we need washer, you dupa!" she said.

Mr. Jaczynski dropped his head, and let out a sequence of what Jack believed to be Polish swears. He smacked his hand against the big box and said, "What do I do?"

"Take it back. Get washer."

And with that, she was gone. Mr. Jaczynski did not move at first, but made his way around to the other side of the box and began pushing it back to whence it came.

"Hey!" Jack yelled.

Mr. Jaczynski turned and looked for the source of the sound, but found no one.

"Over here! In the window!"

"Oh, there you are. Hello, Jack. What is it?"

"What are you doing?"

"Taking this *bzdura* machine back where I got it."

"Where'd you get it?"

"That store on corner."

"Why now? You get a good deal or something?"

Mr. Jaczynski laughed and said, "Have you seen what is happening in city?"

"Of course."

"Then you know what I pay. I just wish I grabbed right one the first time."

He lowered his shoulder and again started pushing the box slowly down the street, the cardboard shredding at the base. Jack watched until he passed the neighbor's house and then turned away, shaking his head.

The situation would have been comical if it weren't so tragic. The city was burning. People were dying. The Army and National Guard were patrolling the streets and for what? So people could get free appliances? Jack felt like he'd somehow landed in an episode of the Twilight Zone, albeit without Rod Serling's purple narration. He couldn't find the connection between the blacks, having dealt with brutality and other forms of repression for years in Detroit and cities all over the country, fighting to gain some semblance of equal societal footing and the mob mentality and unconscionable behavior he was witnessing.

It was then that Jack decided that even midnight was not soon enough. He flung open his closet doors and haphazardly grabbed whatever clothing was within reach. Down came the suitcase from the top shelf and quickly it was stuffed with whatever would fit.

After one final look around his room, he took a deep breath, and stepped out into the hallway. He anticipated a spirited argument with August, who had been planted in front of the television since the riot's inception. It was a small price to pay to leave this alternate Detroit, one devoid of the soul that he'd always known.

He made it all the way to the door before August spoke.

"Where you goin'?"

"I'm leaving."

The senior Kerner looked haggard, more so than usual. On the TV was an aerial view of the city from earlier in the day when the billowing smoke could be seen for miles. To Jack, it looked very much like the footage of Vietnam.

"With the girl?" August said, tipping a fresh bottle of bourbon to his lips.

"Yes. Should you be drinking? Don't you have to go to work tonight?"

"After all this," August said, pointing at the television, "you still want to associate with these people."

"Pamela has nothing to do with this…insanity. Neither does Franklin."

"You think that in times of war, because this *is* a war-don't kid yourself, their allegiance will be to you and not their own kind?"

"All I know is that she loves me and I love her and I can't stay here anymore."

"You think *I* want to be here? As soon as they round the last Negro up, I am leaving to the suburbs. Shoulda done it years ago. I saw this comin'. These people just didn't realize how good they had it."

He took another swig. "And now they've gone and messed it all up."

"It's not just them. It's everyone. The whole city has lost its mind."

"Always cutting them too much slack."

"I just saw Mr. Jaczynski pushing a looted dryer down the street."

August said nothing.

On the screen, a reporter stood in front of an apartment building on the corner of Euclid and Twelfth.

"*A four year old girl was killed today in this apartment building by a stream of machine gun fire from the National Guardsmen's tank. Allegedly, the Guardsmen, assuming a flash in the window to be sniper fire when in reality its source was a lit cigarette, opened fire with over ninety bullets, striking the young girl dead.*" There was a grainy image of a tank rolling down Twelfth Street. Jack opened the front door.

"This is it for us, you know," August said. Jack stopped, but did not look at his father.

"You're eighteen. Not my problem anymore. Remember that when you come crawling back from wherever it is you're going."

Jack walked out the door. The sun had taken respite beyond the western horizon.

Jack pounded the King's front door. It opened and he was face to face with the barrel of a six shooter.

"Mrs. King!" Jack said, arms raised, dropping the suitcase to the ground.

"Oh, Jack! I'm sorry!" she said, lowering the gun in her trembling hands. There were tears in her eyes.

"What is going on? Where is everyone?"

"Mr. King is at his parents' house with Franklin, standin' guard with the shotgun. He left Pammie and me here with this thing and told me to fire at anyone that tries to get in."

"Oh. But, why are you crying?"

"It's my mother. These maniacs have gone n' set her neighbor's house on fire."

"On Chandler Street?"

"Yes. Her house is fine for now, but the fire department said it could be two hours before they get there. Two hours! The whole block could be up in flames by then."

"What are you going to do?"

"What can I do? I told her to hose down her siding hoping that it'll keep it from catchin' fire."

"Where's Pamela?"

"That's the worst of it. She's on her way over there now."

Jack's heart dropped into his stomach. "What?"

"She loves her Grammy. I begged her to stay, but she refused. She wouldn't even take the gun. She can be so stubborn."

"When did she go?"

"You just missed her."

Jack leapt from the porch. Within seconds he was sprinting full speed down the sidewalk. Just before Woodward was a squad car. The cops had nabbed someone on the sidewalk. As Jack got closer he could see that it was Mr. Jaczynski. He hadn't gotten far.

"Him. That boy knows me! I am no criminal! Tell them Jack! Tell them I am good man!" Mr. Jaczynski shouted.

Jack put his head down and ran.

Isaac and Reggie Howard were sitting on their porch listening to an AM news station on a radio Isaac had looted from an electronics store on Monday morning. With each new tale of the devastation, Isaac's smile grew larger and larger. Reggie was neither smiling nor frowning. The events at the blind pig had rendered him numb. Everything was hazy, dreamlike.

Isaac turned the volume down and tapped Reggie on the shoulder, drawing him from his stupor.

"Look over there," Isaac said, pointing in the direction of the King/Kerner residences. Jack had just walked out onto the porch with a suitcase in his hand.

"What you think he's doin'? Lookin' for his sweet thang? Well, she gone, loverboy!" Isaac cackled.

"She is?" Reggie was able to muster.

"Yeah. She ran by couple minutes ago. You was right here. You daydreamin' or somethin'?"

Reggie shook his head in an attempt to clear the fog. "I...I guess."

"Well, wake the hell up. I think this our chance to get back at his honky ass."

"Get back at him?"

"Yeah. What's wrong witchu? He stole yo' girl, remember?"

"Oh."

They watched Jack jump from the porch. He sped by their house, not noticing the two sets of eyes glued to him.

"Get up. Let's follow him," Isaac said. "An' bring yo' gun."

He popped up from his seat and down the porch steps. Reggie slowly got up from his chair, still expressionless. He tucked the Colt .38 revolver that Isaac had given him into his jeans. Though his legs propelled him down the street, he wasn't really there.

When Jack turned the corner at Woodward the heat stopped him like a punch to the stomach. He felt as if he'd walked into a blast furnace. The beauty salon across the street was engulfed in flames that cast the avenue in flickering light. A dark gray plume rose high above the structure, ever expanding. Three firefighters were crouched in the road around the hose dousing the inferno with a powerful stream. Flanking them were gun-toting National Guardsmen, eyes peeled wide for snipers.

Both groups looked weary and on edge, and when a loud popping sound came from the building, the lead fireman dropped the hose. Left unattended, it pirouetted in mid-air, spouting water indiscriminately about the avenue. The captain of the Guardsmen shouted commands and the men, mostly green young boys roughly Jack's age, swiveled their heads to and fro, scanning the rooftops for the source of the sound. When no sniper was found and the hose was corralled, they resumed their positioning. The firemen began aiming the stream at the adjacent building, a hardware store. The salon was a lost cause.

Jack, mesmerized by the insatiable appetite of the fire and the futility of man trying to control it, had temporarily forgotten his quest. He came to just in time to sidestep a fleeing looter. The young, black man was carrying a turntable and was feverishly trying to evade a patrolman hot on his trail. The man tripped and the turntable fell to the pavement, breaking into several pieces. Resolute, he got back up and took off again, with the cop just behind. Jack regained his focus and started south down the road.

The path was littered with broken glass. Most of it appeared to be from the windows of looted stores; the rest from liquor and Stroh's beer bottles that had most likely been looted, as well. Jack gingerly stepped around it and peered down the street for Pamela.

A flatbed truck came traveling slowly north. In the bed of the truck were two men with bullhorns. As they approached, Jack recognized their announcement as a call to disperse. The two men were very familiar. One was Congressman John Conyers and the other was Willie Horton, Detroit's starting left fielder. Their celebrity apparently earned them no sanctuary, as an array of bottles and rocks came raining down on them. Not all took part in the attack, but nobody made a move to quell it, either. Luckily for the men, the driver was able to escape the area before either man sustained injury.

Jack pressed on and, up ahead, he thought he saw her, but in the darkness, it was hard to be certain. He called out to her but, at the same moment, an ambulance sped by, sirens blaring, rendering his voice all but muted. He made his way to her as fast as he could. When he reached her, he put his hand on her shoulder.

"Who the hell is you?" a startled and angry woman spun around to chastise him.

She put her hand on her hip and wagged one contemptuous finger in his face.

"You can't be runnin' up on a woman, touchin' 'em if you ain't know 'em."

"I'm sorry. I thought you were someone else," Jack said.

"Yeah, you all sorry. Go on, now."

She turned away from him, and a small child of about seven years ran up to her carrying a table lamp. He had been in the furniture store at the corner of Euclid.

"What is this? You know momma said orange. This is red. Go on back in there and get an orange one."

The boy ran back into the mostly gutted store, tossing the red lamp aside in the process.

There she was.

About a block further down the road he saw her. She was under a streetlamp at the corner of Virginia Park and Woodward, and it looked as if she was gauging the traffic for the perfect time to cross to the west side. Jack sprinted ahead, broken glass digging into the soles of his sneakers. He shouted her name, snaking his way through the onlookers and kibitzers. She heard his call and her face lit up when she saw him. He wrapped his arms around her diminutive waist and squeezed. They shared a kiss that suggested they'd been displaced for years rather than hours.

"What are you doing runnin' around out here on your own?" Jack said.

"My Grammy needs me. Her neighbor's house is burnin'."

"I know. Your mom told me."

"My mom?"

"I went to get you and she told me that you'd left."

"Get me? I thought we were leaving at midnight."

"I can't stay here any longer."

"Ok, but not before I check on my Grammy. I have to know she's safe."

Jack thought he saw something in her expression, doubt perhaps.

"Hey," he said, placing a hand on her cheek. "Are you sure you want to do this?"

"Do what?"

"This. With me."

She matched his gaze with an intensity that Jack would never be able to get out of his mind. "Jack Kerner, I love you. I will always be with you."

At that moment they were both pulled into the brush underneath the sign for the Algiers Motel.

He could hear her screaming from somewhere nearby, but could do nothing to help. He was being whisked away by some unseen force. His shirt had slid up over his eyes, putting him in the dark and exposing his chest and back to a nonstop assault from every rock, pebble and stick he encountered.

"Right there's good," someone said in a deep, intimidating and very familiar voice.

The dragging stopped and Jack was lifted to his feet. He attempted to flee, but his assailant wrapped his arms tightly behind his back.

"Drop the shirt," the voice commanded.

His captor complied. The scene came into view. He was in a dark alley between the Algiers Motel and the Manor House. The smell was foul, as they stood just a few feet from a dumpster and a grease collector for the motel's kitchen. The ground was damp though it had not rained in days.

Two figures emerged from the shadows. The first was Pamela. She was being led by a very large man and the source of the voice; Isaac Howard. Pamela looked like a child's doll next to the goliath. Her shirt was ripped and there were scratches on her arms and face.

"Pamela!" Jack cried out.

"Jack!"

"Shut the hell up, both a y'all," Isaac yelled. "Reggie, keep hold a him. He's liable to get loose."

"Reggie?!" Jack said, stunned. He tried to turn to face his friend but Reggie locked him into a formidable bear hug that, after a few obligatory attempts to break free, Jack realized he was powerless to overcome.

"All right, now. Ain't this a party! Thass how we do it here in Deeetroit! Ain't no niggers. Ain't no crackers. Just four people havin' a good time on a beautiful night," Isaac said with a smile.

"REGGIE! LET ME GO! THIS IS…CRAZY!" Jack cried out.

Reggie did not flinch.

"But not as beautiful as this fine, Nubian princess," Isaac said. He pulled her to him and ran his tongue slowly up her cheek. She jerked away in disgust, drawing Isaac's laughter.

"Oh, baby, baby. Ain't no need to fuss. I ain't tryin' to be your man. You already got one. He right there. You're big, strong, cracker man."

"Let her go, Isaac!" Jack yelled.

"C'mon now. What fun would that be?"

"It's not a game, Isaac! Let her go! She didn't do anything."

"Oh, no?"

"No. You're just a goddamn bully. You've always been a bully. To me, Frank, even to your own brother. Especially him."

Isaac looked mystified. "Is that so, lil' brother?" he said.

Reggie did not break his silence, though Jack felt his grip slacken just a bit.

"That's what I thought," Isaac said.

"What? He didn't say anything," Jack said.

"Cuz I ain't bully him."

"He's just scared to say it."

"Aww, enough of this shit. This how we gonna do this."

Isaac pulled from his waistband a Colt .45 and forced it against Pamela's temple. She shrieked when the metal hit her skin.

"Isaac, let her go!"

"Ok, Pammie. You got two strapping young lads in front'a you. Now, who's it gonna be, huh?"

She squirmed in his arms, trying to lean away from the gun barrel.

"I asked you a question. What? You think you too good for a nigga?"

He shook her hard, and she lost her footing. He lifted her back up and jammed the gun back against her head.

"Huh, bitch? You got a problem with us. We ain't worthy of your love? Answer me!"

"Isaac, stop this!" Jack screamed.

"Look at him! I want you to look at what you coulda had."

"Isaac!"

"But it's too late." Isaac cocked the hammer.

Jack hooked his right foot behind Reggie's and yanked as hard as he could. The pair came crashing to the pavement, but still Reggie did not let go. He rolled over on top of Jack, and finally the pair met eyes. Jack had never seen Reggie's look so distant.

"Reggie, get off me! He's gonna kill her!"

"Get a hold a him!" Isaac shouted.

Reggie looked back and forth from Isaac to Jack and then finally to Pamela. She was terrified. It was then that Jack saw a flicker of life return to Reggie's eyes.

"Get up, Reg!" Jack shouted.

They both turned their heads when they heard Isaac howl in pain. Pamela had bit him, piercing the webbing between his left thumb and index finger. Isaac dropped the gun, but he was able to grab Pamela by the hair in her attempt to run. He closed his fist within the strands and flung her aside with all of his might. Her scream abruptly stopped when her head cracked against the steel dumpster.

The sound of her skull caving in was blood curdling. Her body crumpled to the cement in an unnatural position.

Jack tried to call out to her, but could produce no sound. He could only look. Reggie did not move, though Jack could feel his muscles trembling.

"Shit, man. Why'd she have to bite me for?" Isaac said, watching a trickle of blood run from Pamela's left ear.

Jack pushed a now limp Reggie off of him and took off towards the wayward gun.

"Uh, uh, uh," Isaac said, beating him to it. He aimed it right at Jack's chest, freezing him in his tracks.

"You sonofabitch! She's hurt! Let me help her," he shouted, boiling with rage.

"No, no. You gonna run and tell the fuzz. I can't let you leave here."

"Ice," Reggie said, speaking for the first time.

"What?"

"Let me."

"You wanna do it?" Isaac said, surprised.

"Yeah," Reggie replied, walking towards his brother.

Isaac backed off. Reggie pulled out the .38 and aimed it straight between Jack's eyes, though it quivered when he stole a glance over at Danielle's body.

"Reggie!" Jack shouted as his old friend advanced on him. "We have to help her! What are you doing?"

A gunshot.

Jack clenched his eyes and waited for the sweet release of death. It did not come. He opened them to see Reggie and Isaac exchange puzzled looks.

"Snipers. Let's get the hell outta here. Place'll be lousy with pigs," Isaac said.

Reggie turned his attention back to Jack with tears welling up in his eyes.

"DO IT, REGGIE!" Isaac shouted.

"You go. I got this," Reggie said.

"You sure?" Isaac said.

"Yeah."

Isaac hesitated for a moment before bolting down the alley and out of sight.

"We were friends," Jack said.

Reggie stepped forward and lifted the gun into the air.

"I know," he said, bringing the handle down on Jack's head with full force.

In that instant, Jack knew nothing but pain. He fell to the ground, inches from Pamela. Barely there, shrouded in starbursts, was her face. He looked into her open, lifeless eyes. He reached out to her touch her lips, but the darkness overcame him, and he slipped into unconsciousness.

CHAPTER XIV
JULY 26, 1967

Jack's eyes opened to nothing. Disoriented and with an intense throb emanating from where Reggie crowned him, he panicked. He tried to gain his footing, but could not. His feet slipped and slid as he drowned in a sea of debris. His lungs rejected the putrid air surrounding him and his heart began to race, which seemed to amplify the pain in his head. Just when he thought he would lose his tenuous grip on sanity, he saw a sliver of light. He reached out to it. Its borders were cold and metallic.

He was in the dumpster.

He pressed the lid up a crack but no further as he heard voices drawing nearer. There seemed to be several men, but he didn't recognize them.

"That nigger didn't even twitch," one said, from what sounded like mere steps away. Then came laughter.

"I don't know guys. We shouldn't have…I've never shot…Oh, God. I think I'm gonna be sick," another said.

Some retching and the splattering of vomit on pavement.

"Oh, get ahold of yourself. You were just doing your job."

"Hey, uh, how we gonna write this up, anyways?" a third voice asked.

"Let's sleep on it. We can figure it out in the morning. Hopefully, by then he'll be done spewin' his guts over there." More laughter.

Jack braved a peek and saw what he thought was a police badge covered with black tape on the one closest to him. Feeling safer, Jack opened the lid. The police spun around and drew their weapons.

"Don't shoot!" Jack said, arms raised.

"What are you doing in that dumpster?" the de facto leader said.

"I don't know. I was attacked and put here, I guess. My girlfriend was lying over…"

Pamela was gone.

He looked to where he remembered her falling, and nothing was there but a small, dark stain.

"Where is she?"

"Who?" the cop said.

"Pamela." Jack jumped from the dumpster and frantically paced the alley, looking everywhere for her.

"All right, calm down. From the looks of that blood on your head, you've taken quite a blow. It's 2:30 now. When were you attacked?"

"What?" Jack said, frenzied.

"I said, it's two thi-, never mind. Why don't I radio to the precinct and find out if anybody picked up your girlfriend?"

"She was right there! She…"

Jack's legs became rubber and he collapsed.

When they arrived at the cruiser, one of the officers got on the radio.

"We just picked up a white male, age…." The cop put down the transmitter and slapped Jack lightly across the face.

"Hey! You! How old are you?"

Jack did not respond. The cop continued, "Let's say seventeen, outside the Algiers Motel in a dumpster. He claims he and his girlfriend were attacked, but there's no girl. Any reports of walking wounded or bodies picked up at or near the Algiers?"

Jack leaned against the cruiser's quarter panel and waited what seemed like an eternity for the voice on the other end to respond. Finally, a static burst came through the line, and a voice that said, "Affirmative. Negro female, aged eighteen, brought to Detroit General at 1:02 A.M. D.O.A."

The cop looked at Jack and said, "You're in luck, son. All they found was a dead coon."

Jack leapt forward, wrapping his hands around the cop's neck. The other two officers immediately pounced on him, driving their nightsticks into his lower back. He fell to the ground and began to sob uncontrollably, his body convulsing with anguish.

"You crazy or something?" the officer said, adjusting his collar.

"One of you cuff this little prick and toss him in, would ya?"

One of the other officers complied. Jack landed face first on the cruiser's backseat.

"You think you're cryin' now, wait 'til I get you down to the tenth," the cop said, settling in behind the wheel.

They drove off as Jack replayed the nights events over in his mind, except instead of a blow to the head, Reggie pulled the trigger.

The chaos inside the Detroit Police Department's tenth precinct mirrored that which was outside its walls. There was no protocol, no infrastructure to contain the hundreds of arrestees. They lined the halls, filled the cells, and were placed wherever there was room. The noise was insufferable with almost nonstop shouting and the omnipresent clang of ringing phones.

"DOWN THAT HALL!" the cop shouted to Jack.

"What?"

"GO!" he said, with a hearty shove.

The cop lead Jack down a dimly lit hall near the rear of the building to the dangerously overcrowded holding cells. Each one was equipped to hold a maximum of ten prisoners but at that moment housed anywhere from twenty-five to thirty.

"FRESH MEAT!" they shouted as Jack approached. Arms reached through the bars, clawing at his clothes.

The officer stopped at one of the lesser crowded cells.

"BACK UP, YOU ANIMALS!" he barked, slamming his nightstick against the steel.

Once the prisoners complied, he opened the door, uncuffed Jack and pushed him in. He stumbled over his feet, and bumped into two large black inmates who were none too pleased. They proceeded to bandy him about like a shuttlecock, ultimately driving him into the corner.

Jack showed no sign whatsoever that he was even aware of his surround. He was so deep inside his own head that he could have been anywhere.

D-O-A.

It wasn't registering. Hours earlier he'd tracked Pamela down on the street so that they might start their lives together. She had told him that she loved him. And he loved her.

Then a realization hit him harder than Reggie had.

It was his fault.

He had led them to her. If he had stayed the course, and waited until midnight like they'd planned, she might have returned from her grandmother's unscathed.

He had killed her.

The room began to spin. He dropped to floor and put his head in his hands. He stayed that way for hours.

By the time Jack had overcome his initial shock, it was 6:00am. His head pulsated, his stomach churned and he didn't dare look at the damage to his torso from his unplanned journey across the Algiers parking lot. Still, as he watched the way most of his fellow inmates were manhandled by the police, he couldn't help but feel he'd gotten off easy.

Many got a nightstick to the head as a welcoming gift to their new home: others, a kick in the ass. Everywhere he looked, he saw split lips and bruised faces, ripped and blood stained clothes, and, with the more serious offenders, missing teeth and cigarette burns.

The blacks were definitely handled more aggressively, though the few whites he saw got more than their fair share. Sex, however, had no bearing on the way the inmates were handled. Many of the women were treated with equally abrasive tactics, especially when it came to frisking, which was being carried out in ways not taught at the academy.

Watching it all served as a welcome distraction for Jack's brain. The officers' tactics repulsed him, but at least it made the pain seem more distant and the image of Pamela's frozen stare emerge less frequently. As time wore on, though, something strange happened.

He started enjoying it.

A little at first, but soon he found himself analyzing each new cellmate for signs of abuse. He eavesdropped on their conversations, waiting for details of nightsticks on wrists and blows to the backs of heads. He was particularly aroused when one prisoner told a tale of how the National Guard made him lie in the street while they pulled the tank within inches of his head.

How he wished he'd been the driver.

An officer approached, bringing with him another future cellmate. The man, who looked to be in his mid-twenties, was roughly the same size as Isaac, big and muscular. He was in obvious physical pain, limping and cradling his right wrist.

"Officer! I'm dyin' here! I think you done broke it!" he said.

The cop said nothing. He unlocked the cell, and shoved him in like the others. The man fell to the floor and crawled up to the bars.

"Help me! I need a doctor!"

The cop looked down on him with derision. "You should have thought of that before you burned down the city, nigger."

As he left, another cop drew near. In his hand he had a manila folder. Taking out his keys, he said, "Which one of you is Jack Kerner?"

Jack found himself in a small cinder block interrogation room. It was colorless and decorated sparely with only a steel table, bolted down, and two folding chairs. A buzzing bulb hung limply over the table.

"Sit down," the cop said, gesturing to one of the chairs. Jack complied.

The cop sat in the other chair and let out a deep, prolonged breath. The bags underneath his eyes were so dark that they looked as if they'd been colored in with marker. He opened the folder in front of him and rubbed at his temples.

"So, you were attacked in that alley?"

"Yes."

"By who?"

Jack took a moment to answer. Isaac's face whirled before his eyes and he could feel Reggie's vice-like grip tighten around his chest.

"No idea."

"You didn't get a look at them?"

"No."

"Well, we know they were Negro. Does that help?"

"Not really."

"A situation occurred just after your attack at the manor house there at the Algiers. An eyewitness said they saw two Negroes leave that alley."

"Oh."

The cop picked up a pencil and jotted some notes down on one of the papers.

"What is wrong with you?" he said.

"Excuse me?"

He looked at Jack quizzically. "You think we don't have enough on our plate with the blacks that we need white kids acting out, too?"

"I wasn't acting out."

"What do you call assaulting an officer?"

Jack shrugged. The indifference he felt towards his current predicament surprised him. He'd never been in trouble a day in his life.

"You have nothing to say to explain yourself?"

"Nope."

The cop took a deep breath and looked at his watch. He cupped his hand over his mouth to hide a yawn.

"Anything that might help us find the guys who killed your girlfriend?"

"No."

The cop flipped through the papers in the folder, not staying on one page long enough to really absorb anything. He shut the folder and got up.

"Well then get the hell out of here. Go home."

Jack thought about the last thing his father had said to him.

"Hey!" the cop said, waving a hand in front of Jack's face.

"What?"

"I said you're free. Now, get out before I physically remove you!"

The cop left. Jack got up and made it about ten feet down the corridor before he froze.

Free.

But to do what, he did not know. Steps away, there was a doorway that would lead him through the main entry and ultimately the front door. He had no idea what lied beyond that door. The life he'd spent eighteen years building was gone. The city was burning. He had no father. He had no home.

He had nothing.

"Look the hell out, kid! What are you doin' back here anyways?" an officer said as he whipped by and entered one of the adjacent interrogation rooms. He was holding a coffee mug, which was not significant in any way. Many of the officers were. What made him unique, though, was that he was smiling.

It was a curious smile, more like a smirk, actually; one that somebody might sport if they were up to something.

He didn't remember moving his feet, but there Jack was, peering into the little window on the interrogation room door.

Inside he found his happy cop as well as one more in addition to a black male prisoner seated at a table similar to the one in the other room. Though muffled, Martin was able to hear their conversation.

"Here. You said you're thirsty. I got you some apple juice," the cop who'd passed him in the hall said. He slid the mug across the table to the man.

He was middle aged, heavy set and had a mostly swollen left eye. When he reached for the mug, his hand was trembled. He put the mug to his lips and took a sip and immediately spit it out.

"That's goddamn urine!" he said, hunched over, retching. The officers guffawed and offered each other congratulatory high fives.

"That's all you animals deserve!" smiley said.

"We ain't no animals! We got rights, you know!" he said.

"You're right," officer number two said. He wiped the smile from his face and offered a stern look to his colleague suggesting he do the same.

"You're right. That was a horrible thing to do. Truly. How about we start over? I'll give you some coffee and we'll talk this out like men."

The man sat up straighter, and wiped his tongue on his shirt. After some deliberation, he offered a slight nod. "I s'pose that'd be all right."

"Good. Well, here's your coffee!" the cop said, tossing the remnants of his steaming cup into the man's face. He fell off the chair onto the tiled floor, writhing in pain.

"THIS IS AN OUTRAGE!"

The officers shared a glance, and then advanced on the man. Cop number two grabbed the man high about the shoulders, pinning him to the floor. He wriggled and twisted, but could not break free. Smiley lifted the man's legs up by the ankles, spreading them wide.

"Do it!" cop two shouted.

It was at that moment, looking into the man's twisted expression of abject fear, that Jack noticed something.

It was Isaac.

Smiley raised his foot up off the ground and brought the heel down into Isaac's testicles. His screech was so loud that every ear in the precinct heard it and could describe it in detail. His face turned purple and he passed out.

Jack backed away from the door, down the corridor and past the holding cell he'd been in. Something had changed. The men inside…

They were all Isaac.

Twenty, thirty men.

All Isaac.

In the main entry he was everywhere. There must have been a hundred of him. Jack approached the front desk where sat a short, fat cop with a thick mane of gray hair. He had in front of him three rotary phones and stack of papers reaching at least a foot high.

"Yes, I'll notify the officers patrolling that neighborhood," he said, hanging up one phone.

Another rang, and then another. He picked one up and said, "Tenth precinct, Atchison here. What's that? You're store's been looted? Where at? All right, I'll have an officer come by. Huh? About an hour, maybe two. Yeah, that's right. Too long? You nuts? Take a look around, bozo."

He hung up the phone. He measured the skinny white kid standing in front of him with the blood matted hair and the spaced out look on his face.

"Whaddya want, kid? I'm busy."

"Sir, some of the officers back there are being a little rough on the inmates."

The mixture of the ringing phones and commotion of all the comings and goings of cops and prisoners created a migraine inducing din. Atchison stuck his index finger into his ear canal and jostled some wax loose.

"Come again?"

"I said, some of the officers back there-,"

Atchison's brow furrowed.

"Now you wait right there, punk," he said, raising his palm. "We got damn near six thousand plus arrested already during this riot, or rebellion, whatever you want to call it. Over two thousand stores have been looted. Pharmacies, liquor stores, gun stores. GUNS, kid. We got an angry mob out there with over two thousand guns reported stolen. They are armed and dangerous. On top of that, the city is burning. Over fifteen hundred alarms were called already. We are trying to coordinate the DPD, state boys, National Guard and Army, four groups that speak different languages, answer to different leaders and have different agendas. The men are tired from pulling eighteen hour shifts. Tired of getting shot at by cowards on rooftops. They're mad about losing one of their own, shot yesterday in front of a damn grocery. And they are mad as hell about losing their city. Now, I'm sure we got some bad apples. What group don't? Rest assured, when all this shit's over, they will be dealt with."

Atchison sat up and leaned in closer to Jack, eyes wide and nostrils flared.

"You take all that, and I'd say my men are doing a HELL of a job. Admirable, even. So forgive me if they occasionally handle some of these lowlife, thieving, arsonist scumbags…A LITTLE ROUGH!" he said, slamming his hands down on the counter.

"Sir, I wasn't trying to rat on them," Jack said.

"No?" Atchison replied, his chest heaving. He plopped back down in his chair and wiped spittle from his moustache. "Well, what do you want then?"

"I wanted to know…where do I sign up?"

CHAPTER XV
AUGUST 1, 2008

"Four and a half years ago, two white Detroit cops were killed by black assailants. One week later, two white, Superior Township men wrote 'courtesy of the fighting whities' on photos of the slain officers and left them at the base of the iconic bronze Joe Louis Fist on Jefferson. Then they covered the fist in a coat of glossy white paint. Why?" Abdul-Tawaab said.

He looked out on a sea of listless, overheated faces, cast in alternating dark and light bars from the early afternoon sun peeking through the blinds.

"Should we cancel class due to heat?" he offered.

"No," they collectively answered, unenthusiastically.

"Then I need an answer. You," he said, calling upon the Indian man in the back row.

"Senseless vandalism, I believe," he said.

"Do you? Well, the magistrate overseeing the case did not. He charged the men with malicious destruction of public property and likened their actions to, and I quote 'cross burning and hate speech' and 'an affirmative threat.'"

"Wow," Darius said.

"Yes. A bold statement. Whether you agree or disagree depends on what you believe the statue is supposed to represent. In its most objective form it is a fitting tribute to African American boxer, Joe Louis, who, after moving to Detroit as a child, became one of the greatest heavyweight fighters ever. His knockout of Germany's Max Schmeling for the title in June 1938 ran roughshod over Hitler's belief that the Aryans were superior in every way. What other ways could this structure be interpreted? Ms. Denson."

Danielle, whose hand had been raised, cleared her throat and said, "A symbol of the Black Panthers, sir?"

"Perhaps. The Panthers adopted the single raised fist as their own. What else?"

Darius spoke up. "How about black triumph over repression, you know, like for civil rights?"

Abdul-Tawaab nodded in agreement. "Another good one. Anybody else?"

Martin raised his hand. "How about a symbol of the violent nature of this city?"

He expected Abdul-Tawaab to critique his response, but instead he stroked his chin and nodded as he had for the others.

"Astute. Detractors of the statue have raised those concerns as well. It is art, first and foremost, and can have as many interpretations as there are people. What cannot be argued, though, is that the actions of those two men were an affront to the black community and a prime example of the fact that this city still suffers from racial division."

He walked around his desk and began gathering his things. Like Pavlov's dogs, the class did the same.

"I would like to remind you that the final exam next week will encompass thirty percent of your grade. Good day."

And with that, he was gone. Martin followed the stream of bodies into the hall.

"Hey, stranger!" someone said behind him.

It was Danielle and she looked absolutely beautiful.

"Stranger?"

"Umm, yeah. We haven't chatted in weeks. You avoiding me?"

He had been. Her brother's grim stare that day in front of the cafe instilled a fear that he was not proud of, yet respected nonetheless.

"Of course not. Why would I?"

"That's what I was trying to figure out."

They walked down the stairs and out of Higgins Hall. The sun was searing and Cass was busy with tank top and sunglass clad students.

Danielle put her own oversized pair on and said, "So…that was our last class before finals."

Martin nodded. "Yep."

Danielle sagged her shoulders and let out an overly dramatic sigh.

"What's wrong?" Martin said.

"Why do I gotta be the man in this relationship?"

NOCTURNE IN BLACK AND WHITE

"Excuse me?"

"Don't mess with me, Kerner. You know... I don't get you. It's like, all semester we hang out, studying and all and it's so obvious you're into me, all stutterin' and fumblin', but here we are, last day of class and..."

"And?"

"And... shit or get off the pot."

She immediately covered her mouth with her hand. A smile crept over Martin's lips. He had never heard her swear before.

"What'd you say?"

"Oh, shut up. It slipped out 'cuz you're makin' me mad."

"But I didn't do anything."

"That's the problem, dummy."

"Wow! First you swear at me, and then you call me names."

"If the shoe fits..."

When she smiled at him it was contagious, disarming. All of a sudden it seemed foolish that he would allow the sideways glances of a seventeen year old or the assumed disapproval of an absentee father dissuade him from pursuing something that felt so right.

"You're right, you know," Martin said.

"I'm always right. Sooner you realize, Kerner, better off you'll be."

"Let's do it, then."

Her face lit up. "F'real?"

"Yep. *Second* second date."

"When?"

"I don't know. How about tonight?"

"Tonight works."

"Ok. Pick you up at seven. I know this great place in Royal Oak that-
"

"Absolutely not."

"What?"

"You got a whole list of 'I nevers' that we gotta take care of, remember? We doin' the 'D'. I pick the places."

Martin bowed to her. "Yes, your highness."

"Oh, quit your foolin'. Pick me up at six, not seven. We got lots to do."

She rifled through her purse for a moment, and came out with a pen and a gum wrapper. She jotted something down on the wrapper and handed it to Martin.

"That's my address. Don't be late."

At 5:20, Martin sprang from the shower in the middle of some improv scatting, which then segued into a peculiar pectoral dance in front of the mirror. After a quick towel dry, he bounded across the hall and into his bedroom.

He likened his ease of mood to a skydiver's immediately after the leap. The anxiety had passed. He'd committed to the fall. The only thing left to do was enjoy the scenery.

After locating the perfect combo of blue jeans and faux-vintage t-shirt, he pirouetted in front of his bedroom mirror, examining himself at all angles. Satisfied, he grabbed a generous dollop of pomade and began molding his hair. Once he'd achieved the desired messiness, he peeked at his bedside clock.

It was 5:30.

He grabbed the Chrysler's keys and bolted for the back door. Stepping outside into the still simmering heat, he felt there was nothing in the world that could spoil his mood.

"Where you goin'?"

He had forgotten about his father, yet there he was, limping into view from the shadowed garage.

"Nowhere," Martin said. It was the first word he'd said to Jack since their altercation.

"Bullshit," Jack said, working at his bad hip.

Martin sighed. "Not that it's any of your business, but I have a date and I'm gonna be la-,"

"A date? With who?"

"Someone from class," Martin said, with no effort to hide his irritation. He had neither the time nor the inclination to fritter about with small talk.

"A woman, right?"

"Of cour-, wait. Why am I talking to you? Goodbye."

"You getting flowers?" Jack said, undeterred by Martin's multiple attempts to extricate himself from the conversation.

"No."

"Candy?"

"I don't have time for this," Martin said, walking off.

"You like this mystery girl?"

Martin stopped, having only made it three steps toward the Chrysler. The thought of Danielle temporarily made the hostility dwindle. "Yeah. I do."

"Well, then. You can't show up in that old Chrysler, empty handed."

"I'll grab some flowers at the gas station."

"Why don't you take the GTO?"

"What?" Martin said, flabbergasted.

"You want to impress her, right?"

Martin scrutinized his father's face for evidence of a ruse.

"Don't mess with me, Jack."

"You know how to drive a stick, right?"

"Yeah. No thanks to you."

Jack reached into his pocket and pulled out the keys. "Be careful with the clutch. It sticks a little."

Martin did not move.

"Come on, now. Don't just stand there with your pecker in your hand," Jack said, smirking.

Martin crept forward like a fawn to a palm full of seed.

"Where you takin' this girl, anyways?"

"I don't know. She's picking the places," Martin said, reaching for the keys dangling from Jack's outstretched hand. "All I know is that we're going somewhere in the city."

Jack snatched the keys back.

"Detroit?!" he said, his brow furrowed.

"Yeah, why?"

"I'm not lettin' you take that car into Detroit. No way."

"What?"

"You drive around down there in a car like that and it'll get stolen…or worse, caught up in some drive-by."

"Of course it would," Martin said, emphatically dropping his hand.

"It would! Believe me, I was a cop in that cesspool of a city and I-,"

"THIRTY YEARS AGO!" Martin bellowed. He was furious, but not at his father, but at his own naïve self.

"Yeah, and nothing's changed."

"And neither have you. You know, I'm gonna be late. I don't have time for this shit."

He turned and marched down the driveway.

"Martin!" Jack yelled, but the conversation was over.

Martin slammed the Chrysler's door and over cranked the starter. His anger then took control of his right foot, driving the accelerator to the floorboard. The wheezing engine propelled him down the street, onto Nine Mile and ultimately I-75. He drove aggressively, whipping across lanes at well over the posted speed limit. He was the subject of several horn blasts and the occasional middle finger, but he was oblivious. His mind was fixated on how someone in his father's position, someone who had spent his adult life emotionally neglecting his only son, could so flippantly throw away every opportunity to begin making amends.

It took until he'd taken the Davison ramp towards Brightmoor, Danielle's neighborhood, before he started to feel at ease again.

But it was short lived.

He'd been so caught up in his own thoughts that he hadn't realized the Davison freeway quickly morphed into Davison West, a surface road.

He was exposed.

The six lane thoroughfare was ripe with overgrown lots and boarded up homes. There was one, just past Rosa Parks Blvd, then another, and another. He'd gotten so comfortable at the campus in the corridor that he'd forgotten about this Detroit. The real Detroit.

The one from the eleven o'clock news.

He could feel the decay around him. He could almost smell the hopelessness in the air. It reminded him of that fateful night driving down Chene on route to T-Mar. But that street was abandoned. A vestige of a different era. This one was busy with activity.

"Where are they all going?" Martin asked himself as he approached the red light at Linwood.

Other than liquor stores and the occasional fast food restaurant, there was nothing for the people. Yet there they were.

And they were watching him.

They were waiting to pounce. He was sure of it. The old black man in the too big for him suit at the crosswalk, the two boys on bikes in front of one of those 'You Buy, We Fry' fish places, and especially the driver of the car inching up closer on his right. Panic was choking him off and he knew if he looked over, he'd see a pistol aimed right at him.

Green light.

He floored the accelerator, weaving in and out of lanes until he reached I-96 and the relative safety of its concrete oasis.

He took the exit at Evergreen just as his pre-printed directions suggested, but it wasn't a decision he came to easily. He was tempted to keep going until he'd passed out of Detroit, loop back around the city to Hazel Park and just forget about the whole thing. But he didn't. He owed it to her to follow through.

He owed it to himself.

He turned onto Lyndon street and immediately wondered how someone as vibrant as Danielle, someone so luminous, could have come from a place so drab, so desolate.

The neighborhood looked uninhabited. Nature had taken over what man had forgotten. The grass and weeds grew tall, infiltrating the cracks in the sidewalks and driveways and snaking up the sides of the homes. The leafy arms of the trees and shrubs, left unattended, reached high and wide without order or purpose. Dandelions provided the only splotches of color amidst the depressing landscape.

The carcasses of several homes were decorated with the words 'GAS CUT' and 'W/OFF' spray painted on the siding in big bright yellow letters. Others were boarded up or in varying states of disrepair.

He turned on Danielle's street and found her house halfway down the block. Hers and the one immediately north were the only two occupied lots on her side of the street. The house was modest but well kempt. The siding looked like it had recently been given a fresh coat of light blue paint and the lawn was neatly groomed. A robin occupied a stone birdbath lying just beyond the front gate.

There were bars across the windows.

Martin eased the Chrysler up the narrow strips of broken cement that served as a driveway and parked. After a final once over in the rearview mirror, he got out.

"Who's over there?"

He nearly jumped out of his skin.

The voice was feminine but stern and sounded as though it had come from his left. He saw a figure in shadow seated on the porch swing next door.

"Yeah, you! Whatchu doin' there?"

Martin noted there was no one else around.

"Me?" he said.

"Yes, you, boy. Get over here and let me get a look 'atcha."

Martin hesitated.

"Today, son!"

Her tenor suggested it was best Martin not argue. As he approached her porch, she slowly came into view. Martin was so taken aback by the woman's disfigurement, he stopped short of climbing the last step.

"Go on. Get it out yo' system," she said.

"I'm sorry, I didn't mean to stare," Martin said, trying to look anywhere but at the black woman's severely burned face. It was no use. His eyes kept drifting back to her hairless scalp and the unnatural plastic-like smoothness to her skin. Her left lower eyelid drooped, and part of the nostril was missing. It was difficult to judge, but Martin guessed the woman's age to be fifty or so.

"Stare. Don't stare. Don't bother me none. Can't tell no difference."

Her corneas were clouded over. She was blind.

"You done?" she said.

"Yes, ma'am. I'm sorry."

"'Nuff apologizin'. Now it's my turn'a get a look at you."

"Umm…"

"Get over here," the woman said. She held her hands out in front of her and Martin stepped forward. The woman's fingers danced around his face.

"Ok, then," she said, satisfied. "Answer the question."

"What question?"

"I asked you whatchu was doin' next door. You one a Tyreke's idiot friends?"

"No, ma'am."

"Naw, didn't think so. You too polite. And you're white."

Martin was confused. "How can you tell?"

She offered only a boisterous, full chested laugh as explanation.

"Now," she said, after regaining her sensibilities, "answer the question."

"I'm here to pick up Danielle for a date."

"Oh, that's lovely. I sure do love that little girl. You show her a good time, now."

"I will," he said.

He lingered, unsure of what to do.

"Go on. You don't keep a good girl like her waitin'."

Martin obliged. On his way back to Danielle's, he looked back just once. Though she was blind, he swore she was watching him. Moments after Martin rang the doorbell, Danielle emerged looking more beautiful than he'd ever seen. She had on a pair of blue jean shorts that hugged her curves and a loose fitting halter, embroidered with a retro flower print. Her black hair bounced on her shoulders as if it were fit with springs.

"You ready?" she said to Martin.

"As I'll ever be."

"Let's go then."

She locked the barred screen door behind her and followed Martin to the passenger side of the Chrysler where he opened her door.

"Ooh, so gentlemanly," she said, with a toothy smile.

"But, of course," Martin said.

He got in and immediately caught her staring at his legs.

"What?"

"Jeans? It's like ninety degrees out."

"I know. I'm an idiot."

"That's why I like you."

"Because I'm an idiot?"

"Yep." She leaned over and playfully squeezed the spot just above his right knee.

"Nice jeans, though," she said.

"Yeah, yeah."

She laughed and so did he.

"Ok, driver. Take me to the DIA!" she said.

Martin parked the Chrysler in the underground lot adjacent to the Detroit Institute of Arts. On the way to the steps leading back above ground, Danielle positioned herself so close to him that their fingertips grazed each other several times.

"So…whaddya think?" Danielle said, once they reached street level.

Martin glanced up at the regal white structure before him. It stood directly across the street from the only slightly less impressive Detroit Public Library. "I've seen this building before. We go to school right by here."

"I know, duh. But, I bet you haven't been this close."

"No, I haven't. It is a striking building. Very elegant. Is that all marble?"

"Yes. Designed by Paul Phillipe Cret, the museum opened in 1927."

"Wow."

"I did some research so I could be a proper guide to you on this, your very first time in the city."

She curtseyed.

"Impressive," Martin said.

"I know, right? But it's nothing compared to what's inside."

She walked ahead, taking the steps to the entrance two at a time. He followed her after briefly pausing to take in the cast of Rodin's Thinker facing Woodward.

Once inside, Danielle guided him to the Great Hall. Battle armor lined the walls, with doorways on both sides leading to various galleries. The wide berth was bathed in natural light from the many windows beneath the arched ceiling.

On to the Diego Court she led him. The space was named after Diego Rivera, the artist who painted the series of murals that covered the walls. It was empty save for Danielle and Martin. He drifted from her, moving from wall to wall to examine the paintings, craning his neck to take in the smaller panels near the ceiling.

"Cool, huh?" Danielle said.

"Very cool. This is crazy intricate. It must have taken years to paint."

"Two, to be exact."

"Oh, I forgot you've researched everything in this place. So, tell me something interesting about it."

"Well, Edsel Ford, Henry's son, commissioned Diego Rivera to paint it in the early thirties. Even though it's kinda like the crown jewel of the Institute now, when he was finished, people weren't too impressed."

Martin walked across the marble floor and examined the mural on the North wall. It depicted an auto assembly line. The men flexed their sinewy arms, working in tandem with the machines to piece together America's wheels.

"Why not?"

"I guess it was supposed to represent the spirit of Detroit's industry, but some people took it as a window into Rivera's Marxist leanings. They especially didn't care for the nudes. It was considered pornographic for the time."

"Nudes?"

"Over there," Danielle said, pointing over to East wall. Martin tipped his head back and noted them.

"Ahh, I see."

"Martin Kerner, you pervert!" Danielle said, with a coy grin.

"Please. Those women look like amorphous blobs."

"That not your type?"

"Ahh, no."

"Well, then. What is?"

"Hmm...let me think," Martin said, tapping his finger to his chin and pretending to ponder her question. Feeling bold, he shortened the distance between them until the tips of their shoes were inches apart. He reached around her back and placed his hand on her waist. Like a plasma globe, he swore he could feel electricity when his fingers met the small bit of skin just below the hem of her top.

He leaned in.

"Martin," she said, pressing her hand to his chest. She gestured with her eyes for him to turn around.

They were not alone.

Behind him were upwards of ten elementary aged children who found Danielle and Martin far more interesting than the murals. Their chaperone, a frumpy, dull stick of a woman, was not amused.

"This is a family museum," she said, with her arms crossed over her chest.

Martin blushed and said, "Yes, I'm sorry. We were umm...I mean-."

Danielle grabbed his hand and dragged him out of the court and down a corridor that branched off the Great Hall. He had to jog to keep up, or risk letting go of her hand, which he had no intention of doing. After getting a bit of distance between them and the children, she stopped.

"What did you think you were you doing back there?" she said, slyly.

"Those kids appeared out of nowhere. They must be, like teleporters or something."

"No, they walked into the room, rather noisily I might add. You were too busy trying to be smooth."

"Trying and succeeding?" Martin winced.

Danielle raised her eyebrows and chuckled. "Sure. Anyways, I don't give it up on the first date, so you know."

"This is our second date."

"Shoot. That's right."

A devilish grin came over Martin's face.

"Don't get presumptuous. I never said I did anything on a second date, either" she said, walking on. "Come, we're wasting time. I got lots to show you."

He followed her down the corridor towards a large oil painting of calla lilies. She turned around and said, "It's the third date where anything goes."

After having whisked Martin around the museum in a rushed and chaotic mini-tour of her favorite works, they ended up in a small gallery featuring art of the late nineteenth century.

"This room has my favorite piece in this whole place," she said.

"Let me guess. That Van Gogh."

"Nope."

"Really? I'm actually surprised that's here," he said, wandering over to it.

"Why?"

"I mean, I would expect this be in New York or the Louvre or something."

"It's right where it belongs. Anyways, the one I love is by James Whistler. Come look," she said, summoning him.

The painting was titled *Nocturne in Black and Gold, The Falling Rocket.* The pair stood before it without saying a word for over a minute, before Danielle looked up at Martin, eager for his interpretation.

"So…" she said.

Martin opened his mouth, but hesitated, wanting to choose his words carefully.

"It's nice."

"Nice?" Danielle sneered.

"I don't know. It's kind of sloppy."

"Are we looking at the same painting?"

"What? It's nice, but we saw Rembrandts, Matisses, Warhols, that Van Gogh..."

"So? Here, take another look. If you really try, you can see the bridge over the Thames. And down there, the people. When I was a little girl, I'd close my eyes and pretend I was one of them, on the riverbank. I could hear the launch of the fireworks, and feel that anticipation before they'd explode and fill the sky in brilliant light. I wanted to be there, reaching up for the falling embers."

"No offense, but all I see is a big black mess."

"Well, I feel sorry for you," she said. Her voiced lacked that usual vigor Martin had grown accustomed to. Neither moved nor spoke for a few awkward seconds. Martin was caught in limbo, wondering if it best he continued browsing or stay tethered to where he was.

"I'm hungry. You wanna go eat?" she said, breaking the silence.

"Sure."

She walked out of the gallery and Martin followed, absolutely sure he'd blown it.

They drove mostly in silence down Woodward towards downtown. Danielle directed Martin to an ivy covered building on Montcalm St which housed a tavern. She popped out to get them a table and he parked the car about a block away. Once inside, he found the place to his liking. It was busy but not overcrowded, and elegant without pretension. He found Danielle seated at a high top in the corner.

"Nice in here. I like the old school tin ceiling and dark woods. And these windows really offer good views of the street," Martin said, trying to jumpstart the conversation.

"Yeah. It is nice," Danielle said, gazing out the aforementioned windows.

"And that library behind the bar. It would be cool to just curl up on that couch with a good book and a beer."

"Umm hmm," she said, this time peering up at a small plasma television broadcasting the baseball game. Detroit was beating Tampa early, 1-0.

"I'll bet this place gets bumpin' when there's a home game with the stadium right near-, Hey, Danielle," he said, waving a hand in front of her face.

She snapped out of her delirium, appearing a little embarrassed.

"Everything cool?" he asked.

"Yeah. Fine."

The waitress came over and took their drink orders. They both ordered beers. Martin a Bud Light, and Danielle a vanilla porter from a local brewery.

"Vanilla porter. That sounds interes-,"

""Back there at the DIA...," Danielle said, cutting him off.

"Ahh, yeah. About that. I didn't mean-,"

"When you said that the Whistler was a sloppy mess, I was going to say that, while I think you are a dummy who wouldn't know a masterpiece if it smacked you in the face...I really appreciated your honesty. It took guts to disagree with me. It tells me you are your own man, capable of making your own decisions and...it's kinda sexy."

"It is?"

"Mmmhmm, and...it inspired me."

"To do what?"

"I want to do this right. You know, this," she said, gesturing between them.

"This, as in, like, our date?"

"Us...well, if there is gonna be an 'us.' I want to start off just dripping honesty. No secrets."

"Fair enough. Ask me anything."

"Your dad. Spill it."

The waitress dropped off their drinks and Martin took a large gulp.

"It's simple really," he said, wiping his mouth of the froth. "He's an asshole, a drunk and a bigot."

"Wow!" she said, surprised.

"How about yours?"

"Well," she said, taking a gulp of her own. "I got you beat. Never met him and hope I never do."

172

"What happened?"

"He left when my mom told him she was pregnant. How's that for an asshole?

"I don't know if I'd say you had me beat. Why don't we call it a draw?"

"Sure. My turn. The logical next topic would be moms."

Martin tensed up.

"Unless…" Danielle said, noticing.

"No, no. This is good. I like that we're doing this. My mom, she…she was awesome. Kind, nurturing, supportive."

"Was?" Danielle said, wincing.

"Brain cancer. Couple years back."

"Sorry. If it makes you feel any better, my mom passed, too."

"That actually makes me feel worse. How did she go, if you don't mind me asking?"

"Drugs."

"Oh…I'm sorry…I-,"

"It's ok. I'm not ashamed. My mom was a soldier. She fought her addiction her whole adult life. Was clean for fifteen years after Tyreke was born, then fell into it again two years ago. Crack mostly. I was raised by my neighbor for the first four years of my life."

"Not that lady on the right?"

"Yeah?" Danielle said, confused. "You know Ma Laika?"

"It's not like I know her. She kinda gave me a once over when I got to your place."

"She feel up your face?"

"Yeah. It was a bit odd."

"Naw. It's just how she sees."

They both took another sip of their respective beers.

"She musta liked you."

"Why?"

"Cuz she didn't chase you off with her big stick."

"What?"

"Yeah. She keeps it under her chair. She must have chased four or five of my dates away over the years. Runnin' down the sidewalk, wavin' a big ol' branch at 'em."

She chuckled and said, "It's kinda funny actually."

"Not for those boys."

"Maybe not, but they were douchebags anyways. She knew it, too. She can always tell."

The waitress came back and took their food orders. They both got sandwiches with sweet potato fries.

"How'd she get the…" Martin said, gesturing to his face.

"During the riot, her house got set on fire. She lost her mom and little sister. She was only a kid herself at the time. A neighbor pulled her out, but she's been blind ever since."

"So your mom left you with a blind woman?"

"Guess she thought it was better than being with a crack addict. I never felt unsafe with her. We'd just sit on her porch, sippin' Vernors, sometimes with a little scoop of vanilla, and listen to the radio. And when there wasn't nothin' good on, we'd just sing."

"Sing what?"

"Motown. Smokey, Diana. She'd always put me up on her lap and do "My Girl" by the Temptations."

A warm smile came to her lips as she remembered those lazy summer afternoons on Ma Laika's porch. Martin watched her and finished the last sip of his Bud Light. He set the empty pint glass down and glanced around the room. It had become much busier and the noise level had risen accordingly. The crowd was a mix of young and old, black and white. Some were in casual attire, others in fancy dress, presumably coming in for drinks before a show at one of the nearby theaters.

"So you said your mom got clean after getting pregnant, so where was Tyreke's dad through all of it?"

She shrugged her shoulders. "She got knocked up at some crack house over on the East side during one of her rough periods. She said she had no recollection of ever hookin' up with anyone. If anything, that might have been her wake-up call."

"I see. What's he like, anyway? Your brother."

Her eyes lit up with genuine pride. "He's a good kid. Crazy smart, too."

"Really?"

"Yeah. He's like you. A brilliant mind. You and him would probably get along real well."

Martin pictured the death stare he got from Tyreke that day in front of the café, and seriously doubted their compatibility. "I'm sure we would. So what's so smart about him?"

"For starters he's a really bangin' writer. He's always comin' up with these stories and poems. They're so good. Oh, and he tutors me on my college math even though he hasn't even started his senior year yet."

"Cool. So he's been able to stay away from the drugs and gangs and stuff."

"After watching what my mom went through with drugs, there's no way he would get messed up in that. There's probably nothing in the world we both hate more. Plus, I work a ton so he don't have to worry about slingin' dope."

"You do? Where?"

"I tend bar at this dive just around the corner from here. The money ain't that good, though. I want something classier. The Kahn-Hudson Hotel is supposed to be reopening with a couple restaurants inside. I might try to get in over there."

"The what hotel?"

"On Washington."

Martin gave her a blank stare.

"Nevermind," she said.

"Yeah, sorry. I know about four Detroit streets now. Woodward, Warren, Evergreen, and Chene."

"Chene? Why do you know that one?"

Martin thought back to that snowy night with Dan Schoenfeld. He did not feel that it was the best time to be admitting that at his lowest point he drove in a snowstorm in the middle of the night looking for drugs, especially after hearing about her mother.

"I think I saw it on a freeway sign. Anyways, it's cool you work so your brother can just focus on school, and not get caught up in the crime like I'd bet a lot of kids in a rough neighborhood like yours do."

"My neighborhood ain't rough. Sure there are a few vacant homes, but I don't think it's any worse off than most."

Martin thought differently, but decided not to debate it. He had offended her earlier at the art museum, and he didn't want to do it again. Lucky for him, that's when the waitress returned with their food.

She set the plates in front of them and took their next drink orders. Danielle ordered something called a Ghettoshocker and Martin switched up to the porter. They each took a bite from their sandwiches.

Martin looked up at Danielle with a look of utter seriousness.

"I'm sorry," he said, with a mouthful of mahi-mahi.

"For what? That neighborhood comment? It's no big d-,"

"Sorry for you that you didn't order this."

He took another bite. "It's probably way better than that chicken parm."

She smiled. "I don't know. This is pretty darn good."

He held his sandwich in front of her face. She hesitated and took a bite and then moaned in delight.

"That *is* really good," she said.

"Right?"

"Here, try mine." She offered Martin a bite, which he gladly accepted. They debated the merits of each sandwich and steadfastly declared that their own was superior. They laughed and ate and drank, forgetting temporarily the poor hand they each had been dealt in regards to their parents.

After another round and some of the best conversation Martin had ever had, they made their way back to the car.

"Let's cross a couple 'I nevers' off your list before we call it a night. Cool?" Danielle said.

"Cool."

Martin followed her directions as she navigated him around the city's confusing spoked-wheel street design. Park to Madison to Beaubien to Gratiot, she pointed and proselytized with an infectious enthusiasm.

Around Campus Martius Park they circled, where Danielle bragged about how her city's ice rink was bigger than that puny one at Rockefeller Center. Then south on Woodward to Jefferson they went where she made Martin loop around so he could get not one, but two extended looks at the Joe Louis fist they'd discussed in class.

"And finally…" Danielle exclaimed as she guided Martin back north on Woodward. "The pièce de résistance. The iconic Spirit of Detroit!"

Perched on his right was a twenty-six foot tall bronze man in a loin cloth. He was on his knees, hunched over with his arms spread wide.

"Oh, I've seen that before," Martin said.

"In person?"

Martin shook his head sheepishly. "I must admit it is much bigger than it looks on television."

"Uh huh. Cross it off the list."

Above the man's right shoulder, carved into the façade of the Coleman A. Young Municipal Center was the Seal of the Detroit. Martin squinted at the words with a confused look on his face.

"What does *Speramus Meliora Resurget Cineribus* mean?"

"It's Latin," she said.

"I got that part. Latin for what?"

She shrugged. "I'm sorry. The free portion of the tour is now concluded."

"What? You don't know?"

"We thank you for your patronage," she continued, with a Stepford-like grin on her face. "And do remember, tips are not expected but are always appreciated."

"Creepy."

"Whatever," she said, smacking him playfully on the shoulder. "Hang a right up here, Jeeves. We can cruise Greektown on the way to the freeway."

Martin complied and it was almost midnight when they finally pulled back into her driveway. On the street in front of her house was Tyreke's Grand Prix.

"So you spent the evening in the 'D' and you survived. You're such a brave soul," Danielle said.

"I know. It was a harrowing experience, but I came through."

"It doesn't have to be over."

"No?"

"You wanna come inside?"

Martin wanted nothing else more in the world than to come inside and finally feel those lips against his and that electricity when his fingertips met her skin, but that Grand Prix deterred him.

"Isn't Tyreke home?"

"Yeah, but its Friday. I'm sure he'll be leavin' soon. He's always out with his boys."

Almost on cue the front door opened and he came, dressed in an oversized plain white t-shirt and a pair of so low they defied gravity khaki shorts. His navy blue baseball cap was pulled down low and to the side as before, but even in the meager light, Martin could just see Tyreke's eyes were on him.

"See, he's leaving. Come," she said. She opened the door and got out. Martin did as he was told, and got out as well. He stayed back by the car, though, instead of following her towards the house.

"Where you been?" Tyreke said.

"Me and Martin went downtown for dinner and a couple drinks. Where you goin'?"

"Dinner and drinks?"

"Yeah."

"With him?"

"Yes," she said, this time in a firm tone. She wasn't interested in a continued dialogue with him on her choice of dating partners.

He scoffed and shook his head.

"I'm out," he said and jumped down from the porch to the walk. He strode to his car, only to stop when Danielle called after him.

"What, Dani?"

"Where you goin'?" she asked.

"I ain't know. Get some food or some shit."

"Oh, damnit!" Danielle shouted, covering her mouth in a failed attempt to prevent the already escaped swear from coming out.

"What?" Martin said, confused by her outburst.

"I screwed up. My plan was to take you to Lafayette to finish the night off. I completely forgot, and we drove right past there, too."

"What's Lafayette," Martin asked.

Tyreke busted out laughing. He leaned on the fence to keep from falling over due to the hilarity of it all. Martin found his reaction to be a bit exaggerated.

Over his fit, Tyreke was able to get out, "Who ain't know Lafayette 'round here? Where you been livin', bro?"

"Hazel Park," Martin said, still confused.

"Martin, Lafayette is a coney island. THE coney island," Danielle said.

"Oh, I see. Another time, maybe."

"Yeah. I guess so."

Danielle's face lit up with epiphany.

"Or..." she said, locking eyes on her brother.

"Or what?" Tyreke said.

"Or you can run down there real quick and bring some back."

"Aww, hell no! I ain't drivin' all the way there just-,"

"It's fifteen minutes. Martin will go with you," she said.

Martin and Tyreke exchanged quizzical looks.

"I, uhhh..." was all Martin could get out.

"Hell to the N-O. No. I got shit to do," Tyreke added.

"Excuse me Martin," Danielle said, pulling her brother aside.

"Need I remind you that you owe me one?" she chided him.

"F'what?"

"Your little stunt on Cass the other day."

Tyreke resisted at first, but when Danielle gave him the wide eyed scowl he'd seen since childhood, he knew she meant business.

"Fine," he said, begrudgingly.

"Then it's settled," she said, turning back to Martin.

"It is?" he said, still unsure of what had just transpired.

"You boys have fun. Oh, and get me some fries, too. Ooh, with chili!"

She went inside the house and closed the door. Tyreke stomped over to his car, muttering under his breath. Martin looked at Tyreke and shrugged. He said, "Hey, man. I didn't know anything about-,"

"Just get in the car, homeboy."

Tyreke got in the Grand Prix and slammed the door. Within seconds the engine was running and the bass was rattling the trunk. Martin took a deep breath and looked around. He walked over to the car and before he got in, he pulled the Chrysler's key fob from his pocket and pushed the lock button twice.

CHAPTER XVI
AUGUST 2, 2008

Each time the beat dropped, everything within the Grand Prix's dingy gray interior vibrated; the seats, the rearview mirror, the rolling papers in the cup holder. Martin swore he could even feel his intestines shifting within his abdominal cavity.

They left the neighborhood and pulled out onto Evergreen and then onto the eastbound ramp for I-96. When the beat dropped again Martin reached his limit. Knowing it was an action not likely to be appreciated by his companion, he reached over to the radio and lowered the volume.

"What the shit?" Tyreke bellowed.

"Man, it's too much. There's no way I coulda rode all the way downtown with the whip bangin' like that."

"You don't touch a nigga's stereo, dawg."

"Sorry, bro."

"Bro?" Tyreke scoffed.

"What?"

Tyreke offered only a sideways glance as a response.

"Seriously. What?" Martin asked.

"You funny."

"Funny how?"

Tyreke leaned back in his chair with just his right hand on the wheel. He said nothing.

"C'mon, yo. What I do?" Martin said.

"Yeah, that. Right there."

Martin was confused.

"Tyreke, man. I know this isn't what we both want to be doing right now, but you gotta give me something. I'm not about to do the whole *Goodfellas* scene with you."

Tyreke fixed his steely gaze at the moonlit concrete expanse before them. The freeway's fourteen lanes, seven in each direction, were sparingly occupied.

"Whatever," Martin said.

Tyreke sighed. "You funny cuz you talkin' all gangsta."

Martin let out a scoff of his own. "Gangster? How?"

"You talkin' bout bangin' beats and whips and shit."

"That's gangster?"

"Then you called me yo' bro."

"Why is that bad?"

"Cuz I ain't yo' bro!"

"I didn't mean it in a hood way."

"No? Who else you call 'bro' recently? Huh? Yo' tennis partner at the country club? You go up to yo' financial advisor and say,'Yo, bro. I need you to get me s'more a 'dat GE stock. Hook a nigga up.'?"

"Wow!" Martin said, shaking his head.

"Naw. That shit was you tryna' act hood."

Martin opened his mouth to deliver a scathing rebuttal, but decided against it. For one, Danielle had thrown them together into this situation for a reason and he was pretty sure it wasn't to fight with each other. Also, the more he thought about it, he realized Tyreke was right.

"Look, man. I can tell you have a problem with me but it doesn't have to be this way. So, I'm sorry if I offended you. I guess, subconsciously my speech just assimilated to what I perceived you wanted to hear. I didn't mea-,"

"Blah, blah, assimilated, blah, blah...bullshit," Tyreke said, mocking him.

"What? What are you doing? Are we five years old?"

"Now you tryna' act all high and mighty with your big ass words."

"What? Assimilated?" Martin said, now agitated. "According to your sister, you're a wunderkind-, oh sorry. I mean, boy genius."

"Don't patronize me, man."

"Patronize? That's a big word."

"Motherfucker, I know what assimilate means, *and* wunderkind. But *you* didn't know I knew that. That's you tryna' use language as a means to marginalize me."

"No. That was just me talking."

"Why I wanna talk to some slummin' ass suburban white boy, tryna' cross 'fuck a nigger bitch' off his bucket list?"

"Don't call her a ni-!"

Tyreke reached across the cab and grabbed Martin by the collar.

"Dontchu dare!" Tyreke yelled. The Grand Prix followed his momentum across the center lane.

"What are you doing!" Martin yelled, his hand wrapped around Tyreke's narrow wrist, trying to wrestle the hand from his collar.

"I should kick yo ass right here!" Tyreke yelled. The Grand Prix continued to veer right.

"Are you out of your mind? Watch the road!"

"Fuck you!"

A light caught the corner of Martin's eye. He craned his neck around and saw a large semi barreling down in the slow lane. A lane both vehicles would soon occupy.

The driver flashed his high beams.

"Tyreke! Move the car!"

The semi closed in. Two hundred feet. One hundred. Still, Tyreke ignored Martin's pleas. "Come up in my spot with my sister and then start droppin' nig-,"

The cabin was filled light and the only sound in the world was the semi's thunderous horn. Martin braced for impact and his almost assured death. The impact did not come, though. The Grand Prix rocked side to side from the wind current generated when the big truck sped by on the shoulder.

Tyreke, seeming dazed, relinquished his hold on Martin's shirt and slumped into the driver's seat once again.

Martin adjusted his shirt and straightened up in the seat. He could feel his heartbeat in his throat.

"Goddamnit!" he said, his voice shaking.

"Wouldn't a' happened if you kept yo' mouth shut," Tyreke said, attempting to come off nonchalant, but the tremor in his voice suggested otherwise.

"Yeah, well…because you gotta be so hard, you almost got us killed."

Tyreke turned from him. For the next several miles there was silence until, thankfully it was broken by the ring of Tyreke's cell phone.

"Whatupdoe," Tyreke said to his caller, apparently over their close call. "When you gonna come through wit' dat fine ass of yours?"

Due to their close quarters, Martin found it impossible not to eavesdrop.

"Oh, I'll get the stuff. I'mma 'bout to run up in the spot now."

Martin watched the exits fly by through the windshield. Davison, Grand River, Joy Rd. Right as they approached the ramp to merge onto I-94, Tyreke finished his conversation.

"Yeah, girl. I see you in a minute. Y'know I'mma 'bout to tear it up, too."

He had a big smile on his face when he put the phone back in his pocket, but his expression returned to a hardened façade once he noticed that Martin was looking at him.

"Was that your girlfriend?" Martin asked.

"Naw. Just some bitch I be fuckin' wit'."

"There's that word again. How come every girl has gotta be a bitch?"

"You the grammar police?"

"Didn't your dad ever tell you that's not a way to refer to a woman?" Martin said. As soon as it was out of his mouth, he regretted it. He had forgotten that Danielle told him Tyreke never met his father.

"No, cuz I ain't know the mu'fucka. So I'm sorry that no one ever told me to talk all proper and shit, like your rich ass daddy."

"My dad is not rich. You keep sayin' stuff like that. I come a from blue collar, workin' class suburb. There's no Caddy in our driveway and I've never been to any country club. Anyways, my dad is a certified prick. Any advice he ever gave me wasn't worth shit anyways."

"Yeah, well, at least you know what he looks like."

As they approached downtown, the traffic picked up, albeit slightly. They passed the Trumbull Ave exit.

"She know you call her that?" Martin asked.

"Who? Shanice? She call *herself* that. She's say that she my 'main bitch'. She wrong, but that's what she say."

"Still seems like you shou-."

"It's just a word, yo!"

Martin briefly contemplated letting it go, but only briefly.

"All right. If words don't matter-,"

"Goddamn! You don't shut up, do you?"

"If words don't matter, how come you almost got us killed over two little syllables."

"Hold up. Hold up. Nigger ain't just two syllables."

"No?"

"Hell, no! Quit that actin' all ignorant. You know it ain't the same."

"Ok, fine. I'll admit that. But why? Both terms are used to degrade."

"Not if we use 'em, they ain't. For us, they terms of endearment."

"So the word's meaning changes based on the skin tone of the speaker?"

"Absolutely."

"Objectively, it should be the same. I guess I don't understand that."

"Well, maybe it ain't for you to understand."

Tyreke took the Chene Rd exit.

"Whoa, whoa! This ain't downtown!" Martin said, panicked.

"You mad, bro? I just gotta make a quick stop. You'll get your hot dog."

"It's not that. It's just…"

"What?"

Though the roads were dry and the weather warm, Martin felt a chill and anticipated the Grand Prix spinning out as the approached the gas station on the corner. He didn't respond to Tyreke, who did not press him further. Martin just looked out the window at the blighted streets. They were remarkably unchanged from the version in his mind's eye from that fateful night.

Tyreke turned left on Farnsworth.

As the alley approached on Martin's right, he was certain they *had* been struck by that semi, he was dead and now in his own personal Hell. It was the only logical conclusion as the probability of Tyreke just happening to take them down the same streets was just too low. He pinched his arm, hard enough to cause himself to wince, to no avail. He was alive, though at that moment, he took little solace in that.

Tyreke turned right onto Mitchell St. and brought the Grand Prix to a stop in front of a small, two story, brick house. A light was on inside. It was the only home on the block that looked occupied. The house to the left was boarded up, and 'keep out' was spray painted on the plywood that served as a front door.

"All right. You stay put. I'mma just uh…, you know. I be right back," Tyreke said. He reached behind his seat and grabbed a backpack, which appeared empty to Martin. He stepped out of the car, but before he could close the door Martin said, "Wait! I'm not sitting in this car on this street by myself."

"I'll only be a minute. Not even. Look, I parked you under the street light. You'll be fine. Anyways, if some big, black, scary nigga rolls up on you, just play dead." He laughed.

"Not funny, man."

Tyreke tossed the keys on the driver's seat.

"Circle the block or some shit if you gettin' freaked. Just don't leave my ass."

He shut the door and walked up the path to the stairs where Martin lost him in shadow. Martin reached over and picked up the keys. He jiggled them to and fro within his palm. The clanging of the metal distracted him from his paranoia until he looked around and realized how alone he was. He peered out his side window, and found nothing but darkness and the silhouettes of scattered pine trees.

He was getting hot.

Martin put the keys in the ignition and cracked the windows. A light breeze trickled in. Martin closed his eyes and let it pass over him. With each breath, he could feel some of his anxiety fading away until he heard it.

He opened his eyes and leaned his ear to the window. It was barely audible, but mixed in with the cricket's summer serenade was a low, guttural reverberation.

A growl.

He looked around him, and the street was as empty and forgotten as before, but the snarl continued. And it was close.

Before he knew it, he was standing in the street with the keys splayed between his fingers as a makeshift weapon. He should have been scared, but he wasn't. Maybe it was curiosity. Maybe delirium. But something carried him across the pavement and up the stairs to the porch of the house next door to Tyreke's acquaintance. He stepped over a pile of broken glass and peered into the home's paneless front window. He could see nothing, but the snarl was immediate, ravenous.

With a shaky hand, he pulled his cell phone from his pocket, and turned on the flashlight. There, in the corner of the abandoned home's foyer, amidst a pile of garbage, was the source.

A pit bull.

He noticed Martin and the snarl stopped. He was white, and had a black spot circling his left eye. He measured Martin with his head tilted slightly to the left. There were what appeared to be entrails, glistening with blood, dangling from its mouth. Martin followed them down to the floor, and found the remains of a small puppy. The pit bull, deciding that Martin was not a threat to its dinner, lowered its head back into the puppy's abdomen and resumed its feast.

Martin retched, and stumbled backward on the broken glass. He nearly tumbled down the steps, but was able to catch himself. He crouched down and put his head between his legs. With his eyes clenched shut, he sucked in and released the humid night air, fighting the urge to vomit.

"Hey yo, Flip," Tyreke said as he stepped into the front room.

"Whatupdoe," replied Phillip 'Flip' Washington, from his perch on a purple, faux-leather couch.

The elder cousin to Temarious 'T-Mar' Washington, Flip wore an unrepentant scowl and an all blue jumpsuit that clung tightly to his oversized, muscular frame. Around his neck was a questionable looking chain adorned with a garish 'F' and in his left hand, a 9mm Beretta. Tyreke offered him dap, and sat opposite him in a matching purple faux-leather recliner.

Spread before them on a white oval pressboard coffee table with gold trim, was an assortment of narcotics. Each was neatly packaged in small baggies, for ease of distribution.

"So, you got anything for me?" Flip asked.

Tyreke reached into his pocket and pulled out a roll of bills held together by rubber bands. He handed it to Flip, who quickly peeled back the corners of the bills. Satisfied, he set the roll down on the table by the drugs.

"You doin' good work, my nigga" he said. He pointed at the pharmacologic menagerie on the table. "This shit yours. I'mma need you to move it quick. Got a big buy this week and I gots to have the cheddar."

"I feel you," Tyreke said. He picked up the baggies with the pills and rocks and stuffed them in the backpack.

"Real talk, though," Flip said. "You pushin' weight like a mu'fuckin' pro. Used to be chasin' my ass up and down Schoolcraft, 'bout ten years old shoutin' 'Flip! Flip! Lemme be in yo' crew.' Now look atcha."

"'preciate ya."

"How's the old hood, these days? Them Fenkell Lordz givin' you any shit?"

Tyreke shook his head.

Flip nodded. "Good. Wish I could be there to move all this myself, but I gots to hold it down over here, look out for my aunt and lil' cuz 'til Temarious get out."

"When is that?"

"He up for parole in a minute. We'll see. The gun, them pills...if I ever catch the mu'fucka who set his ass up..."

Flip's expression grew dour. As he drifted off to some dark recess in his mind, Tyreke fidgeted uncomfortably in his chair and recalled how Flip had garnered his moniker.

Initially Phillip became Flip due to Temarious' inability to pronounce Phillip properly as a toddler. But that was just amongst family. The streets didn't christen him Flip until later after he'd risen through the ranks of the drug game. Once word spread of his tendency to abruptly flip from a state of calm to one of rage, often for seemingly innocuous offenses, the name stuck. Tyreke, as a star-struck youth, had dismissed the stories of unmentionable horrors cast down on Flip's enemies as urban fable, but the pall that had just overcome Flip's face suggested their validity was entirely plausible.

Flip began again, having returned from whatever murky place he'd gone. "Keep it up, lil' nigga. I see big things fo-,"

There was movement just outside the window. Flip grabbed his gun and jumped off the couch. He tucked behind the curtain and took a peek.

"The shit?" he said.

"What? Someone movin' on you?"

"Shit, no. Looks like some white boy fuckin' around next door. Another'a these ruin porn mu'fuckas."

Tyreke went to the window, and when he saw Martin stumbling over the glass and nearly falling, all he could muster was 'shit' under his breath.

Flip turned to him, casually waving the pistol around like an extension of his hand. "You know him?"

"No...well, I guess so. He came with me."

Flip crossed his arms over his puffed out chest, and raised his eyebrows, waiting for an explanation.

"He ain't my boy, or nothin'. He's just some white boy my sister's chillin' with," Tyreke said.

"What?" Flip said, seething.

"I...uh...,"

Flip stepped up into Tyreke's chest.

"One of my niggas ain't gon' have no sister messin' round wit' no cracka'."

"I already told her. I-,"

"You end that shit. Now."

"I'll try."

"No try. You end it. Or I will."

Just like that, the props for moving the drugs were gone. No more waxing nostalgic about the good old days on Schoolcraft Rd. All that was left was the way Flip's index finger stroked the trigger of the Beretta.

"I will, yo. I wi-,"

At that moment, a pigtailed little girl, Tyreke guessed her age to be no more than six, came bounding into the room. She was wearing pink pajamas with a fairy on the front.

"Whatchu doin' Phillip?" she asked, rubbing her eyes.

"Latrice! What the fu...Why you outta bed?" Flip said, tucking the pistol into his pants. The little girl jumped on the couch, and picked up the money roll. She tossed it up and tried to catch it, but it fell to the carpet. She giggled and picked it up, only to toss it and drop it again.

"Latrice, get upstairs," Flip shouted.

A voice came from upstairs. "WHAT'S ALL THE SCREAMIN' BOUT?"

"LATRICE IS OUTTA BED, AUNTIE! AND I GOT BIDNESS," he shouted back.

After a short delay, the voice bellowed, "LATRICE, GET YOUR BUTT BACK TO BED!"

The little girl, after dropping the roll a third time, huffed and puffed, and made her way back upstairs and out of sight.

Tyreke walked over near the couch and picked up the roll of money. Flip snatched it out of his hand, and stuffed it into his pocket.

"Get the fuck outta here and move that shit," he said.

Tyreke grabbed the backpack and rushed out the door.

"Get yo' head out yo' ass and let's roll," Tyreke shouted. Martin lifted his head and saw Tyreke sprinting towards the Grand Prix. He got in and tossed the backpack, pregnant with its newfound weight, behind the driver's seat.

"Come on, homeboy, or you'll be walkin'."

Martin stood up on rubbery legs and gingerly made his way to the car. He got in and handed Tyreke the keys.

They were barely half a block southbound on Mitchell when Tyreke smacked his hand against the dashboard, startling Martin.

"Why you have to get out the car? Huh? Why couldn't you stay your ass in the car for five minutes?"

Martin, still trying to settle his stomach, was confused. "What's the big deal?"

Tyreke shook his head. The image of Flip's Beretta waving around in his right hand was all he could think of. "You shoulda just stayed in the car, man."

"Well, I heard a noise and I had to go check it out. Now I wish I had ignored it."

"What noise?" Tyreke said.

"I heard a snarl or growl coming from that house next door. So I went up there and there was a pit bull eating another dog in there. A puppy."

Tyreke stared straight ahead without so much as a blink. "Mmmhmm," he murmured.

"Mmmhmm? That's it? That was crazy. I about fell off the porch and threw up, and all you say is mmmhmm?"

"I seen worse."

"But it was eating one of its own. You'd think it would have some innate mechanism to prevent doing that."

"Only thing innate is survival," Tyreke said.

Neither of them spoke again for several minutes. Martin watched Tyreke merge the Grand Prix back onto I-96, this time going west, toward Brightmoor. He leaned back and looked at the bag behind Tyreke's seat.

"What's in the bag?"

"Don't concern you," Tyreke said.

"Right. Rough neighborhood, in and out of the house in a couple minutes...I got a pretty good idea of what's in there."

"Like I said...it don't concern you."

"It'll concern me if we get pulled over. Try to at least keep it under eighty."

Tyreke didn't say anything, but he did just as Martin advised. Once they past the Davison interchange, Martin said to Tyreke, "You're sister paints an entirely different picture of you. Academic. Writer. Model citizen."

Tyreke was silent.

"And you know what's messed up?" Martin continued. "You came at me for acting gangster, when you are doing the same exact thing."

"I am gangsta."

"No, you're not but I can tell you *wanna* be, for some ungodly reason. The clothes, the talk, the scowl. You got that all down pat. But, you're a fraud. Gangsters don't use words like 'marginalize' and 'endearment'."

Tyreke sighed, and said, "And you are the authority on what is or isn't gangsta? Whatever. And anyways, you can go ahead and stop what you're doing, cuz I ain't hearin' it."

"What?"

"You're tryna' to do that cracker thing where you come down from the suburbs on your white horse like some savior."

"No, I'm not."

"Yeah, you are. Well, you know I don't need your help. If I wanna write, I'mma write. If I wanna push weight, I'mma do that, then. And, you know what else? I'mma talk gangsta if I want and that don't *preclude* me from being smart."

"I don't see why-,"

"You don't need to see shit! That's the beauty of it."

Martin sat back and shifted his attention out his window. The lines on the pavement flew by at a speed faster than his eyes could follow, but he kept trying nonetheless. He was never one to accept failure lying down.

After a few minutes, he turned to Tyreke and said, "What about J. Lo?"

"What?" Tyreke said with a look of complete bewilderment.

"Didn't she say the 'N' word in one of her songs?"

"Yeah...so?"

"Well..."

"She's Latina. They fall into a kind of gray area."

"I think I'm like ten percent Spanish. Does that make it ok?"

Tyreke slid his cap off his head and ran his hand down his tight fade.

"What about Asians?"

"What about 'em?"

"Are they allowed to say it?"

"No. Man, I don't know. Why? You ten percent Asian, too?"

"No."

"This guy..." he said, acting exasperated but Martin saw a slight grin breaking through his tough guy front.

"What about if I wanted to say the name of the rap group N.W.A.?"

"Man, what's your problem?"

"I want to know. Plus, I've never had this long of a conversation with a black guy before. I'm taking advantage."

"How you even know N.W.A? Don't you listen to like Garth Brooks, or some shit?"

"Well, yes...but I know N.W.A. It's classic west coast hip hop."

"All right. You wanna know how you'd say their name?"

"Yeah."

"You'd say N.W.A."

"So I can't even say it then."

"Nope. Sorry."

"Can I say N-word Wit Attitudes?"

"You can, but that's some clown shit," Tyreke said, allowing himself a subdued chuckle.

"Yeah, you're right," Martin said, matching him with one of his own.

Tyreke pulled the Grand Prix onto his street and parked in front of the house. Walking up the driveway, Martin realized they'd forgotten the coneys.

"Aww, man! We never went to Lafa-,"

"Hold up," Tyreke said, with a hand to Martin's chest. "Look, you seem like a good dude. Little confused but decent. I can tell. Real recognize real. So, I'mma give it to you straight."

"Before you go on, let me be straight with you first."

"A'ight. Go ahead."

"I was giving you shit back there and…it was a bit hypocritical. You see, I got caught up in drugs once, in college. In fact, it's weird, but it was right down the street from where we just were. Scariest night of my life. The dealer was this absolute nut-job. T-Mar, I think his name was."

"What!" Tyreke said.

"He ended up getting' arres-,"

"STOP!"

"What?" Martin said, confused. "I'm just being hon-,"

"MOTHERFUCKER, I SAID STOP!" Tyreke shouted, pulling a Glock 9mm pistol from his waistband.

"WHOA!" Martin said, stumbling back against the Chrysler.

Tyreke glanced at the house and the light on in the bedroom and then finally up into a sky full of stars.

"Un-goddamn-believable," he muttered, shaking his head.

"Look, man. I don't want any tr-,"

Tyreke stepped forward. "Stay the fuck away from Dani, Ok? And for that matter, stay out the D," Tyreke said.

"What? Why?" Martin said, noting a lack of conviction in Tyreke's eyes. "I thought, I mean…it seemed-,"

"Just go! Get yo' ass north of Eight Mile!"

Martin, confused as he was frightened, took one look at the reflection of moonlight dancing off of the 9mm's stainless steel body and knew that his night was over.

He got in the Chrysler and sped off, treating stop signs and red lights as mere suggestions until he reached I-96.

CHAPTER XVII
AUGUST 4, 2008

He was purposefully early.

At Higgins Hall, he took the stairs as he had so many times before, but instead of turning left down the corridor towards class and the final exam that would determine his future, Martin went straight towards the elevator bank. On the south wall was a showcase that housed flyers for upcoming events at the University. Martin perched in front of it and feigned interest in an ad for some type of African tribal drum and dance show called Ngoma Za Kongo. After a few minutes, she passed by. A wave of sadness came over him. He waited another minute to ensure she'd be settled in before making his way to class himself.

She was up top, right corner. Luckily for him, there was an open chair down left. With his head low, he slouched to it and sat. He turned his body away from her to avoid any risk of eye contact.

Abdul-Tawaab entered the room and set his briefcase down on the desk. He opened it and pulled out a stack of papers. Very deliberately, he handed out the stapled packets to each student, licking his index finger in between to separate them.

Martin was the last person to receive a test packet. Abdul-Tawaab loomed over him, packet extended. Martin grabbed it, but it did not immediately come free from the professor's grip. The lag was almost imperceptible. The casual observer may not have noticed at all, but Martin had to tug just a little to get Abdul-Tawaab to let go.

The professor took a few steps to the center of the class and brought his brawny hands together in a booming clap. The startled students' heads popped up and their pencil scraping ceased.

"You have fifty minutes," he said. "When you are finished, you are to place the test face down on my desk."

Within seconds, the graphite symphony commenced again. Martin examined the test's front page. In the top right corner was a space for his name, the name of the course in the top center, and below it was a single question; *Have race relations improved, worsened or stayed the same in Detroit since the 1967 riots?*

Martin flipped through the rest of the packet and was astonished to find nothing but blank sheets. That was it. His grade for the course, and therefore his future as a lawyer, was riding on answering a single question in such a way to appease a man that seemed to be out to get him from the first day of class, and who more than likely had an arbitrary standard known only to him on which the answer to the question would be judged. With a deep breath, and a crack of his knuckles, he began.

After ten minutes had elapsed, all Martin had come up with was "FUCK YOU." It was written in big block letters, albeit faintly for ease of erasure. He looked up and saw Abdul-Tawaab looking in his direction, expressionless. Somehow this spurred Martin into action. He wrote and wrote, filling all the sheets both front and back. When he finished, it was only 9:41, so he used the remaining time to proofread.

Slowly, the classroom emptied as each student rose up and placed their tests on Abdul-Tawaab's desk. Some smiled at him on their way out, others said "goodbye." He barely acknowledged them, save for the occasional nod.

It was Danielle's turn. Martin dared a glance in her direction. He marveled at her grace as she descended the steps. Even the simplest of things, like handing in a test, she did demurely and in a manner seemingly superior to anyone he'd ever met.

She floated by his desk on her way out of the classroom. At the door's threshold, she turned her head and caught him watching her. He quickly shifted his gaze back to his completed test, shuffling through the pages aimlessly for several seconds before hazarding another look towards the doorway. She was gone, but still he cursed his weak will and his eyes' wanderlust.

After a few minutes, Abdul-Tawaab cleared his throat twice. The first time sounded natural, but the next, which came not ten seconds later, was louder and obviously no phlegm loosening exercise.

Martin looked up to see the professor had risen and was staring in his direction. He gestured for Martin to look around. They were alone.

Martin made one more cursory glance at the test, and then gathered his things. He walked to Abdul-Tawaab's desk and set the test down on the pile with the others, face down as requested. He wanted to say something, one final attempt to get in Abdul-Tawaab's good graces, but he only lowered his head and walked out of the room.

His pace was brisk and his eyes locked on the exit at the end of the hall. He wanted out. Out of the building. Out of Detroit. Out of his father's house. Out of the last three months of his life.

The door to the stairwell approached on his right. He pushed through the gaggles of people and reached out to it, but was stopped when a hand clasped his left wrist. The hand was smooth and mocha colored. The nails were finely groomed and painted a bright red shade.

"Hey, Martin. What's the rush?" Danielle said, releasing his arm.

"Oh, hey. Where'd you come from?"

"I was standing over by the elevators waiting for you."

"Oh."

"How do you think you did?"

"Fine, I guess. We'll see what Abdul-Tawaab thinks," he said with his eyes on the doorway.

"I feel the same way. So…how come you were avoiding me this morning?"

"What? I wasn't," Martin said, with a mostly unbelievable poker face.

"Yeah, you were."

She clutched her notebook to her chest waiting for Martin to look at her, to no avail. His hand reached out to the door, once again.

"Hey!" she said.

"What?" he replied with a hint of irritation in his voice.

Danielle's eyes widened, surprised at his irascible tone.

"Whoa, tiger! I just thought we could talk for a bit."

"About what?"

"Well, can you at least look at me?" she said.

The door opened, briefly giving him a glimpse of the exit he so desired. He moved aside for a group of students to pass and then did as she asked. Her trademarked smile was absent. Her brow, furrowed.

"That's better," she said. "So…what happened Saturday night?"

A collage of images whizzed through his mind. A semi-truck barreling down on him. A gnarled up puppy. The glint of moonlight against stainless steel.

"Nothing," he said.

"Uhh, ok. You were supposed to come back to my place and chill. You know, with the coneys?"

"Oh, yeah. Umm, I just, you know, wasn't hungry anymore."

She looked confused. "That's fine but why didn't you at least come in and say bye instead of just driving off."

She searched his eyes for answers, but again Martin looked towards the door.

"Did I do something wrong?" she pleaded.

Martin started chewing at his lower lip. His breathing became more rapid and agitated.

"Martin!" she said, again grabbing his wrist.

"Just leave me alone!" he shouted, swinging his arm free. Startled, Danielle dropped her notebook to the floor. Heads turned throughout the busy hallway.

"Can't you see? This…" Martin continued, gesturing back and forth between them. "Us. It doesn't work. We don't belong together!"

By that point, all other conversation had ceased. The elevator doors were being propped open by onlookers not yet ready to ascend. Up and down the hall, fresh faces popped out from previously closed doors.

Martin moved from one judging expression to another until he finally landed on Danielle's. Her lips, the ones Martin so longed to kiss, quivered. The brown eyes that he'd gotten lost in began to well up. He turned and threw the door open to escape seeing a single tear stream down her cheek. He bristled past students coming up the stairs and was gone.

Abdul-Tawaab grabbed the papers on his desk and straightened them until not a single stray corner poked out. He placed the perfect stack in his briefcase that lied agape next to him. He brought the lid down and pressed until the clasp clicked. His hand slipped through the leather grip and he brought the briefcase to his side. He took a look around the room for any items left behind by his students. There were many times when he'd come across a purse, a half drunken bottle of Faygo or, in recent years, a cell phone just lying there unattended left behind by some absent minded student. This day there was nothing to be found.

He turned off the lights and exited the room and found Danielle and Martin to his right. Her notebook was lying on the ground in front of her. Abdul-Tawaab decided to lean against the doorjamb and join the onlookers.

Martin shouted at Danielle before storming off and in his wake he left that poor girl alone, at the mercy of dozens of preying eyes. Abdul-Tawaab saw her wipe the tears from her face and then grab her notebook from the floor before darting past him. She flung open the door for the women's restroom and disappeared from his sight.

The murmurs in the hall soon became louder until they reached the level of normal conversation. The bodies which had been frozen in place started moving again, and soon the hall was a hive of activity. If he had stepped out of the room just thirty seconds later, he would never have seen any of it.

But he *did* see it.

He looked down at the briefcase in his right hand and, after some consternation, he marched back into the room and flung open the light switch. He placed the briefcase back down on the desk and dialed in the combination to its locks. The latch popped open and he raised the lid. The stack of papers lied there, still without a single disheveled sheet. He grabbed it, and pulled the packet from the bottom of the pile. In the top right corner was the name Martin Kerner. He placed the remaining papers back in the briefcase and then sat at the desk. From his breast pocket he pulled a black felt tipped marker. He uncapped it with his bared teeth, and he read.

PART II

CHAPTER XVIII
SEPTEMBER 6, 2008

It was the right place.

He checked the scrap of paper on which he'd scribbled the room number.

Room 323, Higgins Hall.

The right place, but it still felt wrong. It was not where he belonged. Nonetheless, there he was, on a balmy late summer evening, staring through the frosted glass pane at the silhouette of the man on the other side clicking away loudly on a keyboard.

He raised a shaky hand and rapped his knuckles on the glass. The keystrokes stopped.

"Come in," Marid Abdul-Tawaab bellowed in his husky baritone.

Martin gripped the cold steel doorknob with his sweaty palm. The door slowly opened, creaking ever so slightly on its decades old hinges. He entered.

Only two of the four walls had any adornment. On one was a singular framed black and white picture of a despondent African American man seated in the back of a squad car bookended by two gun toting white cops. Behind the professor's desk were several small plaques and certificates circumnavigating a diploma from Grambling State University. On the desk was a calendar decorated with ringed coffee mug stains, a late twentieth century computer monitor and an old picture of two rather large black men. They were both dressed in all black.

Black pants. Black leather jackets. Even black berets.

Abdul-Tawaab sat bolt upright in his chair, looking almost regal, a king in his one hundred-fifty square foot domain. He took the briefest of glances at Martin before resuming his work.

"State your business. I don't have all day," he said.

Martin took a seat in a small leather office chair opposite the professor's desk. He found the seat to be quite low and had to look up to meet Abdul-Tawaab's eyes. He pulled the chair's lever for the hydraulic lift, but nothing happened.

"Mr. Kerner, would you kindly stop fussing with that chair and enlighten me on the reason you've interrupted my lesson preparation."

Martin cleared his throat and sat up as straight as he could. "Well, sir," he began. "I've come to dispute my grade."

"Oh, you have?" Abdul-Tawaab said, removing his reading glasses. He sat back in his chair and crossed his arms over his barreled chest.

"I called your office several times and emailed you, as well."

He waited a moment for some type of explanation from the professor on his lack of correspondence, but from the unyielding expression on Abdul-Tawaab's face, he gathered that none was coming.

"And, I need to get the 'A' transferred over to Ann Arbor by Monday or I lose my spot. As it stands, I'm already missing classes."

The professor remained silent.

Martin looked up into the eyes of the black prisoner. There was despair in them, but there was a hint of something else, too: defiance, perhaps.

"I've gone over every word I wrote," he continued, trying not to sound desperate, which he very much was. "And every single point I made...I just don't see how it was deserving of the grade you gave."

"It was 'B' work," Abdul-Tawaab stated, matter of factly.

"I respectfully disagree," Martin said.

Abdul-Tawaab sat forward. His thick and slightly grayed eyebrows turned down, and he said, "So *you* are the one who deems what is and what is not 'A' quality in my classroom?"

"No, sir. I feel a final exam based solely on a single essay question that requires more of an opinion rather than fact based response is flawed by design and open to many interpretations. Having said that, I would venture that I had a firm grasp on the subject matter, and my paper was 'A' quality."

The professor sat back in his chair and resumed his lesson prep.

"Please, sir. Can you at least tell me what I did wrong? Maybe I can explain myself."

Abdul-Tawaab pondered the question for such a long time that Martin did not know whether an answer was forthcoming. Just before he was about to get up and leave, the professor spoke.

"I found your paper to be a work of absolute fiction and an insulting attempt to coddle my sensibilities."

"How do you mean?"

"You wrote what you thought I wanted you to instead of what you truly feel."

"How can you ascertain that? To see inside my head and determine which thoughts are genuine and which are fraudulent?"

"Do you know what the term reaction formation means, Mr. Kerner?" he asked.

Martin shook his head.

"It's a psychology term. More or less it's a defense mechanism wherein someone masters their anxiety-producing emotions and impulses by exaggeration of the directly opposing tendencies."

"I don't follow," Martin said.

Abdul-Tawaab closed his eyes and sighed, as if to display how arduous the conversation had become. He continued, "For example, let's use a child molester. In order to deal with the intense anxiety and self-loathing that behavior may generate, the molester may contribute to a charity for abused children, or lobby for stricter laws against child abuse, et cetera. You understand?"

"I suppose, though I don't get the correlation."

Abdul-Tawaab opened up one of the drawers in his desk and leafed through a folder until he found Martin's paper. He flipped the pages until he reached the desired passage.

"Right here, 'Detroit State University is an island panacea surrounded by a sea of blight where the students and faculty seem to share the same color blindness'."

He scoffed and then said, "And here, 'In the forty some odd years since the riot's first stone was cast, the youth of Detroit are celebrating each other's differences instead of using them as a means to subjugate'. When I read that, I don't believe it. To me it's nothing more than the patronizing musings of someone hiding deep seeded racism. Frankly, I'd expect nothing less from the son of Jack Kerner."

The last sentence brought an acid taste to the back of Martin's throat. He choked it back down and searched for a response. A weak "Wh…what?" was all that he could produce.

"You are his son, correct?" Abdul-Tawaab asked.

Martin nodded.

"The Jack Kerner who was once a Detroit Policeman?"

"Yes, but that was a long time ago. Before I was born. What does he have to do with this?"

"You are aware of your father's rather controversial exit from the department, yes?"

"I asked him once, when I was younger. All he said was that he didn't have the stomach for police work."

"JESUS CHRIST," Abdul-Tawaab shouted. He sprung from his chair and paced the small area behind his desk with a fury that frightened Martin.

"Why is this my responsibility?" the professor asked himself while rubbing at his eye sockets.

"What, sir?"

"It should come from him."

"Whatever it is, I wish you'd just say it. Obviously, if he hasn't told me yet…whatever it is, he never will."

The professor's pacing slowed and he tried to regain some degree of the calm dignity that he usually carried himself with. He settled back into his chair and said to Martin, "This may irreparably damage how you regard your father."

"You cannot damage what's already destroyed."

The professor looked Martin square in the eyes and said, "So be it."

Over the next half hour Abdul-Tawaab laid forth an altogether different history of a man Martin thought he knew.

"Jack and a childhood friend, Franklin King, both joined the Detroit Police Department shortly after the last riot fire was extinguished in 1967. The two officers, however, took completely different career paths through the department. Franklin received multiple commendations within the first few years which led to promotion to investigator in late 1971," he said.

"Commendations for what?" Martin asked, not aware that man he was asking about was the same Franklin King who came to his rescue that night in the alley a few years prior.

"He received one for stopping an attempted robbery of the tour bus belonging to the band Jethro Tull outside of the Grande Ballroom in February of 1969. At around 9:00pm, while on patrol down Grand River, King saw two perpetrators armed with crowbars hanging around the bus. He observed and ultimately confronted the men. They attacked him but King was able apprehend one without drawing his weapon. The other man was arrested when back-up arrived. King's restraint from using excessive force under duress was used by the city as an example of the kinder and gentler post-riot Detroit Police Department."

"And what about my dad?"

"Well, Jack Kerner was given no such commendation, to say the least. His first year in the department, he received three separate reprimands for excessive force, each time due to his treatment of black prisoners, which made his participation in the STRESS unit curious."

"STRESS unit?"

"It was an acronym that stood for Stop The Robberies and Enjoy Safe Streets. The unit used mostly white squad members dressed in plain clothes as decoys to lure muggers."

"How?" Martin asked.

"Any means necessary. I witnessed it myself. It was over by St. Hyacinth on McDougall. This white cop kneeled down by the curb pretending to tie his shoe. He must have been lacing it up and then undoing it again over and over for damn near half an hour. All the while he had a wad of bills hanging out of his back pocket. Finally, some fool took the bait and went for it. The cop and a couple more of them that were staking the scene out pounced on him. They didn't kill him, but they came close."

"And nobody had a problem with their tactics?"

"Sure, some did. They were constantly under fire by the liberal community for their violent methods and many blacks viewed them as more dangerous than the muggers they were supposed to be catching. It didn't matter what anybody said. Within months, the unit had led to the deaths of several young blacks, and by the end of the unit's first year the number had climbed into the double digits."

"Did he personally…," Martin said.

"No. But he did get implicated in several lesser beatings. In retrospect, it probably was *because* of your father's violent nature that he was included in the STRESS unit to begin with."

Abdul-Tawaab paused for a moment to collect his thoughts, and continued, "It was December 4, 1972 when the unit was involved in a shootout with a group of young blacks, including an eighteen year old named Hayward Brown. The altercation left four officers wounded, and led to a city wide manhunt. Concerned that Kerner and the other STRESS unit members would act more as vigilantes rather than police, several of the departments more decorated officers were included in the manhunt."

"Like Franklin King?" Martin interjected.

"Exactly. Whether it was their past or by just plain chance, King ended up being partnered with Kerner during the search. It was Christmas Eve, almost three weeks since the shooting, and Brown and his accomplices were still on the loose. These are the facts, but the rest of what I'm about to tell you is based on testimony from the ensuing trial, and much diligent research."

"Who's research?"

Abdul-Tawaab got up from his desk and walked to a small bookcase in the corner of the room. He ran his finger along the dusty spines of several books before selecting one. He dropped it in Martin's lap. On the cover it read *Detroit's Post-Riot Landscape* by Marid Abdul-Tawaab. The professor made his way back around the desk and sat back down.

"Chapter nine is the one concerning the events involving your father. You can keep that one."

Martin shuffled through the book's pages looking for the ninth chapter. He found it, but was only able to read the word 'Murder' at the top of the page before Abdul-Tawaab started again.

"What we know for sure is that King and Kerner began their patrol in the city's southwest area at around 10:00pm. From King's testimony, he stated that Kerner had told him of a tip he'd received regarding the location of Brown and his accomplices. At approximately 10:20, the pair pulled into an alley behind an auto-parts store on Michigan Ave. Within minutes, a small time hood by the name of Roberto Perez emerged from the darkness and Kerner left the cruiser to meet him."

"What did Perez say?"

"Well, he was never found to take the stand at the trial and-,"

"What is this trial you keep mentioning?" Martin asked.

"I'm getting there, boy. Patience is a virtue. Anyways, your father pled the fifth and King stated that he had no information regarding what was said during the meeting. Apparently, your father made it abundantly clear that King needed to stay within sight, but not to join in. He allegedly told him that his involvement would jeopardize the operation because 'spics don't like nigger cops.'"

"That sounds like my dad, but I'm a little surprised that he would say that directly to King's face considering they used to be friends. Actually, the fact that my dad had black friends at all is pretty surprising," Martin said.

"Yes, well their friendship had long since dissolved. There was a falling out between them several years prior."

"Over what?"

"How am I supposed to know?" Abdul-Tawaab said. Martin sensed a hint of defensiveness in his tone.

"All I know is," the professor continued, "that King said the conversation was brief and ended with a suspicious handshake between Kerner and Perez."

"Suspicious, how?"

"King states that after the shake, Kerner's hand was clenched shut and he appeared to transfer something to his back pocket. Only he and Perez really know what or even if anything was exchanged. Again, neither of them took the stand in the trial. It's all speculation, but considering King as the source..."

"So, then what happened?" Martin said.

"Kerner got back in the cruiser and told King that his informant knew for a certainty that Brown and his posse were holed up at the Hotel Linda."

"The one near the bridge?"

"You're familiar with it?"

"I think I saw the sign from I-75."

"Yes. It is mostly low income housing now, but back then it was a proper hotel, albeit a seedy one. So, Kerner parked the cruiser nearby on Hubbard, and both he and King sat for several minutes in silence. King's testimony states that your father was perspiring and his hands were visibly trembling on the steering wheel. Your father made a move to exit the vehicle, but King stopped him, demanding to know the details of the plan. King went on the say that he should have taken the reins being the higher rank, but with Kerner's history in the STRESS unit, he deferred. After some further hesitation, Kerner finally directed King to approach room 313 via the stairwell, while Kerner himself would take the elevator."

"Seems reasonable. Come at Brown from two sides," Martin said.

"They entered the building from the south side main entrance at approximately 10:35. Kerner advised King to wait in the stairwell for five minutes, or if he radioed for assistance, whichever came first. So, King climbed the three flights and waited the five minutes. At 10:42 he entered the third floor hall. He approached room 313. The door was closed, but he heard what he thought was a struggle on the other side of that door. It was locked, so he proceeded to kick it down only to find a white middle aged man in mid coitus with a lady of the night."

"No Brown."

"Or Kerner."

"Where'd he go?"

"That is precisely what King was wondering. He claims that once he left 313, he radioed Kerner but got no reply. He then went back into the stairwell and heard a faint ruckus coming from the second floor. He flung open the stairwell door and saw faces, up and down the hall, peering from their rooms all with their eyes fixed on room 248," Abdul-Tawaab said.

Martin leaned forward in his seat.

"When multiple attempts to kick down the door failed, King resorted to firing two rounds into the door's lock. He then shoved open the door and found a chair had been propped up under the knob."

"And Brown? My dad?"

Abdul-Tawaab took another of his patented lengthy pauses before proceeding.

"There were two men in the room. One was your father. He'd been beaten pretty badly, but had managed to pull himself to the bed. He was shaking uncontrollably. And he was covered in blood."

Martin was speechless.

"And the other man was Isaac Howard, known locally as 'Ice'. He was dead, lying face down on the hardwood floor. Flaps of skin on his head had been ripped open from repeated blunt force trauma."

Martin could not meet the professor's eyes. Though he had nothing to do with the actions of his father, the shame he felt was buried deep within his chromosomes.

"King's testimony states that he immediately cuffed Kerner to the bedpost, who offered no resistance and then radioed to the precinct to notify them of the situation. He said the scene was quite gruesome, and he found it hard to maintain his composure, but he began to look around the room for clues. Other than obvious signs that a physical struggle had occurred in the room, the only thing out of the ordinary was the white powder on Howard's body. It was everywhere. On his nose and cheeks, his shirt and fingers."

"Powder?"

"Well, it turned out to be cocaine, and also the main defense for your father during the trial."

"How?"

"Well, Howard's body was taken to the Wayne County Medical Examiner. A Dr. Walters was the physician on staff that night, and after giving the body a once over, he stated that Isaac Howard's death was from blunt force trauma to the head."

"So, unless my father had a plausible scenario for why he beat Isaac Howard to death, he should have been put in jail, right?"

"Precisely, and the sad thing about it is that his explanation was flimsy at best. On the police report, it states that after his initial shock, your father was able to articulate what had happened. He swore that Perez told him Brown was in that room, and that he never told King to go to 313. He stated that upon arriving at 248 he knocked and a black man opened the door a sliver. He could not identify who was in the room as the lights were off, but he could see a suspicious white residue on the man's fingertips."

"He couldn't make out the features but he could see the cocaine?"

"I said it was flimsy at best. Anyways, the man slammed the door in his face, which your father said gave him justifiable entry into the room. He claims he radioed King, which King denies, and then he busted the door open. According to the report, the hallway light illuminated the room enough for Kerner to realize he'd been given a false tip. He recognized the man as Howard."

"He knew him?"

"Yes, they grew up across the street from one another."

"Wait a second. Did this Isaac sometimes go by the name Reggie?"

Abdul-Tawaab looked momentarily stunned by the question, but quickly retorted, "No. Ice was his only known nickname. Why...Why do you ask?"

"Oh, it's nothing. I just have heard him say the name 'Reggie Howard' before. Not Isaac, or Ice."

"What does he say?"

"Something about how it's all Reggie Howard's fault. It's probably nonsense. I've only heard him say it while he's drunk."

"Yes...well, the report goes on to say that Kerner demanded to know where the drugs were. Howard stated that he had none, but, according to your father, was clenching something in his right fist. Kerner demanded that Howard open the fist, to which Howard refused. After repeated requests and still no compliance on Howard's part, your father pulled out his .38 and aimed it at him."

"So far, my father's claims seem reasonable. So how did Howard end up dead?"

"He says that he slowly advanced on Howard, and that Howard kept backing up, until he bumped into the end table and lost his balance. Your father then pounced on his prone victim and attempted to wrestle free what Howard had in his fist. In the struggle the cocaine was spilled all over Isaac and his clothes, but the struggle persisted. According to your father, nobody gained the upper hand until he delivered, as he says, three blows to Howard's head with the butt of his Smith & Wesson."

"I take it you believe there were more than three blows?"

"That's the crux of the problem. Walters, the Medical Examiner, in his initial report stated that Howard was bludgeoned to death, and that the assailant delivered no less than fourteen blows."

"Fourteen? That's a lot different than three," Martin said.

"Yes. It's the difference between attempting to subdue a prisoner, and murder."

"Ok, so how did the cocaine become the basis for my father's defense?" Martin asked.

"During the trial, Dr. Walter's explained that he'd gone over the body a second time on December twenty-sixth. His reasoning for the repeat examination was that he admittedly did a rush job on the body when it was delivered to him on Christmas Eve, due to wanting to get home to family. This second exam led to him changing the number of blows to the head to three, matching your father's claim, and the cause of death to acute myocardial infarction. He stated that Howard's years of cocaine and alcohol use ravaged his heart, and the struggle with Kerner led to his death."

"Is that not possible as well?"

"It would be, but the toxicology report did not show any evidence of cocaine in his system."

"But what about the powder all over his nose?"

Abdul-Tawaab shrugged his shoulders and said, "And I have from a very reputable and close source that Howard never in his life dabbled in any narcotics. Malt liquor, yes. The occasional joint maybe, but no hard drugs."

Martin put together all the pieces of the puzzle, but he still wanted to hear Abdul-Tawaab just come out and say it.

"So what do you think really happened, then?" he asked.

"I think your father knew Howard would be in that room and deliberately sent King on a wild goose chase to buy himself some time. I think he planted the drugs, which were provided by Perez during their suspicious handshake. I think he delivered the original fourteen blows and I think that's why Howard died, not of some supposed heart attack. I think Walters was pressured into changing his tune by the higher ups, be it the police chief or the mayor. I think they were scared that they might have another riot on their hands if word broke that a white cop beat an unarmed black man to death in cold blood. And, above all else, do you know why I think this wasn't just a drug bust gone bad?"

"The chair," he said.

"Precisely. When King broke into the room, he said a chair had been propped up against the door. That is pre-meditation."

"I guess the only thing not computing for me is motive. Who was this Isaac Howard and what could he have done to provoke-,"

Abdul-Tawaab rose up and pierced Martin with his black irises. "What difference is motive to such a heinous end?" he bellowed.

From Martin's low position in the broken chair, the professor looked ten feet tall.

Having no answer, and feeling uncomfortable with the professor's hulking presence looming over him, Martin got up and went to the door. Before he left, he turned and said, "Whatever happened to Brown?"

Abdul-Tawaab had sat back down, and his eyes had shifted to the old computer monitor. Without looking away from the screen, he said, "He and his associates got into another shooting with the police on December twenty-seventh that year, killing one officer and critically wounding another. A month later he was arrested for firebombing a birth control clinic."

Martin nodded and left the room.

Feeling numb, Martin found himself wandering, step by step through the empty halls of Higgins Hall, painstakingly attempting to rationalize the fact that his dream had been shattered. There was no coming back from a history like that. There were no words he could have said that could even slightly mitigate the fact he was the spawn, not of a run-of-the-mill suburban racist, but of a cold blooded killer.

He never had a chance.

Eventually, he found himself near the elevator bank. There was a placard on the wall with the number one on it. He'd apparently walked down two flights of stairs without knowing, his mind too busy for such trivialities as location.

He continued towards the door never once lifting his eyes from his shoe tops.

"Excuse me," he said, after he'd inadvertently bumped into someone entering the building.

"Martin?"

It was Danielle.

"What are you doing here? Shouldn't you be in Ann Arbor?"

His mouth dropped agape but no words would come forth.

"Are you ok?" she asked, immediately reading the despair in his eyes.

"It's too late," he said, barely above a whisper.

"What is? What's going on?"

"There is no fixing this."

"Abdul-Tawaab?" she asked.

Martin nodded. He was on the verge of tears.

"Oh, Martin," she said.

She hugged him.

"Talk to me," she said.

"I...I...wouldn't know where to start."

She released him.

"How about at the beginning?"

Martin's initial reaction was to deny her request, get back in the Chrysler and drive away. But, the more he thought about it, he realized he had nowhere to drive to. He did not want to go home only to spend arguably the worst day of his life with his father. There was nothing for him in Ann Arbor except an old couch. By his account, the only thing he had left in the asset column was Danielle, and that was only by the grace of her good nature.

"Ok," he said, handing her Abdul-Tawaab's book.

She was confused.

"What's this?"

"The beginning. I'll explain."

"I think I'm gonna need a beer for this. You want a beer?"

"I've never wanted one more."

"Ok. Let's go."

They stepped out into Higgins Hall's shadow. She led the way, first south on Cass and then a right on Hancock.

"Where are we going?" he asked. He'd driven the residential street before, never once seeing a bar.

"I figured we could grab a beer at the Dally," she said.

Martin arched a single eyebrow and said, "The Dally? Is that a bar?"

"No, the street festival. You know, The Dally in the Alley. "

Martin's eyebrow rose even higher. "The what in the what?"

"My God, Kerner! You need a 'Detroit for dummies' book so every time I say something, I don't get that dopey confused look from you."

They continued westbound. Martin squinted his eyes against a sun creeping its way down toward the horizon.

"Why don't you try those?" Danielle said, pointing to the sunglasses hanging from his collar. "You don't look nearly as cute making that squinty face."

The fact that she still found him cute briefly distracted him from his problems, but managed to create a completely new one; he was once again falling under her spell. Her dark brown skin. The way she owned that white tank and blue jeans. He couldn't help himself.

He put on the sunglasses.

"Better?" he asked.

"Much. Now let's get you that beer. I think there's a booth over on Forest."

Martin nodded and followed her down the street. Standing at the corner of Hancock and Second, he could see a crowd of people milling about a few blocks west. A light breeze carried with it the faint sound of pulsing electronic rhythms. He tried to focus on the music, the sunshine, and especially Danielle, but his mind started to drift back to his father, and his abject failure to secure the 'A'.

Danielle traveled south on Second for a few steps before she realized Martin was not following her.

"The beer booth is down there," she said pointing to where, indeed, a beer booth stood.

Martin did not move.

"Hey," she said, coming back to him. "What's wrong?"

"I don't know if…I mean, my head's really jacked right now and…last time we talked, it was-"

"No!" Danielle said, grabbing Martin's hands which he'd held tightly wound into fists at his side.

"No, no, no! This is not about that. This is about the fact that you need a beer and I need a beer and you need to tell me all about what that ass Abdul-Tawaab did back there. That is it! I ain't even hearing none of this other stuff. OK?"

Martin nodded.

She worked at his fists, peeling the fingers back one by one. In his left hand she found the scrap Martin had written Abdul-Tawaab's office number on. Perspiration had caused the ink to run, rendering the writing illegible.

"You need this still?" she asked.

Martin shook his head.

"Ok," she said, tossing it to the wind. "Let's go."

The beer was from a brewery that, unbeknownst to Martin, was just a couple blocks away. Danielle ordered for the both of them and paid, as well.

"My treat," she said.

"Why?" Martin asked.

"'Cuz I'm a nice girl, and you've had a rough day."

They raised their plastic cups and toasted. Martin took a large gulp and let out a refreshed, "Ahh."

"Good beer?" Danielle asked.

"Quite."

They strolled west down Forest, past a stage where a skinny, white guy in Capri khakis and horn rimmed glasses led a band through a raucous cover of a *Kick Out The* Jams, a song by Detroit's own MC5. This particular version omitted the original's famous expletive laden opening call to arms, presumably to appease the family friendly nature of the festival.

"Over here. It's quieter," Danielle said, waving Martin along past a booth where an old black man peddled African inspired jewelry, to a picnic bench tucked behind a food truck.

They sat there for a while, content to take in the ambience and people watch, just enjoying each other's company. When they'd finished their beers, Martin insisted he get the next round. "That's fine," Danielle said. "But only if you also bring me some food, too. A girl's gotta eat, y'know."

"What do you want?"

"I want the greasiest, most unhealthy thing this truck's got."

"Deal," Martin said.

He returned with the beers and a gigantic basket of fries topped with pulled pork, sour cream, and oozing with processed cheese sauce.

Danielle dove right in.

"Mmm...perfect," she said, wiping cheese from the corner of her mouth. "Now...tell me about Abdul-Tawaab."

"Well, I guess it all starts with chapter nine," Martin said, opening up the professor's tome. He began to read.

When Martin closed the book and looked up, he was genuinely surprised to see that the sun had almost set. The block was now lit by festive lights strung along the thoroughfare, and from those used to illuminate the vendor stands and stages. He looked into Danielle's face, expecting to find her asleep for having talked at such length, but she was wide awake, her mouth slightly ajar.

"Holy shit…I mean, crap!" she said.

"I know. I'm sorry. I didn't realize that chapter would be so long."

"Do you think it went down like the prof says?" she replied.

"Yes…no…I don't know. I mean, he probably did it, but I am having a hard time figuring out why."

"I mean…that's crazy, right?"

Martin nodded. They both looked straight ahead, not really focusing on any particular thing. They remained that way for some time until their silence was broken by the crunch of a power chord as another local rock band started their set on the Forest Ave stage.

Martin raised his cup to his lips, but it was empty as was Danielle's. He got up and tossed the cup in a garbage can. Danielle met him there and waved him along to the south entrance of the alley that lends the festival its name. On the stage nearest them was a foursome of young black men in matching suits doing impeccable a cappella renditions of old Motown songs.

She leaned in and cupped her mouth to Martin's ear.

"I'm gonna go-,"

"I figured you might," Martin said, cutting her off. He had an expression of melancholy, which looked out of place considering the festive nature of the surround.

"Figured I might what? I was saying I was going to get us another round." Danielle replied, confused.

"Oh. I thought you might leave after what I said," Martin said, having difficulty meeting her eyes. "You know. All the stuff about my dad."

"And why would that make me want to leave?" she asked.

"You know. The whole 'apple doesn't fall far from the tree' thing."

Danielle put her hands on her hips and looked up into the twinkling expanse and sighed. "If you want me to go, then just tell me, ok?" she said.

"I don't want you to go."

When she lowered her gaze back to Martin, the hurt in her eyes froze him. "Then stop saying stupid shit. That's all you ever do. Stupid shit in the hall at school and stupid shit just now," she said.

Martin waited for her to cover up for her swear, but she never did. He said, "I just thought-,"

"I know what you thought," she said. "You thought that just cuz' your dad is a racist jerk that I'd think you were too. I mean, give me some credit. I've known you long enough now to figure out that you're a decent guy. The problem is that *you* don't realize it."

"How do you figure?"

She stepped up and grabbed Martin by the cheeks, turning his face down putting them eye to eye.

"Let go of him, Martin. You are your own man. What he did does not define you."

"I know."

"Do you? It seems like you are still a scared little boy to me."

She pushed away from him and disappeared into a crowd of slow dancers. For a moment he could see her, her bright white tank top peeking through the bodies swaying to and fro to Smokey Robinson's *Ooh, Baby Baby.*

Then she was gone.

He tried to move. He attempted several times to lift his right foot from the alley's cracked pavement and put it in front of him. Each time, though, it stayed planted.

He thought he saw her again, except when he took a closer look, he found that it was a different tank top clad girl. He drove his fist into his thigh, as if trying to mechanically stimulate his will.

On stage the charismatic front man massaged the crowd with Smokey's words. As Martin, still frozen, listened along, he couldn't help but think that the lyrics, an agonized plea for the return of a lost love, were somehow meant for him.

All of a sudden, Martin's feet began to move. He jostled his way through the dancers. Down the alley he ran, nearly careening into a telephone pole. He rushed by vendors peddling their Detroit themed t-shirts. He dashed by a local art showcase. When he passed a beer stand nestled into a garage, he saw her. She was walking briskly about to make the turn towards Hancock St.

When he reached her, he wrapped his arms around and squeezed.

"Martin!" Danielle yelled out, pressing her palms into his chest in effort to break free from his grasp.

He was relentless, though. He held on to her as if his life depended on it. His face nestled into the space where her neck and shoulder met.

"Martin," she said again, though quieter. Her hands slipped down from his chest, and met behind his back. She interlocked her fingers and pulled in closer. Their breathing synced up and they stood there, while passers-by flowed around them without paying any mind.

Danielle lifted her balm coated lips to Martin's ear and whispered, "Come home with me."

He removed his face from her shoulder and looked into her eyes. They pleaded for him to say yes.

"Your brother?"

"He's at a friend's for the night."

Martin released her from his grip and stood before her without saying a word. He reached his right hand out and found her left. They walked hand in hand back towards campus and his mother's Chrysler with the sounds of the Dally slowly fading away behind them.

Though it only took fifteen minutes for Martin to navigate from the garage on Cass to Danielle's driveway, it felt three times that long. After merging onto I-96, his thoughts splintered. He fought his overactive mind by trying to occupy it with mundane tasks like studying the myriad of billboard advertisements for personal injury lawyers and counting each and every pothole they encountered.

It was to no avail.

Euphoric at the possibilities of what lied ahead, Martin also felt a growing sense of dread. He was unsure whether it arose from concern for his safety in her wretched neighborhood, or, more likely, the fact that the night would eventually transition to morning and with it would come a seemingly insurmountable set of obstacles.

"So...Tyreke's not home?" he said, as he took the Evergreen exit.

"I already told you he wasn't. Why?"

Martin chose his words carefully. "I just don't want to ruffle his feathers. I don't get the impression he's too fond of me."

Danielle reached over and put her hand on Martin's right knee. Her touch caused a shockwave of electricity that could be felt all the way to his fingertips.

In her most calm and reassuring voice Danielle said, "I'm sure he likes you as much as a brother can like some guy that's into his sister."

Martin pictured Tyreke's pistol and thought otherwise. He didn't speak on the subject further. He turned on Lyndon like he had a month before. His eyes darted to and fro surveying the dark street. Up ahead, he saw movement that caused his muscles to tense up.

"Are you all right?" Danielle asked, feeling his leg stiffen.

Martin took a moment to respond as he was trying to determine what it was he saw. His imagination conjured up a gun wielding street thug or a salivating rabid cannibal dog. As he approached, though, he recognized it was just a tree branch shifting in the light breeze next to a road sign that read 'STOP AHEAD'.

"It's a tree," he said.

"What's a tree? Are you ok?"

Martin quickly glanced at Danielle barely long enough to make eye contact before turning his attention back to the road. "Yeah. I'm good," he said forcing a smile.

"You don't seem good. You're driving like twelve miles an hour, and looking around like an army sniper scout in Iraq or something."

He looked at the speedometer. She was close. He was going fifteen miles an hour. He sped up to twenty-five until he reached her house, where he turned and parked the car in the driveway.

The street was empty, the only light coming from Danielle's porch light.

When Martin shut off the engine, the quiet was palpable with only the sound of their breathing to break the silence. Danielle made the first move, applying more pressure to Martin's knee. He turned to her and allowed a genuine smile to cross his lips.

"You ready?" Danielle said, with her right hand resting on the door handle.

"For...?"

"To go inside." She flashed a toothy smile of her own.

He put his hand on hers and squeezed, which she took as a sign that he was ready.

She led him by hand up the walk, and only let go to sift through her purse for her keys. She unlocked three separate locks. One on the black iron barred screen door and two on the steel storm door.

Part of him expected the interior of the home to be in ruins like much of the neighborhood. Fire damaged. Water damaged. Neglected. When she flipped the light switch, he found the home to be none of those things.

It was modest, but tasteful.

Luminous white walls featured several hung photographs. A matching microfiber couch and recliner, both well-worn but clean, perched against one wall. A faux-wood television stand held up a small plasma.

Martin felt a twinge of remorse for his prejudicial leanings. He should have known Danielle would never live in squalor.

"It ain't much, but it's home," she said, arms out wide in presentation of her abode.

A brief notion that Danielle had read his mind came to Martin, which caused a delay in his response. Danielle's arms fell to her sides.

"I mean, I know it ain't the Ritz…" she said. Her smile faded.

Martin saw this and quickly retorted. "No, no, it's…nice. Really nice. Clean, too. I'm sorry. I got lost in thought looking at that photograph. Is that your mom?" He pointed at a framed picture above the television. A woman stood with her arms wrapped around child versions of Danielle and Tyreke on a beach. Danielle took a step toward the picture.

"Yeah. That's Moms. That was like ten years ago."

"Where was it taken?"

"Belle Isle. We'd go down there all the time… well, when she was goin' good, anyways."

"There's a beach on Belle Isle?"

Danielle let out an exasperated groan. "Put it on the list."

Martin smiled and shrugged his shoulders.

She laughed and stepped to him. "Come," she said, grabbing his hand and leading him down a hallway branching off the living room.

"This isn't the way to Belle Isle," he said.

"No. It isn't."

She opened a door and flipped on the light. The room was unequivocally pink. Pink walls, bedspread, curtains, linens. There was even a pink bathrobe slung over the post at the foot of the bed. Embroidered on it was the word 'Pink'.

"It's so pink," he said.

"What color did you expect it to be?"

"I don't know what I expected."

"I like pink. All girls do. Even black ones," she said, slyly.

"Duly noted."

She walked to her bed and hopped on. She leaned back against a mountain of throw pillows and crossed her legs. Martin stayed in the doorway, his eyes moving around the room taking everything in. A small banquet table with folding steel legs served as her desk. On it was a mug filled with pens and highlighters, her textbooks, and several small trophies.

"You're making me nervous just standin' there. Sit with me."

Martin stepped into the room, but instead of meeting Danielle at her bed, he went to her desk and picked up one of her awards, a five inch tall crystal pyramid with a sturdy marble base.

"I got that one freshman year for writing the best essay on how to curtail the violence in the city."

"Looks like nobody took your advice," Martin said, setting the trophy back down.

She sighed and said, "Would you just get over here?"

Martin obliged, seating himself at the foot of her bed.

"You look positively miserable."

"What? Why?" Martin said.

"You're over there like you got a rod up your butt. You need to loosen up."

She scampered over to him and put her hands on his shoulders.

"What are you doi-," Martin said.

"Shh. Just relax. You've had a rough day."

"You don't have to-,"

"SHH!"

Danielle spent the next fifteen minutes compassionately kneading every muscle until it relented to her touch. Martin closed his eyes and focused on her finger's dance. He bathed in the soft, jasmine tinged fragrance of her perfume. His posture slackened and he slouched forward.

He was putty.

He opened his eyes when he realized that he could no longer feel her touch. He turned to look for her and found that she had returned to her place on the pillow mound.

"Wow," he said.

"You're welcome."

He moved his shoulders up and down and rolled his head from side to side. "That was amazing. I think I needed it."

"No doubt. I thought you were gonna fall asleep there at the end."

"I probably could have."

Danielle grinned and let out a deep, satisfied breath. She turned and looked at the small digital clock next to her bed. It read 11:20.

"Speaking of sleeping, I'm getting' kinda tired," she said.

"Oh," Martin said. "Well, I guess I should get going."

She leaned forward and grabbed his wrist.

"No," she said, quickly pulling away. She sat back again and tucked a loose strand of hair behind her ear. "I mean, you can stay for a while. I actually don't mind, considering Tyreke's gone, and all."

"Oh," Martin said. "Sure. I can stay for a bit."

"Cool. I'mma change. Be right back," Danielle said, springing off the bed and into a bathroom that joined her and Tyreke's rooms. In a flash she was back, clad in a pink tank top, matching pajama shorts and a smile that stretched from ear to ear.

"That's better," she said. She reached her pillow mound and began tossing them, one by one, down to the foot of the bed before sliding underneath the covers. She nestled on her side facing the window, and pulled the blankets to her chin. Martin did not move.

"Can you hit that light, please?" she said.

Martin got up from the bed and flipped the switch by the door. The room became an inky black, save for a slew of glow in the dark stars affixed to the ceiling. He shuffled his way back to the bed, arms extended, without bumping into anything. As soon as he sat back down, Danielle said, "No shoes on the bed."

Martin slid them off and lied down several inches from her on top of the covers. For several minutes neither of them moved, Martin on his back, eyes agape taking in the galaxy above him.

"Can you hold me?" Danielle whispered.

Martin was unsure if she had really even said it, or if his brain had fabricated the sound. Nonetheless, he shifted on to his side wrapped his arm around her form. She pressed her body into his as much as was allowed with the blanket barrier between them.

Martin dove his face into the thicket of her hair. He inhaled her. A slight sigh escaped Danielle's lips. The moment was perfect. A snapshot of what could be.

An engine roared.

They tensed up, their serenity stolen.

The squeal of tires.

It was immediate, just outside the window. Their breathing stopped.

A flurry of gunshots.

Danielle let out a petrified scream that was barely audible over the uproar. The shots came in bursts with only brief respites between.

Crashing glass and splintering wood could be heard amongst the cacophony, but none of this registered with Martin. All he could focus on was Danielle. He pulled her in closer. She trembled in his arms, the spasms more violent with each new burst. Finally, after what seemed like hours, but in reality only a few seconds, the shooting stopped.

Martin listened for another burst but it never came. There was the faint sound of laughter and then, after a few seconds, the engine roared again and the car was gone.

Danielle was still trembling. Her breathing was shallow and erratic.

"Danielle," he whispered.

She did not reply.

"Turn to me," he said.

She did, slightly. He caressed her face and felt moisture on her cheek.

"Hey, it's over. It's ok," he said, still whispering.

She was unable to speak. For the next few minutes he held her tightly and rubbed her back until she gained control of the spasms.

When her breathing returned to a normal pace he asked, "Was that a drive-by?"

She nodded. After a few seconds, she cleared her throat and said, "It happens sometimes."

"Huh. For a second I could've sworn it was something else," he said, calmly.

"What else could it have been?"

"It kinda sounded like fireworks."

She didn't say anything, but Martin could sense her questioning him.

"So, when it was happening, you know what I did?" he said.

She sniffled and said, "No."

"I closed my eyes really tightly and tried to picture myself on the banks of the Thames like that painting you like."

He leaned in and pressed his lips to her tear coated cheek, just below her left eye.

"Only I couldn't do it, because I've never been to London. So I pictured the Detroit River instead. And the Ambassador instead of the London Bridge."

He kissed her face again, this time below the right eye. She raised her face ever so slightly to accept him.

"You did?" she said.

"Yeah. It was the grand finale. The colors lit up the sky and I watched the embers float down to the river until they disappeared."

"Yeah?"

"Yeah. It was…it was beautiful."

He leaned again, this time pressing his lips to hers. They were moist and salty from her tears. Nothing would ever come close to matching the taste. He held their mouths together in attempt to make an indelible map of the surface of those lips in his mind.

Eventually, he broke the kiss and pulled back ever so slightly, content to feel her breath on his face. Danielle grabbed the blanket at its edge and tugged. It did not budge with Martin's weight on it. She pulled again, this time more forcefully.

"What are you doing?" he asked.

"Come."

She tugged again, and this time Martin stood up. He pulled away the covers and went inside.

CHAPTER XIX
SEPTEMBER 7, 2008

Martin awoke to a flash accompanied by excruciating pain radiating over his right eye.

He was falling.

He crashed hard onto Danielle's bedroom floor. Disoriented, he opened his eyes and saw Tyreke looming over him with his right fist cocked back. Martin turned at the last second and the punch merely grazed the side of his face.

A startled Danielle sprang up and screamed at the sight of her brother attacking the man she had fallen in love with.

"TY! STOP IT! STOP! WHAT ARE YOU DOING?"

Tyreke ignored her and went about swinging wildly at Martin. His form akin to one of those inflatable tube men often seen at used car lots.

"TYREKE! GET OFF HIM RIGHT NOW!" Danielle shouted. She searched for something to throw at her brother, but found only pillows. She pelted him with them, one after another. With Tyreke pausing his onslaught to deflect them, Martin sat up and grabbed him by the wrists.

"LET ME GO!" Tyreke yelled.

"TYREKE! RELAX, MAN," Martin implored.

"FUCK YOU! I TOLD YOU! I SAID STAY AWAY!"

Tyreke tried again to wriggle himself loose, but could not. He stood up, but still Martin held firm.

"Tyreke, let's talk this thr-," Martin attempted to say, but his sentence was cut short when Tyreke exploded forth, plowing his knee into Martin's abdomen.

His diaphragm spasmed and all of the air was driven from his lungs. The pain was extreme, exacerbated by each breath. Tyreke jumped to his feet, shifting his weight back and forth from one foot to the next. He was elated.

"That's what's up! I told you. Didn't I tell you?" he said, leaning over Martin like Ali over Frazier.

Martin writhed around on Danielle's hardwood floor trying to gain his bearings. He reached out to her desk's cold metallic leg and gripped it. Using it as support, he attempted to rise, but the table was too weak to support him. It capsized, raining down an assortment of books, highlighters, and various awards. The pyramid shaped trophy fell at Tyreke's feet. He picked it up and again pounced on Martin, who, lying face down, was in no position to defend himself.

"Oommph," escaped Martin's lips, as once again Tyreke forced out all of his air.

"You a stupid mu'fucka," Tyreke said, shaking his head. "I told yo' ass. I know I did."

He raised the pyramid high above his head and held it there for just a split second before its inevitable descent. The pause allowed Danielle one last effort at stopping her brother.

"TYREKE BRYANT DENSON!" she shrieked.

Tyreke's head dropped down and he let out a guttural moan increasing in volume and intensity until his lungs were empty. He stood up and tossed the trophy harmlessly aside.

"Why, Dani? Why you wanna go and do that?" he asked with his head still down, his voice calm.

It took her a moment to respond. Her heart was pounding in her chest. She had never seen her brother act like that.

"Do what?" she said, wide-eyed.

He turned to her. "Say my name like that. Like moms used to."

"Are you kidding me?" she said. She threw the covers to the side and leapt from the bed, advancing on him with purpose.

"YOU...AL...MOST...KILLED...HIM," she shouted, slapping him about the head and chest.

He cowered from her. "HEY YO! QUIT IT!" he said, side stepping her to the corner of the room.

She did not follow him. Instead she attended to Martin and helped him to his feet. She pulled a highlighter from the collar of his shirt and tossed it aside.

"You ok?"

Martin went to a full length mirror Danielle had on the back of her door and did a self-assessment. Other than the purple right eyelid, he was no worse for wear.

He turned back to her concerned face and said, "I'm good. Just a black eye."

"See. He fine. And I wasn't gon' kill him, anyway. Jus' scare him, is all," Tyreke said. He was as far as he could possibly be from his sister without knocking out a wall.

Danielle said nothing. She only looked at her brother with unknowing eyes. To Tyreke, it was worse than any words she could've said. He shifted his gaze everywhere in the room other than at Danielle but he could not escape the look. It gnawed at him, an itch from deep within his own skin, until finally it broke him.

"WHAT? WHAT? DAMNIT! SAY SOMETHING!" he shouted.

"What…was…that?"

"What you mean?"

"What DO you mean?!"

"Sorry. What DO you mean?" Tyreke said.

"Are you playin' with me? I mean, why'd you come in here all crazy and start wailin' on my boyfriend?"

"Shit, Dani! So now he's your boyfriend?"

"Watch your mouth!" Danielle retorted.

Tyreke pouted like a toddler. Danielle had an almost maternal way of cutting through his braggadocio.

She pointed to a spot at the foot of her bed, and directed her brother there with her eyes. After he had sat down, she crossed her arms over her chest. Her right foot began vigorously tapping on the floor.

"Now explain yourself."

"I just don't like the dude. He ain't right for you," he said to the tops of his shoes.

She was surprised by this. "What about him isn't right for me?"

Tyreke did not lift his gaze from his shoes.

"It had better be more than just his skin color."

Tyreke didn't flinch.

"Look at me, Ty," she commanded.

He slowly raised his chin, and did as she asked.

"Is that the reason?" Her toe stopped tapping.

Tyreke looked Martin up and down and then back to his sister. "First off, yeah. It was. But not no more. I'm off that. It's 'cuz he's a dope head."

"WHAT?" Martin burst out. He looked at Danielle out of his good eye, and was happy to see that she was struggling to contain a chuckle.

"Tyreke. What are you talking about? Martin ain't no dope head."

"It's true. He told me himself."

"Come on. He did not. Martin?"

Martin put his right hand over his heart and said, "I swear I am not a dope head."

"See. There's no way-,"

"He told me when we were going to get the coneys. He was like, 'Oh, when I was in college I used to come down to the hood and buy all types of shit.'"

"I never said-,"

"I mean, when he said that, all I could think of was…" Tyreke's head dropped down and he started sniffling. "Was…moms, you know?"

Danielle looked over at Martin, though this time her expression was that of doubt. She went to her brother's side and put her arm over his shoulder, drawing him to her bosom.

"It's all right, Ty. I'm sure you misheard him. Martin would never do something like that.

"Of course not," Martin said. "What I told him was that in college I went to this rough neighborhood off Chene with the *intent* to buy drugs. I was going through a rough patch, and I…I don't know what I thinking. It seemed like a good idea for a moment, but when I got down there, I couldn't do it."

Danielle looked up at him with an expression of disgust, betrayal. "It's true, then?"

"What? No. I just said I didn't buy them."

Danielle stood up from the bed and took a step forward, closer to him. "But you went down there to buy drugs. You just said it."

"Well, yeah. But I didn't do it."

"You attempted to, though," Tyreke added from behind his sister. His eyes were bone dry.

"What attempt? Either you buy 'em or you don't. I met the guy, told him I wasn't interested, and that was that."

"I can't believe this," Danielle said. She put her hand to her lips for a brief moment before pointing to the door.

"I want you to leave."

"Danielle. Come on! Let's talk about-,"

"GO!" she shouted. There was a crack in her voice. She turned from him and went to her brother. He stood up and embraced her, all the while eyeballing Martin from over her shoulder.

In shock from what had just transpired, it took Martin a second before he could will his body to leave.

Down the hall he went, past Tyreke's room. Out of the corner of his eye he spotted the backpack resting on Tyreke's bed.

And it was full.

He told himself to keep on moving down the hall. To walk out the front door, and down the porch steps. To get in the car and drive. To go anywhere. Hazel Park and back to his father. Ann Arbor.

Anywhere.

But he found himself next to Tyreke's bed. And his hand was on the backpack's zipper, slowly sliding along its toothed grooves. He looked inside.

The look on Tyreke's face when he saw Martin return with the backpack was that of sheer terror. He broke the embrace with his sister and tried to get to Martin but it was too late. Martin had tossed the backpack to the floor and its contents were strewn about.

Danielle picked up a small plastic baggie that had come to rest on her left foot. It was filled with little blue pills with smiley face imprints. Tyreke quickly snatched it from her and shoveled it and its brethren into the backpack, but the damage was done.

"Tyreke, give me the backpack," she said.

He clung it to his chest, unwavering.

"NOW!"

He sighed and handed it over. She opened it up and peered inside. She reached her right hand in and pulled out Tyreke's pistol. She held it up between her thumb and index finger just long enough to get a good look at it. She dropped it back in the bag as if it were burning through here fingertips.

She calmly handed the bag back to her brother, and turned around. She walked to her bed and lifted the covers. She climbed in and turned her back to the both of them.

Tyreke looked at Martin, and then back to his sister.

"Hey, yo Dani. Let me expl-," he said.

"Get out," she said, quietly. "Both of you."

Tyreke looked at Martin and shook his head. "Look what the fuck you did." He went through the shared bathroom to his room and closed the door.

Martin took one last look at Danielle's shape underneath the blankets before leaving the house.

He started the car and slowly slipped it into reverse. He glanced in the rearview with his one open eye only briefly before hitting the gas.

A horn blast pulled his mind away from Danielle's bedroom back into the here and now. He slammed on the brakes, narrowly missing a large panel van.

The van came to a stop just in front of Ma Laika's house. The driveway was occupied by two Detroit police cars.

After determining it to be safe, Martin reversed the Chrysler into the street, but instead of heading south, towards I-96, curiosity led him north towards the commotion next door.

The front window laid in a million glistening pieces all over the porch and lawn. The shutters splintered and pock marked. Inside, Martin could see several cops moving about with no apparent sense of urgency. Their eyes were fixated down, at something out of sight.

All of a sudden an angry man popped into Martin's view, rapping on his window. Martin fumbled at the switch for a moment before lowering it.

The man, the driver of the van he narrowly missed, was white, in his early forties. He compensated for his baldness with thick eyebrows and a handlebar mustache. He was wearing a short sleeve white shirt and black slacks.

"You better look both ways kid, or else you're gonna get yourself hurt."

"Yes, sir. I'm sorry," Martin said, sheepishly.

The man scoffed and walked away. "He's sorry," he said, to his partner, a similarly dressed man, though a considerable belly hung over the waistband of his black slacks.

"I'll bet," the partner said. "Hey, help me with this thing."

The 'thing' he was referring to was a gurney. The two men wheeled it up Ma Laika's walkway and into the house. It was then that Martin noticed the word 'coroner' on the van's hood.

He slowly pulled away down the street, stealing another glance at the house when he reached the corner. The last thing he saw was a white curtain waving in the breeze, reaching out through the gaping chasm in the home's façade as if it were attempting to escape what was inside.

Martin guided the Chrysler down his old familiar ash-lined street, the leaves only hinting at the chromatic metamorphosis they soon would undergo. Somewhere along the way, he'd made up his mind to return to Ann Arbor. Though it had only had an old couch in Abigail Joplin's extra bedroom to offer, it was still more than he had there in Hazel Park.

Or Detroit.

Before he could go, he knew he'd have to gather his belongings. That meant going in the house, and the potential of an encounter with his father, who, after the revelations in Abdul-Tawaab's office, he had even less desire to see than usual. He could only hope that Jack had really tied one on the night before. If he had, he was unlikely to be awake.

He parked the Chrysler and walked up the driveway's slight grade with the keys in one hand and in the other, Abdul Tawaab's book. He gently inserted the key into the door's lock and gingerly stepped inside. He looked left and right and found no signs that his father had already waken. The television was off, as were all of the lights.

He was a cat burglar, tip toeing through the house, cursing every creak and groan underneath his feet until he reached the bedroom. He closed the door and slowly released the knob, feeling every ping of its internal spring.

He took a deep breath and that's when he saw himself in the mirror. He looked like shit.

He was wearing day old, wrinkled clothes, his hair was disheveled, but worst of all was the eye. It had swollen completely shut. Though he couldn't explain why, he took solace in the fact that it looked as bad as it hurt.

He made haste packing his things and took a quick inventory around the room to ensure that nothing was forgotten. Satisfied, he wrapped his hand around the brass knob and turned it.

Still, no sign of Jack.

His backpack and laptop case over one shoulder, and his laundry sack over the other, he stepped out of the bedroom. Instead of a direct route down the hall, through the kitchen and out the door towards whatever life he still clung to, he took a detour to the bathroom. The throb over the entire right side of his face had become unbearable.

He set down the laundry sack on the tiled floor, and slowly opened the medicine cabinet. It squealed on its hinges, causing Martin to wince. He waited for a few seconds, expecting to hear sounds emanating from his father's bedroom, but they never came.

Inside the cabinet was a half used tube of toothpaste, some antacid tablets, two toothbrushes and a bottle of Advil. He snatched the pills, but just as we was about to close the cabinet door, he spotted a small red bottle that had been hidden by the Advil.

His mother's oxycodone.

He opened the cap, and saw a few dozen pills in the bottle. He paused for a moment, spinning the bottle absentmindedly in his palm before dropping it too inside the laundry sack.

He was moving again, down the hall and past the threshold into the kitchen. He glided over the linoleum floor, miraculously missing every creaky spot and reached out to back door's handle.

"Where you going?" a booming voice let forth from the living room.

"JESUS CHRIST!" Martin cried out. His belongings tumbled to the floor.

Jack Kerner rose from his recliner in the living room, working his bad hip with one hand, and holding a glass that contained a small amount of a brown liquid with the other.

"WHAT THE...!" Jack exclaimed, a look of genuine shock on his face. "What happened to your face?"

Martin was still trying to process the fact that he was not in the car on the way to Ann Arbor, and instead facing the star of Abdul-Tawaab's chapter nine. He decided to forego answering his father's inquiry to begin picking up his things.

"HEY!" Jack persisted.

Martin sighed and said, "Its 5:00 somewhere, right Jack?"

"Answer the question," Jack said, waving Martin's chiding away with a dismissive flip of his wrist.

"Why are you even up now, anyway?" Martin countered.

Jack set the glass down on the kitchen table. "Up? I never went to sleep." It showed. The dark circles under his eyes were far more pronounced than usual.

"Why not?"

"Quit dodging and tell me what happened to you?"

Martin looked down at the floor, again disregarding his father.

"YOU CAN'T STAY OUT ALL NIGHT AND COME TRAIPSING IN AT 10AM LOOKING LIKE YOU GOT HIT BY A TRUCK WITHOUT TELL-,"

"I GOT IN A FIGHT, OK?" Martin shouted back.

"WITH WHO?"

Martin shook his head vehemently and reached out again for the door handle. "I'm not doing this. I'm not getting in a shouting match with you. My head's pounding and I have to g-,"

"Fine. Fine. We won't shout. We can just talk," Jack said, arms up in surrender. He pulled out a chair from the kitchen table and sat down. He gestured for Martin to do the same.

Martin could see the Chrysler through the screen. It was just sitting there, waiting to take him away. But he didn't step outside. That silver ribbon on the fridge tugged at him. Before he knew it he was seated opposite his father at the table.

"Ok, then," Jack began. "Who hit you?"

Martin put his hand to his face. "My girlfriend's...I guess she's my girlfriend...anyway, her brother."

"Your girlfriend's brother. And why did he do that?"

"The truth?" Martin asked.

"Of course."

"Well...honestly I believe it's because I'm white," Martin said. He watched the wheels turn in his father's head.

"You mean she's..."

"Black. Yeah."

"Black," Jack said. He slowly rose from his chair and wrapped his hand around the whiskey glass.

"Mmmhmm," Martin affirmed. He sat back in the chair and waited for the fallout.

"I knew this would happen with you going to school in Detroit. That Godforsaken place…," Jack muttered to himself.

For a moment, Martin thought that his father had taken the news rather well, but that was before the whiskey glass sailed across the kitchen, shattering upon impact with the wall. Brown liquid splattered on the wall, staining several of the ducks' white feathers beige.

Martin pushed away from the table and stood up.

"That's it. I'm done," Martin said.

"No, no, no. Sit back down. I'm sorry. I just…" Jack said, trailing off.

"Just what?" Martin said, still standing.

Jack rubbed his temples as if the news delivered him an instant headache. "I just don't want anything to happen to you. You don't understand. Nothing good can come with associating with those…those people," he said, with a look of disgust on his face.

"Yeah, well, don't fret. It's over now."

"It is?"

"Yes."

"Good."

Martin chuckled. "Thanks for the compassion."

"It's not like that, Martin. You're better off. Look at your face. They aren't like us, son."

Martin nodded dismissively and turned his attention back out the screen door.

"Plus, I'm sure it was just some summer fling that didn't have legs anyways," Jack added.

"How would you know?" Martin said, squinting at the old man. "You don't know the first thing about me!"

"Of course I know you. You're my goddamned son!" Jack said, seeming to take offense.

"What difference does that make? You're my father, and it took a complete stranger for me to find out who *you* really are."

Martin reached into his backpack, and pulled out Abdul-Tawaab's book. He tossed it onto the table in front of his father.

"What's this?" Jack said, picking it up without taking his eyes off of Martin.

"You should start with chapter nine. I found it to be very enlightening."

Jack opened the book and located said chapter. His brow furrowed with each sentence he read. He turned the page. His eyes darted across line after line, his expression growing angrier and angrier. He licked his finger and turned to the next page. And the next.

And the next.

He was frenzied. Martin stood in astonishment that the pages weren't being ripped from the binding. Then, he snapped the book shut and slammed it to the table.

"WHERE DID YOU GET THAT?" he demanded.

"My professor, the author gave it to me."

Jack paused to look at the name on the cover. "THIS ABDUL-TAWAAB?"

"Yep."

"WHO THE HELL DOES THIS GODDAMNED A-RAB THINK HE IS?"

"He's not an Arab."

Jack was confused. "He's not. Then what is he?"

"He's black."

"Black?"

"Yeah. And because you hate blacks, he thinks I do too. So that 'A' I needed to get into law school was never gonna happen."

Jack, after a good ten seconds inside his own head, asked, "How old is he?"

"What? I don't know. What difference does it make?" Martin said.

"Ballpark."

"Older. About your age."

Martin watched all the color drain from his father's face and his eyes turn to glass. Jack fumbled about for the kitchen chair, and when he found it, he didn't sit down, per se. It was more like all of the muscles in his body went slack, and he collapsed into it. His mouth mumbled silent nothings.

"JACK!" Martin yelled to his father.

Jack did not reply. He just picked up the book and again turned to chapter nine, though in a much more deliberate pace.

"JACK!"

He offered no response. He looked like he had seen a whole army of ghosts.

"TALK TO ME!"

" ... "

"Fine. If I walk out that door right now, I'm never coming back in this house again. You hear me?"

Jack muttered something that sounded like "It can't be" but Martin was unsure.

"What did you say?" Martin asked.

" ... "

Martin took a deep breath and sighed. He gathered his things and opened the door. He looked back over his shoulder at the silver ribbon on the refrigerator and said, "I'm sorry. I tried."

He would never step foot in the house again.

CHAPTER XX
OCTOBER 31, 2008

It was 6:15 and Tyreke was sprawled out on his bed flipping through a dog-eared copy of *Huckleberry Finn* by what light the descending sun snuck through the slats of the blinds. He dragged a highlighter over a single word, and muttered to himself, "Another one! This dude be wildin'!"

He put down the book when he heard Danielle's keys rattling in the front door's myriad of locks. When she passed by his bedroom door he sprang from his bed. He hadn't seen her all day.

"Hey, yo. Dani!"

She entered her bedroom without responding and closed the door emphatically. Tyreke heard the lock trip shortly afterwards.

"Dani! C'mon, now," he said, unsuccessfully trying the knob. "We ain't…I mean, we haven't talked all day!"

"What do you want?" she shouted back.

"Nothin'. You know…just wanted to see what's up."

She said nothing in return. Tyreke draped the copy of Huck Finn over his face and took a deep, exasperated breath. He lowered the book and took a glance at its cover. It displayed a young boy sitting on a raft with a large, overall-clad black man paddling behind him. In the background, a burning orange sun was setting over the Mississippi.

"I was just readin' Huck Finn, again. Y'know, for the second time. Got a big test next week."

"…"

"You ever read this book?" he asked. "I can't believe how many times this white boy Twain drops the word 'nigger' in this thing. He's all, 'Nigger Jim' this, and 'Nigger Jim' that."

"…"

He sighed and shook his head.

"C'mon, Dani. Talk to me."

"I have nothing to say to you."

"I been goin' to school. Ain't missed a day since-,"

"Good for you!" she shouted to her brother. "Leave, me alone!"

"I just got one question."

"What?" Her tone was of extreme annoyance.

"You get that job? The one at the Kahn?"

After a lengthy pause, Danielle said, "Yeah. I got it."

Tyreke smiled. He was happy for her even though at the moment she wanted nothing to do with him.

He went back to his room feeling almost jubilant. While his conversation with Danielle was brief, and through closed doors, it was the most they had spoken in weeks. It was, if nothing else, a step in the right direction.

Propped up on his pillow, he opened up the book to begin reading again. Before he read a single word, he put it back down. He knew that to really get back in Danielle's good graces, he needed to commit fully.

He picked up his phone.

It was time to make a call he'd been putting off for too long.

It rang several times.

"What nigga?" Flip sniped. Tyreke thought he seemed more agitated than usual.

"Hey, yo Flip. Whatupdoe?"

"The fuck you want?"

Tyreke's muscles tightened.

"Uhh...this a bad time?"

There was no response. After a few seconds, Tyreke proceeded cautiously.

"Yo...I called 'cuz I was think-,"

"He ain't make parole!" Flip erupted.

"What?" Tyreke said, confused.

"They all on some bullshit 'bout he a fuckin' danger to the muthafuckin' public."

"Who?"

"T-Mar! He just called me. Gonna be another couple years 'fo that nigga sees the outside."

"Shit, dawg. I'm sorry."

Tyreke was sorry about T-Mar, but more so that he'd picked that moment to announce his resignation from the drug game.

"Danger?…Shit. Fo' a couple pills and a strap?" Flip continued, incensed. "They want some danger? I'mma show 'em some danger when I find that cracka' that got him-"

"Are we there yet?" interrupted a very high pitched and excited little voice in the background.

"Almost, baby" Flip said, the jagged edges in his voice smoothed out.

"That Latrice?" Tyreke asked.

"Yeah. I'm tryna' take baby girl out trick or treatin' and now this shit."

"You drivin' out this way?"

"Hell, no! Run up on a buncha busted ass houses, fuckin' stray dogs and shit. No, we just rolled past Eight Mile. Gon' take Nine. Gotta keep a safe distance from the hood."

"Oh, ok."

"Whitey got the candy. Just gotta go get it. Right, Latty?"

"Whitey candy!" Latrice yelled, quite enthusiastically.

Flip burst out laughing. It was loud, boisterous. Tyreke could hear Latrice laughing as well.

After one of those lengthy sighs that often conclude long fits of laughter, Flip said, "Ahhh, shit. I needed that. Anyway, lil nigga, what was you sayin'?

"Oh, nothin'. Forget it," Tyreke said.

"Fuck that, nigga. You called me fo' a reason. Out with it."

Tyreke sat at the edge of his bed, strongly considering making something up on the spot. That fit of laughter, though, convinced him to go forward.

"Well, f'real…I was thinking 'bout getting' out. You know…out the game."

Silence, then more laughter.

First, just Flip, but then Tyreke swore he heard Latrice's tiny voice mixed in there, as well.

"Flip?"

"Ahh…Whatchu think? You can give two weeks notice and then bounce?"

"I don't know…I just-,"

"Nah, nigga."

His voice dropped two octaves.

"I ain't even close to done witchu."

And he was gone, leaving Tyreke with nothing but silence and the dark. The sun had completed its descent.

When another political ad championing the black candidate for the United States Presidency came on, the third in the last hour, Jack Kerner buried his thumb into the remote's off button. The picture and the voice that had so angered him were extinguished.

He felt a brief sense of pride for his insignificant little protest, that is until he realized it had left him in the dark, the only sound his own breathing. It was another reminder that he was alone and probably for good after the last dustup with Martin. It was unsettling. So much so, that he began tracing the power button on the remote, considering giving the television a chance to redeem itself. Just as he was about to press it, he heard a vigorous tapping at his front door.

"Who the hell…" he questioned, rising up, beer in hand.

He wrestled with the locks for a moment before pulling the door open to find Barack Obama himself standing on his stoop. His features were exaggerated, cartoonish. He was wearing a striped sweater and ripped jeans, and stood easily six feet four.

"Can I help you?" Jack asked the Senator.

"Give me some candy, man" Obama said, through the slit that served as a mouth.

"Candy?"

"Yeah, man. It's like, Halloween."

"What's with that shit-eating grin?"

"Huh?"

"How old are you?"

"You got your light on, old man, so…are you gonna, like, give me somethin' or not?"

"Get the hell out of here."

"Pssh…asshole," Obama said, before leaping off the stoop, kicking over a potted plant in the process.

Jack watched Obama sprint across his lawn until he was out of sight. He cupped his hand over his eyes and pressed his face to the glass to survey the street.

The neighborhood was teeming with superheroes, princesses, pirates and the like. They ran about, oozing enthusiasm, dragging behind them their sacks of processed sugar. A smattering of parents trailed behind the kids, sipping coffees and carrying swords and wands and other superfluous accessories.

Jack's mind drifted to Martin's childhood. He searched for the memories of walking those streets, shuffling through the rainbow of fallen leaves with his own son. He tried to recall Martin's costumes, a football uniform or a mutant turtle perhaps, but could not. The images weren't there. Everything after '67 was just a memory soup. The alcohol had liquefied it all. Every now and then something would drift to the surface but when he tried to hold on to it, it would trickle through his hands.

He opened his eyes and cocked the can back to his lips, vanquishing it. He wrapped his hand around the cold steel door and just before it shut he heard a tiny voice from his stoop.

"Trick or treat," it said.

Jack pulled the door open again and found a smiling little baseball player looking back at him. The little boy, who couldn't have been more than four years old, had a beaming smile and eye black on his cheeks.

Jack smiled at a woman, presumably the boy's mother, standing behind the boy. He then crouched down to meet the boy at eye level and said, "So what are you supposed to be?"

"A baseball player!" he shouted, jubilantly.

"Oh yeah? And what team are you on?"

The little boy set his pillowcase down on the ground and pointed to the old English 'D' on his chest.

"Oh, you play for Detroit?"

"Yeah."

"That's marvelous. So what's your name, son?"

"William," the boy said, struggling to pick up the pillowcase without removing his mitt from his left hand.

"Wow! Did you know my favorite player's name was William?"

"Really?"

"Yeah. Well, Willie actually. Willie Horton. Have you heard of him?"

The boy shrugged his shoulders and looked to his mother for help, but she shrugged right along with him.

"It's ok. It was a long time ago."

The boy lifted the pillowcase up as a not so subtle reminder to Jack the purpose of the evening.

"Oh, yeah. The candy. Look, kid. I'm sorry, but I don't have any…" Jack said, a finger going to his lips. "Wait a sec. Just hold on. I'll be right back," Jack said.

He recalled the day Martin had returned from Ann Arbor. Surprised by Martin's thin physique, he had made a point to fill the house with food. The next day he'd purchased the only things he could remember the boy ever liking; boxed macaroni and cheese, salami, and chocolate. Martin never touched any of it. The salami Jack had ended up eating himself, but the chocolate remained.

Jack swung open the pantry door and sure enough, next to the boxed macaroni was a bag of Sanders chocolates. Jack grabbed the bag, and a beer for himself from the fridge, and returned to the door where the little baseball player and his mother had been joined by a vampire and a fairy, each with pillowcases in hand waiting for their share.

"Wow! We got a whole big group of you out here now. Well, hang on. Let me open this thing," Jack said tearing into the plastic bag. He stepped out onto the porch and dropped a few of the chocolates into each child's bag.

"There you go. Now don't go eatin' all of it tonight. You'll get a bellyache."

"We won't," the children said in unison.

"Now what do you say, William?" the mother said.

"Thank you!"

"You're welcome, son," Jack said.

The children sprang from the porch, one by one, and made their way to the next house. Jack stepped back inside and closed the door. He smiled and cracked open his beer, downing half its contents. Back into the kitchen he went. He polished off the remainder of the beer and set the empty can down on the counter. For a moment he closed his eyes and just stood there, listening to the symphony of children's voices coming from outside. He opened his eyes and glanced down at the bag of chocolates in his hand.

With a fresh sixer of beer, he went back to the front door and opened it wide. A brown accent chair with wooden peg legs that had accumulated a fine layer of dust since Diane had died was dragged over to the landing. Jack sank into it and cracked open another beer.

Martin awoke to a gentle nudge. He clenched his eyes shut and grunted some polysyllabic nonsense before turning over and digging his face deeper into his pillow.

"Martin," a voice said from over him.

He did not move. He couldn't. Just the act of turning had jostled his stomach contents to the brink of eruption. A rail spike was lodged in his right temporal lobe. His mouth was full of cotton.

The nudge returned, though now more a shove.

"Martin! Get up!" the voice said again, annoyed.

He managed to turn back around, choking down the bile at the back of his throat. A haloed figure loomed over him. From the light overhead he could discern it was a female in a nurse's outfit.

It was his mother.

"Mom?" he said, reaching out to her.

"What?" Diane said, withdrawing from his touch as if he were leprous.

"Mom! Don't go!" he urged, watching his mother recede, her halo fading. When she sat down in the rattan Papasan chair opposite Martin, her features had morphed into that of his dreadlocked roommate, Abigail Joplin.

"Abby?" he said. He sat bolt upright, swinging his feet to the floor. The left struck something, but he did not address it immediately. Instead he focused on the pain that the change in head position had brought on. He winced and mashed his fingers into his temples.

"Martin!" Abby yelled out, pointing at the floor by Martin's feet.

He looked down and saw that he'd knocked over a fifth of Jack Daniel's. A steady stream of the brown liquid poured over the carpet. By the time he had lifted the bottle, Abby had already retrieved some towels and began sopping the whiskey up.

"I'm sorry, Abby. Here let me get-,"

"I got it!" she snapped.

He sat back and watched, not knowing what else to do. When she finished, she stood up and surveyed the stain.

"Well, that's not coming out," she said, tossing the soiled towel aside.

"I'll pay for it. Hire a cleaning service or something. Here…," Martin said, pulling his wallet from his back pocket. Inside were seven dollars and his driver's license.

Abigail sighed and looked up at the ceiling.

"I can get the money. I'll get a job or someth-,"

"What was that?"

"What?"

"You called me 'mom'?" There was a look of repugnance on her face.

"I don't know. I mean, I just woke up and my head was pounding and the light was there and-,"

"But still…"

"I know! I know! It's weird."

"It's hella weird, Martin." She was pacing the room, her arms crossed.

"What do you want me to say? It was an accident."

"But, I don't even know how you could…I mean, what the…"

"Maybe it was the nurse outfit. My mom was a nurse, you know."

"I'm sure her uniform looked nothing like this one."

Martin examined Abigail's outfit and determined that she was correct. It was extremely low cut. Paired with a push up bra it left little to the imagination up top. The short skirt and pinstriped leggings didn't look like typical hospital issue, either.

"No. I guess not. Yours is a little-,"

"Sluttier?"

"I wasn't going to say that, but…yeah."

"Well, that's the whole point. It's a slutty nurse costume."

"Why are you wearing that?"

Abby shook her head. "Oh my God. You don't even know what day it is, do you?"

"Friday?"

"Yeah. The thirty-first. Halloween?"

"Oh. Isn't it a little early to head out, though?"

"It's 7:00!"

"It is?" Martin said, stupefied.

Abigail went over to the window and drew the shades. The streetlamps were on and Martin could see a slim waxing crescent of a moon just above the tree line.

"I slept until 7:00?"

"More like passed out," Abigail retorted.

Martin turned his attention from the window down to the stain by his feet. He stayed that way for a while, causing an already antsy Abigail to become further agitated.

"Martin!" she called out to him, but he was no longer there.

"Look...I know I said you could stay on the couch here until you figured things out...," Abigail said.

She walked to the couch and sat down next to him, pulling down at her hem to cover her underthings, and then up at the lapel to conceal her cleavage. Martin hardly seemed to notice.

"...but it's been almost two months and..."

Her voice drifted to him from some distant place.

"...drinking every night..."

His eyes shifted from the stain to the pillow he'd slept on. The pillowcase was fraying at the end. He twisted the fibers between his index finger and thumb.

"...sleeping until, well like 1:00 usually, but 7:00?"

Then his focus moved to Abigail's Jim Morrison poster. Jim seemed so free with his arms out wide like wings.

"I'm sorry to say this, but..."

Abigail placed her hand on Martin's shoulder. She pitied him. The dark circles under his eyes. His pale skin. His cheek imprinted with pillow marks. All of him.

"...you need to move out."

He did not so much as blink.

"Did you hear me?" she said, shaking him.

"Huh?" he said, his consciousness returning.

"You have to go."

"Yeah. I understand."

"You do?"

"Of course. Gimme a week. Two, tops."

Abigail nodded and stood up, again first adjusting her hem, then the lapels. She looked relieved.

"Ok, then. So...I'm guessing you aren't going to any Halloween parties tonight, right?"

"No. Stayin' in."

"Yeah, well..." she said and walked away, her absurdly high heels clicking away at the kitchen floor. She opened the front door, but before she left she turned back to look at him.

"Have fun," Martin said.

"Thanks," she said, and she was gone.

Martin stayed on the couch for a minute or two before walking to the corner of the room where his belongings were. He grabbed his laundry bag and sat back down. He dumped the bag's contents before him on the carpet. He sifted through clothing searching for something. Systematically, he shook out each shirt and pair of pants, listening for that familiar rattle. Finally, hidden inside a wrinkled up t-shirt, he found them.

His mother's pills.

"Let's go! Let's go! Let's go!" Latrice shrieked, bouncing up and down on the back seat.

"Ok. Ok. Get out the car, then."

Latrice leapt out onto the grass, and her eyes lit up as she watched all her fellow trick or treaters traipsing around, bags full. Flip leaned to the side and pulled his piece from his waistband. He popped open the glove compartment, and put it inside before meeting his cousin on the lawn.

"Ok, then. Lead the way," he said.

She dashed up the driveway of the nearest house and onto the porch.

"Trick or treat!" she yelled.

"Shhh, Latty! You don't gotta scream it!"

She smiled back at him and then turned her attention to the door, which, in her eyes, was taking entirely too long to open. Finally, it did and an elderly woman dropped a few pieces of candy into Latrice's bag. She thanked the woman and jumped from the porch, and back down the driveway to Flip.

"So, whatchu get?" he asked her.

"I dunno. Candy?"

"You ain't look?"

"No. I don't care what kind."

"A'ight. Well, let's go. Next one."

She ran ahead of him but then abruptly stopped. He caught up and off she went again, only to stop when she got as far separated from him that she was comfortable with. Arms at her sides, she shouted to him, "C'mon, Phillip! Hurry up!"

"Slow ya roll, Latty. We got time," Flip said, continuing at his own pace.

She huffed and puffed until he once again caught up, and off she sprinted. She reached the next house and repeated the candy receiving ritual.

When she reached Flip at the base of the driveway, he said "So, whatchu s'posed to be anyway?"

"I'm a bunny rabbit!"

"What, like Bugs?"

"No,"

"What, like Roger?"

"Who?"

"Energizer?"

"NOOO! I'm just a fluffy, white bunny."

"They ain't got no black bunny costumes?"

She shrugged her shoulders.

"Next year, we gon' get you a black bunny costume."

"I don't want to be a bunny again next year."

"Well, then black somethin'."

"Ok," she said, and up the next driveway she went. She got her candy and returned to him.

"That bag gettin' heavy? Need me ta carry it?"

"No. You'll eat my candy!"

"Damn right. Carryin' tax."

"I can carry it," she said, swinging the pillowcase over her shoulder.

"A'ight. Lemme know."

They approached the next house and observed a woman at the base of the driveway snatch her son's pillowcase from him.

"What did he give you?" she said, frantically digging through the bag.

"Give me back my candy, mom!" the boy yelled out.

"That man was obviously drunk. Who knows what he did to the candy," she said, still digging. "Here, this is what he gave you. You're not having this."

"But, mom…"

"Oh, be quiet. You've got enough already," she said, putting the candy in her pocket and giving the pillowcase back to the boy.

"Shit," Flip said.

"What, Phillip?" Latrice asked, looking up at him with big brown eyes and floppy white ears.

"That lady crazy. Go on now. Get that candy."

After the last couple drops plummeted from the lip of the can into Jack's mouth, he set it down on the tile next to the other five empties. In his left hand was the candy bag, wherein laid only enough candy for one more trick or treater.

"C'mon down, you're the next contestant on-" Jack said, stopping only when he saw a little black girl in a white bunny costume come running up the driveway and behind her a black man in baggy jeans and a black hooded sweatshirt.

"What the…Oh, hell no."

He stood from the chair and slammed the door shut. He brought his hand down over the switch and snuffed out the porch light, as well. Nonetheless, a little girl's voice came through the door.

"Trick or treat," she said.

Jack leaned against the door, making no move to address the little girl.

"Trick or treat," came the voice again.

Still Jack did not move. A deeper voice, Jack assumed it to belong to the black man, said something to the girl, but it was too muffled for Jack to decipher. Jack waited a few seconds and stepped over to the front window. He peeled back the curtains and saw the little girl in her bunny costume walk hand in hand with the man down the driveway and on to the sidewalk.

He flipped the switch back on.

Flip took his cousin's hand and led her away from the darkened house.

248

"They musta ran outta candy," he said.

"How do you know?" Latrice asked, big eyes looking up at him.

"The light's off. That means they out."

"But, Phillip…"

"What?"

"The lights not off."

Flip stopped and looked back over his shoulder. Sure enough, the light was on.

"Oh. They musta found some mo'."

They turned around and started back up the driveway. Just as Latrice hopped up the porch step, the light went off again. Latrice turned and looked at Flip with a confused look on her whiskered face.

"Hold up, Latty," he said.

He pulled up his jeans and stepped up on the porch.

"HEY, YO!" he shouted, rapping his knuckles against the door.

There was no response from the other side.

"Yo! Why you keep hittin' that light, huh? You got candy or not?"

Still no response.

He knocked again.

"HEY, YO! ANYONE IN TH-,"

"GET OFF MY PORCH!"

"What's that?" Flip said, taken aback.

"AND GET YOUR BLACK ASS SOUTH OF EIGHT MILE!"

Every muscle is Flip's body tensed up, but he did not immediately react.

"What'd he say?" Latrice said, looking up at him.

"Nothing, baby," he calmly said, his chest heaving in and out. "Get back, now, a lil' bit down the driveway, ok?"

"Ok," Latrice said.

She did as she was told, walking slowly down the porch, her pillowcase clasped tightly to her chest, and merged with a small crowd that had gathered at the base of the driveway, unsure of what was unfolding before them.

Gnashing his teeth, Flip muttered under his breath, "Homeboy done picked the wrong fuckin' day…"

He drove his fist into the door.

A shriek collectively was released from the crowd.

"C'MON OUT HERE, BITCH!" Flip shouted.

He delivered another blow to the door. Then another.

"C'MON OUT AND SAY THAT SHIT TO MY FACE!"

Another blow. Then two more. His knuckles had split open and blood was smearing across the cold steel.

"TO MY FACE!"

Flip stood on his tip toes and peered into the house through the door's half-moon window on its upper third. Inside was an old white man holding a small bag of candy backed into the corner of the landing.

"WHAT?" Flip shouted, resuming his assault on the door, but now with his feet.

"MY COUSIN... "

The heel of his size thirteen Air Force One slammed against the door, shaking it on its hinges.

"AIN'T GOOD ENOUGH..."

Another kick. And another.

"FO' YO' CANDY?"

Just as he was about to deliver another kick, one that most assuredly would have unshackled the door from its frame, he heard a quiet sobbing coming from behind him. He turned around to see the tears were Latrice's. Her drawn-on whiskers were running down her cheeks.

"Oh, shit," he said, pausing to catch his breath. "Y'all went an' done it now."

He flew off the porch, scattering the onlookers like pigeons. He scooped Latrice up in his arms and carried her down the driveway. Her tiny body was shaking.

"It's ok, baby. We goin'. We goin'..." he said, gently rubbing her back.

He could see his car parked up ahead underneath a large birch through the light fog that hung just above the pavement. He took several steps towards it but stopped suddenly and turned towards the old man's house. He extended his left hand and made a gun with his thumb and index finger. He closed his right eye and aimed directly at the front window. His hand recoiled ever so slightly when he pulled the trigger.

Martin sat on the toilet seat gazing at the little white tablets in his hand. There were ten of them. He must have counted them a dozen times.

The label stated not to take more than eight tablets per day, so he figured the ten in his right hand, along with the remainder of the Jack Daniel's in his left, would be enough to do the trick.

His heart was thrashing against the inside of his rib cage. His palms were moist, causing the tablets to stick.

There was no point in delaying it any longer.

He took a deep breath and slammed them into his mouth. The bitterness was immediate, bringing with it the harsh memory of that night in the alley. He looked to the whiskey for relief. He took a swig, but the pills refused to go down. Instead, they swam about, disintegrating.

The taste was insufferable.

Martin's abdominal muscles spasmed. He put his hand to his mouth in a fruitless attempt to keep it all in. With one further retch, semi-dissolved pills and whiskey filled the air. Martin's nasal passage singed as the liquor dribbled out of his nostrils. His eyes welled with tears. He stood and went to the sink, frantically cupping water into his mouth. He swished it around, tilting his head back to gargle. He did this again and again until the pain receded.

"GODDAMNIT!" he shouted, slamming his hand down to the sink. One of the oxycodone tablets clung to the uneven scraggle of his beard. He plucked it and threw it into the toilet. He discovered another on his sock, five on the floor and one that had landed in the small waste basket in the corner. The other two were M.I.A.

Martin cleaned them up and stood before the mirror. He dropped his brow and castigated the man he saw for his weak resolve and even weaker stomach. He silently berated him for how poorly he'd executed his own execution. The man accepted his nonverbal chastising for a while, but eventually he stood up tall, chest puffed out. Their failure was not due to lack of will, but to poor choice of method.

Martin agreed.

He snatched the little red bottle from its perch on top of the toilet's tank. He snapped off the cap and looked inside. Shaking its contents he estimated there were roughly another eight to ten tablets inside.

Into the kitchen Martin went, manically opening and closing drawers until he found the mortar and pestle. He set it down on the counter and placed the tablets in the ceramic bowl and set about to grinding. He surgically crushed each tablet into a fine white powder, stopping every few seconds to sift through it for lumps.

Once he had ground the tablets to his liking, he searched for the proper surface to spread the powder out. Not having a mirror, he figured a glass surface would suffice. In his pile of belongings he'd dumped on the living room floor was the answer to his quandary.

He retrieved the framed photo of his graduation and went back into the bathroom with it in one hand and the mortar in the other. He sat on the toilet seat again and very carefully dumped the powder onto the glass. From his wallet he pulled out his license and one of the dollar bills. With the license he chopped out three geometrically equivalent white lines.

His heart began to beat strongly again, though not with the fervor of before. He rolled the dollar bill into a tightly coiled cylinder and pinched it between his thumb and index finger.

Had he started with the line on the right, he may have gone through with it, and Abigail may have come home to find him face down on the tile, dead or nearly so.

But he didn't.

He started on the left. One end of the bill went up his nostril, and the other went to the bottom of the line. He plugged the other nostril and exhaled. That's when he saw his mother standing just to the left of his impeccable line.

Diane Kerner's smile had always been radiant and contagious. Even then, sitting on a toilet with a dollar up his nose, he had to fight the curl coming to the corners of his mouth.

On the other side of the line was a young boy in a robe and tasseled hat. His smile was forced. He was stupid and selfish and too naïve to know when to cherish the moment.

Martin tossed the dollar aside and swept the divisive line and its brethren into the wastebasket. He stood up and went back to the mirror.

The man was there, bearded and gaunt but in his eyes Martin could see something familiar. He turned on the faucet and waited for the water to warm before grabbing a bar of soap and working up a good lather. He applied the soapy water to his face, covering every single follicle.

In his toiletry bag was an old disposable razor. He dragged it across his face. It did not shear the hair so much as it snagged and yanked, leaving behind a patchy red landscape. Droplets of blood emerged here and there. Each pass was agonizing, but Martin did not relent.

Slowly but surely, the razor cleared the hair to reveal the face of that naïve boy, though older and hardened.

Martin dabbed the blood clean, but still, on his arms and shirt, he was spattered with severed hairs. He attempted to pluck and brush them off, but they were resilient. The only way to completely get rid of them was to wash himself clean.

He undressed and stepped into the shower without waiting for it to warm up. Standing there under its cleansing stream, he closed his eyes and recalled the slight rain that he and his mother shared that day. When his mouth again began to curl into a smile, he did not fight it.

Jack released the curtain and backed away from the front window when the angry black man was no longer in sight. He braced himself against the wall, trembling, negotiating with his heart to return to a normal pace.

It took several minutes, but eventually the feeling that he might pass out faded.

"Goddamn coward!" he shouted.

He was ashamed. He tried to convince himself that it derived from failing to stand up to his aggressor. Failing to throw open the door and protect his property, his beliefs, his manhood. But, it was a lie and deep down he knew it. After all, to mentally self-flagellate for not brawling with a man who was less than half his age was irrational. The shame came from somewhere else, somewhere nearer to his core.

He walked back to the landing to examine the damage to the door. He picked shards of wood from the jamb, where the deadbolt had dug a canal. He unlocked the door and opened it, feeling it sag on its hinges. The front was dented and decorated with a collage of bloodied shoeprints.

"Serves you right!" a voice yelled to him.

Jack looked out across his driveway, and that's when he noticed the spectators were all still there. In fact, the crowd looked to have grown.

"Who said that?" Jack shouted back.

A man in the back flipped him off and shuffled a little boy in a Batman costume down the street.

Jack surveyed the crowd. They were pummeling him with silent derision until he couldn't take it anymore.

"WHAT DO YOU WANT? HUH? YOU WANT THIS?" he shouted, launching the mostly empty bag of chocolate towards the mob. It wafted harmlessly to the pavement.

No one moved.

"YOU'RE DISGUSTING!" screamed a woman clutching a small ballerina at her side. There was fire in her eyes.

Jack could think of no counterargument. Instead he shouted, "GET THE HELL OFF MY PROPERTY!" and slammed his broken door.

The glass in the half moon window fractured and fell to his feet in pieces.

"AWW, HELL…" Jack said, and bent over to clean it up. A sharp pain shot down his hip, and he collapsed on his backside with a thud. Seated, he began picking up the pieces, one by one. Several of the shards dug in, causing trickles of blood to leak from his palms. Seemingly unaware of or indifferent to the pain in his hands he continued to pick up the glass. He organized the shards in his palm, piecing them together like a puzzle.

He then stood up, but his hip barked at him again. His hand reflexively went to the wall to brace himself, and the pieces tumbled to floor, their order lost to him.

Jack sighed and walked away. He went straight to the fridge and found that he had drunk the last beer. The pantry was dry as well, the last drop of whiskey long since imbibed.

He closed the fridge and went to the back door. Onto the driveway he stepped, barefoot, ignoring the pebbles imbedding into the soles of his feet. He reached the garage and stepped inside, closing the door behind him.

The ever flickering bulb hanging overhead, Jack sat in his auto sanctuary, sinking into leather creases and trenches that he'd earned through the years. His was at ease, his breathing barely there. It was then, that the man's attack and his own embarrassing rejoinder began to dissipate into the far reaches of his feeble memory. It was then that he began to truly feel at peace. It was then that he reached under the seat for the revolver.

The surge of power he'd felt holding the Smith & Wesson that day when Martin came home was absent. The only thing he perceived were the wispy tendrils of a memory that he'd been there before.

The barrel of the .38 began to graze the skin of his right temple.

Jack knew that, of course, he had been there before. Not in that exact location, but in that frame of mind.

The barrel slid across his cheek towards his mouth where it was received.

He couldn't remember much from that day; in fact he had no recollection of pulling the trigger. Other than waking up in the hospital, and possibly the thin, ever fading scar just above his right temple, he had no reason to believe it happened at all.

The cold steel clinked against his teeth.

But he did wake up in the hospital, and he saw her. She was so young. So naïve. She had no idea of the demons within him.

The hammer slowly tilted back until it clicked into place.

During those few weeks while he was held against his will until he'd proven his sanity to the powers that be, Diane had found a way to worm herself into a place in his heart that he'd long since given up as dead. A place that had only ever been occupied by Pamela.

The trigger quivered under Jack's index finger.

Nothing had filled the void that was created that night outside the Algiers. Not the anger. Not revenge. Not the alcohol. It was all poison. Then Diane came along. Her smile. Her calming presence. She was the antidote. She grabbed him by the shirttail as he was about to tumble over the edge of the cliff.

The trigger slid, ever so slightly, along its groove.

Then, just like Pamela, she too was taken from him. Without her, the anger and alcohol reclaimed power, destroying any possibility he had of reconciling with his son.

And without him, there was nobody.

The barrel of the gun slid deeper into his mouth just before it went off. Had it not done so, the interior of the GTO would have been ruined, blanketed with skull fragments, brain matter and blood that could never be truly wiped away. But the barrel did slide deeper. So deep that it induced a gag reflex, forcing the gun from Jack's mouth and causing the bullet to pass harmlessly through the GTO's convertible top. It penetrated the overhead light fixture before coming to rest in one of the rafter beams.

The gun's report caused such an intense ringing in Jack's right ear that for a moment he thought that the bullet had in fact hit him.

He pressed his palm into the noise, dropping the revolver in the process, but it was of no use. Nothing he could do would silence it. He screamed, but it too was no match for it.

He clenched his eyes shut, fighting back tears, but they came nonetheless. It was an avalanche, the pent up anguish of a life torn asunder by man's fear of the different and his penchant for violence.

Finally, the ringing reduced to a dull hum. When he opened his eyes, he noticed the light.

It was everywhere.

Parts of the garage that he hadn't seen in years were bathed in luminous fluorescent light. Above him, he could see the overhead fixture through the hole the bullet created in the in the convertible top. For years it had contained two bulbs, one dead and the other existing only as a frail, intermittent flicker. At that moment, both glowed brilliantly.

He reached out to the cone of light that passed through the bullet hole. He let his fingers dance with the dust particles it illuminated. He traced the air it passed through all the way to where it landed on the dashboard, just above the glove compartment. Almost reflexively, his thumb traced the button and pushed it in. Inside were two things; the original owner's manual and the Polaroid of him and the twins. He took the picture out and before he knew it, he had pulled his cell phone from his pocket and dialed a number that he'd saved off the caller I.D. from a late night call he received several years prior. A number that he never thought he'd use. After seven long rings, a man answered.

"Hello?"

"Hello," Jack said, stopping to clear his throat. "Is this um…who am I speaking with?"

"Sergeant Franklin King. Who is this?"

Jack's eyes welled again with tears. They drained into his nose forcing a sniffle.

"Hello?" King said.

Jack gathered himself and said, "Frank…it's Jack."

There was a pause before King spoke up again. "Jack?" he said, softly.

"Yeah."

For a while Jack heard nothing but the background drone of a busy office. Though he didn't know Franklin's location, he pictured him seated at a desk inside the tenth precinct. He saw an old photo of him and Martha in a dusty frame on one corner, and an outdated desktop computer on the other. He heard a faint squeal, which he attributed to Franklin shifting his weight in a chair with springs much in need of some oil. Finally, Sgt. King said, "Been a long time, Jack."

"Yes, Frank. It has."

And then nobody said a word. They were two seasoned prize fighters tapping gloves and dancing on the canvas, feeling each other out.

Frank spoke first. "I gotta admit, I didn't expect this. I'm kinda at a loss."

"Believe me, I'm just as surprised as you," Jack said, shifting about in his own chair, in search of a comfortable position that was nowhere to be found.

"You doin' ok, Jack?"

"Oh, yeah. Doin' just fine," Jack said. His voice quivered, belying his words.

"Really? It, uh…well, you sound-,"

"I'm fine."

"Ok, ok." King said.

And again, silence. Each wordless second threatened Jack's tenuous hold on his sanity.

"So, how about you Frank?" he blurted out, failing miserably to hide his frazzled state.

"What is this about, Jack?"

"Just say something, man," Jack said, running his hand through his thinned hair. His fingers remained at the base of his skull, or roughly were the exit point would have been.

"Why? Why now after all these years?" Frank said, a hint of annoyance in his voice.

"Can't you just humor me? All I'm askin'-,"

"I know what you're askin', Jack. It's the same thing I was askin' you for a couple years back, and you blew me off."

Jack sighed and said, "I know. It's just...tonight I..."

"What, you think I owe you something?"

"I don't know, Frank," Jack said, exasperated. "I...I got no one else."

"I wouldn't even know what to say to you. I don't know you anymore. What could we possibly have to talk about, Jack? Huh?"

Jack was on the verge of tears again. "If I woulda came next door ten minutes earlier..."

"Come on, now. Don't do this."

"Do what?"

"Jack...it was a long time ago."

"What? So it's not supposed to hurt anymore?"

"No. Of course not. It hurts like hell. Every goddamn day. I miss her, Jack. She was my sister, my *twin* sister. Hell, I still hate driving down that stretch of Woodward even though they bulldozed the Algiers years ago."

"So, it's ok for you to miss her because she was blood? I loved her, Frank!"

"I know, Jack. But...what's the endgame, huh? What's to gain by dredging up the past?"

"The past is all I got left."

"That can't be true. What about your son?"

Jack scoffed. "Yeah, well...he doesn't want anything to do with me, and to be honest, I don't blame him."

"What happened?"

"He found out about Isaac."

"Shit," Frank said, solemnly. "Well, I guess in this day and age, with the internet and all..."

"There's a book."

"Yeah...Abdul-Tawaab."

"You knew?" Jack said, surprised.

"I've known for a few years now."

"Why didn't you tell me?"

"When, Jack? When was I supposed to do that? We don't talk, remember?"

"I know. I know," Jack said, pausing briefly before adding, "And that's on me."

"No point in placing blame. It is what it is."

"No. You were a good friend, even during...you know, all of it."

"I tried, Jack. I really did."

Another silence came, but, for Jack, this time it brought with it no feeling of angst.

"Hey, Frank," he said.

"What?"

"You ever go see her? You know, over at Woodmere?"

"Every July twenty-fifth and then again on our birthday."

"You think maybe you and I can go together sometime? Maybe grab a coffee?"

For a moment all Jack heard was the squeak of Franklin's chair again.

"Sure, Jack," Frank said. "That'd be ok."

"Good," Jack said. He opened the GTO's door and got out, bringing the photo with him. He made a mental note to get a frame the next time he was out. "Well...I guess that'll do. Have a good night," he said.

"Jack," Frank said.

"What?"

"That boy of yours..."

"Yeah?"

"You should call him."

"I will."

"I'm serious. Family, Jack...family's everything."

"I promise. I'll call. Scout's honor."

"You were never no scout."

Jack scoffed. "Bye Frank."

"Oh, and leave Abdul-Tawaab alone."

"Why would you say that?"

"You know why."

"I'm not trying to get into any trouble. Not at my age."

"All these years and I can still tell when you're bullshitting me."

"Bye Frank," Jack said, hanging up.

He closed the garage door and walked slowly back towards the house, debating whether to follow through on that promise to call Martin right then. Ultimately, he decided to wait. There were a few fires to be put out first. One of which that had been burning for over forty years.

Tyreke was sleeping when the phone rang. The last thing he could remember was reading, but he was burrowed under the covers, the dog-eared copy of Huck Finn on the nightstand. He sat up and grabbed his phone. On the screen was a single word.

Flip.

His stomach dropped at least six inches and his mouth became the Sahara. He took a deep breath and answered it.

"Whatupdoe?"

"You strapped up?" Flip said.

"Uhh…yeah. I got my nine milli. Why?"

"Good," Flip said, ignoring him. "I'mma need you to bring it."

"What? Now?" Tyreke said, panicked.

"Naw…but soon."

"Ok, but fo' what?"

"…"

"Flip?"

With a shaky hand, Tyreke placed the phone back on the nightstand. When it fell to the floor, he didn't bother to pick it up.

He lied down again and closed his eyes in a feeble attempt to go back in time five minutes to a world where that phone call did not exist. Instead, a flurry of images rushed by, each more nightmarish than the last.

Flip's face, eyes ablaze and features twisted with rage.

His 9mm, spinning like a top, before stopping with the barrel pointed directly at him.

Then Danielle.

He snapped his eyes open and stared at the ceiling. He pleaded for exhaustion to overtake him, but it would not. There was no more sleep to be had that night.

CHAPTER XXI
NOVEMBER 4, 2008

Tyreke glanced back over his shoulder at his alarm clock. It was 7:15 and the first glimmer of sunlight was peeking through his blinds.

"Dani! C'mon now! I'mma be late!" he said, rapping on the bathroom door for the third time

"What? You got an early drug deal?" Danielle shouted from inside.

"Ha-ha," Tyreke said, feigning laughter.

Every morning, it seemed, she'd been spending more and more time in there. Tyreke, perplexed, put his ear to the door for clues as to what she was doing. For a while, he heard nothing, but then she flushed and ran the faucet briefly.

When she unlocked his door, he quickly went inside. He caught a glimpse of Danielle just before she escaped into her bedroom. He hastily showered and then dressed. He reached for the knob on the door that lead to his bedroom, but stopped before turning it. Instead, he turned around and went to the other one. The one that lead to his sister's room that he figured almost assuredly would be locked. He twisted it and was surprised when the door swung open.

"What the hell?" Danielle cried out from underneath the covers of her bed.

"Why you back in bed?" Tyreke asked.

"Don't come bustin' in here! What if I was naked?"

Tyreke shivered and said, "That shit woulda sucked."

"Well, get out!"

"Hold up. I just wanna see if you ok."

Danielle pulled the covers tight and drew them up to her chin.

"I'm fine. And how come you can't use the other bathroom? Gotta bother me when I'm in there."

"I didn't want to," he said, meekly into his chest.

"Why?"

"There was a big ass spider in that shower last time."

"Oh my God," Danielle said, rolling her eyes.

"You don't even know. It was huge! I reached for the soap and he just sittin' there chillin'. Almost bit my hand."

"You know, for a killer, you are such a baby!"

"I never killed nobody!" he shouted, a look of genuine hurt on his face. "Now answer me. Why you in bed?"

"'Cuz I'm in bed."

"What the doctor say yesterday?"

"He said…" Danielle hesitated, and looked up at the stars on her ceiling. "He said it's a stomach bug."

"That's some bug. You been throwin' up for like two weeks?"

"Yeah, well…"

"Is it contagious, 'cuz I ain't even tryin' to be getting' si-,"

"I'll be fine. You'll be fine. Everybody will be fucking fine!" she shouted, flipping over to face the wall.

"Whoa!" Tyreke said, unsure if he'd ever heard that word come out of his sister's mouth. It was a hideous sound. Like nails on a chalkboard.

He searched for the right words, but they evaded him.

"You're creepin' me out just standing there. I thought you said you were gonna be late, anyways," Danielle said, her voice muffled from talking into her blanket.

"I ain't leavin' 'til I know you a'ight."

"I just got a lot on my mind."

"Like what?"

"Oh, I don't know. How about the fact that I lost three people that I loved dearly."

"Who?"

Danielle said nothing.

"Ma Laika, but who else?"

"…"

"I know you ain't talkin' 'bout me. I'm right here, Dani."

"You are but you aren't," she said, solemnly. "Everything's changed."

"Yeah, you right. Shit done changed. I'm pullin' straight 'A's again and I ain't dealin' no more." He neglected to tell her about the phone call from Flip.

"You still talk like some banger, though. Anyways, too little, too late."

"Why's it gotta be too late?"

"Speaking of, you are for sure late now."

"Who's the third person?"

"..."

"It ain't, excuse me, it's not Martin, is it? You aren't still hung up on that fool?"

"..."

"You can do better than him. Someone who treats you like a queen. Some Taye Diggs lookin' brother..."

"I don't want Taye Diggs and I don't wanna talk about this anymore. Go to school."

"You work tonight?"

"Yes. Now go."

Tyreke slunk out of her room, gently closing the bathroom door behind him and gathered his things to go. Just before he stepped out the front door, he spotted Danielle's purse on the couch.

"Shit," he said, dropping his head.

He unzipped the front pocket and took out her cell phone. When he found the number, he begrudgingly entered the digits into his phone.

Martin cupped his hand over his phone to try and stifle its vibration in the front pocket of his pressed black slacks. He had turned the ringer off when he entered the Law Library for fear it may go off during the interview. In hindsight, he wished he had just shut it off the completely.

"Do you need to get that, Mr. Kerner?" said the very stern woman who directed administrations for the library.

"No ma'am. Let me just shut this off," Martin said, trying to find the mute button through his pants.

"What if it's an emergency?" the woman said.

"I'm sure it's not."

"Just check." Her features were harsh and cold. Martin was unsure if she persisted because she genuinely thought it may be an emergency, or if she just liked being in control. When she gestured with her slate gray eyes towards the phone in his pocket, he pulled it out and looked at the caller I.D.

"Nope. I don't recognize the number."

"Wonderful," she said, clicking her unpainted fingernails on her desk until Martin shut the phone off and returned it to his pocket.

"I'm very sorry," he said.

"Yes, well, I'm afraid that-," she replied, cut off when her land line rang on the desk. She answered seemingly unaware or just indifferent to her hypocrisy.

Martin waited patiently for the completion to her truncated sentence, though he already knew what it would bring. He would not be offered the job he so desperately needed, not only to pay rent at the shitty apartment he'd found off campus, but to replenish the coffers depleted by Abdul-Tawaab's course. And that doesn't even take into account compensating Abigail for her hospitality and whiskey stained carpet.

She hung up the phone and continued. "As I was saying, I'm afraid the only position available is for a reference desk assistant."

Martin was quite surprised, certain the vibrating phone had derailed the interview. "I'm willing to do anything."

"Hmm. Well, you can start on Thursday. 9:00am." she said, rising from her chair.

"Thank you for the opportunity."

Martin extended his hand, which the director accepted, albeit unenthusiastically.

"That's 9:00am sharp, Mr. Kerner."

"Yes, ma'am."

Martin left her office and stepped into the low hum of hushed whispers that was the Law Library. Everywhere he looked, he saw students bent over massive tomes of legal info and they all seemed to be sharing the same pained and exhausted expression. The anxiety over whatever seemingly unconquerable exam they had awaiting them was palpable.

And he was jealous.

The hostility towards Abdul-Tawaab, the man who'd single handedly robbed him of that communal experience, was absent, though. Martin had taken on a new, much more optimistic temperament and casted off the despair that had weighed him down for months. He no longer saw his becoming a lawyer merely an eventuality, but a certainty. It was only a matter of time.

So he stepped out into the early morning sun, with the notion that he should celebrate. Despite the chill of a Michigan November morning, he headed towards the nearest coffee shop for a frozen caramel cappuccino.

He located one on University and waited patiently in line to order his drink from the pretty blonde girl with a nose ring behind the counter.

"That'll be $4.45," she said.

Martin reached for his wallet in his back pocket, but stopped when he felt the phone vibrate again. He pulled it out to find the same 313 number from before. He hated ignoring calls from numbers he didn't recognize. He feared he'd miss something important. It vibrated in his hand as he deliberated.

"$4.45?" the girl said again, with a hint of annoyance in her voice.

Martin flipped open the phone and put it to his ear.

"Hello?"

"Yo, is this Martin?"

"Yes...who is this?"

"Tyreke."

"$4.45, sir! We have other customers!"

"Oh, I'm sorry," Martin said, snatching his wallet from his pocket. He fumbled through looking for a five. He tossed her the bill and shuffled over to the beverage pick up counter.

"Sorry for what?" Tyreke asked.

"What? Nothing."

"Your change?" the girl shouted to him, waving a fistful of coins.

"Yo, is this a bad time?"

"Keep it!" Martin said, waving her off.

The girl rolled her eyes and tossed the coins into the tip jar.

"Keep what? What the hell you sayin', yo?"

"Nothing. Nothing. I was talking to the...it doesn't matter. What...uh, what's up?"

"Where you at? It's loud as shit."

"Coffee shop in Ann Arbor."

"Oh," Tyreke said, clearing his throat. "Anyway, I called 'cuz...I can't believe I'm 'bout to say this."

"Say what?"

"That you should come down and see Dani. I think she be...I don't know, missin' you, or some shit."

"Missing me how?"

"What you mean how? How you miss someone? She be actin' all down and shit. Layin' in bed all day. Ain't like her."

"Really?" Martin said, feeling compelled to sit. He found the nearest chair and fell into it.

"How do you know she even wants to see me? She seemed pretty pissed at me that day."

"She my sister. I just know."

"Hmm," Martin said. The confusing noise in the coffeehouse was nothing compared to the maelstrom of voices in his own head.

"So whatchu gonna do, playboy?"

"I don't know…I guess I should call her."

"You guess?"

"No. I will. Tomorrow."

"The hell's wrong witchu?"

"What?"

"You got big plans right now?"

"No."

"So you a bitch, then."

"FROZEN CARAMEL CAP!" the barista shouted, holding the drink out in Martin's direction.

"I'm not a bitch, it's just-,"

"Then you must not give a shit and I'm wastin' my time."

"No. That's not it. I…" Martin said, rising from his chair. He pressed the phone against his head and plugged the other ear to drown out the noise.

"FROZEN CARAMEL CAP!"

"It's one or the other. Either you don't care or you a bitch," Tyreke said before adding, with a pause between words for effect, "A pussy…ass…bitch."

"I'M NOT A BITCH!" Martin shouted. Conversations around him ceased. Eyes were trained on him from every corner of the coffeehouse. Tyreke went silent as well, in fact Martin checked he phone to make sure they were still connected.

"Hello?" he said.

"I'm here. You gonna call?"

"As soon as we hang up."

"A'ight. Then we straight."

"Ok," Martin said.

"And I gotta bounce. I got class."

"Hey! Wait a sec."

"What?"

"What about your little toy tucked in your waistband?"

"Naw. I'm off that."

"Really?"

"Yeah. But that don't mean I won't end your ass if you mess with Dani."

"Understood."

"Just make the call," Tyreke said and he hung up.

The phone lingered against Martin's ear for a moment before he returned it to his front pocket. He looked up at the wide eyed barista whose hand was extended in mid-air holding his drink.

"Frozen caramel cap?" she said.

"Thanks," Martin said.

He strode with purpose past the line of patrons. As he reached for the door, a hand, feminine but strong, gripped his arm. He looked up into the eyes of its owner; the library's director of administrations.

"Mr. Kerner!" she said, reproachfully.

"Thursday! 9:00am sharp!" he said, and exploded through the door and into the cold. He marched down the sidewalk, sidestepping backpack clad students, past the salon and the Mexican joint, crossing Church St and the bars he'd so frequently wasted his time and money. Near the apothecary shop, he took a long, slow drag from his caramel cappuccino. An icy shiver ran up his spine that stopped him in his tracks. He shook it off and tilted his face to the sun.

Danielle stood in front of the full length mirror adorning the back of her bathroom door. She turned to the side and pulled up her tank top to just below her ribs, running her hand over her abdomen gently in a circular motion. She was not showing yet, which brought her a modest amount of relief, though she knew she had a month, maybe two, before she would be. To give herself a glimpse into the future, she widened her stance and pushed her belly out. She quickly recoiled. The sight of it, bulbous and distended, terrified her.

Her cell phone rang.

Down the hall she went, to her purse on the couch, unaware of Tyreke's earlier prying. When she saw the number on the caller I.D., her heart fluttered. She sat down at the corner of the couch and pulled her knees to her chin. She couldn't take her eyes off of his name on the digital display. Her hand trembled as she pressed 'accept.'

"Hello," she said, hoping it didn't sound as weak and feeble as it did on her end.

"Danielle?"

"Hi Martin."

"Hi…how are you? You doing ok?" he asked.

"Yeah. You?"

"I'm fine. Is this a bad time. You sound-,"

"What? No, no. I'm…" Her hand went back to her abdomen. "I'm just a little flustered. I didn't expect you to…"

Her bottom lip began to quiver and tears welled in her eyes. She looked across the room at the picture of herself and her mom and brother at the Belle Isle Beach. Though she fought it, the tears slowly blurred their faces.

"Danielle?"

"Yes?" She could not keep the emotion from coming through in her voice and it angered her. She was not the little girl who cried at the drop of a hat. She was stronger than that.

"I miss you," he said, and the levy broke. Tears came pouring down her cheeks. Her chest heaved in and out erratically with her breathing.

"Danielle?"

Sounds came out, but she was unable to piece any of them together into words.

"It's ok. You don't have to talk until you're ready. Ok?"

"Mmmhmm," she said through a sniffle.

"Ok," he said, taking a moment to collect his thoughts. "Then I'll get straight to the point. The last two months have been two of the hardest of my life. They've been shit, to put it bluntly. But it's my own fault. I'm the one who ran away. I went to Ann Arbor even though there was nothing for me here. No job. No school. Nothing. But I did anyways because I was scared. Scared of…shit, everything. Failure. My father. Tyreke and honestly…of you."

Danielle was surprised by his words. She wiped her eyes with her shirt and said, "Me?"

He inhaled deeply and slowly released before answering.

"Did I ever tell you about the deer?"

"No."

"Oh. Well, this one time, during freshman year, I was pulling an all-nighter and my brain was just fried."

"Ok…"

"It was during finals, like mid-December. Studying for sociology was kicking my ass, so I decided I needed to take a walk, you know to get some fresh air. I grabbed a granola bar to snack on and rushed out of my dorm wearing only shorts, a sweatshirt and flip flops."

"Why didn't you put on a coat?"

"I told you. My brain was fried. I didn't even think about it until I stepped outside and, holy shit, was it freezing! There was probably four inches of snow on the ground, and remember, I was wearing flip flops. My toes were numb in seconds. So, I turn around to go back inside to get my shoes just in time to see the door slam. And after midnight you had to slide your I.D. keycard to get in, but of course I left mine in my room. I had to go all the way around the building to the main entrance. So I started walking. I'd only taken like three steps when I saw a flicker of movement in this little patio outside the administration building. It was hard to see from a distance and with the snow falling in my eyes, so I had to make a decision: ignore it and get my freezing ass back in the building, or investigate and risk frostbite."

"You chose frostbite," Danielle said, having gained some control over her tears.

"Yeah, well at the least the risk of it. Anyways, as I approached the patio the figure of a deer came into focus. I thought it to be quite strange that a deer would be on campus, so I kept advancing on it, slushing through the snow in my flip flops, to get a better look."

"Hadn't you ever seen a deer before?"

"Of course I had, but they were always way out there in some field or dead on the side of the road. This was different. It was only thirty feet away."

"So, what happened?"

"It saw me and we both froze."

"Literally and figuratively."

"No, I'm sure it was quite comfortable. The deer was wearing its coat."

"Terrible. Just terrible," Danielle said, grinning.

"Yeah, that was bad…Anyways, I thought it would take off, but it didn't. It just stared at me. I looked around to see if there was anyone else witnessing what I was, but the patio was deserted. All the while it never took its black eyes off me. I could see hot breath pluming from its nostrils. Snowflakes would land on its hindquarters and disappear. Every few seconds, the muscles would twitch, ever so slightly, underneath the fur. That's how close I was. It was absolutely stunning."

"What was?"

"The deer. It was so beautiful. I'd never truly appreciated that beauty until I really looked at it. Soaked it in. All I can say is that I was transfixed. My mouth was agape and I no longer felt the cold."

"Nice."

"And then it grunted at me."

"Excuse me?"

"Yep. I couldn't tell what it meant, because I don't speak deer, but yes, it absolutely grunted at me."

"Deer don't grunt."

"No? Then what sound do they make?"

Danielle thought about it for a second, but for the life of her, she couldn't remember ever hearing a deer make a noise. Martin took her pause as a concession of defeat.

"That's what I thought. So…at that point, I decided I needed to be closer to the deer, to share that moment in time with it. To ingrain myself in its memory and it in mine. To be a part of its existence. To do that, I figured I needed an offering. That's when I remembered the granola bar. I went to grab it from my pocket and all it took was that slight movement and the deer took off."

"Sucks."

"But the thing is, it didn't run away completely. It just hid behind some bushes about twenty feet further from me. I watched it for another minute until finally I remembered how cold I was, and then I went back inside."

"Is that it?"

"Yes. I suppose it is."

"Umm…I'm sorry. I mean, it's a beautiful story, but I don't see the relevance."

"The deer and I shared a moment. But it could have been so much more. Fear, though, wouldn't allow it. I walked away disappointed, and it went hungry."

"All because it ran."

"Yeah. But I guess I shouldn't have been surprised. Running is in their DNA."

"And what about you?"

"I guess…if you're told a lie over and over again for your entire life, even though deep down you know it to be untrue, you start to believe it."

"Your father?"

"Yeah, but not just him. It's the whole damn city."

"I know."

"Except I never fully left, Danielle. I never stopped thinking of you and I wanted to tell you that I'm not scared anymore. I need to see you. Tonight."

"Tonight?" she blurted out, in shock.

"Yeah. Do you not want to see me?"

"No. I really, really, really want to see you. Tonight is fi-, CRAP!"

"What?"

"I have to work tonight. Crap! Crap! Crap!" Danielle repeated, slamming her fist to her thigh.

Martin chuckled at her demonstrative, yet PG exclamation. "It's ok. I can meet you after."

"I don't get off at the Kahn until ten, though."

"The Kahn? The Kahn-Hudson? You got that job?"

"Yeah."

"Cool! What's it like?"

"Let's just talk tonight. I have…lots to tell you."

"Ok."

"Oh, and I might be able to switch and get off earlier, but I don't know. I have to call the other hostess."

"That's fine. Just let me know."

"I'll text you a time, ok?"

"Sounds good."

"Martin?" Danielle said as she got up off the couch and walked down the hall to her bedroom.

"Yeah?"

She opened her closet door and pinned the phone between her head and shoulder. She needed the use of both hands to sift through her clothes for the perfect outfit.

"Why call today? I mean, after all this time?"

"Honestly?"

"Yeah."

"Tyreke called me this morning."

"HE DID? THAT LITTLE..." she trailed off, unable to conjure a non- expletive laden ending to her thought.

"Why are you mad? If he hadn't, I might still be hiding in the bushes."

"I suppose. But still...I'm gonna have to talk to that boy." The smile on her face contradicted her severe words.

"Not before you talk to your coworker."

"I know. Let me hang up and call."

"OK. And Danielle?"

"Yes?"

"I love you."

She closed her eyes and smiled the most she had in months. "I love you, too."

She tossed the phone to her bed and pulled from her closet a lacy white, knee length cocktail dress. She twirled across the hardwood floor, pressing the dress against her body. A tiny squeal escaped her lips, which surprised her. She was never the type to squeal, or twirl for that matter.

She stopped in front of the mirror where she examined herself for the second time that morning.

"No white after labor day," she told her mirrored self, wagging her finger. She turned to get a look at her profile and said, "Screw it. I look good."

Then she pushed her belly out, and held it. Unlike before, it didn't bother her. She was no longer afraid.

Jack Kerner was in the same place he was every day at 9:00am since his talk with Franklin: the sidewalk. A brisk walk had become a part of his morning routine. He'd have much rather been jogging, but the walk was all his hip, and his fifty-nine year old knees would allow after a lifetime of neglect.

He looked up through his condensed breath and saw his house approaching on the right. Just as his feet hit the driveway, Robinson, that old bastard, emerged from his front door, equipped with a thermos of coffee and a judgmental stare.

"Hiya doin', Jerome?" Jack said, with a wave.

Robinson stopped in his tracks, paralyzed by Jack's greeting. From the look of the man's frozen features, Jack feared the man was mid-stroke. Finally, though, he grumbled something that sounded like the word *fine*, before shuffling off to his Mercury to do whatever it is that old men do.

Jack went inside to continue with the next step of his newly adopted ritual: a long, hot shower. He found the water to be cleansing both physically and spiritually. He became more focused, eager to tackle the day's activities. Up to that point, they had been mostly just the seemingly endless list of trivial, yet necessary, things that he'd ignored since Diane had died. Changing furnace filters, new batteries in the smoke detectors, not to mention replacing the damaged front door.

But, that day was different. He had two long overdue conversations to have and he knew they would be taxing. He was apprehensive, and his anxiety had muddled the serenity the walk and shower normally brought him.

He lingered after shutting the water off, breathing in the steam until a chill started to come on. He dried off, dressed and ran a comb through his thinning hair before starting off to the kitchen to brew a fresh pot of coffee. Caffeine had replaced alcohol as his drug of choice. He was putting away four to five cups per day. The jitters and occasional runaway heartbeat were no fun, but he still preferred them to the hangovers.

Before long, the java's dense aroma had permeated the kitchen. Jack poured himself a healthy cup and sat down in his recliner.

The first sip burned, as it always did, but he was too engrossed in his own thoughts to wait for it to cool. He took another sip and pulled out his phone. He pressed the necessary buttons and waited. It barely completed one ring before an excited sounding Martin answered.

"So are we on for tonight?" he said.

Jack squinted at the display to make sure he'd dialed the right number.

"Excuse me?" he said.

There was a brief pause before Martin said, "Oh, shit."

"Martin?"

"What do you want Jack?" Martin's tone switched to defiance, anger.

"Who did you think was calling you?"

"That's none of your concern."

"Don't you have caller I.D.?"

"What? Yeah…of course."

"Was it that girl? What was her name?"

"I never told you her name."

"Tell me now."

"Why?" Martin said, but when no reply came, he relented and said, "Danielle, ok? It's Danielle."

"Is that who you thought was calling?"

"What do you wan-,"

"Was it her or not?" Jack said, the calm in his voice never wavering.

"Yes! Yes. I don't need another lecture on the evils of the black community, or any other topic for that mat-,"

"Good. I'm glad."

Martin scoffed. "Glad about what?"

"Do you love her?"

"Don't toy with me, old man. I've just now gotten over some pretty shitty stuff, and I don't need you trying to mess with my head."

"It's a simple question."

"Yes! I do. More than anything. What is this? Are you drunk?"

"No, Martin. Only coffee in my cup. Today is day four of my sobriety."

"Really?" Martin seemed legitimately surprised. "Four days, huh? What's the over under on you making the week?"

"Martin, I don't want to fight."

"Then hang up."

Jack breathed a heavy sigh and rose from his chair. He began to pace the room.

"Do you remember when you asked me whether or not I loved your mother?"

"How could I forget? It was the moment I realized how stupid mom was for-,"

"YOU SHUT YOUR DAMN MOUTH!" Jack shouted, the only time he would lose his temper during their conversation.

Martin didn't say a word, from shock or obedience Jack couldn't tell. Either way, Jack quickly spoke up for fear that Martin may hang up.

"I didn't mean to yell. It's just…you shouldn't ever say that about your mother. She was…she was a lot of things, damn near every one of 'em good, but stupid ain't one of them."

"I didn't mean it that way."

"I know. You were just takin' a dig at me, which is what you do and that's my fault."

"What's your fault?"

"For not teaching you how to be a man."

"So, now I'm not a man?"

"Don't be so defensive. And don't go twisting my words when I'm trying to apologize."

"I haven't heard anything resembling an apology."

"Well, can you give me a chance to speak without some snide remark?"

"Hang on a second."

"For what?"

It took Martin a few seconds to respond. "I just got a text."

"From her?"

"Yeah. So, go ahead. Let's hear it."

"I'm sorry, ok?"

The words came, but not without difficulty. When he said it again it felt more natural, sincere. "I'm sorry a hundred times over."

"For what? For the fights? For the countless birthdays and recitals and games and award ceremonies you missed? Be specific, Jack. It's a little trite without context."

"For all of it. I'm sorry for all of it. I'm sorry…how did you put it…?"

He paused.

"…that I was never a loving husband and father…and instead…an alcoholic asshole."

"Wh…what did you say?" Martin asked, the defiance stripped from his voice.

"You heard me."

"How…why did you say-,"

"I was there, son. You didn't think I materialized from that row of trees just in time for the picture, did you?"

"Yeah…I kinda did."

"I got there late. I stayed in back in the vestibule. And afterwards…well…what was there to say? You were right."

"I had no idea. I didn't mean for you to hear that."

"Yes you did."

"Maybe I did. But why did you have to get that drunk? It was my graduation day. I was the goddamned valedictorian!"

Jack heard the hurt in his son's voice. He hated to bring him more pain than he already had. But it had to be done. Too much time had already been fritted away on grudges and falsehoods.

"Your mother told me that morning about the cancer."

"What?"

"She never wanted anybody to worry. Never wanted anyone to do anything for her. She just did and did and did for everyone else, at the expense of herself. For weeks she'd been so restless at night with the headaches that she was keeping me up, too. I finally told her to stop being silly, and just go to the damn doctor. Hell, she worked at a hospital. 'Just go,' I said. She resisted at first, but I convinced her. Well, you know the rest."

"You found out that day? She didn't tell me until after I left for college? That was months later."

"If it was up to her she never woulda told anyone. Didn't want to inconvenience anybody with her dying, I suppose. Anyways, we both decided to wait so you could enjoy your last summer before college."

"That sucks. You kept me in the dark."

"What would you have done about it?"

"I don't know. I…"

"I loved her, Martin. Maybe not in the Hallmark sense, but I did. It pains me to this day that she died. She was too good a person to have to suffer like she did."

"Then why did you say what you did? That she was like a nurse to you?"

"Because, in a way, she was exactly that. She found me when I was drowning in my own loathing, and managed to keep my head above water every day after."

"She told me how you met, you know. At the hospital."

"Did she say why I was there in the first place?"

"Yes."

Jack wasn't surprised. It would be just like Diane to try and make him a sympathetic figure in Martin's eyes. Anything to bring them closer after her death.

"I was weak. I had no one and-,"

"You don't need to go into detail. I understand."

"You do?"

"More than you know."

"What's that supposed to mean?"

"Nothing."

"Is everything all right over there?"

"Yeah, yeah," Martin said, dismissively. "I'm fine. I got a job, or at least I think I do. I'll find out Thursday morning, I guess. Still reading the case studies in prep for when I apply next year."

"That's really why I called."

"What do you mean?"

"I'm going to visit your professor, this Abdul-Tawaab, today to speak about your grade."

"There's no point. He's not gonna budge."

"We'll see. He may be more receptive to me."

"Good luck with that."

Nobody spoke for a while. The conversation up to that point had been strenuous for both of them and the brief respite was not unwelcome.

"I truly am sorry, Martin," Jack said, breaking the silence. "I've been everything you said I was that day, and probably more. But, I wasn't always this way. I used to be...well, I used to be a lot like you, only without the brains. You get them from your mother."

"How were you like me?"

"I was engaged once before. Pamela King. She grew up next door to me."

"You were?"

"Yes. I was eighteen. She was the sister of my best friend Franklin. You've met him."

"I don't know anybody by that name."

"Sgt. Franklin King. He called me the day you met in an alley in Detroit."

"Ahh…that's how you knew! I should've known it was some old cop buddy that told you."

"Anyways, she was my first love, and no matter how much I cared for your mother, she could never take Pamela's place. Nobody could."

"Why didn't you get married, if you loved her so much?"

"Because she was murdered right before my eyes."

"Oh…shit."

"Yes, well…"

"By who?"

"Isaac Howard."

"So that's why you-,"

"I'm not going to talk about that night, if that's where you're going."

"Ok. Can I ask you one thing, though?"

"Go ahead."

"Who's Reggie Howard?"

"His brother. He was my age. We actually were friends, or at least I thought we were. That all changed when he stood by and let his monster of a brother take her from me."

"Did you try to tell the cops?

"It was during the riot. It was chaos. I was scared they'd botch the case somehow and he'd get off. Plus…forget it. You wouldn't understand."

"Try me."

Jack sighed and said, "If it was Danielle, and you had to watch the life fade from her eyes…watch the future you saw together destroyed…you would want justice. I'm not sure that means life in prison."

"I understand that just fine, but, forgive me, I still don't understand how that makes you like me."

"I'm not gonna spoon feed you."

Jack waited for Martin to piece it all together.

"That cop. Franklin King. He was black," Martin said.

"Yes. Still is, as far as I know."

"That means his sister…"

"Uh huh."

Martin could only laugh. "Mom was right. I don't know you at all."

"No, you don't. That's something I mean to fix going forward."

Martin was quiet. Jack knew his son would require time to process everything and he meant to give him all he needed.

"I'm going to go, now," Jack said. "If you ever need anything, anything at all, just call."

"There is one thing."

"Name it."

"Can I borrow the GTO?"

"What?"

"Never mind. I shouldn't have asked."

Jack laughed. "No, no. It's not that. I'm just surprised. When?"

"Tonight."

"I'll make sure it's gassed up."

"Really? Just like that?"

"Just like that."

"And what if I said that I was going to take it downtown?"

"That's fine, Martin."

"Downtown Detroit."

"Just watch that clutch. It sticks."

Jack waited for Martin to say something, but nothing came. Somehow, he felt that was better than if he had. A slight smile came over his lips as he sat back down in his chair.

"I might be gone but the garage door will be unlocked and I'll leave the key on the console."

"Ok."

"All right, then. I'll umm…we'll talk soon.""

"Thanks, Jack."

"Goodbye, son."

He put the phone back down on the table and picked up his coffee. It still burned but he guzzled it nonetheless. He needed the caffeine for the mental edge. That conversation was just an appetizer compared to what was in store for him.

He set down the mug on the table next to Abdul-Tawaab's book. He then pulled open the drawer where he used to keep the TV Guide, back before there was a whole channel to tell you what's on. The drawer now held an assortment of dried up pens as well as a notepad that somehow had made its way into the house from a dentist's office in Madison Heights that he'd never been to. He sifted through the drawer until he found what he was looking for: a black felt tipped marker. He uncapped it with his bared teeth and picked up the book. Across Marid Abdul-Tawaab's name he drew a thick black line.

Tyreke got Flip's text while in his calculus class.
PIK U UP UR CRIB 6PM.
After it came, focusing on the limit definition of a derivative became a near impossibility. He waded through the rest of classes and managed to make it home without crashing his car in a fit of panic.

Luckily for him, Danielle was not there, and with her working until her date with the white boy, he had a good chance of avoiding her altogether. The last thing he needed, as he'd painstakingly tried to restore normalcy to their relationship, was for her to see him taking off with a nefarious character such as Flip.

After eating a whole sleeve of saltines in a failed attempt to settle his nervous stomach he lied down on his bed. He contemplated every way he could foresee the night's events unfolding. He looked at it this way and that, flipped it over and back again, and still he saw no scenario that he'd walk away unscathed. The game just didn't work that way.

Brightmoor didn't work that way.

When the horn announced Flip's arrival, Tyreke didn't believe it.

"No fuckin' way!" Tyreke said to the 5:43 on his bedside clock's face.

"I need more time!" he pleaded.

The horn blared again, this time a long, incessant blast.

Tyreke leapt from his bed fueled by pure adrenaline and crawled to his closet. He fumbled through his collection of shoeboxes for the one that housed his gun. The horn blared again and again, as if Flip was communicating in Morse code for Tyreke to get his ass outside.

He tucked the piece into his waistband and darted through the house to the door. Before slamming it shut, he took one long forlorn look around the house, knowing full well that it might be the last time he would.

Jack stood in front of a heavy oak door with a frosted glass pane on which HH 323 was printed in block letters. He tapped gently on the glass and awaited a reply that would not come. He could see the shifting silhouette of Abdul-Tawaab behind the glass. He knocked again, harder.

"Before you break the glass, I'll have you know office hours were over at 5:30," Abdul-Tawaab bellowed.

Jack tested the knob. It was unlocked, so he entered. The first thing to catch his eye in the sparsely decorated office was the large framed photo of the African American arrestee. It triggered unpleasant memories of those fateful days. The second was the man he'd come to see, seated with his back to the door and busy filing papers in a small cabinet.

"Either you are deaf or extremely slow. Office hours are over and I have dinner reservations with the dean."

"Hello, Reggie," Jack said.

Immediately the fingers that had been dancing along the file tabs froze. Abdul-Tawaab posture stiffened but he continued to face the wall.

"Been a long time, Jack," he said, slowly swiveling the chair around to meet eyes with his old friend.

Gazing upon Reggie, Jack was reminded once more that time tends to ravage even the biggest and strongest of men. His hair, grayed. His skin, wrinkled. His eyes, though, were just as piercing and intense as Jack remembered them to be.

"Yes, it has. Long time."

"I must say I expected you much sooner."

Jack stepped in and closed the door.

"Lovely place you got here, Reg," he said, running his finger along the dusty spines of an assortment of shelved books. Next to a stack of newspapers called *The Final Call* were several copies of the same book he had on his side table, albeit without a vandalized cover.

"I'm glad my office garners your approval," Abdul-Tawaab said, bitingly.

"Not your office. Your city. Detroit. It looks marvelous."

"Your sarcasm is not lost on me."

"What sarcasm? It's true. I drove through the old neighborhood before coming over to see you."

"I'm surprised you knew the way."

"All I had to do was the follow the smell of gunfire."

"Droll."

"So, what's with the new name?"

"I follow the teachings of the Nation of Islam."

"Like that Farrakhan."

"Yes."

"Isn't that a bit hypocritical?"

"How so?"

"I read your book. In it, you vilify the white dominated society. But then you hitch on with a bunch of black supremacists?"

"That is merely a critique lobbed at us from the ill-informed, but I highly doubt you came here to talk politics."

"No, I came to ask you a question."

"I'm all ears."

"Is this what you wanted?" Jack said, his arms spread out wide.

"What are you referring to?"

"The city wasn't perfect. None are. But damnit, man! Look around you! It's a goddamn warzone out there."

"And how could that possibly be what I wanted?"

"Well you burned the city down to gain control. All these years it's been yours, and you haven't done a damn thing with it. Twelfth St looks just as it did when the rubble was still smoldering."

"I did not light a single fire. Do not put that on me," Reggie said, his index finger aimed like a dart right between Jack's eyes.

"Oh, we both know who was at the blind pig that night. The streets talk, Reg."

For a moment, Jack saw something other than restrained intensity in Reggie's eyes. It was regret, but only a flicker. Had Jack blinked, he would have missed it.

"Come now, Jack. You know your people are just as complicit in this city's decline as we are."

"Ha! You can't be serious."

"You don't think your abandonment of the city had anything to do with the state that it's in?"

"What were we to do? You made it quite clear you didn't want us around."

"That was not the purpose of the riot. It was a declaration of equality."

"There are better ways to get your point across, I would think."

"Perhaps. But the city was sick. Maybe you didn't see it, being white, but it was a deep, festering infection. The riot was the first step toward a cure. Like amputating a rotting limb."

"The patient's terminal, Reggie."

"I disagree, but even if that were so, at least we stayed. We didn't run and hide from our responsibilities to the community."

"Is that what you think we did?"

"Yes. You ran," Abdul-Tawaab said, rising from his seat. "Like the cockroaches you are, you ran across your precious Eight Mile."

Slowly, he came from around his desk, closing the space between him and Jack. It was then that Jack noticed that while time had taken its toll on Reggie's features, it had done nothing to his massive frame.

"So now we're cockroaches," he said, taking a step backward.

"We shined the lights on the true nature of this city, and you ran. Isn't that what roaches do? Run when the lights come on."

"Ok, we left. But don't go playing the martyr. You had your opportunity to do right by this city but you failed. Admit it."

Abdul-Tawaab scoffed.

"Why are you really here, Jack?"

"You know why I'm here. You squeezed my son because of our history."

"No. He's a liar and a racist, just like his father. I've witnessed it with my own eyes."

"Then why is he on his way to a date with a pretty little black girl? The one he told me he's in love with," he said, taking another step back. His foot hit the base of the book shelf. There was nowhere to go.

Abdul-Tawaab stepped forward.

"Let's keep this civil, Reggie."

"It's Marid Abdul-Tawaab!" he shouted, grabbing fists full of Jack's shirt with his goliathesque hands.

"WHAT HAPPENED THAT NIGHT?" he shouted. His eyes were alight with a rage that had been pent up for almost forty years. His nostrils flared and his breath blanketed Jack's face with heat and the faint smell of stale coffee.

"WHAT ARE YOU DOING!?" Jack said, attempting to pry himself free. It was of no use. Abdul-Tawaab's grip was vice-like.

"HE WAS MY BROTHER!" Abdul-Tawaab said, violently driving him back.

Jack's teeth rattled in his jaw when his head met the cinder block wall. There were stars dancing around Abdul-Tawaab's head. Still, Jack was unwilling to submit to his assailant. He found his footing and leaned into his assailant's face.

"HE WAS A MONSTER!" he said, and the next thing he knew he was airborne. Abdul-Tawaab lifted him from his feet and drove him to the unforgiving tile floor. His hip exploded with pain, but it was nothing compared to the discomfort of having the full brunt of Abdul-Tawaab's weight come crashing down on his abdomen. Whatever breath he had stockpiled was quickly expelled from his lungs. He struggled to regain it as there was no room for his chest to expand. He wheezed and pulled, but it was a losing battle.

"WHAT HAPPENED THAT NIGHT!?" Abdul-Tawaab yelled, his voice pinging off the walls.

"HE...USED TO...BEAT YOU!" he managed to push out.

Abdul-Tawaab wrapped his hands around Jack's neck and squeezed.

"TELL ME!" his thumbs digging into Jack's Adam's apple.

"HE...K-KILLED...H-HER!"

Jack was losing his grip on consciousness. The stars had disappeared and were being replaced by a slowly growing black curtain. Abdul-Tawaab's face floated above him in a tunnel.

"I lo...loved herrr..." Jack said, slipping away.

"SO DID I!" Abdul-Tawaab cried out.

And then all of a sudden the immense weight on Jack's chest lifted. The hands around his neck vanished. The life giving oxygen returned, though barely. It was like sucking air through a coffee stirrer. Slowly, his vision returned as well. It was grainy and forming in patches like a puzzle coming together, piece by piece. Abdul-Tawaab had retreated to his book shelf. He was bent over, breathing heavily facing the wall.

"HEY!" Jack shouted, sounding asthmatic. "FINISH ME OFF!"

Abdul-Tawaab did not move.

"That's what I thought. Couldn't do it then and can't do it now," Jack chided. "Goddamn coward."

Flinching at that last word as if it stung, Abdul-Tawaab still did not turn around. Instead he shuffled his feet towards his desk, head down and collapsed into his desk chair.

Jack attempted to rise when he felt he had enough of his wind back. He wobbled like a newborn foal, bracing himself on the professor's desk.

"Whatever this is between us," Jack said, straightening his collar. "Leave my boy out of it. It's our mess."

Abdul-Tawaab paid him no mind. He reached across his desk for the old photo of Isaac and him in their militant gear and gently traced the frames ridged edge with his thumb.

Jack waited for some confirmation that Abdul-Tawaab understood, but he never got any. So he limped out of the room and down the hall towards the elevator bank and pressed the button. While waiting for the car, he heard a crash come from the direction of Abdul-Tawaab's office. He looked down the hall and there lying on the floor amongst shards of frosted glass was the picture frame.

Tyreke spoke only once until Flip parked the car on the unfamiliar street just off of Nine Mile. When they had taken the exit for I-75 north off of the Davison, he asked, "So, where we goin'?"

The sideways glance he got in return was enough for him to know that it might be best to keep quiet.

After they had been parked underneath the naked branches of a large ash for over ten minutes, Flip finally said something.

"You see that house up there? On the right?" he said, pointing up ahead. "The one with big ass tree in the front yard."

"Sure," Tyreke said.

"Old ass cracker that lives there fucked up Latrice's Halloween."

"How?"

"His racist ass flipped the light off when we roll up."

"Oh, shit."

"Lemme see that strap," Flip said. He extended his hand but never broke gaze from the street. Tyreke handed him the gun. Flip briefly looked it over and set it in his lap.

"Pretty sure he alone. Been by couple times already. Never see anyone else come through," he said.

"We gon' rob his ass?" Tyreke asked.

"Already been inside. Ain't shit worth taking."

"He didn't have no money? No gold? Nothin'?"

"Naw..." Flip said, rubbing the scruff at the end of his chin. "There *was* one thing I found."

"Somethin' we can move?"

He reached into the back seat and pulled out a picture frame.

"What's that?" Tyreke said, confused.

Flip handed it to him. It housed a photo of three people. A woman. A man.

And Martin.

"Recognize anyone?" Flip asked.

Tyreke said nothing, unable to do anything but stare at the framed photo.

"What's wrong, nigga?" Flip said, placing a patronizing hand on Tyreke's trembling shoulder.

"Oh, it's all right. You can tell Flip. It's that cracker that was runnin' round outside, ain't it? The one you let get all up on your sister."

Tyreke, still unable to form words, meekly nodded.

"Yeah. I thought so," Flip said, sitting back again.

"Was the first thing I saw when I bust in there. That pic. I was like, 'that's that cracker. That's him.' Thing is...more I looked at it, more I kept thinkin' I'd seen him before, y'know, before that night at my crib."

Tyreke, frozen stiff, watched Flip slowly wrap his fingers around the Glock's grip.

"Pop open the glove box," Flip said, using the gun to relieve an itch above his ear.

"Wh...what?" Tyreke muttered, terrified at the thought of where this was going.

"Goddamn glove box, nigga!" Flip said, pointing to it with the barrel.

Tyreke did as he was told. Inside was a stack of napkins from Tubby's sub shop, some rolling papers and an old cell phone.

"The phone. Peep that last photo."

Tyreke opened up the phone's gallery. He scrolled all the way to the end where he found a dark picture of a thin, white man.

"Who dat?" Flip asked.

Tyreke had absolutely no idea who the bearded, gaunt man was.

"I don't kn-,"

"Aww, c'mon now. Zoom that shit in."

As the image grew, Tyreke realized that the man behind the beard was once again Martin Kerner.

Flip could read the recognition in his face.

"That's right! Him again."

"I don't...whose phone is this?" Tyreke asked.

"T-Mar's. You see..." Flip said, reaching the gun across the cabin until it grazed the skin of Tyreke's left temple. "He always snapped a pic before a deal in case some shit went down. And as you know...shit..."

He lowered the barrel to Tyreke's chest.

"Went..."

Then to his abdomen.

"Down."

The barrel came to rest in Tyreke's crotch.

He squirmed and pushed back into the seat, but the barrel was zeroed in.

"Now, you wanna tell me why your sister's boyfriend is in T-Mar's phone?"

"I...I..." Tyreke squealed, waiting for the moment when a bullet would rip through his manhood.

At that moment, Flip grabbed Tyreke by the head and slammed it against the window.

"YOU KNEW!"

"NO!" Tyreke screamed as Flip forced his skull on the glass. "I DIDN'T!"

He was sure at any second his head would break right through.

"DON'T PLAY ME, NIGGA!"

"I'M NOT, FLIP!"

Flip loomed over him with crazed eyes, examining every inch of Tyreke's face for signs of deceit.

"Nigga, I ain't even fuckin' witchu. We Brightmoor and all that, but I will straight up spray your shit all over this mu'fuckin' car if you playin' me."

"I swear, Flip!" Tyreke contended with what was the best poker face he could muster under the circumstances.

The cabin was filled with light.

Up ahead a car approached. Flip shifted his attention from Tyreke to watch it park in the street in front of the old man's house. As he saw someone emerge from the car and walk up the driveway, he released his grip on Tyreke's head and sat back behind the steering wheel.

"You ready to prove it?"

"F-fo sho'," Tyreke said, exhaling deeply. His hand briefly went down low to confirm everything was still there.

"A'ight then. You know whatchu gotta do."

He dropped the pistol in Tyreke's lap.

"What? You mean pop the old man?"

"You said you wanted out. Well, this how you get out."

Tyreke slowly reached for the Glock with a shaky hand. He had carried the gun for a couple years up to that point, but only because it was what he thought he was supposed to do. Everyone he knew had one. He'd never even fired it, let alone shot someone.

"When?" he said, stalling.

"Now, nigga! Whatchu think?"

"No. I just…"

"Just what?"

"I…I was thinkin' is this really the best way to do this?"

"Oh, you runnin' shit now?"

"No, but this old man, is that who you really got beef with?"

"Hell yeah, I do. Woulda murked his ass right then if weren't no crowd watchin'."

"I feel you. But this dude…" Tyreke said, flipping the image open on the phone. "This dude the one who got T-Mar locked up. Ain't he the one we should we takin' out?"

"We do the old man. It's payback for what he do to Latty and it'll send a message to the white boy. Plus, he right here and the white boy ain't, so…" Flip said, reaching over and opening Tyreke's door. "Quit tryna' get out this shit and move."

Tyreke placed one foot on the pavement, then the other. Up ahead was the house of a man he'd never met, a man who he held no ill will towards, but nonetheless would die at his hand.

He closed his eyes.

"What if I knew where the white boy was gonna be tonight?"

"Say what?" Flip sneered.

"He gon' be downtown. With my sister."

"I thought I told you to end that shit."

"I *did*, but she…she do what she wants."

He dared a glance back into the car, expecting to see Flip seething. Instead he looked contemplative, calm.

"Downtown, huh?" he said, again stroking the stubble. "That's perfect."

Tyreke subtly pumped his fist at his side. He needed now only to send Flip on a wild goose chase for the evening, and no one would have to die, at least for one day.

Cones of light came piercing the dark in front of the old man's driveway, followed moments later by a low rumble and the glimmering, metallic body of Old Detroit.

"Shit!" Flip yelled.

"What?"

"Fuck you mean, what? He leavin'," Flip said, fumbling at the keys in the ignition. He turned them and the engine came to life.

"So?" he said, swinging his feet back into the car. "I thought we were going after the white boy?"

"We are," Flip said. A sinister grin had taken possession of his face.

"Right after the old man."

Martin stepped cautiously up the driveway to the garage, a part of him expecting to open it and find nothing inside. He could see Jack changing his mind, deeming Martin too green a driver, Detroit too dangerous, or worse, Martin's choice of companion too black to lend him his precious GTO. That was always how it had been with him and Jack: a series of disappointments.

When the door was lifted, though, his doubts were extinguished. Before him stood thirty-five hundred pounds of pure Detroit muscle.

Up until that morning, it had been the only thing in the world that Martin believed his father ever, truly loved. Taking in the Pontiac's elegant curves, Martin began to feel smitten as well. He walked along the passenger side, allowing his fingertips to lightly graze the iridescent blue paint. He marveled at the gleam flashing off the rally wheels.

Leaning against his father's underused workbench to get an all-encompassing view of its mighty berth, he recalled the hate he'd felt as a child towards the car. It had been Jack's mistress, stealing him away from his rightful place in the house with his wife and child. Martin often even fantasized about one of the towering ashes crashing down on the garage during a late summer storm.

Standing before it now, the veil of contempt had been lifted. He could see that the hatred had always been misplaced. The GTO, an inanimate object, was bereft of feeling or intent and had been nothing but a symbol of his father's inadequacies as a man.

He got behind the wheel.

The interior was a snapshot from an era long since passed accompanied by a faint aroma of Armor All and skunked beer. Everything was in showroom condition other than the sag in the driver's seat springs and a curious dime sized hole in the convertible top. He inserted the key into the ignition and turned it. The boisterous eight cylinders filled the garage with sound. Martin wrapped one hand around the wheel and the other on the floor shifter. He could not help the shaking in his left leg as he slowly eased off the clutch. After a near-stall, Martin steered the GTO out of its hibernation and into the night.

They turned right onto Nine Mile. About five car lengths ahead, Tyreke could see the GTO's octet of thin horizontal taillights as it glided down the road, its driver blissfully unaware of the peril that lurked behind.

He momentarily broke surveillance to steal a glance at Flip. On the surface, he appeared calm and composed, as if stalking and hunting another human being was commonplace. The only thing that suggested that he may have flipped, as the streets had murmured he was given to do, was the intensity with which he gnawed at his lower lip.

The GTO slid into the left lane.

"Shit. I can't see him. Can you?" Flip said, his view obscured by a giant F-350 pickup.

Tyreke could, but he hesitated admitting it.

"DO YOU SEE HIM?!"

"I..."

"You better look around this goddamn truck an' tell me whatchu see."

Tyreke shifted over to the right, feigning difficulty.

"He there," he said, with resignation. "look like he gettin' on 75."

Flip sneered and jerked the car over into the now vacant right lane. He floored the gas pedal until he had space to cut off the big truck. The man behind the wheel laid on his horn, which did not even register on Flip's radar. He followed the GTO onto the southbound freeway's service drive.

"Grab that strap," he said, still gnawing at his lip. Tyreke wondered whether he was impervious to the pain or if the pain was the whole point altogether.

He picked up the gun.

"What we gon' do? We getting' on the freeway."

"*We* ain't doin' shit. *You* gon' pop his ass soon as this traffic light up."

The freeway was fairly congested and Tyreke knew that even in his agitated state, Flip was unlikely to make a move with so many witnesses. As they passed Eight Mile, then Seven, the frustration grew on Flip's face. Still, the traffic remained heavy. Tyreke silently appealed to the traffic gods that it stay that way.

Past Detroit.

Downriver.

Into Ohio, for that matter. However long it took for Flip to give up.

One look, though, at that now bloodied lip told him that it wouldn't matter if they followed that car all the way down 75 to Florida. Eventually Flip would get his man.

Slowly, traffic lightened and when they passed the Caniff ramp, the freeway basically emptied. It was as if everybody all of a sudden needed a kielbasa fix and grabbed that exit towards Hamtramck.

"Here we go, nigga," Flip said, gently pressing down the accelerator.

Tyreke watched the GTO get closer and closer on his right side. Meanwhile, the gun grew heavier and heavier.

"A'ight, now. Aim for the mu'fucka's dome. Pop-pop and we out. Ready?"

Tyreke nodded as if he was, but it was a lie. He'd never be.

He wasn't a killer.

Even the rumor that Ma Laika's drive-by had been meant for him, rendering him at least indirectly responsible for her death, made him sick to his stomach. Still, he hadn't pulled that trigger. Her death was not by his hand. This man's would be. There was no preparing for that.

The GTO's back bumper was even with their front. Then the back wheel. Tyreke wrapped his hand around the gun's grip, and gently placed his index finger on the trigger.

"Raise that shit, nigga!" Flip shouted.

Tyreke lowered the window. Wind whipped across his face, smearing the tears that had welled up in his eyes. His arm slowly began its ascension as the silhouette of the man emerged in the GTO's window.

He looked down the sight.

"Forgive me Dani," he muttered under his breath, before slowly adding pressure to the trigger.

"SHIT!" Flip yelled, braking hard.

Tyreke lurched forward, nearly hitting his head on the dash. His arm hung out the window, the gun precariously dangling from his hand. He looked up to see the GTO shoot forward five car lengths.

"Pull it in! Pull it in!" Flip yelled.

Tyreke quickly pulled the gun back into the cab of the vehicle. "What happened?" he asked.

"5-0!" Flip said, straightening up in his seat.

Tyreke turned around and saw a cruiser about six car lengths behind. "Where'd he come from?"

"No clue. Goddamn state boy."

"What we gon' do?"

"We ain't doin' shit cuz we ain't *do* shit. We just two niggas out drivin'."

Flip changed lanes to the right, directly behind the GTO, making sure to use his signal.

The blue Ford approached on the left. Tyreke's heart was beating so rapidly that it became hard to discern individual beats.

"Eyes forward and keep that piece down," Flip ordered.

Tyreke did as he said.

The cruiser pulled even with them. Flip sat upright, chest out, with both hands on the wheel.

"Ten and two, bitch! Keep movin'!" he said, but the cruiser did not budge from its position. Up ahead, the GTO passed the exit for East Grand Blvd.

The cruiser's flashers lit up.

"Shit!" Tyreke yelped, forcing his eyes to their absolute corners. He didn't dare turn his head.

"Slide me that strap, nigga!"

Tyreke placed the gun on the seat between them. Flip slowly picked it up.

"You picked the wrong nigga…" he said, lowering his window.

Inch by inch, the barrel ascended.

"…to fuck with."

Just then, the cruiser's engine screamed and it exploded forward. Within seconds it had darted across three lanes and up the I-94 onramp.

And it was gone.

"Thass right, nigga! Thass right!" Flip shouted at the now distant cop.

Tyreke put his hand to his chest and, for a moment, felt a sense of relief wash over him. But one look at his companion glowering through the tops of his eyes at his now distant prey extinguished it. And when the gun was directed back across the seat, he knew that this night would only end with someone dead or in jail.

Franklin King finished the last bite of his coney dog and dropped a couple dollars down on the table.

"Delicious, as always," he said to the woman behind the counter.

"I'm glad you enjoyed them," she said with a smile as warm as the famous chili topping the coneys.

"Y'know, for years, I couldn't have 'em. Yeah. First time I came home with them onions on my breath, Martha, she flat out told me; it was her, or the coneys. 'Course I chose her."

The waitress smiled politely, wiping the counter with a damp cloth.

"I, uh…I told you that before. Didn't I?" he said, sheepishly.

"Yeah, but I don't mind listenin'. Here…" she said, handing him a napkin. "You got a little…"

She pointed in the general direction of his face.

He wiped at the corner of his mouth and the napkin came away smudged yellow.

"Mustard," he scoffed.

"Goodnight, Frank."

"Goodnight," he said.

He stepped out into unseasonable warmth. Though the sun had long since set, the temp was hovering near sixty degrees. So, instead of clutching his lapels close to his chest, bracing against a typical November chill, he strode down Michigan Ave with his coat flapping in the light breeze.

And he was happy.

It wasn't due to the weather, or the coneys, scrumptious as they were. It was because of the fact that, earlier that day, he was able to cast a vote for presidential candidate that looked like him.

Now, he was no fool. Obama's blackness was not the only reason he'd garnered his vote. Franklin had seen many a black leader fail his very own city, and to have voted for him solely because of skin color would have been just as indefensible as to vote against him for that same reason.

No, Franklin had liked what Obama said in the debates all the way back to the primaries. How he'd carried himself.

His demeanor.

Those were the reasons he got his vote. The fact that he was black, too: that was just gravy.

Franklin eased into his seat and flipped on the radio to the AM news station to catch the latest election results.

"…only thirty-two percent of Ohio precincts reporting, but so far the numbers are favorable for candidate Obama. Other battleground states such as Virginia and Indiana also leaning his way, though it's still early. It's still anyone's guess which way Florida will swi-,"

He flipped off the radio.

"Martha baby," he said, smiling. "I wish you were here to see this."

He pulled the cruiser from the curb in front of the old shoe repair store and started eastbound down Michigan. He turned right on Griswold and then left on Larned. The streets were deserted and most of the businesses were closed for the night, but that was fine by him. He had no particular destination in mind. He just wanted to be there, as he felt the election was as much about Detroit as the country as a whole.

So he drove.

Through Lafayette Park, Eastern Market, feeling the city's pulse through his tires, drifting through the steamy breath emerging from its sewers, relishing in the moment.

The GTO exited at Mack Ave with its pursuers right behind.

"A'ight. Enough playin'," Flip said. "Soon as we get an opening, this shit ends."

The GTO turned right onto the avenue and settled in the far left lane. Flip pulled behind and to the right. Tyreke shifted in his seat, preparing to take the shot.

"Hell you doin'?" Flip said.

"What?"

"Whatchu mean 'what'?" he said to Tyreke with a crazed look in his eyes. "He in the left lane. You think I want you leanin' over me, blastin' that shit right in front my face?"

"No. I-,"

"Ignorant-ass nigga!"

He squeezed the wheel so hard, Tyreke wondered how it didn't break off in his hands. They passed a green light at St. Antoine and another at Beaubien, all the while the GTO stayed to the left.

"Motherfucker!" Flip howled, seemingly vexed at why the driver wouldn't just move over to better facilitate his own death.

Up ahead, the light at Woodward was a tired yellow. The GTO hit the gas, turning left just as it turned red.

"Aww, hell no," Flip snarled.

"Don't do it, yo!" Tyreke implored.

Flip floored the accelerator.

An old, haggard woman wrapped in several layers of filthy rags pushed a shopping cart filled with junk onto the crosswalk going northbound. One step after the next, right into their path.

"FLIP!"

Tyreke covered his face.

The impact sent the woman's belongings, an assortment of bottles and cans scavenged for the ten cent deposit and some cardboard that most assuredly would have been fabricated into a makeshift shelter that evening, soaring through the air. The mangled cart landed on the grassy median, looking like an amateur piece of public art.

The tires chirped and skittered across the pavement as Flip forced them southbound. Tyreke spun around to see what carnage lied in their wake. The woman stood statuesque in the middle of the road, either still trying to process what had just happened, or paralyzed by life's cruelty.

"You almost killed that woman!" Tyreke cried.

Flip said nothing. He was singularly obsessed with one thing and one thing only; revenge. A homeless woman and her garbage simply did not matter.

He quickly shrank the divide between them and the GTO.

"You ready?" he asked, inching up to his white whale from the center lane.

Tyreke nodded, taking his hand off the pistol for a moment to wipe the sweat on his pants. He looked around. Theirs were the only two cars on the seven lane span.

"A'ight, nigga. It's yo show," Flip said.

Martin had just completed the left on onto Woodward when his phone vibrated in his lap.

It was his father.

"You callin' to check up on me?" Martin said.

"No, no. I just wanted to see how she's handling. I haven't taken her out in quite a while."

"Other than almost stalling as I pulled out of the garage, it's been fine. You do have to adjust to a car this big, though. The hood goes for miles."

"That wasn't even a full size model back then."

"And it is kinda tough to keep this phone pinned against my shoulder and shift."

"Well, we didn't have cell phones back when I bought her. No crazy navigation or mp somethin' or others, either."

"Mp3."

"Whatever... so, did you open her up?"

"I don't know what that means."

"Punch it. Hit the gas. You know."

"Oh. No, not really. I didn't know if that would be cool..."

"What's the point of drivin' a muscle car if you're gonna baby it?"

"I don't know."

"Well, drop her into first and get on her, then."

"What, right now?" he said, looking to the right, then left for any sneaky cops potentially hiding in the shadows, ready to pounce.

There were none.

"Why not?" Jack said.

"Ok. Let me put you on speaker," Martin said, dropping the phone back into his lap.

"I need two hands for this."

By the time they hit Erskine, they were in position. GTO on the right, no onlookers. Tyreke knew he was out of excuses.

It was time.

He hung the shaking gun out and aimed at the back of the man's head. Looking down the sight, the color of the man's hair gave him pause.

It was brown, not gray.

"You sure it's him, Flip?"

"What?"

"Can't see his face with his cell pressed to his ear, but the dude don't look old."

Flip wiped at the film coating the inside of his windshield and squinted.

"SHIT!" he screamed, slamming his hand on the dash.

"GOD! DAMN! MOTHERFUCK!" he continued, punctuating each syllable with another slam.

Tyreke cowered against the door.

"WHO THE HELL IS THAT?" Flip pleaded. He was borderline hysterical.

Tyreke shrugged his shoulders.

"LOOK AT HIM!" Flip ordered.

Tyreke straightened up and did as he was told.

"Hard to say. Could be anyone."

"NO! I told you. Ain't nobody come by there! He alone!"

"I mean, maybe it's some nephew or a friend from work, or maybe…"

It was then that the man they'd been following lowered his phone and turned his head.

"HOLY SHIT! IT'S HIM!" Flip bellowed.

"No, no…it…it," Tyreke mumbled, aghast at seeing Martin's face.

"IT'S HIM! POP HIS ASS!"

Tyreke didn't flinch.

"NOW!"

Wide-eyed, Tyreke shifted his gaze from Martin to the pistol in his hands to Flip. Back, forth and back again.

"AHHHH!!" he screamed, swinging the gun across the cab, aiming directly at Flip's chest.

Flip looked down at the barrel and scoffed.

"You lil'…" he said. "I knew it. I knew you were in on this shit. Why else you want out the game?"

He turned and stuck out his chest.

"Ok, playa. Nice big target. Do it."

Tyreke tried to. He commanded his finger to pull that trigger, pleading with it to do so, knowing full well it might be his only option. But the finger wouldn't budge.

"That's what I thought," Flip sneered.

Ahead, the GTO shot forth like a rocket, filling the air with a throaty rumble and painting the cement with twin patches of rubber. Tyreke glanced in its direction, momentarily taking his eyes off of Flip, but a moment was all it took.

Flip's left fist crashed into Tyreke's right cheekbone, fracturing it immediately. He collapsed backward into the door, dropping the gun to the floor in the process. Flip chuckled and sat back in his chair.

And floored it.

Tyreke, fighting against the pull of unconsciousness, felt his body being driven into the seat by the car's surge. He had no control of his limbs, his only reality being the pain radiating across his face and boring through his skull. He remained in limbo until a sensation near his feet drew him back into the here and now. He opened his eyes, a struggle heretofore unknown to him, and looked down.

What he saw was Flip, his face mangled by fury, reaching across the cab and frantically scouring the floor for something. With his brain barely functioning, it took Tyreke a few seconds to figure out what that something was.

The gun.

The car veered wildly back and forth across multiple lanes as Flip groped about. Tyreke, slowly regaining himself, knew that if Flip found it he was dead. He reached behind and fumbled around for the door handle. He located it and yanked. The dome light came on, illuminating the Glock poking out from underneath Tyreke's seat.

Flip grabbed the gun, but before he could raise it and fire, Tyreke flung open the door.

And leapt.

The world flipped over on itself repeatedly. Down was up and up was sideways. Every bone in his body took its turn slamming into the pavement until, mercifully, he caromed over the curb and came to a stop at the base of a defunct dollar store at Charlotte St. Unable to corral the spinning in his head, nausea overcame him and out came the saltines in a pile on the sidewalk.

His chest heaving in and out, he wanted nothing more than to lie there motionless so as not to exacerbate the indescribable amount of pain that had engulfed him, but he knew he could not.

He reached into his pocket to retrieve his phone.

"Shit!" he yelled out, staring at the ravaged screen. "Shit, shit, shit!"

Having no clue what the white boy's number was he dialed the only one he knew by heart; Danielle's.

"C'mon, c'mon..." he muttered, putting the phone to his ear. The few second lag from when he hit 'send' until he heard that first ring was agonizing.

"No voicemail! No voicemail!"

Just when he thought she wouldn't answer, her voice came over the line.

"Ty? What's up?"

"DANI!" he exclaimed.

"What? Is something wrong?"

"He's coming!"

"Who?"

"Flip!"

"Flip? That fool from the neighborhood?"

"He's gonna kill him!"

"Kill who?"

"Oh, shit! Shit, Dani!"

"Ty! What are you saying? You're scaring me!"

"You gotta warn him!"

"WHO?"

"Martin! Me and Flip was followin' this old blue convertible...it was supposed to be some old man! I didn't think it'd be him, Dani! He's gonna kill him!"

"OH MY GOD!"

"Call him!"

And the line was dead.

Slowly, he slid down the wall until he felt the soothing cool of the sidewalk on his fractured face. He curled up his legs and he cried. Nobody paid him any mind. To the onlookers cruising down Woodward Avenue, he was just another vagrant. Another insignificant lost to the streets.

The GTO fishtailed for a moment, the rapidly spinning tires unable to gain traction. When they hooked up, the car shot forward. Martin banged into second gear, chirping the tires again. The pull was exhilarating. The needle kept rising on the speedometer as the streets flew by. Third gear. Then fourth. The landscape blurred. The vacant lots on his right. The new condos on his left. They were just colors bleeding together.

When the needle hit ninety, he started on the brakes. Fun was fun, but he had no desire to miss his date and spend the night in jail on a reckless driving bust. By the time he hit the I-75 service drive, he was a law abiding citizen again.

"Hello?" a voice said from his lap.

"Sorry," he said, again pinning the phone between his head and shoulder. "Forgot about you for a sec."

"I understand. It's easy to forget about things when you're behind that wheel."

"That was pretty wicked. I must admit."

"She sure sounded good on my end."

Neither spoke for a moment, seemingly content just to share the same silence. Martin passed by both the Fox and State Theaters before making a right on Adams.

"So...you almost there, then?" Jack said.

"I think so," he said, navigating the GTO around the curve of Grand Circus Park onto Washington Blvd. "Like half mile away."

"Ok, good," Jack said, a smile coming through in the tone of his voice. "Well, I'm almost home, myself, so I suppose I'll let-,"

"Hang on a sec. Getting another call," Martin said.

After a brief pause Martin continued. "I'm sorry. You were saying?"

"Was it her?"

"Yeah, but it's fine. I'll see her in a minute."

"What time you tell her you'd be there?"

"6:30."

"Then you're late."

"It's 6:25."

"Five minutes early is late for a date and you never want to keep a good woman waiting."

"Oh, yeah? Where were these pearls of wisdom before?"

"I don't know, son. I don't know."

Martin passed the Grand River intersection and could see the Kahn-Hudson Hotel up ahead on the left.

"All right, I'm at the hotel. I should go."

"Hotel, eh?" Jack said, a hint of innuendo in his tone.

"For drinks. Nothing crazy?"

"Ahh. Ok, have fun."

"Dad?"

"Dad? You haven't called me that since you were a boy."

"No. I guess I haven't," Martin said, pulling to a red light at Michigan Ave.

"Well, what is it?"

Martin looked off to his left and at the picturesque, tree lined boulevard and the hotel's glowing façade with the myriad flags above the golden entrance swaying in the gentle wind.

"I wanted to say thanks."

It took Jack a moment to respond.

"You're welcome, son."

Martin hung up and when the light turned green, he maneuvered the GTO eastbound onto Michigan and then back onto Washington to the hotel's valet drop.

And there she was.

Bursting through the revolving doors, she looked as stunning as ever in a lacy, white dress. But, something was definitely off. She was waving her arms as if she was on fire, frantically pointing at something behind him. Her features, normally delicate and graceful, were grotesquely contorted with terror.

Her lips moved but the sound was drowned out by the screeching of tires coming from behind him. Even still, it was obvious she was screaming.

After a while, Franklin King found himself back on the same little strip of Michigan Avenue whence he'd begun his election night victory lap. And what he saw there, like much of Detroit, was downright Dickensian. On his left languished a blacked out, two story brick cube that housed a nightclub. Its sole purpose seemed to be to provide a haven for gun-toting gangbangers to mix it up. On his right stood a shining example of what Detroit used to be, and what could be again; the recently refurbished Kahn-Hudson Hotel. He stopped at a red light at Washington and watched the door men and valet boys do their thing.

And in front of him, waiting to make a left was something he hadn't seen in ages; a pristine blue 1967 Pontiac GTO. Just like that, he was eighteen again, watching his best friend bring his brand new car up West Philadelphia Street.

"Can't be," he said, squinting to get a look at the driver. The lights from the hotel's façade glared off the GTO's windshield, obscuring his view.

"Is that you, Jack?"

The first bullet shattered the driver's side window and entered Martin's left shoulder, driving him hard to his right. The wound immediately burned as if he'd been stabbed by a white hot fire iron.

NOCTURNE IN BLACK AND WHITE

Danielle froze mid-sprint just feet from the car at the sound of the gunfire. Martin, confused and mouth agape, searched her petrified face for some level of understanding.

Two more shots rang out.

One bullet pierced the GTO's steel and lodged itself in the base of Martin's left lung. Blood ejaculated from his lips and painted the dash and windshield. Martin tried desperately to stay locked in on Danielle's face, but everything was blurring around her. The world came in and out in waves.

Pain was the only constant.

The final bullet came through the now opened window and came to rest inside Martin's skull just above his left ear. Martin's body went lax and splayed over the console. The pain was gone. There was no panic. There was nothing, and then even that was gone, too. He was no longer there.

"This is Sgt. King. Shots fired! Corner of Washington and Michigan. Repeat. Shots fired! Request back-up!"

Franklin King threw open his door and sprang from the cruiser. Within seconds, his gun had been drawn and he was off and running.

The perpetrator attempted to flee the scene, only he didn't get far. Two lanes of the boulevard were blocked by a still running Lincoln MKS that a frightened valet driver bolted from upon hearing the shots. There was only a sliver of space between its front bumper and a line of parked cars. The shooter attempted to squeeze through and failed.

"C'mon outta there, hands up!" Franklin ordered, approaching the mess of twisted metal with his gun trained on the driver's side door. "Don't make things any worse for yourself!"

No response came from the vehicle.

Pandemonium had ensued outside of the hotel. The wealthy suburban restaurant goers and the street people collectively sought cover, terror knowing no socioeconomic status.

King continued to close in. As he passed the GTO, one of the panicked on-lookers nearly ran right into him.

"Watch it, girl!" he said to the young woman in the lacy, white dress.

She was frenzied and paid him no mind. She flung open the GTO's door and let out a blood-curdling scream.

King looked in the car.

"Shit," he muttered, recognizing Martin from that night in the alley.

"One of you! Get her away from the car!" he yelled at the throng.

Nobody moved.

"Now, goddamnit! And call this boy an ambulance!"

Several of the onlookers pulled out cell phones and started dialing.

Angrier than ever, he marched to the wreckage and sidled up against the car's driver's side quarter panel.

"Get the hell out that car! Arms to the goddamn stars!" he shouted.

Not a peep from inside the car.

King breathed out a deep sigh and swung the gun into cab.

The car was empty.

There were traces of blood on the seat and steering wheel, but no shooter.

He stood up, his head on a swivel, and scanned the faces of everyone in sight; the huddled masses near the hotel entrance, the scattered onlookers up and down the street, everyone.

The man leaning against the deli on the corner at State Street looked suspicious, but then again so did the two teenagers a half block up on the grassy median taking videos with their phones.

The shooter was all of them and none of them. Precious time was ticking away.

A scream.

King spun around and saw its source was the girl. A large black man had both arms wrapped around her and was violently ripping her from the GTO.

"Hey! Don't hurt her. I just need her away from my scene!" King commanded. He lowered his weapon and approached them.

"NOOO!! NOOO!!" she screamed, writhing around beneath the man's clutches. Her legs furiously kicked at the space around her.

A shoe went flying into the bushes.

"I said take it easy, buddy!" King implored, more vociferously. "Just get her back to the hotel!"

The man remained silent, towing the girl not towards the hotel but southbound towards Michigan Ave.

"I SAID TO THE HOT-,"

King stopped when he saw the blood.

It was right there seeping from a gash above the man's left brow.
King quickly raised his pistol and aimed it at the between the man's eyes.

"Let her go, or I will end you! Right here and right now."

"In front of all these rich, white folks?" the man scoffed. "You ain't
goin' spoil they dinner."

"Now!"

"Can't you see they the problem? They come down here actin' all
high and mighty, eatin' they food, buyin' they drugs and then what?
What about my nigga T-Mar? Huh? What about him?!"

He pulled the Glock from his waistband and pressed it to the girl's
temple who, seemingly all screamed out, mustered only a whimper.

"Goddamnit, son! Let the girl go!" King said, approaching with
trepidation.

"Hell no! She the problem, too! And that mu'fucka in that car. And
the old man. And Ty!"

King saw mania in his eyes. Something else, too. Sadness. Perhaps
fear.

"I have no idea what you're talking about," King said. "Just let the
girl go, and we can discuss this like men."

"Naw. I don't think so," he said, still backing away. "How 'bout
instead you put your piece away."

"You know I can't do that."

"Well, I guess it is what it is, then."

The man reached the intersection and changed direction, heading east
down Michigan Ave.

King followed from a safe distance, his gun laser focused between the
man's frenetic eyes while high above, the hotel's guests rubbernecked,
backlit and behind glass, secure in their position.

Slowly, their dance continued down the avenue until the man reached
the entrance of an alley that bridged a parking garage and the seedy club
King had passed earlier. He took one look down its length and was gone.

King stood frozen in place for a split second before sprinting after
him. Huffing and puffing, he threw his back up against the concrete
corner. Slowly, he poked his head around and saw the man about fifteen
yards from the alley's end and beyond that a parking lot chock-full of
potential getaway cars ripe for the plucking.

He stepped into the alley.

The crack of the gun's discharge was booming, amplified by the surrounding cement walls. The bullet hissed by King's head, nearly removing his left ear. He took cover, launching himself back behind the wall.

"Shit!" King said. "Where the hell is my goddamn back-up?"

Marid Abdul-Tawaab was no longer hungry. He'd lost his appetite somewhere between when Jack Kerner knocked on his door and when he'd had his old friend by the neck. Therefore, at that moment he could think of about a million things he'd rather do than grin through some meal exchanging inane small talk.

He wanted to call and cancel.

It would have been easy to make up some falsehood about a flat tire, or a migraine or something of that nature. But his dinner mate was the soon to be retired Dean of the College of Liberal Arts and Sciences and if he had any aspiration of becoming his successor, canceling was not in his best interest.

So he drove the little over two miles from the campus to the restaurant at the Kahn-Hudson Hotel, where the Dean was no doubt checking his watch and already halfway through his second Manhattan. All the while, Abdul-Tawaab could not get Kerner's visit from his mind. He had been waiting years for that encounter. He'd rehearsed what he would say.

How it would go.

Needless to say, in his mind it had never played out with him on his hands and knees scooping up pieces of broken glass.

He had become someone else in that room. Nothing like the version of himself that he'd cultivated with cold precision for over forty years, and more like the version that had emerged when Isaac returned from prison. He was violent, short tempered.

Just as Isaac had wanted him to be.

After all these years, he was still subconsciously seeking the approval of a dead man that he was quite sure had resented his very existence.

Abdul-Tawaab pulled onto Washington Blvd. Up ahead, he could see a crowd in front of the hotel. It appeared to him that they were gawking at a fender bender.

"Anything to delay me further," he said, gritting his teeth.

As he got closer, it became more apparent that it was no mere fender bender. The people looked skittish, if not downright frightened. A mob was trying to force its way through the revolving doors.

He came to a stop in a vacant spot adjacent to the tree lined median across from the hotel.

That's when he saw it.

"It can't be…" he said, laying eyes on the GTO's glimmering blue finish.

Suddenly the petrified screams of the horde rushing the hotel were extinguished and the surround melted away. He was eighteen again on West Philadelphia street. And there she was, smiling so brightly in the passenger seat. That smile, so pure, so unfiltered, so genuine, was what had catapulted his jealousy of Jack Kerner, one borne of run of the mill teenage angst, to a much more dangerous level.

He stepped from his vehicle.

"Kerner?" Abdul-Tawaab said, more to himself than anyone else.

Then he noticed the bullet holes.

"Shit!"

Back now in the present, he hurried forth crunching broken glass under his feet.

He looked inside.

"Oh, no. Oh, God no," he said, staring at the bullet riddled body of Martin Kerner.

He flung open the door and examined him. From what he could tell, there were three wounds, all bleeding profusely. A shallow pool was forming in the crux of the driver's seat. Against hope, he held his fingers to neck.

"He's still alive, but barely," he said to himself, feeling the faintest of a pulse.

He stood up and looked out over the roof of the vehicle at the frozen onlookers.

"Someone get over here and help me!" he bellowed to them. Nobody moved.

"You!" he said to one of the valets. "Get over here!"

The boy shuffled over to the car.

"Help me get him up," Abdul-Tawaab commanded. The valet wavered just for a moment upon seeing all the blood before complying.

"Ok, ok. Now, listen to me very carefully. I need you to apply pressure to the wounds. When I say pressure, I mean really lean into it. We have to control the bleeding if he's to have any hope of staying alive."

"Y-yes, sir," the boy said, meekly, looking back over his shoulder.

"DO YOU UNDERSTAND?" he roared.

"YES, SIR!" the valet barked back.

Abdul-Tawaab was puzzled when the valet again looked over his shoulder.

"What are you looking for?"

"The shooter!"

"He's nearby?"

He nodded. "He got some girl. Just dragged her around the corner."

"Who…what girl?" Abdul-Tawaab asked, already knowing the answer.

The valet shrugged. "She's young, pretty. Musta known this guy, way she was screamin' and cryin'."

"How long they been gone?"

"You *just* missed 'em. Some cop chasin' 'em down Michigan, but…"

"But what?"

"He ain't gonna get him."

"Why not?"

"Cuz he old."

"How old?"

The valet looked back at Abdul-Tawaab and said, "'bout as old as you."

The professor glared back at him and whipped off his overcoat. Without even the hint of a struggle he tore the sleeves clean off and held them out to the valet.

"Use these to absorb the blood. One around the head and one around the chest."

The valet began with Martin's head, tying the sleeve as best he could with trembling hands. Martin's body again started to slip.

"Keep him upright!" Abdul-Tawaab demanded, reaching in to untangle Martin's feet.

Peeking out from under the seat was something metallic. Abdul-Tawaab wrestled it free.

Jack Kerner's old Smith & Wesson.

Abdul-Tawaab's pulse quickened.

"Which direction did the shooter go?" he asked, wrapping his fingers around the cold steel.

The valet pointed east.

"That way. Towards downt-,"

The pop of gunfire filled the night air. The crowd in front of the hotel let out a collective shriek. Within seconds, Abdul-Tawaab had already taken several steps towards the sound of the shot. His pace was gradual at first but he was quickly into a slight jog. He reached the corner of the Kahn-Hudson and tucked up against the wall. He poked his head around and saw an older black man, presumably the cop, halfway down the block. He was backed up against a parking garage, his gun drawn.

"Give it up! This is a no-win situation!" the man yelled out, though Abdul-Tawaab heard no conviction in his voice.

He considered running to officer's aid, but being a strange man holding a gun, decided against it. No, his only means of helping was to reach the other end of that alley before the shooter.

He sprinted across the avenue and then alongside the wall of a budget hotel that sat at the intersection's southeast corner. He drove his body forward, pushing long hibernating muscles to their very limits, until he reached the building's end.

Pausing briefly to gather some air into his now burning lungs, the weight of the gun became apparent.

"What am I doing?" he said, looking down at the revolver in the grip of a hand that couldn't possibly be his own.

He contemplated walking away. Just dropping the piece to ground and leaving.

'Coward.'

That's what Kerner had called him and he knew leaving would do nothing but reinforce that narrative, one that he himself had spawned through his own inaction that fateful night.

He turned the corner, stepping cautiously with his aged but still sinewy arms extended and the gun aimed straight ahead. As he approached the alley's opening, he prepared himself to shoot whoever it gave birth to.

He was no more than ten feet away when he heard footsteps approaching. One by one they fell, synced up with the pounding in his chest.

Finally, the shooter emerged. He was facing east, side-stepping with his prey towards the parked cars. Abdul-Tawaab stood in shadow, marveling at the size of the man's back, whilst fear and righteousness jockeyed for control of his right hand.

Slowly he raised the pistol and aimed. Right there, between the shoulder blades.

But could not pull the trigger.

The man reached the nearest vehicle. As he wound up to smash the butt of his gun through the car's driver's side window, the girl's face came into view.

It was Danielle, which Abdul-Tawaab knew it would be. She wore an expression of despair, and her limp extremities followed suit.

The crash of the window did not even garner a blink of her forlorn eyes as she seemed to have long ago resigned herself to her plight.

But then she saw him.

The life returned to her face. Her eyes, now filled with a restrained hope, locked onto Abdul-Tawaab's pleading him for a chance.

Before he knew it he was moving again. Cautiously he strode forward as the man fumbled for the car's lock.

Ten feet away.

Then five.

He took one more step, but still did not pull the trigger. Instead he offered Danielle a subtle nod. She looked momentarily confused, but when her brow furrowed and her lips tightened he knew she understood.

Just as the man pulled the door open, she clamped her jaw around his wrist.

"AHHH! YOU BITCH!" the man shouted.

She wriggled free, but only for a moment. The man grabbed her by the hair, but before he could do anything more the butt end of Kerner's old police issue .38 came down on his skull.

The man wobbled in place, a thin stream of blood cascading down his face. His eyes landed upon Abdul-Tawaab but before he could process the sight of this new unknown pursuer, they rolled backwards up into his sockets and he crumpled to the ground in a heap.

"You! Drop that weapon!" Franklin King shouted as he darted down the alley.

The man tossed the gun aside as told.

"Now," King said, arriving on the scene. "Put your hands on that trunk and stay there!"

The mystery man with the graying temples shuffled over the would-be getaway car and put hands to steel.

King loomed over the fallen perpetrator, shaking his head in disbelief. "Ho-ly shit."

He bent down and felt for a pulse.

"Well, he's alive," he said, prying the piece from the shooter's hand. "You're lucky for that."

He then picked up the old .38 the man had tossed aside and tucked it in his waistband.

"This is where you explain to me what in the holy hell happened here."

"I hit him with that pistol."

"Ok, but where did you even come from?"

"I arrived at the hotel moments after you began your pursuit."

"That's wonderful," King said, wrapping the shooter's flaccid arms behind his back and cuffing them. "But how does that lead us to where we are now?"

"The valet said you were the only officer trailing the suspect. I thought I might be of some assistance."

"I had him," King said, unable to even convince himself.

"But let's say I didn't. Assistance should come in the form of trained police officers. Not some fool runnin' 'round with a gun, playing vigilante!"

"No, but I wasn't about to allow someone to get away w-,"

"People gettin' killed here every day," King said, slowly rising. "Almost three-hundred this year. Where were you on all them?"

"Look, am I in some kind of trouble?"

"Don't know yet. Turn around and let me get a look at you."

The man did as he was told. There was something strangely familiar within the crags and wrinkles in his face.

"The victim," he said, "the boy in the car...I know him. Personally."

"Old brother like you? How you know some young suburban kid?"

"He was my student."

And it clicked.

"Your student?" King said, slowly advancing on the man.

"Yes."

"Reggie?"

The man looked back at him with his own brand of scrutiny. King could feel him scouring his face, beneath the pain etched in from years of witnessed horrors to find the neighbor he once knew.

"Frank?" he said.

"Oh my…," King said, trailing off.

It was all either of them could manage. They just stared, in mutual paralysis unable to believe their own eyes. They might have remained that way for some time, had their concentration not been broken by the wail of approaching sirens.

"Where's the girl?" King asked, snapping out of it.

"She…" Reggie said, looking around. "She must have run off."

"Go get her before she completely louses up my scene."

"But…" Reggie said, looking down at the shooter who was beginning to stir.

"You're fine," King said just as a squad car came storming into the alley.

"In fact…you probably saved my ass. Now go and find that girl."

Reggie nodded and took off towards the hotel.

The cruiser sped down the alley and came to a screeching halt a few yards from where King stood. Two young, uniformed officers popped out.

"Over there," Franklin said, directing them to their man. "He was unconscious but he's coming to. Better get him in back of the car before he becomes a problem. You got it?"

"Yes, sir," one of them said.

"I'm going back to the scene," he said, handing the shooter's piece to the other cop. "Is the victim still with us?"

"Yes, sir. Medics are working as we speak."

"Where they gonna take him?"

"Detroit General."

"Ok. Don't take your eye off this one. Not for a second."

King walked away, towards Washington Blvd. After a few steps, he pulled his cell from his coat pocket and dialed.

"Jack, please answer," he told the ringer.

"Hello?" Jack Kerner said. His voice was muffled.

"Jack?"

"Yeah. Frank, what is it?"

"Where are you? You sound like you're in a goddamn wind tunnel."

"I'm outside the old house. *Our* old house. On West Philly."

"What the hell are you doing there?"

"Was in the area. It looks empty."

"Jack."

"What?"

"It's Martin."

There was a pause. "Go on."

"He's been…"

"Spill it, Frank."

"The car's all shot up, Jack."

"Never mind the goddamn car! How is my boy!?"

"He's on his way to Detroit General."

Jack Kerner hung up. Frank sighed and put the phone back in his pocket.

Standing at the alley's corner, plastered all over the wall he saw posters of Barack Obama. It was the same pencil portrait over and over, colored in beige, red and blue, each with a single word in big, bold letters at the bottom. Some said 'HOPE'. Others, 'CHANGE'.

One of the posters had been vandalized. Underneath Obama's face, someone had changed the 'H' in 'HOPE' to an 'N'.

"Clever," King said, tearing it from the wall. He crumpled it up and tossed it into a nearby dumpster.

He stepped towards the boulevard, but noticed another poster had been vandalized. It was right at the corner, plainly visible to all who drove northbound on Washington.

The 'C' and 'E' in 'CHANGE' had been blacked out. A noose had been drawn in, as well, snaking in from the corner and wrapping around the Senator's neck. King raised his hand to tear it down, but then dropped it to his side. He shook his head and kept walking.

He reached the scene of the shooting just as the paramedics were loading Martin into the ambulance. Police were everywhere, some huddled together in tight circles, others directing people this way and that in attempt to wrangle the chaos. To his right, near the hotel's entrance, a sizeable group of gawkers remained, their mortified faces bathed in alternating red, then blue hues by the ambulance's flashing lights.

To his left, he found Reggie seated at the base of the statue of General Alexander Macomb that stood watch over the intersection.

And with him, the girl.

He had his giant arm wrapped around her shaking body. And he was gently rocking her.

As King drew closer, he could hear his old friend say "It's going to be all right, Danielle."

He repeated it over and over, as if that somehow would make it less of a lie.

"Reggie," King said.

His old friend rose. He got the girl to her feet and they all met near the GTO.

"She ok?" King asked. The girl looked like an extra from one of those zombie movies. Dried blood was painted across the front of her formerly white dress and she had a look of complete stupefaction on her face.

"A little rattled, but I think she'll be ok," Reggie said.

"What about that blood?"

"It's not hers."

"No?" King said, pointing to the thin stream that was seeping down the girl's inner right thigh. "That looks fresh right there."

The girl's eyes came to life. She took one look down and then back at the men. With both hands on her abdomen, she opened her mouth but managed no sound before her legs gave out beneath her.

CHAPTER XXII
NOVEMBER 5, 2008

To Jack Kerner, time had become an enemy. It had decided to carry on at its own glacial pace, knowing full well that each second not knowing if his boy would live or die was pure agony. Five hours had been frittered away, and in the process Tuesday had become Wednesday, like nothing at all was askew.

Like there was no urgency whatsoever to move things along.

How he wanted to rip the infernal clock above the vending machines off the wall and smash it into a million pieces. Anything to not have to watch those little hands mock him.

Click by click.

Instead, he sat in his hard plastic chair diverting his eyes in search of a distraction. The faces of his waiting companions offered no solace. They all seemed to share the same quiet misery, their dulled eyes turned up to a corner television tuned to a twenty-four hour news station, which only served to perpetuate their gloom.

On the side table to his left were several months-old magazines and his growing collection of Styrofoam coffee cups. And on his right sat Sgt. Franklin King, a friend that he'd not laid eyes on in over thirty years.

Their reunion had been to that point subdued, not that they weren't both grateful to finally be in each other's company. It was the gravity of the situation that had rendered them all but mute.

When the clock's minute hand trudged forward to reach the three, Jack spoke up.

"Frank, go home. It's a quarter after twelve."

King took a sip from his own Styrofoam cup and said, "I'm not going anywhere."

"Go. Get some sleep. There's nothing else you can do here."

"Jack, I want to be here," he said then adding, "and I got nowhere else to be."

Jack spent the next fifteen minutes watching the whirring hospital employees do any number of things that didn't pertain to him and his son. Eventually, a young doctor, maybe six or seven years older than Martin, stopped at the nurses' station and picked up a chart.

"Kerner," he said plainly, without looking up.

Jack sprang from his seat and approached him with ten of the most difficult steps of his life.

"Martin Kerner?" he asked.

The doctor double checked the name on the chart.

"Yes. And you are?"

"His father."

"Follow me."

The doctor led him into a small consultation room equipped with nothing but a circular table and three chairs. One wall had windows looking out over the hall and waiting area. The others were bare save for a poster preaching the importance of hand washing.

"Please sit," the doctor said, directing Jack to one of the chairs.

"No. I've been sitting in that room for over five hours. Just say what you gotta say."

"All right," he said. "Your son is in a coma."

His words came so matter-of-factly that it was immediately apparent that his fresh out of residency arrogance had not yet given way to the empathy of experience.

"What…" Jack choked out, peering through the glass at a furiously pacing Franklin King. "What does that mean, exactly?"

"He has sustained three gunshot wounds. The one to the shoulder is minor. He should recover from it fairly well. The other two, however, are far more complicated."

"Complicated how?"

"When he arrived we immediately got him to our top thoracic surgeon. She removed the bullet from his collapsed lung and attempted to repair the damage."

"And…"

"The majority of the lung's lower lobe had to be removed. Afterwards, he appeared to be breathing on his own, but then the respiration slipped into a Cheyne-Stokes pattern."

"In English!" Jack said, growing agitated.

"It's when the breathing gets progressively deeper and faster, and then gradually slows. For some, it can stop altogether. We've got him on a ventilator for the time being and we will be monitoring him closely for emboli and thrombosis."

"And the third wound?"

"His head. We were able to remove the bullet and luckily it was in one piece. That minimized the collateral damage to the cortex."

"Is he…in pain?"

"He feels nothing. We have painkillers on the ready in the event he wakes up."

"So, what now?"

"He just left recovery. In a minute you will be able to see him, if you like, but keep in mind that he has gone through Hell. It may be disturb-,"

"Will he live?" he said, feverishly wringing his hands.

"Sir, it would be reckless of me to try and predict-,"

"Will he live, damnit?" Jack said, pounding his fist on the table. "And not some vegetable feeding tube shit! Actually live."

The doctor gazed out the door, as if contemplating an exit before searching the pages of the chart for an answer that wasn't there.

"Look, Mr. Kerner," he finally said. "Gunshots to the head are never easy. They can change people. Now, your son, he was shot here," he said, pointing to a spot just above and behind his left ear.

"It's called Wernicke's area and it helps with language processing. That means *if* he survives, on top of any physical rehab, he'll have to learn how to communicate all over again."

Jack dropped his gaze down to his hands. The wringing stopped, replaced with a slow tracing of the long crease that bisected his left palm.

"Is there anythi-,"

"Where is he?" Jack said.

"Well, the nurses over there would have that infor-,"

Jack quickly exited the room leaving the doctor there to linger, momentarily perplexed.

Franklin met Jack in the hall.

"So...what did he say, Jack?"

"Coma."

Franklin shook his head and exhaled deeply.

"I'm so sorry, Ja-,"

"Ok, ok. Stop right there. I said 'coma' not 'dead'. This ain't gonna be some pity party."

"Sorry. I didn't mean to-,"

"Nurse!" Jack called out to a woman just beyond the counter. "I want to see my boy!"

"Sir! Keep your voice down. This is a hospital."

"You want quiet? Take me to my boy."

The nurse stopped in front of one of the identical looking rooms along the sterile, gray corridor.

"Your son is in here. *Do* be quiet, as most of our patients are sleeping," she said, leaving the men alone.

Now standing at the threshold of the room, the anger Jack had felt over the wait and the TV news and the know-it-all doctor, all of it, was gone. Replacing it was a sense of numb acceptance.

"You comin'?" he said to Franklin, peering into the room. A floor length curtain shielded everything but Martin's feet from view.

"I don't think so, Jack. You...you go on in. I gotta make a call, anyways."

Jack regarded his long lost friend for a moment and then stepped into the room.

He was instantly struck by the symphony of blips and beeps and then the deeper, grotesque sound created by the rise and fall of the ventilator's pneumatic air reservoir.

Its grating hideousness was only exceeded by the sight of the machine's tentacle like projection protruding forward and snaking its way down Martin's throat.

Jack could not bear to look at it even as he knew that that it was the only thing keeping Martin alive. He went to his son's bedside, turning from the mechanical abomination, and lightly placed his hand on his gauze wrapped head.

Leaning in close, he placed his lips near Martin's ear and whispered to him.

Two sentences short and concise.

He then straightened up and gripped Martin's hand with his own. He shook it firmly, two pumps, and made his way to the door. Upon entering the hall, he found Franklin about fifteen or so feet away. His back was to Martin's room and he had his phone pressed to his ear.

"Mmmhmm. Good. I'm glad to hear," he said, not aware that Jack was just steps behind. "Abdul-Tawaab still there?"

Jack loudly cleared his throat.

King turned around. "Ok, I gotta go. I'll be up there in a minute."

He returned the phone to his pocket. "Whoa, whoa! Why so fast?" he said.

"I said what I needed to say. What else is there to do?"

"I…I just thought you'd want to be spend some ti-,"

"What's this about Abdul-Tawaab?"

Franklin ran his hand across his gray stubbled chin. "Jack…I-,"

"Why the hell is Reggie here?" Jack seethed, his words coated with napalm.

"He goes by Marid now."

"WHATEVER THE HELL HIS NAME IS!"

"Shh!' Franklin said, pulling Jack towards the elevator bank. "You've got to calm down before they kick you ou-,"

"Calm down!? Calm down!? My boy's lying there full of holes!"

"I'm sorry. I didn't mean-,"

"A goddamn machine's the only thing keeping him alive and you want me to calm down?!"

"Jack,"

"And that sonofabitch…after what he did-,"

"JACK!"

"What!"

"Shut your damn mouth for a second!" Frank shouted.

He looked up and down the hall for any potential offended and found none. "What that sonofabitch did…" he continued, quietly. "You don't know the half of it."

"Enlighten me." Jack said, with crossed arms.

Frank took a deep breath.

"The perp. He had her. He was draggin' her across Michigan Ave like it was nothin'. He'd already shot up the car, so I knew what he was capable of. And I…" he scoffed. "I was useless. Couldn't take him on foot. Couldn't take the shot without risking hitting her."

"And?"

"Once he took her in the alley, I was out of moves. Bastard buzzed me, too."

"Really?"

"Another couple inches and we wouldn't be havin' this conversation. And just as he's about to jack a parked car and be gone, he just showed up outta thin air."

"Reggie?"

Frank nodded. "Thin fucking air. Clocked the dude over the head. Knocked him out. Saved that girl's life."

Jack stood stupefied. He had no idea how to reconcile this story of selfless heroism while still feeling the unflinching grip of Reggie's arms around him as he watched his love die.

Maybe he wasn't the only one capable of change.

"And Jack," Frank added. "He saved your grandchild's life, too."

Jack's eyes widened.

"That's right. Danielle's pregnant. You're gonna be a grandpa."

Jack's trembling hand went to his heart.

"You shittin' me?"

Frank shook his head.

"I'm gonna be a grandpa," Jack stated, as though it could not be confirmed until he himself said it. Tears immediately filled his eyes.

"You are. Congrat-,"

Jack leapt forward and embraced his old friend. Franklin reciprocated, feeling a subtle tremor as Jack gently sobbed.

"I just got off the phone with the uniform that's been watchin' her," Frank said, patting Jack's back. "She's awake now, so I'm going to go talk to her. You wanna come?"

Jack broke the embrace and stared up at the blur of the fluorescent lights, fighting the tears' downward trajectory across his cheeks.

"I do," he finally said, wiping them away with a swipe of his sleeve. "I absolutely do."

The officer seated outside Danielle's room immediately jumped to his feet at the sight of Franklin King approaching.

"Sgt.," he said, standing bolt upright.

"Relax, officer," King said.

The officer's posture slackened.

"How is she?" King asked.

"Seems ok. Been talking a lot."

"Talking to who?"

"Her brother for a while. Nurse is in there right now."

"Her brother?"

"Yeah. While she was asleep, her cell kept going off. Finally, one of the nurses answered. It was him. He was lying on the sidewalk off Woodward less than a mile from here."

"Excuse me?"

"Yeah. Apparently he was in the car with our perp. They got into a bit of a skirmish near Erskine, and he fled the vehicle."

"What kind of skirmish?"

"He got his ass kicked basically. Face all swollen. Walkin' all hunched over. I'm surprised he made it here on his own."

"Did you get a statement?"

"Yes, sir."

"Good. Where is he now? I'd like to talk with him."

"You just missed him. Nurse took him to get his face looked at."

"You go find him and stick to him like glue in case one of Flip's associates come lookin'."

"Yes, sir."

The officer walked off, leaving the two men alone in the hall.

Franklin gestured towards the room. "You ready?"

Jack, having gained control of his emotions, nodded in affirmation.

King entered first and Jack followed closely behind. Danielle was sitting up on the bed, barricaded in by a wall of pillows. Though her eyes were slightly puffy from crying, Jack could see the graceful beauty that Martin had been so taken by.

A nurse stood beside the bed holding Danielle's hand in both of her own.

"Everything is going to be ok, dear," she said.

Danielle managed a bit of a smile.

"Did you need anything else?" the nurse asked.

Danielle shook her head and the nurse left.

Franklin walked over to the side table and retrieved a tissue. "Here you go, honey," he said, offering it to her. She accepted it graciously.

"Sgt. King?" she said, dabbing at the corners of her eyes.

"Yes?"

"Is...is Martin..." was all she could get out. It was as though she really didn't want to ask the question for fear of the answer.

"He's hurt pretty bad," Frank said.

"He's alive?"

"Yes, but he's in a coma."

She looked down at her abdomen and ran her hand over it in slow circles. After about a minute she said, "But he's alive," to no one in particular.

When she looked up Jack was surprised to see that in her eyes was not despair, but a steely resolve.

"And, what about you?" King asked.

"What?" she said, adrift in her own thoughts.

"You and the baby are ok?"

"Oh. Yes. We're fine."

"What about the blood?"

"They said I have a urinary tract infection. That in combination with the stress..."

"Ahh. I see," Frank said. "Well, that's a relief. I'm really glad to hear that."

"Can I ask how far along you are?" Jack said.

"Umm...about two months," she said, looking upon him as if until then she'd been unaware of his presence in the room. "I'm sorry, who are you?"

"Oh, that's my fault," Frank said, apologetically. "I forgot to introduce him. Danielle, this is my old friend, Jack."

Jack went to her bedside and offered his hand. "Lovely to meet you," he said. "I'm Martin's father."

"What!?" she said, revolted. She ripped her hand from his grasp.

"Get out," Danielle said firmly.

"I'm sorry?" Jack said, confused. Palms up, he backed away from her bedside. "Did I-,"

"Out! Now!"

He and Franklin exchanged puzzled looks.

"Danielle, what's this all about?" King asked.

"It's his fault. All of this," she said, her voice getting agitated. "He thought *you* were driving that car! It was *you* he was after!"

"Who?"

"Flip!"

Jack could only shrug his shoulders.

"Halloween!?" she said.

"Shit," Jack muttered, the color leaving his face.

"What, Jack?"

"What kind of a psycho does that to a little girl?"

She was bordering on hysteria.

"Now, wait a minute," Jack pleaded. "I can explain."

"GET OUT!" she screamed.

Frank grabbed Jack by the coat and rushed him out of the room. "Hey, what are you doing?" Jack said, unable to wrestle free of Frank's grip.

"You heard her. She wanted you gone," he said, dragging Jack to an empty waiting room across the hall.

"Let me back in, damnit!" Jack implored. He was frantically pacing the room like a caged animal. "I need to explain-,"

"You need to leave her be," Frank said, blocking the doorway. "The last thing she or that baby needs is more stress."

The mention of the baby froze Jack in place.

"So what's this about a little girl?" King asked.

"Shit, Frank. Do we need to do this?"

"Yes, we do."

Jack said nothing.

"Jack!" Franklin bellowed.

After a long pause, Jack sighed deeply. "I was passing out candy and this little girl and her thug of a...whatever he was to her-uncle, brother, I don't know...When they came to my stoop, I closed my door and shut off my light. And when they walked away, I flipped it back on."

"What? Why?"

"I don't know why," Jack said, angrily turning away. Still, he could feel Franklin' stare, how it bored into the skin on the back of his neck.

It was unbearable.

"Because she was black, ok!" he exploded, spinning back around.

He expected Franklin to be wearing a look of abject disgust, like he'd gazed upon a monster, because Jack very much felt like one at that moment. Instead Franklin was calm, expressionless.

"Did that make you feel good, Jack?" Frank asked.

"No. It didn't. I was drunk and they weren't from the neighborhood and I just wanted them to…"

"To what?"

Jack shrugged. Exasperated, he found a chair along the wall and sat.

"You know he nearly kicked down my door," he said, staring down at the tops of his shoes.

"Well, I'd a done worse."

"Sometimes I wish he had. I wish he would have busted it down and just ended it all right then and there."

"C'mon. Let's not start with that kinda talk."

"Why not? Everybody'd be better off right now if he had. Martin, Danielle…even you. You'd be home sound asleep."

Frank said nothing.

"I mean, shit…I almost ate a bullet later on that night."

"Wait…wasn't that the night that you called me?"

Jack nodded.

Frank left his perch and sat down in the chair adjacent Jack's. He leaned his head back until it rested on the mauve-papered wall and stared up at the dropped ceiling tiles.

"Well, if you're aim's still anything like our academy days, you probably woulda missed."

For a moment, Jack wondered how Franklin could possibly had known, but one look at the slight grin forming at the corner of his old friend's mouth made it apparent that he was just old fashioned ball busting.

"Like you were some sharpshooter?" he said with a smirk as slim as the circumstances would allow.

"Top of the class."

"Bull-shit," Jack said, mirroring Frank's leaned back pose.

The pair sat silently for a minute or so before Jack spoke up. "What are you doing here with a bastard like me? After what I just said, you should be running for the hills."

"That? That's not you," Frank said with a dismissive wave of his hand.

"How do you know? We haven't spoken in thirty some odd years."

"I just know."

Jack scoffed. "Yeah, well. She doesn't," he said, pointing at Danielle's room.

"And neither will that baby unless you do something about it."

"I can't let that happen."

"No, you can't."

Jack stood up.

"Where you goin'?" Frank said, his hands quick to the armrests ready to jettison his body forth should Jack make any attempt back in that room.

"Don't worry. I'm going home. I'm tired. And I suggest you do the same."

"In due time. I still want to talk to the brother," Franklin said, rising though without any sense of urgency. He adjusted his belt to the base of his convex belly.

Jack stepped into the hall.

"All right, then. If you want to reach me, I'll be here tomorrow and, well, probably all the tomorrows for the foreseeable future."

"Sounds good."

Down the hall, the elevator car announced its arrival with a monotone bing. It was no louder than typical, but without the usual hum of activity in the hall to drown it out, it rang out like warning blast.

Jack turned around and watched the elevator doors slowly pull apart, screeching along their tracks. A shoe poked out. Then the leg that belonged to it. Gradually the form of Marid Abdul-Tawaab emerged into the hall.

He took a few steps with his gaze down, his attention solely on the vending machine coffee cup his left hand was raising to his puckered lips. He recoiled slightly at the coffee's heat before looking up.

He froze in place.

"Jack..." Frank said. He reached out for Jack's sleeve but he was already out of reach.

"Jack!" he said again, with more than a hint of consternation in his voice.

Jack, continued on, unwavering.

Abdul-Tawaab did not flinch, seemingly acquiescent to whatever comeuppance was soon to befall him.

Jack closed the expanse between them. Ten feet. Then five.

Abdul-Tawaab stiffened upon his arrival, but the blows he anticipated to rain down upon on him with a lifetime of pent up aggression never came.

Instead, Jack stopped just short.

And extended his hand.

Abdul-Tawaab looked down at it, puzzled. He glanced down the hall to Franklin King for an explanation, but got none.

He accepted Jack's hand and they shook. Two firm pumps and it was over.

"Thank you," Jack said, and he walked into the open elevator car.

Abdul-Tawaab could only stare, stupefied as the elevator doors again screeched on their tracks, encasing Jack inside.

CHAPTER XXIII
MARCH 1, 2009

When the elevator doors opened and Jack emerged, Franklin King sprang up from his chair. He appeared to be a tad over excited, presumably due to the big news Jack had promised when they'd spoken the night before.

"Hey there, old-timer," Jack said.

"Aren't we the same age?" Franklin said with a friendly clap of Jack's back.

"Yeah, yeah," he said, smiling

They started side by side down the corridor.

"So, what's this big news you dragged me all the way here for?" King asked.

"What do you care? You're retired now. What else were you gonna do on a cold, drab Sunday afternoon?"

"I had a recliner and some leftover Buddy's pizza with my name on it."

"Well, for gracing me with your presence, I'll buy you lunch. Okay?"

"I can live with that."

It was the first time Jack had visited Martin while the sun was up. Out of respect for Danielle, he'd avoided coming during the day, knowing that she often visited between classes.

It was unusual for him to see the hospital so alive. Nurses and doctors zipped along, their immaculate white sneakers squeaking against the tiled floor.

"So…what's the news?" King asked again as they maneuvered through the masses towards Martin's room.

Jack reached into his coat pocket and, after a bit of fumbling around, pulled out a single chrome plated key. He held it up for Franklin to see.

"A key," he said, unimpressed.

"Uh huh."

Franklin shrugged. "Am I missing something?"

"It goes to my new house."

"Oh. Well, congratulations, I guess."

"Thanks."

"What's it got to do with me?" Franklin said, mildly perturbed.

"West Philly."

"What?" Franklin said, skeptically. "You didn't."

"I did"

"You playin' with me?"

"Closed on it this past Friday."

An ear to ear smile filled Franklin's face. "Well, I'll be damned. Never in a million years did I think…"

"Yep," Jack said, with his own to match. "Already met one of my neighbors, too."

He pointed towards the waiting room just ahead. Seated there cross-legged with his face turned up to the television was one Marid Abdul-Tawaab. He rose when he noticed Frank and Jack approaching.

Frank looked from Jack to the professor, and then back to Jack, again.

"He's your neighbor?" he said, flabbergasted.

"Thanks for coming, Marid," Jack said to Abdul-Tawaab. The pair shook hands.

"She in there still?" Jack asked.

Marid nodded and then extended his hand to Franklin. "Hello, Franklin. How've you been?"

"Good, good," King said, shaking Abdul-Tawaab's hand absentmindedly. "So…you still live on West Philly?"

"Moved back after my mom passed."

"Huh," Franklin said, shaking his head. He still wore a look of complete astonishment.

"So when are you moving in, Jack?" Marid asked.

"Took some stuff over there this morning. Couple small boxes. There's a few things that need attending to before I can fully move in. Plumbing, mainly. Damn thieves broke in and stole all the copper."

"That, unfortunately, is an epidemic around here," Abdul-Tawaab said.

"I'm sorry, but this," Frank said gesturing to the two old friends who more recently had been sworn enemies, "it's all a little much for me to take in."

"Well, Frank. All I can tell you is…," Jack started before pausing to find the right words. "Forty years is a long time."

Franklin nodded in approval, those six words seemingly enough to appease his curiosity.

"You decide which half you're going to live in," Marid asked.

"Kerner side. It's funny. I thought as soon as I stepped foot in there, I'd realize what a mistake this whole thing was. You know, like I would be sharing a home with ghosts. But it wasn't that way at all. It just felt like home."

"What about the King side?" Franklin asked.

Jack shared a knowing look with Abdul-Tawaab before responding, which got Franklin's detective sense all abuzz.

"I've got a plan for the King side," Jack said. "But enough jabbering out here in the hall. You guys ready?"

"Ready for what?" King asked.

"When you are, Jack," Abdul-Tawaab said. He and Jack started towards Martin's room.

"Wait a sec. Didn't he just say Danielle was still in there?" Franklin asked.

"Yep," Jack said.

Frank watched the pair walk away, all the while the wheels turned in his head.

"Hang on a sec," he said. Jack and Marid stopped and turned around.

"I see what you're doing. You're gonna go in there and-,"

"Yeah, yeah. You always were a great detective," Jack said.

"I don't know if that's such a good-,"

"Frank, you're not here to give me permission. You're here for support. You gonna back me up, or not?"

"You know I will, you stubborn S.O.B." Frank said.

"Good. Then if you're ready…" Jack said, waving him along. After a brief hesitation, Franklin joined them just outside Martin's room.

Jack entered first, with the other two men close behind. The curtains were mostly drawn, with only a slight separation allowing a hint of the day's gray inside. The television was on. The low murmur of the local news broadcast helped to drown out the mechanical sound of Martin's life giving machines. Danielle had pulled a chair to Martin's bedside and had fallen asleep in an awkward position with her body slumped over and her right hand gripping Martin's through the bars of the bed railing. A faint drool spot had formed on her sweater where her mouth and right shoulder met.

She stirred upon hearing the men enter the room. Her eyes fluttered and eventually settled directly on Jack. Startled, she released Martin's hand and sat upright.

"What are you doing here?" she said, wiping at the corner of her mouth.

"I came to talk to you," Jack said in as calm of a voice as he could muster.

"I have nothing to say to you."

Jack was discouraged at how the mere sight of him had immediately drawn her ire.

"It won't take long," he persisted. "I just wanted to-,"

"This is *my* time," she said, pointing at the watch on her wrist for effect. "You are interrupting *my* time with him. I thought we had an understanding."

Her eyes began darting around the room until they settled on her purse sitting on top of the heat register. She stood up and went to it, which is when Jack got a look at her growing belly.

"Oh, wow. Look at…" Jack said, choking up at the sight of it.

Danielle slung the purse over her shoulder and turned to him fully intent on tearing into him further but something about the way he was looking at her belly, and by extension her child, softened her. It was never really in her nature to be that way, anyhow.

"You have fifteen minutes," she said. "I'm going to go to the cafeteria and get a hot chocolate. When I return, I would hope you'd be gone."

She put her head down and walked right past him.

"Wait!" he pleaded.

Franklin stepped into her path and she stopped.

"Why don't you just let him say what's on his mind," he said.

She sidestepped him but then encountered Marid Abdul-Tawaab filling in the doorway.

"Yes, Danielle. I think you should sit back down," he said.

She could see in his eyes that he was in no hurry to get out of her way, so she sighed and retreated to the chair. She dropped the purse to the floor and sat down, crossing her arms over her chest.

"Go on then," she said, annoyed.

Jack offered his old friends a thank you nod and then pulled a chair over from the corner directly across Danielle's. Before he sat, though, he went to Martin's bedside and cupped his son's hand in his own. He held it for a moment, eyes closed as Danielle looked on. She was a little surprised that someone who was capable of actions so heinous, could, in one simple gesture, look so warm and loving.

Jack carefully placed his son's hand back down on the bed and took his seat facing Danielle.

He took her hand.

"What are you-," she said.

"I'm going to tell you what I came here to tell you, and then you can say anything you want or nothing at all. Ok?"

She nodded.

Jack hesitated, aware of the gravity of choosing his words wisely. For a moment, the only voice in the room was that of the news anchor on the television.

"*There was a bit of rustle today at a Detroit city council meeting regarding the expansion of Cobo Center, a deal many consider paramount to bringing much needed convention money downtown.*"

Jack began. "I'm not who you think I am. The man that Martin told you about, assuming he paid me enough mind to even speak about me at all. That man…he's not me."

"*A very vocal crowd of citizens taunted some predominantly white speakers with chants of 'Go home'.*"

"Back in '67 I lost someone very dear to me. She was my everything. My friend. My lover. My future. And she was black."

Danielle immediately wore a look of shock, though she remained silent. She was never one to interrupt, but even if she'd tried, the words would not have come.

"If you don't believe me, you can ask Sgt. King. It was his sister, Pamela."

Danielle looked at Franklin who nodded just slightly before dropping his gaze to the floor.

"When she died, I lost my way. I became somebody else. Somebody filled with hate and rage…"

"Council President Monica Conyers, who presided over the hearing, took part in the haranguing, as well."

"And I did things. Horrible things. Things that keep me up nights. And I drank. Anything to kill the pain."

"Things really came to a boil when a suburban Teamster official suggested that the deal would create more good-paying jobs for union workers."

"I let my anger consume me. I lost my job because of it and it nearly killed me, but I was lucky to find someone who loved me a lot more than I loved myself. We got married and had Martin…"

"President Conyers, the wife of Congressman John Conyers, seen here on a flatbed attempting to calm an angry throng during the 1967 Detroit riot, replied, 'Those workers look like you; they don't look like me.'"

"But I was a terrible father and husband. I was never there, and when I was, I was distant, cold. Martin's the man he is because of his mother, not me."

"In what was likely an attempt to placate the crowd and Conyers herself, the man mentioned President Barack Obama's campaign message of unity…"

"It all came to a head that Halloween night when I did something I never thought I was capable of. It was despicable and I know damn well it should be me lying in that bed…"

"…to which Conyers warned, "Don't you say his name here."

"But there's nothing I can do to change the past. That's not why I'm here."

"Then why are you here?" Danielle said.

"The incident is another reminder of the city's longstanding racial divide. One hopes that it does not derail the redevelopment of-,"

Her voice was abruptly cut off. Jack turned around and saw Abdul-Tawaab taking his hand from the television's power button and returning to his post near the door.

"I'm here about the future," Jack said.

"Who's future?"

"My grandchild's."

"Ok…I'm listening."

Jack took a deep breath.

"I think you and the baby should move in with me."

"Ha!" scoffed Danielle, breaking her hand free from Jack's.

"Now hear me out," Jack said.

"Are you serious?"

"I really think it would be best."

"I think you've gone and lost your damn mind."

"I bought a house here in Detroit. My old house. It's a duplex. I'd take one side, and you and the baby can take the other."

"I ain't even hearing this," she said, abruptly rising and going to the window. She pulled the curtains open and looked out over the expanse of Dolan Park and the cars driving along Beaubien St. A few rays of sunlight were peeking through all of the gray.

"What? You think you can raise that baby by yourself?" Jack said.

"Just about raised my brother myself," Danielle said, still with her back to him.

"That doesn't mean that you should. Not when you don't have to."

"I got Tyreke."

"For now. But what about in the fall? Marid told me that he got accepted to Ann Arbor? How much help will he be from there?"

Danielle said nothing.

"And that neighborhood of yours. Sgt. King here tells me they like to shoot up the homes of old blind women there. Is that a place to raise a child?"

Danielle turned around to face him. There were tears in her eyes. "You got all the answers, huh?"

"No, Danielle. I don't. Far from it. I just want what's best for that child. Now, my son…" he said, stealing a glance at Martin. "He's a fighter. He will come out of this, I promise you that. And he will be ten times the father I ever was, but until he does, please…I just want to…"

Jack trailed off. He couldn't take his eyes off Danielle's belly.

"How many weeks are you?"

"What?"

"How far along?"

"Twenty-six."

Jack took a precarious step forward and slowly reached out his hand. "Can I?"

"I…I suppose."

Jack gently put his hand on Danielle's belly.

"Any kicks yet?"

Danielle smiled. "Yeah. Last couple weeks I been feeling them."

"Diane, Martin's mom, would always say 'Jack quickly put your hand here' and she'd grab my hand and put it on her belly and say 'there. Did you feel it?' but I never did. She was so excited, though, that I'd lie and say I did."

Jack leaned over, bringing his face inches from her belly.

"Hey, little guy," he said in a comforting voice Danielle never would have guessed was inside him. "It's grandpa. Little cramped in there, I'll bet, but don't worry. You'll be out soon enough and I can't wait to meet you."

"It's a girl," Danielle said.

Jack slowly rose. "A girl?"

"Yeah."

Jack beamed.

"You here that?" he said to King and Abdul-Tawaab. "A little girl."

They confirmed that they had indeed heard.

Jack turned his attention back to Danielle. "You know, if you haven't thought of any names yet, I have a suggest-,"

She embraced him.

Jack's body seized. She'd sprung forward and buried her face in his chest so quickly that he had hardly a moment to process it. He looked to his compatriots for guidance, but they offered none.

"I'm sorry," she said, softly sobbing, her tears seeping through Jack's shirt.

"My dear, you have nothing to be sorry for."

He returned the hug, wrapping his arms around her like she was his own blood. Marid tapped Franklin on the shoulder and gestured to the door. Franklin nodded and took one step, until something in the window drew him back in. He tip-toed carefully around Jack and Danielle so as not to disrupt them. The sun had broken through parted clouds to bathe the city in a shimmering light. But that was not what had caught Franklin's eye.

It was the snow.

It was only a dusting at first, but the longer he watched, the heavier it came. The flakes larger and larger.

He could swear if he looked hard enough, he could see their individual patterns. A blanket began to form over Dolan Park's neglected patches of dirt and crabgrass and it wasn't long before Franklin could hardly see its imperfections.

And there, behind him, laid Martin, coupled to a pneumatic reservoir whose rise and fall provided only the slimmest of chances.

And there, were three scars, deep and painful, but no longer the wounds that once seemed insurmountable.

And there, at the base of his dormant left arm, were his fingers, curled inwards with the nails meeting the skin of his palm and the thumb crossed tightly over top in an unmistakable form.

And there, deep within his cortex, were the words he'd once been told, untethered to any conscious understanding.

Hope for better things. You will rise from the ashes.

References:

Fine, Sidney, *Violence In The Model City: The Cavanagh Administration, Race Relations, and the Detroit Riot of 1967.* 2007

Finley, Nolan. "Elect A Crazy Council, Get Crazy Results." *The Detroit News,* March 1, 2009.

Countless message boards and the racist trolls that populate them.

Photo credit: Rinka Patel

Erik Belcarz was first published back in 1995 with a poem lamenting the Major League Baseball strike. He then took a brief hiatus from writing in order to focus on graduating high school, then college, marrying his dream girl and starting a family. He resides and practices as a Doctor of Optometry in the Detroit suburbs, though some of his most cherished memories were borne within the confines of the city (a near death experience on Clifford St. notwithstanding).